PENGUIN BOOKS

You'll Never See Me Again

You'll Never See Me Again

LESLEY PEARSE

PENGUIN BOOKS

PENGUIN BOOKS

UK | USA | Canada | Ireland | Australia
India | New Zealand | South Africa

Penguin Books is part of the Penguin Random House group of companies
whose addresses can be found at global.penguinrandomhouse.com

First published by Michael Joseph 2019
Published in Penguin Books 2020

001

Set in 12.15/14.44 pt Garamond MT Std
Typeset by Jouve (UK), Milton Keynes
Printed and bound in Great Britain by Clays Ltd, Elcograf S.p.A.

A CIP catalogue record for this book is available from the British Library

ISBN: 978-1-405-95142-5

www.greenpenguin.co.uk

I dedicate this book to Carsten Frasch for being such a good sport in bidding in a charity auction to be a character in the book.

Carsten's real-life personality made it a joy to invent a fictional character, as he has all the qualities that make a first-class hero. I do hope his friends and family in Germany will enjoy how I have portrayed him and realize that I grew as fond of the fictional Carsten as I am of the real man.

I

Hallsands, Devon, 1917

The wind and heavy rain coming right off the sea rattled the cottage windows and pounded on the glass. Betty shuddered; she'd lived in this village her entire life, and seen the destruction the sea was capable of, but she'd never felt so menaced by it before.

'If you've got anything about you, you'll get down there and rescue what you can!'

Betty almost jumped out of her skin at the sharp order from her mother-in-law. She'd been so engrossed in watching the terrifying sight of huge waves crashing on to the beach far below, licking up to where her own house stood, that she hadn't heard Agnes come into the room. Her mother-in-law's threatening tone was even more disturbing than the scene beyond the window.

'But it's almost dark,' Betty protested. 'It's far too dangerous to go there now.'

'So, you are happy to lose all your belongings, and my son's, and sponge off me once your house is gone?'

Betty couldn't think of anything worse than being forced to live permanently with Agnes. She was a cold-hearted, mean-spirited shrew of a woman, and the only reason Betty was in her house now was because she'd come to see her husband. Martin had been staying with his mother and grandfather for a month now, since being sent home from France suffering from a leg wound and shell shock.

In truth there wasn't much point in visiting him. He spent all day hunched in a chair by the fire; the only thing that could rouse him from his stupor was a sudden loud noise. When the door banged he would dive to the floor, gibbering in terror.

'Of course I'm not happy to lose everything, but everyone else in the row has left their homes to find shelter somewhere else for the night. They say tonight's high tide will sweep the whole street and all the houses away.'

'Quite so, but you've got a few hours yet. Stop being so feeble and get down there.'

Betty glanced anxiously at the scene beyond the window. The sky was like lead, the sea the same colour, but as the huge waves uncurled to show peaks of pure white they reminded her of a savage dog's teeth. As she was the daughter of a fisherman who had lost his life at sea, she knew better than anyone how cruel it could be.

When she looked back at Agnes, she saw she had picked up a lump of bread dough and was kneading it on the table. She was attacking it with such force her knuckles were white, and Betty could imagine one of those large, rough fists slamming into her face if she didn't obey her.

'I'm not sure I can even get down the lane,' Betty said fearfully. She had experienced enough rough weather in her life to know that when the path was wet and strewn with shingle, it was treacherous. She suspected that the strength of the wind could send a wave high enough to snatch her up and toss her into the sea.

'Rubbish, don't be so pathetic,' Agnes snarled at her.

'You've always been spineless, I don't know what my son ever saw in you.'

Betty went over to her husband, putting her hand on his shoulder, but she knew she could expect no help and support from him; he wasn't even aware of his wife's presence, let alone that his mother was nasty to her. His physical wounds might be healed, but it seemed the mental ones would remain forever.

Many people viewed his problem as a ruse to escape being sent back to the front. But Betty knew what ailed him was as real as the wild sea outside. God only knew what horrors he'd been subjected to in France, but they were vicious enough to rob him of his strength, his health – even knowing what it meant to be a husband.

'Why are you always so hateful to me?' Betty asked Agnes. She knew she was pushing her luck asking such a thing. The woman was as quick to slap as she was to humiliate. 'I've never done anything to you.'

Agnes's lip curled back. 'You're so mealy-mouthed. You think you're better than anyone else, especially since you got that new job.'

Betty took her cloak down from the peg by the door. She *had* been lucky to get the housekeeping job in Kingsbridge. A girl of twenty-two, whose only real skill was helping her father to fish, wouldn't expect to get such a position. But at her interview she'd gone all out to convince Mrs Porter she could do it and, surprisingly, the woman had agreed to give her a trial. Perhaps she was just a little smug that she'd made the grade. But wouldn't anyone be?

Yet if Agnes hadn't insisted Betty hand over half

Martin's army pay, she wouldn't have needed another job; she could have made some extra cash gutting fish, making new crab and lobster pots, here in Hallsands. As it was, she had an eighteen-mile round trip to Kingsbridge on a muddy lane full of potholes. She left in the dark and came home the same way. And now the pittance Martin got for being invalided out still had to be shared.

Suddenly Betty didn't care how dangerous it would be to go down to her house. Anything was better than being in this poisonous atmosphere with such a spiteful harridan and the shell of the man she had married.

'I *am* better than you,' Betty said as she pulled her hood up and secured it. 'But then almost everyone is. If I don't come back, it will be on your head.'

She didn't wait for the abuse and violence she knew would follow her retort, but opened the door quickly and left. For the first time in ages she had to stifle a giggle at her own daring; it felt good to strike back, even if she was going to regret it later.

Betty guessed it to be nearly four in the afternoon, as it was almost dark. She was well used to being in the dark, so her eyes soon adjusted, but the wind was another matter. It tore at her cloak, trying to pull off her hood, and buffeted her against the cottages she passed. But once she was on the narrow lane down to her home, she became really scared.

The wind and rain hit her, full in the face, so hard she could barely breathe, and so much shingle had been thrown up at the last high tide that it was extremely hazardous underfoot. She had to take tiny steps, feeling her way cautiously and praying that a big wave wouldn't come just yet.

Finally, she reached her cottage. She had been born here, as her father Bert Grainger had been before her. She'd mourned a baby sister who died at two months old, and three years later her mother died after a miscarriage. Betty and her father had become very close after that; she'd fished with him, kept house and helped mend his nets. They were a tight-knit duo, yet he'd been delighted when sixteen-year-old Martin Wellows arrived in the village with his widowed mother. They were to stay with his grandfather, and Martin soon became friends with Bert's daughter.

Martin asked Bert to teach him to become a fisherman, and in the process, he very quickly became like the son Bert had always wanted. Betty remembered that first year being so happy for all three of them. She had Martin's company, her father got a helper and a stand-in son, while Martin learned so much from Bert. There was a great deal of laughter and good-natured banter between the three of them as they sorted the catch and mended the nets, and Betty sensed that Martin was reluctant to leave them in the evenings and go home to his mother.

She couldn't say exactly when she fell in love with Martin, her feelings for him seemed to grow more intense with each passing week. Martin asked Bert if he could marry her when she was sixteen, and Bert laughed joyously, saying if he had to pick a husband for his daughter, it would be Martin. Yet her father still warned her about Agnes; he said Betty would need to be strong and stand up to her, or she would crush the life out of her.

Martin moved in with Betty and her father when they married, and for the first year of their marriage Betty was so happy that Agnes's sharp remarks, her meanness and spite could be laughed off. But then disaster struck when Bert was lost at sea. Martin felt responsible for the accident. He felt he should have insisted his father-in-law wore his safety harness when the sea became mountainous, but although Bert had always made Martin wear his in rough weather, Bert often left his off. Swept away in darkness, he wasn't even visible for any attempt at rescue, but Martin still felt he hadn't done enough.

It was almost three weeks before Bert's body was washed up further along the coast.

That was such a terrible time, and if it hadn't been for Martin's love and strength, Betty felt she might never have got over it. But he said their life together had to go on, he took on another experienced fisherman in their boat, and got Betty to come too when the weather wasn't too wild. The pair of them loved their little cottage. On summer evenings they would sit on a bench outside looking at the view of the sea, talking about how lovely it would be when they were blessed with a baby.

Agnes had used the tragedy of Bert's death remorselessly to point out that her son should've become a carpenter, like his own father, a much safer profession. Yet as she was living at Tern Cottage, with Ted, Martin's grandfather, high up on the cliff, they didn't have to see her much.

But then war broke out in 1914, and by the end of 1915 Martin felt compelled to join up with other men in the village. The last thing Betty remembered him saying as he was leaving was, 'I'll come back stronger, more determined to put Mother in her place, and we'll make our baby.'

It was somewhat ironic that she remembered that promise so clearly. And now, two years later, here she was, risking her life at his mother's orders, and Martin was sitting by the fire, oblivious to the danger she was in.

The front door of her cottage was bent like cardboard from the barrage of seawater, partially split by the force of the wind and hurled shingle. As Betty pushed it open, it fell drunkenly inwards on to the stone floor. Three or four inches of water had already flooded in, lying there dark and still, a dank smell reaching her nostrils. Betty had taken the two fireside chairs and the rug upstairs before she left on the previous day, in the hope that the storm would blow itself out. Yet she had sensed even then, as all her neighbours had, that there would be no reprieve this time. Maybe last night's high tide hadn't destroyed their homes, but a second extremely high tide and a bad storm would mean that by tomorrow morning the walls and windows would be gone, the furniture floating out to sea.

Even now Betty could hear the cottage walls creaking in the wind, and she knew she'd have to be quick. Picking up her skirt, she waded through the water to a candle left on a shelf, lit it and then climbed the already rickety, damp stairs. She grabbed a carpetbag from beneath her bed and stuffed what she could into it. All of Martin's belongings were already up at Tern Cottage, and it was just that realization which set her thinking.

Agnes knew there was nothing of Martin's here, so why had she taunted Betty into coming down here? Was it in the hope she'd be swept away?

But surely no one was that wicked?

The more Betty thought about it, the more she sensed that was exactly why Agnes had goaded her. So why not give the crone her heart's desire and not go back? She could easily slip away now under cover of darkness.

This cottage had been owned by her father, so it had passed to Betty and Martin on his death.

A dilapidated cottage wouldn't be worth anything, of course, but there could possibly be compensation, because some years ago massive amounts of shingle had been taken from the beach here to sell to Plymouth harbour. This had weakened the village's defences against the sea. With no one to fight their corner against the powerful and greedy businessmen responsible, the cottage owners had done nothing in the past. But Agnes was made of the right stuff to tackle them. She was like a terrier with a bone where money was concerned, so she could be relied on to fight for compensation for her son.

Standing there by the spluttering light of the candle, listening to the sea and the wind roaring, Betty asked herself what there was to keep her here in this village.

Her parents were gone, and while there were people here she'd known all her life and was fond of, they could never make up for being forced to live with a spiteful, cruel woman who carped incessantly. And there was Martin. She loved him, but he was now a sad, traumatized wretch who sat all day rocking himself. He didn't even speak to her – let alone wish to make love to her – and if she stayed, she would be looking after him forever.

It was undoubtedly cruel to run out on him, and if it wasn't for his mother she wouldn't even consider doing so. But there was no way she could spend another week, let alone years, under the same roof with such a bully. Agnes had always resented Betty for taking her son away from her, so this way she could keep him for herself forever. Martin would be unaware his wife had gone.

Betty had never owned much, but she scooped up a string of green glass beads hanging on a nail on the wall. They had been her mother's; her father had given them to his bride when they got married because they matched her eyes. Betty's eyes were green too, and she had her mother's red hair and pale skin. On the nightstand there was the photograph of her parents on their wedding day. It had faded, but their youthful faces still seemed to gleam with expectation. Perhaps it was as well they hadn't lived long enough to see this cottage they'd loved so much fall into the sea. To know that their daughter had to run away to keep her sanity.

It was only then that Betty remembered the money hidden beside the little fireplace. When she got the housekeeping job in Kingsbridge, she knew Agnes would insist on Betty supporting her, as Martin had done. She told the woman she earned five shillings a week, when in fact she earned six, and each week she tucked away a shilling in a little bag behind a loose brick.

The brick was difficult to get out with only candlelight to see by, and when her fingers finally touched the small linen bag, she snatched it up and tucked it into the bodice of her dress. She guessed there was something in the region of three pounds in it. She had always intended it to go towards a new fishing boat when Martin came home from the war. But he was unlikely ever to go fishing again, and she wasn't stealing, it was her own money.

Suddenly she heard the window downstairs crash in. She had to go now, or she might be washed out to sea.

Putting the carpetbag on to her shoulder, she went carefully down the stairs. She paused near the bottom, holding her candle aloft and looking in horror as a huge wave came hurtling into the cottage. Like a greedy white-tipped hand, it snatched up a wooden stool and retreated with it. Betty knew she must rush out then, through the water, before the next wave came.

She was barely out of the door, and just a few steps up the lane, when an even bigger wave came. This time it filled the doorway, and seconds later the bedroom window was swept outwards with the force of the water, a chair riding and spinning on the crest of the wave. If she had still been in there she would've been snatched up along with the last few sticks of furniture.

Terror made her rush to the top of the lane. Once there, she paused to catch her breath and take stock. All her old neighbours had gone to take shelter in either the mission hall or a friend's home; no one else would be crazy enough to come out in this weather, so she wasn't going to be spotted. Her boots were soaked through, as were the bottom of her dress and cloak. In a short while she would be freezing cold, but she would have to bear that.

The main thing would be to get beyond Kingsbridge by morning, to be safe from running into anyone who knew her.

As she passed the end of the lane, she glanced sideways towards Tern Cottage. She imagined Martin moving his chair closer to the fire, trying to block out the roar of the wind and the sea. She was certain his mother would be laying the table for tea and pretending to show some concern that Betty was taking so long.

Betty smirked at the mental picture. She didn't want to trudge for miles, cold and wet, but she had no choice. If she wanted everyone to believe the sea had swept her away, she must keep going until morning and then invent a new story about herself.

'You'll never see me again,' she said aloud, looking towards Tern Cottage. 'May God forgive me for doing something so wicked. But you are to blame, Agnes Wellows!'

2

As the first weak strip of daylight appeared on the horizon, Betty staggered up a narrow-rutted lane towards a dark shape she hoped was a barn. The rain had stopped about an hour ago, but she was soaked through and the wind was whistling through her wet garments right to her skin. It felt like she'd walked a hundred miles, yet she knew it couldn't be more than twenty. She didn't know the road very well, but she hoped she was near Totnes.

She had never been so exhausted or cold, and she was starving too. The last thing she'd eaten was a slice of bread and dripping, not long before Agnes goaded her into going down to the cottage. She'd passed a horse trough earlier and drank from that, but the cold, hunger and her wet clothes were not as important as being able to rest. She felt as if she was on the point of collapse.

The only way she'd managed to walk the last mile or two was by working on a story about herself in case anyone questioned her.

Saying she was a widow, her husband killed at the Somme, was what she'd decided on. It wasn't very original, but then almost every family in England was mourning someone killed in France. She knew enough about Martin's regiment to carry this off too, and she thought she would say she was making her way to Bristol to look for work.

But she was very aware she would need far more detail

ready in her head: where she'd come from, her relatives, and the kind of work she was used to doing. If she accidentally let slip about Hallsands and fishing, someone might remember that a young red-headed woman went missing from there recently and had been presumed drowned.

Betty had been brought up to be truthful, so lying wasn't going to come easy to her. She wasn't sure whether faking her own death was a crime, but it was certainly wicked to leave a sick husband, even if her mother-in-law had provoked it. Yet she was determined to get over her qualms and embark on a new life.

Thankfully, the dark shape was a barn. To her joy it wasn't locked, and was full of bales of hay. The sweet, warm smell as she opened the door was a welcome reminder of happy times as a child, helping with the haymaking. She climbed up the bales, took off her wet outer clothes and spread them out to dry. Then, after slipping on an almost dry dress from her bag and wrapping herself in her spare shawl, she burrowed into the hay bales and fell asleep almost instantly.

She woke suddenly when something touched her face. To her shock she realized it was a rat – and judging by the squeaking there were many more, close by. Rats and barns went together, everyone knew that, but the thought of one touching her made her skin crawl, and she jumped to her feet, stamping to make any further rodents scurry away.

When she'd arrived at the barn at daybreak, she could see the interior quite clearly as there were thin, narrow slits in one of the walls, up by the roof. But to her surprise the barn was now in total darkness, which meant she'd slept all day.

Gathering up her things, which although not quite dry, were not sodden any more, she felt remarkably cheerful. She fumbled for dry stockings in her bag, put them on, laced up her boots, dragged a comb through her hair and retied it with a ribbon, then picked up her bag, cloak and shawl and cautiously felt her way down the bales.

Agnes came into her mind. She had been terrified of rats; she liked to tell horror stories of them biting babies' faces while they were in a crib. Betty wondered how Agnes would have coped with a rat touching her. Even now, she was probably regaling neighbours with tales of how she'd begged her daughter-in-law not to go to the cottages one more time. No doubt she would practise being grief-stricken at the tragedy, but Betty suspected that many of the neighbours would see through her act. They'd be kind to Agnes, purely because of Martin and his grandfather, but Betty could imagine what they'd be saying behind the woman's back.

Perhaps it was as well the rat had woken her; it was better to walk on by night, to remain unseen. But her stomach was so empty it hurt, and she had no idea what time it was, or how long it would take to reach a shop where she could buy some food.

She was just about to the leave the barn when she smelled apples. Groping her way in the darkness towards the smell, she found some crates. As she ran her hands over the apples' smooth skins, she sensed how much care had gone into storing them for the winter. She took only four, sure the owner wouldn't begrudge her. As she walked back down the rutted lane, far more nimbly than she'd staggered up it the night before, she bit into one.

It was sweet, juicy and delicious. The taste, feel and smell of it brought back a sudden and unexpected memory.

She was fourteen, going off to the Harvest Festival at the chapel with her father. She was wearing her best dress, moss-green wool, with a hair ribbon to match. Mrs Holdway, a neighbour, had made it for her when she noticed Betty's clothes were all getting too short for her. It felt good to be dressed up, and the Harvest Festival was always a jolly service. Betty had made a large plaited loaf, identical to the ones her mother had always made for such occasions when she was alive. Her father was carrying a basket of potatoes and some carrots that he'd grown on his allotment about a mile out of Hallsands. Many of the men had allotments there, one of which belonged to Ted Wellows, Martin's grandfather.

Betty had heard how Ted had invited his widowed daughter-in-law and her son to stay with him until they found a place of their own. Word had it that the daughter-in-law was a tartar, and Ted was already regretting his kindness. But so far Betty hadn't seen these new additions to the village.

As they approached the chapel a young lad came rushing over to them. 'You are Mr Grainger, aren't you?' he said breathlessly, looking up at Bert. 'I'm Martin Wellows, and Grandpa said if I asked you politely you might take me out fishing with you.'

Betty remembered thinking how nice Martin looked; he was fair-haired, with sea-blue eyes and clear rosy skin. He was well dressed too, in a brown tweed jacket and dark grey trousers, his shoes so well polished she could see the October sun glinting on them.

'I'll give you a try,' Bert said with a smile. 'You are the image of your father. We used to fool about together when we were your age.' He turned to Betty then and introduced her to Martin. 'She might be a girl, but she's got the sea in her blood too. You two will get on right well.'

Martin grinned at Betty and shook her hand. Then he had to rush back to his mother, who was coming up the hill.

'Nice lad, so like his dad,' her father said thoughtfully as they went into the church. 'It's cruel how nature takes the good ones first.'

Betty knew he wasn't only referring to Martin's father but to his own dear wife, Betty's mother, and she resolved to ask more questions after church.

As they filed out of the little church after the service, to Betty's surprise, Martin sidled up to her and pushed something into her hand. It was a bright red apple.

He put his finger to his lips to warn her to say nothing. 'Four o'clock, up here,' he whispered.

Betty was amused at this secrecy. Much later, of course, she was to learn that poor Martin couldn't speak to anyone freely without risking his mother's wrath. But the gift of the apple touched her, and later, when she ate it, she found it was the sweetest, juiciest one she'd ever tasted.

That was the day they become friends. She was fourteen, he was sixteen, thrown together by circumstance, or was it fate? Two years later, in 1911, they were married.

'If only he hadn't enlisted,' Betty sighed, as she polished off a second apple. He didn't have to; as a fisherman he was in a reserved occupation. But at twenty-two, he said it was his duty to king and country to go. Betty understood he really wanted adventure, and had a fierce need to see places beyond Devon, but she gave him her blessing – believing, as everyone did then, that it would soon be over.

Ted, his grandfather, became ill just two months later, while Martin was still doing basic training. He managed to get some leave, but even then Agnes berated him for staying with Betty, and not with her, at Ted's cottage.

Betty remembered Martin's response to her. As always, he was calm and measured. 'Mother,' he said, 'Betty is my wife. We made our home together with her father when we got married. I feel sad you have Ted to care for now, but you owe him that for taking us in when we had nowhere else to go. My place is with my wife now. I'm sorry, but that's the way it has to be.'

Betty was proud of him for standing up to his mother; she was a formidable woman, and only the very brave dared cross swords with her. But that act of courage and defiance hardened the woman's heart even further against her daughter-in-law. She had taken against Betty at first because, as she saw it, the girl and her father had lured Martin into fishing when he was supposed to be a carpenter, like his father. She had been very fond of saying Martin's father would be turning in his grave at his son's betrayal. Then she blamed Betty for her son enlisting, claiming she'd made him think that war was exciting.

Ted Wellows confided in Betty's father once that he hadn't wanted to take Agnes in when his son died of lung disease. He'd even suggested Agnes went into service and left Martin with him. But along with being a shrew, Agnes was also a snob. Her husband, Frank, had been a fine cabinet maker, well respected as a craftsman in Plymouth, and until he become ill, they'd had a good standard of living. But two years of sickness had depleted all their savings and, come the end, Agnes was selling her furniture just to eat and pay for Frank's medicine. But hardship didn't have a mellowing effect on her – she still had no intention of being a servant to anyone.

Maybe she believed her father-in-law had enough money to pay for the apprenticeship she wanted so badly for her boy. But Ted too lived a hand-to-mouth existence, as almost everyone in Hallsands did.

Agnes ought to have been grateful to Ted for taking her in, and should have made the best of the situation she found herself in, but her sour face and sharp words alienated her from her new neighbours.

Yet however much of a come-down she thought Hallsands was, Martin loved it. He had his grandfather to help him through his grief at losing his father, he quickly made friends with other boys, and then he met Betty and her father and took to fishing as if he'd been born to it.

Fishing was virtually the sole occupation in Hallsands and everyone, from the youngest to the eldest, did their bit to help. Children were sent up on to the cliffs to watch for shoals of fish and to give the signal for men to sail their boats out to cast the huge seine nets. Everyone in the village rushed to the shore to help pull in the nets and sort the catch.

The best fish was packed into boxes to be sold, others would be eaten by the villagers, and the poorest quality were put aside as bait for crabs. The crabs and lobsters were caught in baskets made from withers, and then kept alive until they could be taken by boat to the London markets.

Of all the children in the village Betty Grainger was the one people smiled about the most. With her tousled mop of red curls, her sparkling green eyes and a smile as wide as Salcombe estuary, she was beguiling.

Even as a little five-year-old she could beat bigger children in the race to the cliff top to act as lookout for shoals of fish. She was never afraid of the sea, and thought nothing of wading in up to her chest in even the coldest weather to help pull in the nets. When her mother died of blood poisoning after a miscarriage, she was sad, but stoic, and although only eight years old she took responsibility for household chores and looking after her father without ever complaining.

So when the villagers saw Betty and Martin becoming friends, two youngsters who had each lost a parent, they were happy for them.

Agnes didn't dare voice her feelings aloud when her son and Betty began courting, but her face gave her away anyway. She once said to a neighbour that she couldn't see what her son saw in 'that impudent, carrot-haired tomboy'. That remark went right around the village, and it only served to make Agnes even more unpopular.

Betty and Martin were married on a sweltering day at the end of May in Stokenham church. Although they had the chapel in Hallsands and went there on Sundays, most people were true to the Church of England and so went to Stokenham church for weddings, funerals and christenings. But after the wedding service it was back to Hallsands for the celebrations on the green outside the chapel. Miss Evans, the retired schoolteacher from Huckham school, where Betty had gone, made her a wedding gown from an evening dress she'd had as a young woman, and the neighbours pooled together to get the ingredients to make a wedding cake.

The celebrations went on till it was dark. Jack Farmer, an itinerant musician, came and played his fiddle, and everyone – from the youngest to the eldest – danced till they dropped. Bert arranged to sleep at a neighbour's cottage for a few nights so the young couple could have the house to themselves.

Everyone in the village wanted 'happy ever after' for the young couple. But in December of the following year, Bert was washed overboard from his boat in a horrific storm.

The tragedy affected the entire village. Fishing was a dangerous occupation, everyone knew that. Each time a boat sailed out, there was always a chance that someone could be swept overboard. To make the tragedy even more distressing, his body wasn't discovered for almost three more weeks, washed up further along the coast. Bert Grainger was one of the most popular fishermen in the village, and people really felt the loss of their friend and neighbour. He was hard-working, kind-hearted, generous with his time, a man who loved to sing and laugh, a good example to the young men of the village and admired by the older ones. As he'd lost his wife, and a baby daughter before, it was thought no further tragedy could strike him; in fact, on the day of Betty and Martin's wedding, they'd teased him and said it was time for him to marry again.

There was only one person who seemed unaffected by his death, and that was Agnes. She even tried to use his death to her advantage by saying she thought she should move in with the young couple. But Martin stood firm and refused to let her. Ted Wellows once again suggested Agnes went into service in Kingsbridge. He even said he wanted his house back for himself.

But Agnes made no attempt to find work; she claimed Ted needed her to look after him, even if he denied it. As a result, Ted spent more time at the London Inn to get away from her. Betty remembered, when Martin enlisted, how he'd told his mother he could no longer support her on a soldier's wages. She got very angry with him and said his father would have been ashamed of him. Betty felt she could easily slap the woman for being so idle and nasty. But to keep the peace, Betty told Martin she would give Ted half the money he sent home, for Agnes's keep. Later, she got the job in Kingsbridge too. She did wonder how on earth she would have managed if she had found herself pregnant after Martin's last leave.

Thankfully, that hadn't happened, and although Betty had missed Martin desperately, she liked her job in Kingsbridge. Mr Porter was an insurance man, his wife a little scatter-brained, but she had a sunny nature and appreciated Betty's help running her house. To Betty, her employer's house – a pretty villa with modern conveniences like a bathroom, inside lavatory, gas lighting and well-appointed scullery – was a joy to look after.

When Martin came home from France with a severely damaged leg, it was clear he wouldn't be able to get up and down to their own house, so Ted suggested he stayed with him and Agnes. They didn't know then that Martin's mental damage wouldn't heal along with his leg and other more minor injuries. Betty needed to keep her job too – she had to help provide for both Martin and Agnes – so Ted resigned himself to the fact that this was his lot now: a damaged grandson and a harpy who would never change.

Ted had been out when Agnes ordered Betty to go to her home and rescue her belongings. Betty knew he would've been distraught when he got home and found she was missing. He would also be suspicious that Agnes was responsible.

'Poor Ted,' Betty murmured to herself. 'As if he didn't have enough to put up with.'

Walking through the darkness didn't seem half as awful as it had the previous night. The wind was cold, but it was dry. She heard the occasional owl hooting, cows moving around in the fields, and saw a badger crossing the lane right in front of her. There were cottages here and there, but no lights were on, and a dog barked at only one farmhouse. She plodded valiantly on, her mind on the new person she was going to become.

'Mabel,' she said aloud, and smiled because she'd had a friend when she was five years old by that name, and she'd always thought Betty a very plain name. 'Mabel Brook. And I come from Plymouth. My husband, Peter, was killed at the Somme . . . but I can't bear to speak about that, it's too painful.'

It *had* been too painful to talk about what was wrong with Martin. When he was first shipped back to England and she visited him in hospital in Plymouth, she imagined that once his body was mended, he'd be back to normal. His leg was mended now, but he remained in a chair, seemingly unable to understand anything.

Even the doctor couldn't suggest any remedies, and it became so bad that sometimes Betty wished he'd died in Flanders as a hero, rather than spending the rest of his life as he was now. Though that seemed a terrible thing to think, as if she didn't love him.

That love had never diminished, but it was love for the strong, funny and loving Martin who went off to France, not this broken shell of a man by the same name. She felt guilty that she cringed at the terror in his eyes when he heard a loud noise, and she was irritated that he appeared to have no knowledge of who she was, or how he'd felt about her. She hated, too, that people pitied her for losing a real man and being left with a deranged child.

'I'm an only child, my father died six years ago . . .' Betty – or Mabel, as she must think of herself from now on – told her story out loud as she walked. 'Since then, I've looked after my sick mother. She died just recently. I felt I had to leave the sad memories in Plymouth and start again. I'll make a good housekeeper or a plain cook. Or I can work in a shop, as I'm good at figures.'

She was so engrossed in this new story that she hadn't noticed it was growing light again. When she did notice, it occurred to her that she must have left the barn in the middle of the night, not early evening, as she'd supposed.

'No wonder you felt so rested,' she thought. Just ahead of her she saw a milestone saying Totnes was only two miles further on. Her plan was to find a room there for a night or two, study Situations Vacant columns in the newspaper, then decide where to go next.

As Mabel, she walked down the hill towards the river in the centre of Totnes. Along with terror at the prospect of being stopped by someone who knew her, she felt a flurry of excitement, remembering how she'd come here with Martin soon after they were married.

They'd gone with her father on his fishing boat to Dartmouth, early in the morning, to deliver some crabs and lobsters, and to pick up a spare part for his boat. Leaving him there, and with the promise they'd be back by five, they caught a paddle steamer up the River Dart to Totnes.

It was a beautiful, hot and sunny June day, and it was lovely to just sit in the sun watching the fields and tiny villages go by. They were both enchanted by Totnes, so many little shops and incredibly old houses, all crowded together in a very higgledy-piggledy manner, and Martin bought her a straw hat with a string of artificial daisies around the crown.

They got a pork pie from a butcher's and a bottle of lemonade, and nothing had ever tasted as good as that impromptu picnic sitting by the river.

They didn't have time to explore up the hill as the boat trip took longer than they'd expected. But she remembered Martin saying they'd come back there one day and explore the rest of the town. They never did.

But exploring the town was the last thing on her mind now. She needed to find a safe place to stay, to get her off the streets. Aside from being spotted by someone who knew her, she was afraid her disappearance had been reported and the police were looking for her. She pulled the hood on her cloak right over her head, hiding her face, and cowered in alleys when she spotted a policeman. When a man tapped her on the shoulder, she nearly jumped out of her skin, but all he wanted was to ask her the way to Dartington village. He made her feel so scared she couldn't even tell him she didn't know.

By ten that morning, Mabel had already eaten a quantity of fatty bacon stuck between two thick lumps of bread, washed down with three cups of tea, in a little café by the market. She had to sit down, as her feet ached, but it was terrifying to be sitting so close to other people. She kept her head down and didn't meet anyone's gaze. Each time the café door opened she imagined a policeman coming in.

But a chance remark she overheard, about the library, made her think it would be a good place to while away some time in the warm. They always had newspapers to read – ideal for not only finding out about how badly Hallsands had fared during the night, but also advertisements for rooms to let. She didn't think anyone who knew her would be likely to go to the library; many of the older people in Hallsands couldn't read or write.

About six other people who looked a great deal more destitute than her were already in the little reading room of the library, and there was quite a fug of pipe tobacco, wet wool and unwashed bodies. Mabel went right down to the end of the room, away from the stove and people, and opened *The Times*.

There were three or four column inches on the damage to the houses at Hallsands on the night before last. There was even a photograph showing the lane down to the sea, including a small bit of her house. It was an old photograph taken the time before, when the high tide had damaged the cottages. Clearly no one had yet been down there to check on more recent damage or to take pictures.

She scanned through the paper; between reports of overcrowding in hospitals, with the constant influx of wounded men brought back from France, details of scarcity of many food stuffs, and the revolution brewing in Russia, she saw reports of flooding in several other seaside towns in Devon and Cornwall. Then she picked up the local newspaper.

There was far more about localized flooding here, rivers that had burst their banks, roads and the railway closed. But again, Hallsands only warranted a few lines. For a moment or two she felt a bit queasy, wondering what would happen if the house hadn't been washed away and Agnes found out she'd been in there and taken clothes and other things.

But common sense said that was so unlikely, as the waves had been roaring in through the door as she left, and it wasn't even high tide then. The only real things she had to worry about for now were the risk of being recognized and the urgency of finding a cheap place to stay.

There were only houses, no rooms, to let in the newspaper, and all the situations vacant required a character.

As Mabel walked down the hill towards the river, keeping her head down and the hood of her cloak partially over her face, she passed a sweet shop with a board outside, advertising things for sale, jobs and accommodation. She stopped to look, almost holding her breath in the hope of there being something right for her. There were three 'rooms for working men, dinner included'. Another one offered accommodation in return for light housekeeping duties. But that wouldn't do, as she had no intention of staying more than two or three nights.

Finally, almost hidden by a card offering gardening work, was one that was just right. Bed and breakfast, down on the quayside. It claimed to be 'warm and comfortable' and 'best rates'.

She had no idea what best rates meant. But she liked the sound of warm and comfortable. After jotting down the address, she nervously continued down the hill.

Quay View on the Strand was, as she expected, one of the three-storey houses she'd passed earlier that morning, right by the river. Not a smart house, but neither was it the worst in the row. The white paint was dingy, but then it was January. On the plus side, the windows sparkled and the brass on the front door was gleaming.

Mabel rang the bell and the door was opened almost immediately by a stout lady with a very red face, her hair covered by a blue checked turban.

'Have you a room vacant, just for two or three nights?' Mabel asked. 'I'm on my way to Bristol, but I thought I'd take a breather here.'

'Come in out of the cold,' the woman said and smiled. 'I don't get many guests at this time of year. So you can have my best room. I'm Mrs Halliwell.'

Mabel was very scared when Mrs Halliwell invited her into her kitchen for a cup of tea. It crossed her mind that the police could have already been round, warning guest-house owners she might ask for a room.

That idea faded once she was in a very cosy and warm kitchen. Mrs Halliwell was truly welcoming, and not a bit suspicious. Mabel told her the story she'd prepared, making sure she made it clear she had little money, in case this seemingly good woman turned out to be greedy.

'You poor dear,' Mrs Halliwell said in sympathy. 'A pretty young thing like you shouldn't be having to start a new life in a strange town.'

'These are tough times for everyone,' Mabel said. 'I'm just glad I haven't any children, things would've been really tough then. I'm young enough to make new friends, and I'm not afraid of hard work.'

The room was only a shilling a night, and it was a pretty one overlooking the river, the wallpaper green with white blossom, and a multicoloured patchwork quilt on the brass bed. As Mrs Halliwell showed Mabel the room she bent over to light the fire, already laid in the grate.

'You'll soon be as snug as a bug,' she said, looking down at the flames as they caught the kindling. 'I'll leave you to settle in now. You look tired, my dear, so why not have a little nap? Come and have supper with me tonight, at six thirty? I'm a widow too and I don't much like eating alone.'

It was the kindness of Mrs Halliwell that made Mabel start to cry after the woman had left the room. She lay down on the bed, pulled the patchwork quilt over her and sobbed.

Until then, she hadn't really considered how people she'd known all her life would react to the news that she'd been washed away by the sea. Her neighbours had comforted her when her mother died, cooked her meals and made her clothes. They had rejoiced at her wedding and grieved with her when her father was lost at sea, and now, when they were in despair at losing their homes, she was giving them still more pain by allowing them to think she was dead.

Supposing Martin woke out of whatever place his mind had been in, to remember he had a wife he loved, and then found she was gone? Wasn't that likely to completely destroy him?

Mabel felt sick with guilt, but she couldn't go back now. She'd slammed and bolted that door for all time.

3

As the train chugged away from Totnes station, Mabel felt such a sense of relief.

In the three days she'd spent there, she had been too scared to stay out for more than an hour – and even then, she kept darting into alleyways if she saw someone she thought she knew. If anyone looked at her hard, she wanted to run, and she felt sick to her stomach whenever she saw a policeman. So she'd spent most of the time in her room, alone with her very troubling thoughts about how wicked she was.

Yet staying with Mrs Halliwell was so pleasant. She was the kindest, most generous person, and her home was as cosy and warm as she was. It felt so good to have someone showing concern for her. It was a long time since anyone had done that. But with each day, expecting her face to be on the front page of a newspaper, she lived with the guilt that Mrs Halliwell might be taken to task for hiding a fugitive.

It had made no difference that she told herself her old neighbours in Hallsands rarely went beyond Kingsbridge; she was still scared. She knew many people in Kingsbridge too, including her old employers, and they all came to Totnes to shop.

On her second day in the town, the papers had finally reported on the tragedy in Hallsands. All the houses in the lane were gone, the picture showing only a couple of tottering walls to indicate that these were once people's homes. The journalist pointed out in a strong, campaigning voice that if it hadn't been for developers ruthlessly taking away shingle from the beach below the village, merely to extend Plymouth harbour, this tragedy in Hallsands wouldn't have happened. Mabel thought it was a shame he and other people in authority hadn't started an outcry years ago, when it had become clear how this was going to end. The journalist hammered his point home, listing other occasions when a storm and an unusually high tide had created similar damage.

The developers and the local council have had so many warnings of the dangers. But this time it appears the sea claimed a life too. Young Mrs Betty Wellows, aged only 22, is presumed to have been swept away as she tried to rescue some of her belongings.

Mabel cringed at the editorial that followed.

Betty, with her curly red hair, slight build and ready smile, was popular with her neighbours. She had lived in Hallsands all her life, and in her short life she had become accustomed to tragedy. Her mother died when she was eight; her fisherman father, Bert Grainger, was lost at sea soon after Betty was married to Martin Wellows, also a fisherman. Wellows enlisted in the army in November 1915 and was brought home a few months ago, having been wounded at the Battle of the Somme. He is now a widower, he's lost his house, and it is reported that he is still suffering from the injuries he sustained in France.

Can it be right that people in positions of power, such as these wealthy developers, can ride roughshod over working people's rights, their homes and even their lives? For surely these businessmen are responsible for Mrs Wellows's death and for the plight of all those who are now homeless.

There was even an old, grainy class photograph from Mabel's school. But fortunately her face wasn't at all clear.

While Mabel was pleased that someone was acting as a champion for her friends and neighbours in Hallsands, she also felt a sudden, sharp stab of guilt that there would be those who would be terribly upset that she'd lost her life. All she'd focused on as she left the village was how hateful Agnes was. But her neighbours who'd cared for her when her mother died, her childhood playmates and her employers in Kingsbridge, they didn't deserve the pain of grief.

Yet however guilty she felt about making old friends sad, she was aware that others thrived on drama and it would give them pleasure to boast of their tenuous connection to her. Unfortunately, it would be just Mabel's luck to run into someone who had met her briefly at chapel, in the market, or somewhere equally random.

It was a shame she couldn't stay in Totnes, as she really liked the busy, bustling small town. It had a good variety of shops, including clothing shops which were renowned all over Devon. There were the lumber yards along the river, and boats moored there to bring so many goods to the town. Harris's bacon factory employed a great many people and their food products were sold countrywide.

But she didn't dare stay any longer, and she was just grateful to dear Mrs Halliwell for being so kind. She'd only taken a shilling for her keep. She said Mabel needed money more than she did. Mabel didn't expect to be that lucky in Bristol. It was a big city and she'd been told Bristolians were mean.

Looking out of the train window, she wondered if she would ever see Devon again. The countryside was at its most stark and desolate right now, even the cows and sheep in the fields looked miserable, and many fields resembled lakes because of the heavy rain. But she knew, by March, she'd be daydreaming of lambs skipping around these same fields, buds opening on trees and the banks being covered in primroses and violets. Yet it would be the sea she would miss the most. It might be cruel and violent sometimes, but she'd woken up to it every day of her life; she'd fished, sailed, swam and just sat and watched the incredible majesty of it. She couldn't imagine a life without it just beyond her window.

But Mabel was determined to look forward. The past was gone; today, tomorrow and the future were what counted. Totnes and Plymouth were the furthest she'd been so far, and she expected there were many other towns and cities that were just as lovely. Her plan for now was to put away the memories of Devon – her parents dying, Martin being brought back from France a different man to the one she'd married, and her flight from Hallsands – and seal them in a kind of imaginary box. She would keep it locked until such time as she was able to be objective about it all. Then she would open it again, remember the good times and shed a few tears of sorrow for those she'd hurt in running away. Until that day, she was Mabel Brook from Plymouth, and she was embarking on a whole new life.

*

The first thing to strike Mabel about Bristol, when she came out of Temple Meads station, was the congestion. It had been noisy and smoky in the station, but she was so overawed by the size of the place – the high glass roof over the platforms, the trains belching out steam, a maelstrom of people pushing and shoving to either catch a train or to leave the station – she had assumed, once she was outside, it would be calmer.

But it was worse, with horse-drawn carts, cabs and trolley buses all hurtling their way around one another at what seemed to be breakneck speed. Back in Devon, spotting one of the new petrol automobiles was a rare and noteworthy sight, but here there were lots. The pavements were equally crowded too; people making their way to Temple Meads station, carrying bags or suitcases, jostled with housewives going shopping in the opposite direction. There were flower sellers, boot blacks and newspaper boys. Working men in grubby clothes and flat caps mingled with men in bowler hats and smart suits. Scores of dirty little urchins darted about, their eyes full of mischief. She was glad she'd tucked her purse into a secret, buttoned-up pocket on the inside of her cloak, as she was sure these children were pickpockets.

There were many men in uniform too, either coming home on leave or going back to the front. More worrying still was the number of crippled men, some with a missing leg, hobbling along on crutches, others with bandaged heads or arms in slings. She saw one man who had lost both legs; he was sitting on a wheeled soap box, begging. He had a card hanging around his neck, which read 'Wounded at the Somme'.

But over and above such sights was the noise. Cartwheels, horses' hooves, engines, bells ringing on the trolley buses, traders shouting out their wares. Mabel wanted to cover her ears to shut it out, but it occurred to her she might as well cover her eyes too, so she didn't have to see the poverty and those wounded in France, and even cover her nose against the smells. The most pungent were horse droppings, unwashed bodies, and the stink of the river. She wondered how she was ever going to like living in this town, when right now it was making her stomach churn.

Mrs Halliwell had suggested the St Pauls area of Bristol, to find some accommodation and possibly work, as it was within walking distance of the train station. She said she'd stayed once at a pleasant guest house in City Road.

Mabel turned to look back at Temple Meads station. At school she'd been taught about Isambard Kingdom Brunel, who had designed the railway, but she hadn't been expecting the station itself to be quite so impressive. To her it looked like a splendid palace or a cathedral. It seemed odd that, just outside the forecourt, everywhere was so dirty, smelly and noisy.

Mabel had often heard visitors to Devon describe local people as 'country bumpkins' and, looking around her now, she thought that described her perfectly. The smarter women were wearing fitted cloth coats, or furs; they had felt hats in interesting shapes, often decorated with flowers or feathers. Cloaks like hers and knitted bonnets were only worn by the old or the poor, and few women wore dresses right down to their ankles. Along with being scared, and revolted by the sights and smells, she also felt old and dowdy.

She bought the local newspaper on the way to City Road, but although she wanted to study it right away for any situations vacant, the weather was very cold, and she thought it might snow, so it seemed advisable to find lodgings first.

A couple of hours later, Mabel had found a room. It bore no resemblance to Mrs Halliwell's lovely home; it was just a small shabby room with a lumpy bed, a washbasin, a single gas ring and a gas fire. But it would do until she found a live-in job.

The house was four storeys tall, with only one very grubby bathroom and one lavatory. As there were at least four doors on each floor – her room was on the second, at the back – it didn't really bear thinking about just how many people would be using that one lavatory. But she reminded herself she had always shared a communal privy, and had never had a real bathroom anyway, so she didn't know why she was horrified at the prospect.

Some of the houses in City Road were still family homes, but far more were shabby lodging houses. Yet an elderly woman she spoke to in the grocer's, as she was buying some essentials food stuffs, said that twenty years earlier it had been home to wealthy people. She said that gradually the rich had begun to move further out of the city and she anticipated in a few more years the once fine houses would turn into slums.

That same lady had found Mabel's Devon accent very amusing. 'You sound like a farmer's wife,' she chuckled. 'You just mind people don't take advantage of you or snatch your purse cos they think you're a bit slow.'

Mabel wanted to retort that it was rude to make personal

remarks, but she bit it back; the woman was old, and maybe she meant well by warning her.

The thought that maybe she was a fish out of water in a big city made Mabel feel scared again. All at once, she thought people were looking at her, weighing her up. She hurried back to her room, her heart thumping loudly, locking the door behind her and trembling as if she'd been assaulted.

But the room didn't feel safe. People shouted angrily in the rooms above her, a baby cried constantly, and when she finally plucked up courage to go and use the lavatory it smelled so bad, she gagged.

For the first time since she'd left Hallsands she wished she hadn't run away. Even Agnes's sharp tongue was preferable to the strangers fighting upstairs. If she opened her front door there, the air was fresh and clean, and the only sound at night was the sea below. Here she had the carts, cabs and buses going along the street, drunks and hooligans yelling to each other, dogs barking, loud music and raucous laughter coming from the public house on the corner.

She crawled into the bed to get warm, but even that felt slightly damp, and the sheets the landlady had said were clean on that morning smelled nasty. Was this what life was going to be like from now on?

Huddled in the bed, hungry and thirsty, she was too cold to get the bread and cheese she'd brought back, and however much she wanted a hot cup of tea, she didn't dare go to the bathroom to fill the kettle in case she ran into someone.

The tears came then. Tears of remorse, guilt and loneliness. She'd thought she was heading for an adventure, something better than she had before, but it seemed it was going to be far worse.

Two days later, Mabel walked to Clifton. The wife of the grocer in City Road had told her there were many jobs as kitchen maids, parlour maids, cooks and housekeepers going there. She said hundreds of women had left jobs in service to work in factories since the war began. She recommended Mabel did the same, as the pay was far better than domestic work.

But Mabel didn't want to work in a factory and carry on living in a dirty, noisy boarding house. She wanted the security of working in a private home, a clean, quiet place where she got fed, didn't have to share a lavatory with scores of people, and would be warm. Once she'd found her way around Bristol, she could always leave and get a better job.

It was a cold, crisp day and Mabel had been tempted to put on her best dress and hat. The dress was brown with a cream lace collar and cuffs. The matching brown hat, perched on her head at an angle, looked stylish, and it contrasted well with her red hair. She had made the dress herself, back before Martin enlisted, and he'd bought her the hat to go with it in Kingsbridge. But she'd suddenly realized she couldn't wear such a jaunty outfit; a woman claiming to be a widow, and not in full mourning, would be accused of being 'fast'. So she had resigned herself to wearing the hated old black dress she'd had since her father's funeral, brushed off the mud smears around the hem, tied her bonnet under her chin, and put the dowdy black cloak on too, just to keep warm.

She winced when she saw herself reflected in shop windows. Black drained all colour from her face and made her look ill and old. She wondered just how long she would have to keep up the pretence.

An advertisement on the board outside a tobacconist's in a side street caught her eye. 'Maid of all work required. Call at 6 Harley Place. Good wages for the right applicant.'

Just five minutes later, she was walking through the gate of an elegant, double-fronted, four-storey old house.

She'd asked directions and was told the house was by Christchurch and looked out over the Downs, not far from the suspension bridge. The Downs turned out to be a large grassy area that appeared to go on and on. Looking to her left as she faced Harley Place, she could just see part of the famous Clifton Suspension Bridge. She remembered from school that it was another Brunel design, though he'd died before it was built. She wanted to walk over it, and to explore the Downs. But first she had to get this job.

The front garden was small, but well maintained. She went up the steps and rang the bell. The door was opened by an older woman who was wearing a black dress almost completely covered by a snowy white apron.

'I've called about the position of maid of all work,' Mabel said.

The woman looked her up and down and half smiled. 'You're a country girl!'

It was a statement, rather than a question. But Mabel had a feeling the woman was kindly.

'Yes, ma'am, I'm from Plymouth. My husband was killed in France, and I've come to Bristol to find work.'

The older woman nodded. 'Come on in,' she said. 'It's very cold today. I'm Mrs Hardy, the housekeeper. And you are?'

'Mrs Mabel Brook.'

Mrs Hardy ushered Mabel into a small room just off the large kitchen at the back of the house. The room appeared to be the housekeeper's office; there was a desk beneath the window with a large ledger opened on it, and a brutal-looking spike held many bills. On a trolley was a pile of clean white towels, and a sizeable basket held clothes either waiting to be ironed or mended. Although it was a rather dark room, there was a cheerful fire in the grate.

'Tell me about your last employer?' she asked, turning the seat by her desk around to face Mabel, then sitting down and indicating Mabel was to take the chair close to her. 'I will of course need a character from them.'

'Oh dear! I haven't been employed by anyone,' Mabel said, putting on the most wide-eyed innocent look she could. 'I helped my father, who was a fisherman, until I married, and after that I just kept house for my husband. But now he's gone I felt unable to stay there. I want, and need, a fresh start and work.'

Mrs Hardy nodded. 'I am sorry for your loss, so many women have lost their menfolk in this terrible war. But tell me what you think being a maid of all work means.'

'I imagine it means cleaning, lighting fires, laundry, polishing and possibly helping out in the kitchen too.'

'You imagine right. Can you do all that?'

'I can – and many other things, like mending and ironing,' Mabel said. 'I could catch you a few mackerel too, if we weren't so far from the sea.'

For a moment she thought her little joke was not appreciated, for the woman's face remained stern and businesslike, but then she chuckled.

'I think you'll do fine, Mabel. But just to be sure, two weeks' trial, and if you don't suit, you'll have to go.'

'That's very fair,' Mabel said, and meaning it. 'I won't let you down. Will the mistress want to see me now?'

'No, that won't be necessary. Mrs Gladsworthy is a widow and an invalid. She leaves the staff and the running of the house to me entirely. We don't have a big staff, just me, Mrs Tweed our cook, and now you too, though we do have another woman who comes in now and then to do any rough work. You'll be paid six shillings a month, all found, and a half-day off on Sunday and Wednesday afternoons.'

Mabel had expected the pay to be more; after all, she'd got the same amount for a week in Kingsbridge. But she had been the housekeeper, doing everything, and she hadn't lived in. But 'beggars can't be choosers', as her father used to say.

'I shall expect you to come to church with me on Sunday mornings,' Mrs Hardy went on. 'And your room is up in the attic. Have you a suitable black dress?'

'Only this one.' Mabel indicated what she was wearing. 'It's awfully shabby now, as I've worn it ever since my father died. That was soon after I was married . . . and then of course Peter was killed.'

Mrs Hardy looked at her thoughtfully. 'There are a couple of dresses tucked away upstairs. You could alter one of them to fit you. More importantly, when can you start work?'

'Later today, if I just go back to the room in St Pauls I've been staying in, and collect my things,' Mabel said eagerly. 'Or is that too soon for you?'

Mrs Hardy beamed. 'No, that is ideal. But for tonight you can just settle in and start work tomorrow.'

It was no hardship leaving the room in City Road. Mrs Hardy had shown her the room that would be hers, up in the attic, and it was pleasant, with a brass bed, a dressing table and an easy chair. It smelled fresh and clean, and there was a pretty multicoloured patchwork comforter on the bed, which Mrs Hardy said Mrs Gladsworthy had made as a young girl. She'd also seen the kitchen and the little staff room where she would have her meals. Mrs Tweed, the cook, looked about forty – plump and smiley, as cooks were supposed to look – and said she was glad Mabel was going to join the household and she hoped she'd be happy there. Then just as she was about to leave, Mrs Hardy pointed out the staff bathroom, along the corridor from the kitchen.

'We are blessed here with constant hot water, heated by the kitchen range, and an inside lavatory,' Mrs Hardy said with a warm smile. 'There is also a bathroom upstairs and so in this house there is none of that tedious and back-breaking filling and emptying of baths for the mistress, as I had to do when I was your age.'

Mabel could hardly believe her luck as she rushed down through Clifton to collect her few belongings. To live in a house even nicer than the one where she'd worked in Kingsbridge, to be warm and well fed, to have electricity instead of oil lamps and candles, and to be trusted without supplying a character.

Someone was smiling down on her, and she intended to make sure she paid back that trust by working extra hard.

Within a week at Harley Place, Mabel felt totally at home. She liked her uniform black dress, it was far better quality material than her own dress, and apart from taking up the hem it fitted as if it had been made for her. She had a grey-and-black striped apron to wear when she was doing the fires, and three snowy white ones for the rest of the time. She started work at six thirty, clearing the grates and relighting the fires; there was one in the upstairs sitting room Mrs Gladsworthy used, one in Mrs Hardy's office and one in the staff room. She had been told the drawing room and dining room on the ground floor were only used on the rare occasions the mistress had guests.

While the mistress was having her breakfast in her sitting room, Mabel cleared the fire in her bedroom, relaid it and lit it, made her bed and put her clothes away. She had met her new employer on her first day and felt deeply sorry for her. She was in her late forties but looked older because she was crippled by rheumatism. There was an oil painting of her as a young woman in the drawing room. She had been lovely then, in a pink ball gown with an hour-glass figure, startlingly blue eyes and long, golden blonde hair. Her eyes were still lovely, but her hair was white and her back bent.

Mrs Hardy had told Mabel that until the mistress's husband was killed in a riding accident in Leigh Woods, some ten years earlier, she had been a keen horsewoman and loved to play tennis too. Up until then, she'd only had odd twinges of rheumatism, but almost as soon as he died it flared up, incapacitating her completely at times. The only time she felt better was in warm weather, and in fact her doctor had recommended she move to a place with a milder climate.

'She won't do that, because her husband is buried at Christchurch. She says she can't bear to leave him,' Mrs Hardy said. 'I look after his grave for her during the winter months when she can't get out. I'd worked for them for over ten years before Mr Gladsworthy died. It is so sad. They were the golden couple, invited out all the time – in fact, no social event was complete without them – and they had so many parties here. If only they'd been blessed with children, maybe she wouldn't have sunk so low that the rheumatism took hold.'

Mabel murmured her understanding, yet she couldn't help but think of all the poor people she'd met who had lost a wife, husband or child, and because of their situation they just had to get on with life. But at least Mrs Gladsworthy hadn't become a tyrant, believing she was the only person in the world to suffer and grieve. In fact, she had sympathized with Mabel losing her husband, and said she hoped that she would find a measure of new happiness here in her home. Mabel doubted many rich women like Mrs Gladsworthy cared a jot about their servants' happiness.

Mabel was happy. Maybe there was more cleaning to do here than at her job in Kingsbridge, but she didn't have the long walk there and back in all weathers. Back then, she'd also had her own house to look after, and she had to do whatever Agnes demanded. Her mother-in-law made her scrub the living-room floor every single day; she expected the fireside rug to be taken out and beaten too, with no regard for Mabel having already done a hard day's work.

Here it was quite different. Mrs Hardy rarely pulled her up on anything – in fact, she complimented her all the time. Mrs Tweed made delicious meals; Mabel had never been so well fed, and even if Cook did pry a bit too much about her past, she was kindly. It wasn't even a long day, as Mrs Gladsworthy liked her supper at six, and once her tray was taken away, she didn't ring again for anything else. Mabel did any washing-up left in the kitchen once Mrs Tweed had left for her own home, and then she stayed by the fire in the staff room, off the kitchen, to read or do any mending required. Mrs Hardy usually stayed up in her office, doing her accounts, but sometimes she came down later and she and Mabel would have a cup of tea and a chat.

It wasn't just the easy work that Mabel liked about the job, or the warmth and decent food; she loved the house too. Mrs Hardy said it was Georgian, as most of the houses in Clifton were, though that meant little to Mabel. She liked that it was light and bright, with elegant large windows, dainty furniture, soft carpets and so many lovely oil paintings that the Gladsworthys had collected over the years. She particularly liked one of a pretty harbour at sunset; the sea and sky had an orange tint that reminded her of how the sea had sometimes looked back home in Hallsands. Mrs Hardy said it was Weymouth and that before Mr Gladsworthy's death, they used to stay for the whole of August in a cottage there.

Sometimes when Mabel went upstairs to put more coal on the fire, Mrs Gladsworthy would talk to her. She always wore black, because she was still in mourning. Ten years was an awfully long time to be in full mourning, but at least her dress was beautifully cut, with pin-tucks down the bodice, and she wore pearl earrings and a pearl brooch at her neck.

'Did you feel that you wanted to die when your husband was killed?' she asked one day.

Mabel didn't really know how to respond.

'I don't remember exactly how I felt,' she said carefully, yet remembering all too clearly the day she'd visited Martin in hospital and been completely shocked that he didn't seem to even remember who she was. 'I think I was kind of numb for a while. It didn't seem real.'

'I imagine it's a bit different if your husband is a soldier. You know it could happen. But it never crossed my mind that Mr Gladsworthy would go before me, and in a riding accident.'

She looked so dejected, Mabel felt bad she was claiming to be a widow too. 'I expect you feel very lonely now,' she ventured gingerly.

'Yes, I do,' she sighed. 'So many of our old friends don't bother with me any more, it's very hurtful.'

'I'm so sorry, ma'am,' Mabel said. 'But maybe they think you don't want to see anyone. Couldn't you send them a letter inviting them to tea?'

'That is an excellent idea,' Mrs Gladsworthy said, and gave a little tinkling laugh. 'I should be ashamed of myself, complaining to you of all people.'

Mabel knew straight off that her employer meant she had so much, while Mabel had nothing.

'But I'm not in pain all the time, ma'am, like you are,' she said.

'What a sweet girl you are,' Mrs Gladsworthy said. 'I'll make more of an effort to contact my old friends in future.'

By the time the first warm day arrived in May, Mabel felt as if she'd be content to stay in Harley Place forever. She felt so fortunate to have found herself safe and secure in a job she liked. Clifton was a treasure trove of interesting shops, beautiful houses and so many parks and open spaces.

Yet by moving to a big city she had come to see how ignorant she was as a result of the cloistered life she'd led in Devon. She could sail a boat, swim like a fish, grow vegetables, cook and clean, but she'd never been anywhere else, and all her neighbours and friends were just like her.

She recalled that when war was declared, she hadn't understood what had started it. She vaguely recalled something about a prince being shot, but that seemed a very flimsy reason for thousands of innocent people to be killed.

But then she hadn't even really grasped the scale of the carnage in France, not until Martin was wounded. His wounds were mild when compared with the other soldiers in his ward, who were blinded, maimed and had missing limbs.

To address this ignorance, she now read *The Times* every day and borrowed books from the diverse collection in the drawing room, often asking Mrs Gladsworthy for her recommendations. But for now, the war and world events were her main interest. She had a personal interest, of course, in the battle of the Somme as Martin had been wounded there, and she was horrified to read that on just the first day of the battle 19,000 British men had died. An even longer battle had taken place at Verdun, with the Germans bleeding the French army dry.

Closer to home was the Easter Rising in Ireland, in 1916, something she'd never even heard about at the time. Although she didn't fully understand Ireland's wish for independence, she was impressed by Padraig Pearse, one of the founder members of the Irish Volunteers. She loved his courage and how he exclaimed at his court martial, 'You cannot conquer Ireland. You cannot extinguish the Irish passion for freedom.' He was holding a crucifix in his hand as he was executed.

She read about German U-boats, and how Tsar Nicholas and his family were arrested by the Bolsheviks in Russia. The menace of Zeppelin airships had been an ongoing problem since 1915, but it wasn't until the first daylight bombing raid in London, in June of 1917, when the death toll rose to 162 deaths and hundreds injured, that people really began to feel the war was entering England.

Yet in all that she read, the most distressing thing of all to Mabel was the long lists of soldiers who had died in France. They were someone's husband, father, brother or friend, and most were so terribly young, men like Martin who had left England thinking it would be the greatest adventure. Then there were the even greater numbers of wounded. What future would they have, with a missing limb or lost sight?

On her daily trip to the shops, across the road in The Mall, there was hardly a woman in sight who wasn't either in full mourning or wearing a black patch on her sleeve to signify she'd lost someone close.

But as sad as it was to hear the roll call of new deaths of

local men at church each Sunday, and to read in the newspaper about the conditions at the front, the poverty here in Bristol was even more disturbing, because it was right in front of her, not across the English Channel.

When she walked down to the city centre, she was confronted with it. Not the mild kind of poverty she'd known back in Hallsands – shabby clothes and a breakfast of bread and dripping – but real poverty, hunger etched on gaunt faces and dead-looking eyes. Back home, no one would let a neighbour starve if they fell on hard times; they would share what they had. But here, people wore rags and shoes that were split open and tied on to their feet with string. She had seen men hideously disfigured, presumably by shrapnel in France, and people crossing the road to avoid any contact with them. Poor women lurked in doorways, and although she knew nothing about prostitution, instinctively she knew these women were offering themselves for sale because they had no other way of surviving.

As for the children, it was terrible to see their grey, thin faces, bare feet even in the February snow, and running sores on their limbs. She asked herself, and indeed Mrs Hardy, why the government cared nothing about the plight of these children, and made no provision for the men who had been seriously injured while fighting for their country, leaving them no choice but to beg on the streets. Mrs Hardy just shrugged, she had no answers.

Seeing such sights had made Mabel realize that her former life in Devon might have been tough, yet she could be proud that there was a tradition of caring for others in the community she'd been born into. She remembered, when her father was lost at sea, how the other fishermen made a collection to help her, just as they'd helped her father years before when her mother died. There were plenty of people wanting to help Martin too when he came home from the war, but Agnes never let them through the door. The silly woman felt shell shock was something shameful, so she hid it from those who might just have been able to help heal his broken mind.

Despite her happiness in her new job and home, Mabel did get days when she fervently wished she'd stood her ground when Martin came out of hospital and refused to let him stay with his mother. Maybe if she'd taken him to their house and held him tightly in her arms at night, the security of that might have helped him.

But as spring slipped into summer, she thought less and less about her old life, and in the evenings when she had no sewing to do, she borrowed books from the drawing room and immersed herself in them. She listened to the way Mrs Hardy and Mrs Gladsworthy spoke and tried to copy them. Cook teased her about it and said not to copy her, as she'd get a Bristol accent that was far uglier than a Devon one.

Mrs Gladsworthy's painful joints had become easier once the weather grew warmer, and Mabel volunteered to take her for some short walks. The first one was to the suspension bridge and back. Mabel had been over it many times since she began work in Harley Place, and marvelled that such a delicate-looking, beautiful bridge could take such heavy traffic.

She voiced that opinion to Mrs Gladsworthy as the woman clung to Mabel's arm.

'I've never before met anyone as young as you taking an interest in the engineering of bridges,' her employer remarked with surprise.

'I've become interested in architecture too,' Mabel said with enthusiasm. 'Clifton has so many fine houses, Georgian like yours, and Victorian ones too. Further down, in the middle of Bristol, there are other buildings far, far older.'

'You've no doubt discovered that wealthy folk built houses in Clifton in the 1800s to escape the terrible smell of the docks,' her mistress said with a little laugh.

'Yes, I did, and so many of them were slave traders too,' Mabel said. 'That was a bad period of history, wasn't it? Just as this war is too, so many men sent out to France to die. No one seems to be able to say what good will come out of it, either.'

'You sound as if you've been following the Suffragettes,' Mrs Gladsworthy said.

'I've been reading about them, and what they say makes complete sense to me. Women should be allowed to vote. What stupid person thought that a woman is incapable of deciding for herself without a man to guide her? Lord knows, men expect us to be cooks, cleaners, child minders, teachers, nurses and gardeners, which proves we have exceptional abilities.'

'But the Suffragettes are so strident,' Mrs Gladsworthy said, pursing her lips in disapproval.

'They've had to be, in order to get politicians to listen. Besides, they've shelved their stance on voting for now and are concentrating on encouraging women to work towards the war effort. I saw a woman driving a tram the other day. I think it's right we should get opportunities like that.'

'Oh, Mabel, please don't tell me you're going to leave us to drive a tram?'

Mabel giggled. 'No! I'm really happy working for you, but I wouldn't mind learning to drive a train, though.'

'I suspect, when this war is over, women's lives won't be the same any more,' Mrs Gladsworthy said thoughtfully. 'Once you let a cat outside the house, it refuses to stay in. I think it might be the same for some women. Perhaps that is just as well. Because with so many young men being killed in France, there won't be enough men left to become husbands and fathers.'

'I never minded being just a wife,' Mabel said, and suddenly a sharp memory came to her of Martin rushing up from the beach and the fishing boat, and twirling her around in his arms, because he'd missed her.

All at once it struck her that she was unlikely to experience such things ever again. She wouldn't dare to get involved with a man for fear of having to admit she was married. Or not admitting it, and then committing bigamy.

Mrs Gladsworthy put her hand on Mabel's arm comfortingly. 'No, I'm sure you didn't, but someone will come along and sweep you off your feet, you'll see. You are far too young and pretty not to marry again.'

Mabel smiled, but it was forced. Was her future really to be spent alone, for fear of someone finding out her secret?

4

November 1917

A loud noise woke Mabel with a start. She got out of bed and went to the door to listen. All was quiet. She knew she hadn't dreamed the noise, so what was it?

She thought it could be a burglar who was now lurking somewhere, hoping that no one had heard him break in.

Creeping down the narrow attic stairs, she reached the floor where the housekeeper's and the guest bedrooms were, then heard another sound. This time it was more like a groan, and it was coming from the floor below, where Mrs Gladsworthy had her suite of rooms.

Mabel ran down the next flight of stairs to reach Mrs Gladsworthy's bedroom. She knocked, but then turned the knob and went straight in. In a ray of light from the landing she could see Mrs Gladsworthy on the floor in her white nightdress. Assuming she'd fallen out of bed, Mabel flicked on the light and rushed to her, to help her up.

But one look at her face was enough to know this was serious. Her face was contorted, all slack and drooping on the right side.

'Hold on,' Mabel said. 'I'll get Mrs Hardy.'

It took only a moment or two to leap up the stairs to the next floor, and a couple more strides to wake the house-keeper. Mrs Hardy rushed out of her room with a net over her hair, wearing a grey dressing gown. Mabel explained what had happened as they went down the stairs, and how she'd found their mistress on the floor.

Mrs Hardy blanched when she saw Mrs Gladsworthy. 'Put a coat on and run to number ten, that's where Dr Preston lives,' she told Mabel. 'I don't think we'd better move her, but I'll cover her with the eiderdown.'

Mabel ran down the remaining flight of stairs two at a time, her heart thumping, grabbed Mrs Hardy's coat from her office and rushed out the door in her bare feet.

'Come on, come on,' she muttered as she hopped from foot to foot on the doctor's cold doorstep. She saw a light come on upstairs and finally she heard footsteps coming down the stairs.

'Could Dr Preston come quickly to Mrs Gladsworthy, at number six?' Mabel stammered out to the woman who opened the door in her dressing gown. 'She fell out of bed, but we think it's something serious, her face has fallen on one side.'

'I'll tell him straight away. You go back before you freeze,' the woman said. 'Leave the front door open, he knows his way to her bedroom.'

Mabel did as she was told. As she got up to the bedroom, she saw Mrs Hardy was crying as she knelt beside her mistress.

'She doesn't know me, she can't speak, and her pulse is so weak its almost not there,' she sobbed out. 'I think she's had a stroke.'

Mabel tried to comfort Mrs Hardy and asked if there was something she could do. The older woman didn't answer, she was so immersed in her grief, so Mabel stirred up the fire and put some more coal on it, as it was icy cold in the bedroom.

The doctor came up the stairs just a few minutes later, a coat over his pyjamas. He knelt on the floor beside Mrs Gladsworthy and first listened to her heart, then examined her arms and legs. He sat back on his heels and looked at Mabel and the housekeeper.

'She's had a huge stroke, and I'm deeply sorry to have to say this, but I doubt she'll come back from it. If you could help me get her into her bed, that would be kind.'

Mrs Hardy began to cry again, and Mabel went to help the doctor.

'Isn't there something we can do?' she asked him, as she tucked the covers round her mistress. 'What about getting her to hospital?'

'I'm sorry, my dear,' he replied. 'Even at the hospital they could do nothing but make her comfortable. She's had a couple of little strokes in the past, and recovered fully. But this one is so bad, it would be kinder if she did die tonight, as she is paralysed from her neck down. I think you should contact her brother.'

After the doctor had left, Mabel went down to the kitchen and made Mrs Hardy and herself a cup of tea. When she got back to the mistress's room, the housekeeper was sitting with her head in her hands.

'I'm dreading speaking to her brother,' she said, looking up at Mabel with her eyes full of tears. 'I've only met him once, at Mr Gladsworthy's funeral, and he's a very unpleasant man.'

They drank their tea in silence; they were too sad for

any words. They remained there for the rest of the night, Mrs Hardy on the chaise longue and Mabel in an arm-chair. But just as it was growing light, a faint rattling sound woke them. They moved quickly to the bed, only to see their mistress had just slipped away.

They embraced and cried. Mabel might only have been employed by Mrs Gladsworthy for a little less than a full year, but she had grown fond of her because she was so undemanding and caring towards her staff. For Mrs Hardy, who had worked for the Gladsworthys for over twenty years and had no family of her own, her mistress was everything. Her 'Mrs' title was a customary mark of respect for spinster housekeepers.

'I'll get dressed and go back for the doctor, to tell him,' Mabel said, realizing that the housekeeper was too upset to give any instructions. 'Then we'll have a cup of tea, and you can telephone her brother. I'll stay with you.'

Mrs Hardy clung on to Mabel's hand. 'I'm afraid, Mabel. What if he dismisses us?'

'Now why would he do that?' Mabel said soothingly. 'You are running ahead of yourself, for now we just have to telephone him. We need to contact the vicar at Christchurch too, she'll want to be buried with her husband. But it's up to her brother to decide who else must be informed and to make other arrangements, though we can offer to do some of it for him.'

'You are such a level-headed girl.' Mrs Hardy wiped her wet eyes with a handkerchief. 'You are right, of course. Go and get dressed, and I will too. I'll meet you down in the kitchen. Cook will be in soon.'

*

Two hours later, Mabel was in the kitchen with Cook and the housekeeper.

The doctor had been back to issue a death certificate, and Mrs Hardy had spoken to her employer's brother.

'Mr Bedford was quite pleasant – he even seemed upset at his sister dying,' she said to Mrs Tweed, sounding rather surprised. 'I can't believe he's left it to me to arrange things with the undertaker, though. When I said that he needed to choose her coffin, he said he trusted me to pick the right one.'

Mabel had been beside Mrs Hardy during this telephone conversation, and Mr Bedford had spoken so loudly that she heard every word he said. In her opinion, though, he had just been too shocked to be unpleasant; there was something about his loud voice that told her he was a bully who had a low opinion of women.

'Have another slice of fruit cake.' Mrs Tweed pushed the cake closer to them. 'I always think tea and cake make everything better. Did he say when he was coming down? I'll have to plan a menu. The last time he was here, he complained that the meat was tough, and the vegetables overcooked. They weren't, of course, he just likes to be difficult.'

'He said he would come the day after tomorrow, but he said to choose the hymns and ask the vicar if the funeral can be this coming Friday. I wanted to say that's a bit soon to organize everything and let people know, but I didn't dare. Including today, that's only four days.'

'How will we know how many people will come back here for refreshments?' Mrs Tweed asked, looking panicked. 'And if I've got to wait for him to arrive to ask what he wants, and for how many people, that only gives me Thursday to prepare everything.'

'With luck, the undertakers won't be able to do it till next week,' Mrs Hardy said. 'Will you come with me, Mabel? I'm really not up to it on my own.'

The funeral was arranged for Friday afternoon at Christchurch, and the undertaker said he would be sending one of his staff round to lay out the body later that afternoon. Once Mrs Gladsworthy had been placed in her coffin, he recommended it should be placed on trestles in a room of their choice on the ground floor. He said he would see to ordering flowers, not just for the hearse but for the room where the coffin was to be placed. As they were so close to the church, everyone could walk to and from the funeral.

Mr Bedford had agreed to place an obituary in *The Times* and told Mrs Hardy to let other people know. It seemed that was all he intended to do. He had even changed his mind about his arrival and said it would now be on Thursday evening; Mrs Hardy was to make up beds for himself, his wife and their three daughters.

'Well, at least you won't have him interfering with your arrangements,' Mabel said to the other two very anxious women. 'He'll be the one who will look bad if anything goes wrong, not you two.'

Many of Mrs Gladsworthy's neighbours and friends didn't have telephones, so Mabel – who had neater handwriting than Cook or the housekeeper – was charged with the job of writing on black-edged cards, informing them of her funeral. Then she hand-delivered them.

On Friday morning, the day of the funeral, Mabel got

up an hour early, despite having been up extremely late the previous evening, waiting on Mr Bedford and his family. Mrs Bedford was a weak, whey-faced woman who deferred to her husband constantly, and the three daughters – Constance, Faith and Emily, twenty, eighteen and fifteen – simpered and giggled inappropriately. They were also very rude, prying into cupboards and drawers as if it was their own home. All three of them wanted the single room, and the younger sisters sulked when their mother said Constance, the eldest, should have it. Anyone would've thought there was something unattractive about the other, spacious bedroom with twin beds.

Mr Bedford was as unlike his sister as it was possible to be. Short, stout, dark-haired and with a moustache so thick it looked fake. He was also bombastic and very loud. 'Soup!' he exclaimed, as dinner was brought into the dining room. 'One only serves soup at luncheon!'

Mrs Hardy gently explained she was aware of that, but had thought they'd like something warming after a long journey from London on a very chilly day. His only answer to that was a sniff.

He remarked unfavourably on many things – from the gravy, which was too salty, to the wine, which was too dry – but it seemed that he just liked to complain, even if something was perfect.

The undertakers had put Mrs Gladsworthy in an open coffin in the small sitting room, early in the evening of the day she died. They had lit candles all around the coffin, with two large arrangements of lilies either side.

Mabel hadn't liked to ask how they had managed to straighten out the drooping side of her face – some sort of padding, she supposed – but she looked quite lovely, and not a bit frightening. The immediate neighbours began calling to pay their last respects the next morning. As Mrs Hardy had to show them in, it was left to Mabel to spring-clean both the seldom-used drawing and dining rooms, make up beds and generally ensure the house looked inviting to visitors.

As for Cook, she worked solidly, preparing food for both the Bedford family and for people coming back to the house after the funeral. Yet when Mr Bedford arrived, he looked around as if he had an unpleasant smell under his nose, and he couldn't find it in himself to offer one word of thanks to Cook and Mrs Hardy for all their hard work.

Today, the day of the funeral, Mabel had a feeling there was more trouble looming. She'd noticed the way Mr Bedford and his wife had been appraising certain pieces of furniture last night, also the paintings and silver. She had no idea what their own home was like, but she was certain it wasn't as refined as Harley Place, because she could almost taste their greed and glee.

Mabel told herself it was none of her business as she dressed and did her hair. Today was going to be an ordeal, but funerals always were. She just hoped that, on Saturday, the Bedfords would put everyone out of their misery by telling them what was going to happen, and then clear off back to London.

The funeral went as well as any funeral could. Christ-church was around half full – a triumph, considering there hadn't been time for many old friends and family members living a long way away to get there. Also, Mrs Gladsworthy was only able to attend church when the weather was warm and dry, so she had lost touch with some of the congregation. But the vicar spoke of all she had done for the church before she became an invalid; he pointed out the altar cloth she had embroidered and the elegant silver candlesticks she had donated. He said what a kind-hearted woman she was, always interested in other people and ready to help them, and how sad it was that she had lost her beloved husband to a riding accident when he was still a young man.

Mabel's eyes kept prickling with tears, and when she looked at Mrs Hardy, seated next to her, she saw she had tears streaming down her cheeks. Yet Mr Bedford was stony-faced; his own sister dead, and not even a quiver of his lips.

People didn't stay long back at Harley Place. They drank the offered sherry, ate the vol-au-vents, the sausage rolls and the sandwiches. They chatted to one another in low voices, but Mr Bedford, his wife and children made no attempt to mingle with them and discover what they had been to Mrs Gladsworthy.

Mabel became aware, through pinning back her ears and paying attention, that many of the people gathered today were relatives or friends of Mrs Gladsworthy's late husband, and they did appear to be genuinely sorrowful.

'She wrote often,' she heard one very elegant, slender middle-aged lady say to another equally elegant lady of the same age. 'She didn't say that she was virtually housebound; she was always asking about our family, remembering the children's names and wanting to know what they were doing. I feel so bad I didn't suspect she was poorly and rush over here to see her. She must have been very lonely.'

'Sol was her world,' the other woman said in response, leading Mabel to think she must be Mrs Gladsworthy's sister-in-law. 'It was like the light went out inside her after he died. I haven't visited since last Christmas, and I feel guilty about that now too, but it's a long way to come from Dorchester, and to be honest I found it very upsetting here, with all the memories of Sol.'

After everyone had gone, and the Bedfords were drinking tea in the drawing room, Mabel asked Mrs Hardy if Sol had been their mistress's husband.

'Yes, his name was Solomon. He was a lovely man, a real gentleman and very handsome. He was a surveyor and his services were very much in demand. I think Frank Bedford was green with envy that his sister had married so well. Their father was just a grocer, and I believe Frank has quite a lowly job in the Civil Service. I'm really hoping it will turn out that the estate goes back to Solomon's family, as they are such good people.'

She didn't need to add what might happen if the Bedfords inherited. But Mabel had watched Frank Bedford strutting about and felt sure he was already planning to move into Harley Place.

Two days after the funeral, Mrs Hardy told Mabel that she thought they ought to go through the mistress's clothes, just to check that nothing had been put away still stained, or in need of mending.

'I've no idea, of course, what Mr Bedford will decide to do with them, but I'd be mortified if his wife tried any of the garments and found something not quite right. Mrs Gladsworthy was always so particular.'

To Mabel it seemed a somewhat pointless exercise, but a pleasant one nonetheless, as some of the evening gowns were exceedingly beautiful. It gave her the chance to look at them and to hold them up against herself, imagining wearing something so grand.

Mrs Hardy went downstairs to see to something in the kitchen after a little while, leaving Mabel to carry on alone. They had brought a wheeled rail down from the attic, and after she'd checked each gown, she hung it on the rail.

She found a very lovely white voile dress with a ruffled skirt that she felt Mrs Gladsworthy had worn as a young woman. She wished she dared put it on, but she held it up against herself and looked at her reflection in the mirror. She could smell lily of the valley perfume, and she performed a few dance steps, imagining herself at a ball.

All at once a strange feeling came over her. It was like she was drifting off to sleep, and dreaming about a girl dancing, wearing the dress. The man she was dancing with was far taller than the girl, he had dark hair and wore tails and a bow tie.

'What are you doing, Mabel?' Mrs Hardy's sharp question brought Mabel back to reality.

For a moment Mabel was so disorientated she could only gape at Mrs Hardy.

'What is it?' the older woman said. 'You are very flushed. What are you doing with that dress?'

'Nothing! I'm sorry,' she said. 'I suddenly felt really funny and I saw a girl wearing this dress and dancing with a tall dark man wearing tails.'

The housekeeper snatched the dress away from Mabel, looking very suspicious. 'That was Mrs Gladsworthy's special dress. She was wearing it the night she met her husband. It was far too small and rather young for her, but she was sentimental and that's why she kept it.'

'But was he very tall, and was he wearing a tail coat that night?' Mabel asked.

Mrs Hardy frowned. 'Well, yes he was. But I think you probably just need to eat something. Girls your age sometimes faint and imagine things when their stomachs are empty.'

Mabel wasn't hungry. And she really had seen the girl and a man dancing. But she knew it was better to agree she was hungry, and leave it at that.

Perhaps she looked very glum, because the housekeeper put her hand on Mabel's shoulder. 'You are just a little overwrought,' she said gently. 'First the mistress dying, and then Bedford marching in here and making us all feel unwanted. It's enough for us all to start seeing things.'

It was mid-December, over two weeks since Mrs Gladsworthy's funeral, when Frank Bedford arrived back at Harley Place. He had given Mrs Hardy no warning he was coming, and the way he just barged in without so much as a 'good morning' was an indication he might now own the house. With him was another man – tall, slender, silver-haired and carrying a briefcase – and also Mr John Stevenson, who had been a close friend of Solomon Gladsworthy.

After ordering Mrs Hardy to bring him a large whisky – and tea for his two companions, who he didn't introduce – Bedford opened the door to the drawing room, invited the other gentlemen to take a seat, and demanded to know of the housekeeper why no fire had been lit in there.

'Sir, if you'd let me know you were coming, it would've been lit,' she replied. 'Since Mrs Gladsworthy stopped using this room, and the dining room, we only light a fire occasionally to air them.'

'Well, get it lit now,' he said sharply.

'I don't think that's necessary now,' the tall man spoke up. 'My business here won't take long. You said earlier you are booked on the three-thirty train back to London. Hardly worth lighting a fire.'

'Then get the cook to come up with my whisky and the tea,' Bedford snapped at Mrs Hardy. 'And you come in with her.'

Mabel was standing on a stepladder, passing seldom-used pots and pans down from a high shelf to Mrs Tweed to wash, while she cleaned the shelf, when Mrs Hardy came in and told them about what had occurred upstairs. 'One of the men is Mr Stevenson, that portly gentleman with the red face that used to be a close friend of the master. I think the other man is Mrs Gladsworthy's solicitor, but I can't be sure as I only saw him once, years ago.'

'He's come about the will, then?' Mrs Tweed asked.

'Possibly, but he wants to see you – and me, too. We'd better put on clean aprons.'

Mabel climbed down from the stepladder.

'He didn't ask you to come too,' Mrs Hardy said. 'You stay down here and put the kettle on low, in case they want more tea later.'

Mabel nodded in agreement. As the most junior person in the household, she hadn't expected to be included.

*

'Do you think he's going to give us our marching orders?' Cook whispered to the housekeeper as they went up the stairs. Cook was carrying the tea tray, Mrs Hardy the whisky.

'We'll soon find out,' she whispered back.

Mr Bedford had taken an easy chair opposite his companions. But as the two women entered the room, one of the gentlemen jumped to his feet to introduce himself as Mr Fortesque, Mrs Gladsworthy's solicitor. 'I believe you've met Mr Stevenson before,' he said, indicating the portly man. 'He was a close friend of Mr Gladsworthy and is the executor of Mrs Gladsworthy's will.'

After the two women had put down the drinks, Bedford pointed to two seats to one side of his own, but slightly back, as if to make clear they were less important. Then, without any preamble, Mr Fortesque took papers from his briefcase, cleared his throat and began to speak.

'First, I must apologize for not coming to Mrs Gladsworthy's funeral or speaking to you all immediately afterwards, but I was abroad on business and didn't learn of her death until my return. So, I am here today to read the last will and testament of Mrs Elizabeth Gladsworthy. It is dated the eighteenth of July, 1915, and was witnessed by her friend Mrs Mildred Francis, and my secretary Miss Ruth Brown. As I have already stated, Mr Stevenson is the executor of the will.

'I am not going to read every word of it to you, only the parts which are relevant to those here today. But after that, I will give you a general overview of the contents, so that you understand who has been bequeathed what.'

Clearing his throat, he began to read in solemn tones.

'To my brother, Frank Bedford, I leave my home, number six Harley Place. This will include any contents left after the bequests I have made.'

Cook and housekeeper exchanged a quick glance. They had discussed a few days ago that Bedford would almost certainly be left the house, and they doubted he would want to keep either of them on. Neither of them relished working for him anyway.

'To my niece Constance Anne Bedford, I leave my diamond and pearl bracelet,' Fortesque went on. 'To my niece Faith Evelyn Bedford, my gold and ruby flower brooch, and to my niece Emily Lily Bedford, I leave my garnet and diamond earrings.'

The housekeeper glanced at Bedford and saw he was frowning. Had he been expecting more for his daughters? She wondered why they hadn't come today.

'The remainder of my jewellery, furs, clothes and all my personal effects,' Mr Fortesque went on, 'I leave to my sister-in-law, Lavinia Jane Forester, sister of my late husband, Solomon Gladsworthy. I entrust her to share out my effects between herself and my late husband's nieces, who we were both so fond of.'

The solicitor looked up from his papers at this point and paused, taking a moment to make sure everyone assembled was listening. 'Ideally, Mrs Forester should have been here today, but she was unable to make the long journey. However, it is in Mr Bedford's interests to hear about the bequest to her. Now I am not going to read out the next part as it is exceedingly long, and concerns no one in this room. In it Mrs Gladsworthy has listed many of what she refers to as her and her husband's 'treasures' and explains that they either originated from the Gladsworthy family, or they were special items she and Solomon bought during their marriage. They are all to go to Lavinia Forester, on the understanding she either shares them or holds them in trust for her children and grandchildren.'

He looked up again and settled his glasses further back on his nose. 'I have copies of this list of items, one of which I shall be sending to Mrs Forester, and one each for Mrs Hardy, Mr Bedford and Mr Stevenson, so that no mistakes are made about ownership before Mrs Forester can arrange to collect them all.'

Mrs Hardy noted that Bedford's frown had deepened, and his colour had risen. Clearly, he was angry that all the treasures he and his wife had looked at during their time here for the funeral were not going to be his.

'To Mrs Joan Hardy,' he went on, looking straight at the housekeeper, 'I leave the sum of five hundred pounds, and the mews house at the back of Harley Place, along with its entire contents, to secure your future. You have been so much more than a housekeeper to first my husband and myself, then since his death you have been friend, confidant and nurse to me. I cannot thank you enough and wish you every happiness in the future.'

Mrs Hardy couldn't help but gasp; her eyes welled up and the tears spilled over. The most she had expected was perhaps a small item of jewellery as a token of her mistress's esteem, but the pretty little mews house!

But Mr Fortesque was already moving on.

'To Mrs Mary Tweed, my cook, I leave the sum of five hundred pounds and my thanks for all the years you have cooked for me. I wish you and your family happiness.'

The two older women looked at each other, and their excitement and joy were like a waft of warm air entering the chilly room.

Mr Fortesque smiled at the two women, clearly glad to be giving them some good news.

'I will try to wind this up now,' Mr Fortesque said, looking to each of them in turn. 'Aside from this house, which has been left to Mr Bedford, and the bequests to his daughters, the sums to staff and the mews house, the remainder of Mrs Gladsworthy's estate – money, stocks and shares, et cetera – will go to various charities. I have a list of them here.'

Mr Bedford looked at the two women. 'You two can go now and get on with your duties,' he barked at them. His face was red, and his eyes were flashing dangerously.

'Before you go,' Mr Fortesque said, 'I shall be sending each of you letters to confirm what I have told you today. Probate has to be settled before any money is paid out; that is, of course, partly to check there is enough money in the estate to cover it. My advice to all three of you is to do nothing rash until probate has been settled, and if you should leave here do let me know your new address.'

Once back in the kitchen, the two older women stood like statues without speaking until Mabel begged them to tell her what had happened.

Mrs Hardy was so overcome and tearful, it was left to Cook to explain.

'Mr Bedford isn't best pleased,' she added.

Mabel hugged the two older women. 'I'm glad about that, but I'm so happy for you', she said. 'It's lovely to think the mistress thought about you both some years ago when she made the will.'

'What are you three conspiring about?'

Bedford's voice, coming from the passage outside the kitchen, made them all start.

'Conspiring?' Mrs Hardy said. 'Hardly that.'

He came right into the kitchen, his eyes blazing. 'I shall contest the will,' he said. 'It should all have gone to me.'

'I'm so sorry, sir, that you are disappointed,' Mrs Hardy said, her tone silky. 'Is there anything I can do for you now? Something to eat, a pot of tea? Will you be staying the night?'

Mabel sensed how insincere the housekeeper was and wanted to smile, but she didn't dare.

'You needn't think you are all going to do nothing until the probate has gone through, and I move in here,' he snapped at her. 'I shall be checking on you.'

'We will work as we always have done,' Mrs Hardy said. 'You mustn't worry about anything, sir.'

He just stood there, his eyes darting around the kitchen, as if he was looking for something to find fault with.

His eyes fell on Mrs Tweed. 'I'm giving you a week's notice to quit,' he said. 'There is no point in keeping a cook on when there are only two other servants in the house.' He then turned his eyes to Mabel. 'I shall decide what to do about you shortly.'

He swept out then. After just a few minutes, they heard the front door slam behind him.

'Oh, Cook, I'm so sorry,' Mrs Hardy said. 'That was very mean of him.'

Mrs Tweed shrugged. 'I'm not a bit surprised. I'm only

glad it wasn't Mabel or you he ordered to go. I have at least got a home. Even if he'd asked me to stay on to cook for him, I'd have refused. He's a horrible man.'

'You should nip down to the solicitor's office tomorrow and tell them he's fired you. He might not have the right to do that until the probate is settled,' Mrs Hardy said.

'It's nearly Christmas, it will be good to have free time to cook for my own family this year. You'll remember what it's usually like here?'

Mrs Hardy sat down on a chair by the table. 'Yes, well, in the years before the mistress took to staying upstairs. All those nieces and nephews, the parlour games, decorating the house, and so much preparation. But they were happy times, weren't they?'

She looked to Cook and Mabel, and smiled. 'Now let's have a slice of that Christmas cake I saw Cook stowing away. It would be a terrible thing to see Bedford and his greedy daughters eat it all. And Mabel can nip up and get the sherry from the drawing room. Let's celebrate our good fortune.'

Mabel went to get the sherry, regardless of the fact that she had nothing to celebrate. She had no intention of spoiling the happy mood in the kitchen by making them fret as to what was going to happen to her. But she was scared.

5

On the 23rd of December, less than two weeks after his previous visit to number six, Mr Bedford returned at two in the afternoon, using a key to get in. Mrs Hardy and Mabel were in the dining room, packing the last of the china and glass ornaments Mrs Lavinia Forester wanted, and it startled them to see Bedford glowering at them from the hall.

'Good afternoon sir,' Mrs Hardy said nervously. 'Mabel and I are just packing up these last few things for Mrs Forester. She's already taken everything else.'

Mr Bedford stood in the doorway of the dining room, looking astounded that it was devoid of all furniture. 'I didn't expect her to strip the place,' he said with great indignation, touching a mark on the wall where a painting had been. 'She was only supposed to take a few keepsakes.'

Mrs Hardy glanced at Mabel and frowned. Lavinia Forester and Robert, her husband, had called just over a week ago and earmarked all the things they wanted. The following day a removal company came and took the furniture, and all the large paintings and mirrors. Plus many boxes of furs, evening dresses and all Mrs Gladsworthy's jewellery, except the pieces that had been left to Frank Bedford's daughters.

Mabel had helped with the packing up, and Mrs Forester had confided that she would rather give the remainder of clothes and furniture to a charity for those in need than leave anything for Frank Bedford, who she detested.

'I don't want his miserable wife or those ghastly girls of his walking around in dear Elizabeth's beautiful frocks,' she said, then laughed nervously as if she felt she shouldn't really say such things.

She wanted Mabel to take some of the clothes too, but Mabel pointed out she was in mourning and so took only a black wool coat, another black dress and some black, fine-quality shoes that felt like slippers, they were so comfortable. 'Besides, Mr Bedford is likely to take anything else from me,' she explained. 'I'm half expecting him to come and throw me out anyway.'

'If he does, you must get in touch with me,' Mrs Forester said. 'I know people who need help in their homes, and Mrs Hardy thinks very highly of you. But if Frank has got any sense, he'll keep you on, it isn't easy to get competent staff these days.'

Mrs Forester had given Mabel her address near Dorchester before she left, leaving instructions that the remainder of the items she wanted were to be packed and sent on to her.

'As I understood it, sir, Mrs Forester could take what she liked,' Mrs Hardy ventured bravely. She didn't add that just yesterday a man from a charity had come with a big van and taken all the left-over furniture, bedding, clothes, books and kitchen utensils. All that was left now were Mabel and Mrs Hardy's beds, linen for them, a few towels and essentials – crockery, pots and cutlery – plus a table and chairs in the kitchen. 'The jewellery for your daughters is up in your sister's bedroom.'

'I cannot believe that woman would be so grasping,' he said vehemently, shaking his head in disbelief. 'It isn't as if she is in need.'

'Maybe she knows people who are?' Mrs Hardy suggested, and Mabel had to turn away to hide her amusement. 'I'm sure you didn't really want Mrs Gladsworthy's old things? She often used to say her house was cluttered with old hand-me-downs. You can start afresh now.'

Mabel *had* heard her old mistress say such things, but only in jest, as almost every item of furniture had been made by craftsmen a hundred or more years ago. The French clocks, the Persian rugs and exquisite Italian glass were almost priceless, or so Mrs Hardy said.

Bedford made a kind of growl in his throat; he was clenching and unclenching his hands in anger. He probably realized Lavinia Forester had taken everything to upset him.

'There will be nothing for you to do now the house is empty,' he snarled at Mrs Hardy. 'So, you might as well clear off now. She had no business leaving you the mews house, that should've remained with this property.'

'You are dismissing me, sir?' Mrs Hardy gasped in shock. 'Just like that! Before Christmas, after all the years I've worked here?'

'Of course I'm dismissing you, a house devoid of furniture doesn't need a housekeeper. I can't think why you sound so aggrieved, you've had the life of Riley all these years. And I've no doubt you twisted my sister's arm to make her give you the mews house and money.'

A surge of anger erupted in Mabel; the very thought of Mrs Hardy using guile to get the mistress to leave her something was unthinkable. She rounded on the man.

'How could you say such a thing?' she asked. 'Mrs Hardy couldn't have done more for our mistress – and she did it willingly, out of affection, not for what it might bring her. You should be ashamed of yourself! You are the mistress's brother, and yet you didn't visit her when she could barely get out of her bed for pain.'

'How dare you?' he roared back at her. 'I won't take such insolence from a mere maid. Get out of this house, this minute. Out now!'

Mabel remembered all the times she'd taken verbal abuse from Agnes without ever fighting back. She also knew Mr Bedford would get the police to eject her if she didn't go. But she could at least speak her mind.

'I wouldn't want to stay in the same room with such a greedy, self-centred, stupid man,' she shouted back at him. 'No wonder the mistress left almost everything to her husband's family. They deserved it.'

He leapt forward and slapped her face hard.

Mabel wanted to cry, it hurt so much, but she wasn't going to give him the satisfaction. 'So, you are a coward who hits women too,' she retorted. 'It seems you have no saving graces.'

She didn't wait for him to hit her again but ran up the stairs to her room. She wanted to throw herself on her bed and cry – after all, she had no job now, nowhere to sleep tonight, and he obviously wasn't going to give her the month's wages due to her. But her pride wouldn't let her resort to tears.

It took only a few moments to gather herself. She put on the black coat, hat and shoes Mrs Forester had given her, and pushed her old cloak, bonnet and shoes into her bag, along with her other old things. Taking one last look around the room, remembering how happy she'd been here for almost a year, she straightened her back, bit back tears and went down the stairs.

Mr Bedford was standing in the hall. Mabel realized he'd stayed there to prevent her speaking to Mrs Hardy.

'I hope you won't have one happy moment in this house,' she said in a loud voice, hoping that, wherever Mrs Hardy was, she'd hear her. 'But you haven't seen the last of me, I've got to know many old friends of your sister here in Clifton, and I'll soon get another place with one of them. Do pass on my good wishes to Mrs Hardy, I'll be round to see her soon.'

He opened the front door and she could see he wanted to hit her again, but she skipped quickly past him. Once on the doorstep, she turned on her heels and grinned at him.

'I wish you an utterly miserable Christmas!'

She felt a brief moment's satisfaction that she'd had the last word. Then she hurried off towards Regent Street, as if she had a plan.

But that was play-acting. Once she was out of his sight around the corner, she stopped short, her heart racing. She was shaking with shock at her predicament. Homeless, close to tears, with very little money, no character and unlikely to find another job so close to Christmas. Things couldn't get any worse.

Mrs Hardy would perhaps take her in at the mews flat, but the housekeeper had been so busy packing up Mrs Forester's things, she hadn't been able to go in to clean it, or see what she needed for it. The last person to live there had been Mr Gladsworthy's groom, and he'd left after the master's riding accident, as his horse had to be put down because of a severe injury.

At the time the will was read, Mrs Hardy had said that it was over a year since she'd been into the place, and she'd been horrified by the cobwebs and filth. But as much as she'd always intended to give it a good spring clean, she'd forgotten about it.

One thing Mabel knew about the housekeeper was, however nasty Mr Bedford had been to her today, and despite being ordered out, she wouldn't leave number six until she'd completed what she considered to be her duty. That would mean sending off the last parcel to Mrs Forester and cleaning the house from top to bottom.

Unfortunately, Mr Bedford was certain to stay there too, if only to make sure Mrs Hardy didn't take anything from the house. Mabel couldn't go and knock on the front door and offer to clean the mews flat in return for a bed for a few nights.

She knew exactly how much money she had – two pounds, sixteen shillings and sixpence – because she'd counted it the previous day. That wouldn't go far, especially if she wanted to get to Dorchester to ask Mrs Forester for a job. If she went to Mrs Gladsworthy's solicitor, he'd probably side with Mr Bedford – after all, a maid was nothing to people like them. As for Mrs Tweed, the cook, she probably would have helped, but Mabel had no idea where she lived.

It was about sixty miles to Dorchester. Would a train take her there? Everyone said all the train services were disrupted because of collecting up wounded servicemen and getting them to hospitals. With Christmas so close, that would only make it worse, but she could go to the station and ask.

By the time she got down into the centre of Bristol and reached the tram terminus, it was dark. As always, it was full of jostling crowds, and in her present state of mind that made her nervous. There were a great many drunken men lurching about too. The smell of roast chestnuts mingled with horse droppings and stale beer, making her feel a bit sick, so she hastily crossed the town centre to take the shortcut through the backstreets to the station.

Mabel had walked this way to reach Bristol Bridge several times before, but always in daylight. On those occasions she'd found the cobbled streets lined with banks and intriguing small shops, a part of town she wanted to linger in. But now the street lamps were so dim they only lit up a small radius around them, making the shadows beyond look menacing, and she felt there were people lurking unseen in dark doorways. Suddenly she was scared and wanted to return to where there were people and light, but her bag had grown heavy and she reminded herself this way was quicker.

She didn't hear any warning footsteps that someone was behind her. So when a big, smelly hand was clamped over her mouth, and her shoulder held in a vice-like grip, she became rigid with terror.

'Don't struggle or I'll hurt you,' a rasping male voice said. Pressing his body against her back, he pushed her into a narrow, dark alleyway.

The only thought that ran through her head then was that he would spoil her new coat, or even steal it. Later she was shocked that material things seemed so important when he might be going to kill her.

'Now what've you got for me, my lovely?' he asked, and while keeping one hand over her mouth he wrenched her bag from her hand.

He smelled terrible, like he'd come out of a sewer, and she judged from the way he held her he was around five foot ten and strongly built. She hoped that as he began to rummage through her bag, he might loosen his grip on her and she could make a run for it.

Clearly, he'd done this before, because with only a cursory delve into her bag, and finding no purse, he let go of her face, caught hold of her two arms and twisted them back towards him.

'Where's yer money?' he rasped.

'I haven't got any,' she said. 'I've just been dismissed from my job. I'm walking home to my folks.'

He spun her round and pushed her hard up against the alley wall with his body. 'Don'cha lie to me, I knows you got money, I can smell it.'

There was just enough light to see he was dirty and ragged; his face was gaunt and his hair was straggling on to his shoulders. Many of his teeth were missing; only the whites of his eyes showed up clearly. He looked and sounded old, but the strength in his hands and body suggested otherwise.

'You are mistaken,' she whimpered. 'All I've got is a shilling or two in my pocket.'

He thrust his hand into her pockets and brought out the small sum she'd put in there. The rest of her money was in a small linen bag tucked into the bodice of her petticoat.

'You think that fools me,' he roared at her, clearly no

longer worried about silence. 'Where's the rest?' He punched her in the stomach so hard she was winded.

'I told you, there is none,' she wheezed.

He caught hold of her hair and punched her in the face, not once but three times. With that he threw her down on the ground, kicked her soundly in the ribs and stomach and began to search her.

Nothing she'd ever experienced came close to the shock and horror of that man's hands under her dress. He groped around the top of her stockings, into her drawers and up to her breasts. She thought he was going to rape her, there in the filthy alley, but when his fingers finally found the linen bag and tore it from where she'd pinned it to her petticoat, she sensed he was done.

'You could've given me that straight off and saved your pretty face,' he said, leaning over her. 'But cos you never, now I'm gonna teach you a lesson.'

He kicked her repeatedly, until mercifully everything went black.

She came to later, to find herself virtually paralysed with cold. When she tried to get to her feet, pain overwhelmed her. She couldn't even say where the pain was coming from; it was all over. Sinking down again, she cried at her helplessness. She attempted to crawl then, hoping to reach the main street and get help, but although she managed about twelve yards, it was agony – and furthermore, she realized she was going further into the alley, not out of it.

Perhaps she passed out again, because the next thing she became aware of was someone telling her to wake up.

There was a strong smell of urine in the alley and she was so cold she thought the voice was just a dream.

'Come on, open yer eyes and look at me! If you stays 'ere you'll freeze to death.'

This time Mabel was aware the woman's voice was real. She forced herself to open her eyes. She could only see a dark shape looming over her.

'Upsy-daisy,' the woman said, putting one hand under Mabel's arm and pulling her upright. 'My God, someone's given you a right working over!'

The pain of being pulled to her feet almost made her faint again, but she couldn't let that happen. 'He took my money,' she tried to say, but her mouth was so painful it sounded like a mere groan.

'There's some right bastards around here,' the woman said, and picked up Mabel's bag. 'But I live close by, let me get you there and clean you up.'

Every step Mabel took was like red-hot knives being stuck into her; it even hurt to breathe. But the woman had her arm around her to support her, and she encouraged her by saying she'd feel better once she was in the warm. It crossed Mabel's mind that this woman might be intending to rob or hurt her in some way too, but the lure of being in the warm was worth the risk.

She led Mabel down another even narrower alley and stopped at a heavy wooden gate, some eight feet tall, which she unlocked. 'It's no palace but it's warm and safe,' she said, drawing Mabel into a yard that was too dark for her to see anything. From there the woman unlocked another door into the building.

'Home sweet home,' the woman said cheerfully. 'Now just bear with me while I light the gas.'

Mabel hadn't heard a gas mantel being lit since she last went to the chapel in Hallsands. The sound and smell of the match being struck, the gas in the pipe, then the pop as it caught the flame brought back the memory of her old village and kindly neighbours, so sharply that her eyes welled up with tears.

'There, there,' the woman said. 'Don't cry, you're safe now. Let me sit you down and stir up the fire. Then I can bathe your face.'

There were just two rooms; a living room that doubled as a kitchen, and through a door she could see a bedroom. The living room was much the same as many working people's homes Mabel had been in throughout her life. A central table covered with a dark green cloth, the gas light above it. A rag rug in front of the fire and two easy chairs either side of it. The walls were papered, but the pattern had faded and above the back door it was peeling off. A small dresser stood next to a sink; the collection of china on it didn't match, but there was a neatness to the room that was reassuring.

'I'm Nora Nightingale,' the woman said as she helped Mabel to sit down by the fire. 'The Nightingale is made up, as it sounded right for a medium. But don't tell anyone that!'

Mabel gulped and tried to control her sore mouth enough to speak. 'Mabel Brook,' she said haltingly. 'Thank you so much for your kindness. What's a medium?'

'I speak to the dead,' Nora replied, and on seeing Mabel's shock she laughed. 'No, you ain't dead. I'm real and so are your injuries.'

As the gas light grew brighter and the fire responded to a poke and more fuel, Mabel could see that Nora was small and buxom, with untidy fair hair and red cheeks. She appeared to be around thirty years old. It was the face of a country woman, Mabel thought – and like her she wore black, and a wedding ring.

'Are you a widow too?' Mabel asked.

'In a manner of speaking,' Nora said with a little chuckle. She put a kettle on a small gas stove in the corner and then placed an enamel basin, a clean cloth and towel on the table. Next, she gently removed Mabel's hat – which, remarkably, had stayed in place throughout her beating – and her coat. 'Looks like your old man had a few bob. Nice hat and coat,' she said, stroking the dark coat reverently.

While Nora worked on cleaning up her face, Mabel managed to explain the gist of what had happened at Harley Place and that she'd intended to go to Dorchester to get a new job. She also put the woman straight about how she came by the quality coat and hat. Nora didn't comment on anything. Once she'd cleaned Mabel's face and hands, she measured out some brown liquid into a glass, added warm water and made her drink it.

'That will help with the pain,' she said. 'Now let's look at yer body and see what damage has been done.'

A couple of hours later, and despite how much Mabel was hurting, she felt she'd found a real friend in Nora. She was kind and funny, but completely down to earth about people.

'I find most folk are either stupid, selfish, greedy or vain. Some are all four. But then I must be stupid too, as I keep hoping I'll meet someone who ain't like that,' she said as she examined Mabel's injuries. 'I think you've got a couple of broken ribs, you poor love, which will take ages to heal, but the rest is just severe bruising. In a day or two it'll feel better. You'd better stay here with me, cos if you try to walk with those broken ribs, they'll give you gip and never heal.'

'But I can't impose on you,' Mabel said. 'I haven't even got any money to pay you.'

'I don't need paying for being a friend,' Nora said firmly. 'I get a bit lonely at this time of year, and I'll be glad of your company.'

That night, as Mabel lay next to her new friend in her bed, hurting like she'd never hurt before, and unable to sleep, she offered up a silent prayer of thanks. If not for Nora where would she be now? Frozen to death in that alley, she guessed. When she had staggered to the outside lavatory earlier, she saw there was a hard frost. No one else would've taken her in with no money.

Every winter people died in such conditions. She'd been lucky.

Nora still hadn't explained what she meant by talking to the dead. Perhaps she would in the morning. But whatever she did for a living, Mabel intended to find some way of paying her back for her kindness.

By Christmas Eve Mabel could talk more normally, even though she looked terrible, with two black eyes, and was wincing at every step from her bruises and broken ribs. So far, she'd only eaten bread and milk, as her mouth was so sore. But already she felt as if she'd known Nora all her life. And she wanted to keep her in it.

It was Nora's warmth that was so remarkable. Lying in the bed next to her was like lying next to a big hot-water bottle, but it was the warmth of her personality that was outstanding. She was prepared to share everything she had – her bed, clothes, food and the fireside. She didn't judge; even her questions were gentle. She was funny too, though Mabel wished she wouldn't make her laugh so often, as it hurt. But when Nora told her about her past, Mabel wondered how she'd managed to be so forgiving.

Nora was twenty-nine now and she'd come to Bristol from a farming village in Somerset when she was just fourteen, for a position as a maid. She said she'd been happy with the Withall family in Royal York Crescent, in Clifton, for six years, until their son Albert came back from South Africa where he'd been working.

'He pestered me night and day,' she said with a grimace. 'You know, trying to have his way with me. I tried to tell his mother, but she ignored what I said. Then finally he came into my room one night and raped me! I told his father then, but neither he nor his bloody mother believed it was rape. They said I'd led him on and threw me out for being such a slut. Well, I couldn't go home – I doubted my parents would believe me, either – and to top it all, a few weeks later I found I was having his baby.'

'Oh, Nora, how awful.'

'It was! I felt like flinging meself off the suspension bridge, but I wasn't even brave enough to climb on to the railings, let alone jump. I had no choice but to go to the workhouse. There was nowhere else. My baby, a little boy, was stillborn. I think he died because the old crone at the workhouse who acted as a midwife didn't know what she was doing. I was badly torn too, and I wished I could die.'

Mabel put her arms around her new friend, to comfort her. She didn't have the words to express how awful it must have been for her.

'Maybe it was just as well.' Nora sighed, and gave a glum half-smile. 'Bringing a child up on your own is well-nigh impossible. But it made me go a bit mad for a time. That's when I first discovered I could talk to the dead.'

Mabel had almost forgotten that Nora had told her that before. 'Can you? Seriously?'

'Well, not to just anyone. But I do get messages, if I concentrate. I got a message for you while I was cleaning up your face.'

Mabel was flabbergasted, and she wanted to take it further. 'Who was the message from?' she asked.

'I don't know, someone who drowned at sea. He asked me to tell you to stay strong, and that he understood. I thought he said he was called Bert, but I might have got that wrong. Does it mean anything to you?'

Mabel was struck dumb with shock. She wanted to admit it was her father, but she was afraid that if she opened up to say that much, she wouldn't be able to stop, and she didn't know yet if she could trust Nora.

'I had an uncle who was drowned at sea,' she said carefully. 'Maybe it was him.'

'Sometimes wires do get crossed.' Nora shrugged. 'But I have found that messages come through when people are in difficulties – it's like confirmation the spirits are looking out for you. I got a keen sense of you and the sea too. Were you with your uncle when it happened?'

'No,' Mabel said quickly. 'But we lived by the sea in Plymouth. It's a comforting thought the dead do look out for us. But tell me, do you make a living from speaking to the dead?'

'Don't mock,' Nora said sharply. 'Yes, I do.'

Mabel was mortified at hurting her friend's feelings. 'I wasn't mocking, I'm just bowled over by it. It's not something I know anything about.'

Nora's face softened. 'I'll forgive you. People do like to mock. A great many people think people like me are tricksters. It's only when I get messages from someone who means a lot to them, and I couldn't have known about that person, or what they would say, that they begin to believe in me.'

'So how do you do it? Where do you do it?' Here, or in their homes?'

'Sometimes people ask me to their homes. That is usually the best, as the spirits are either there already or close by. Occasionally I might do it here, if someone special asks me, but mostly I do it in a small hall. Then more people come, and if the atmosphere is right the messages come through.'

'But how?' Mabel frowned. 'Is it a bit like dreaming?'

'In a way. If I close my eyes and empty my head of all the usual stuff, just focus on thinking about my audience; it's a bit like falling asleep. They call it a trance. Sometimes I don't even remember what I've heard and said afterwards. I'm doing one on the thirtieth, near here. You can come and see what you think.'

'I look too horrible to go anywhere just yet,' Mabel said. 'I'd frighten people.'

'I've got a black hat with a veil, you could wear that,' Nora said. 'Go on, come, I think you'll find it really interesting. I can't predict what will pop up, though lately it's been mostly messages from husbands and sons killed in France. Maybe your husband will be one of them, but I hope not, as you'll think I'm faking it.'

'What did you mean when you said, "in a manner of speaking" when I asked if you were a widow?'

Nora smiled. 'It's partly because after losing the baby, I felt I never wanted another man to come near me,' she said thoughtfully. 'I dressed like a widow and I found it put men off approaching me. I tell folk, if they ask, that my hubby was run over by a tram.'

She giggled and put her hand over her mouth, as if embarrassed. 'I started the story before war broke out, you see, and I'd read about a man being killed that way in Manchester. It stops people in their tracks, they don't ask anything else.'

Mabel could feel her own confession forming on her lips. She wanted to tell Nora the truth about herself so badly, but she didn't dare. Nora was too kind-hearted to approve of her running out on a shell-shocked man.

Later that evening, it suddenly occurred to Mabel that the experience she'd had while handling Mrs Gladsworthy's dress might be similar to what Nora had described. Did the girl and that man come to her because they were spirits? If Mrs Hardy hadn't interrupted, might she have got a message?

She wasn't sure she wanted to have another experience

like that, but she would dearly love to know if it really was a message from the dead.

They awoke on Christmas morning to hear church bells ringing. Mabel went out into the alley to listen. Her eyes filled with tears, as it was such a sharp memory of Christmas at Hallsands. As a little girl she could remember going up to Stokenham church for the Christmas morning service, walking between her parents with them holding both her hands. The two adult hands, each holding a small hand, gave her a safe, precious feeling. She hoped if they were looking down on her now, they weren't too upset by what she'd done.

The two girls celebrated Christmas with beef stew and opened a box of chocolates one of Nora's clients had given her. They played cards, drank some sherry and talked their heads off. Despite the pain Mabel was in, it was a far happier Christmas than the previous year, when Agnes had been nastier than usual, and Mabel had walked out and gone back alone to her own house.

By the evening of the thirtieth, Mabel was feeling able to walk about; her ribs were still agony if she moved suddenly, but the swelling on her face had gone down and the bruises only hurt when pressed. She was so curious about Nora talking to the dead that she felt compelled to go with her to the small meeting house. It was less than half a mile away, and she needed to try walking again. With Nora's black-veiled hat on, she seemed almost invisible, and that felt good.

A group of about eight women were waiting for Nora outside a somewhat ramshackle hut by the River Avon. They greeted Nora as if she was someone famous. They were respectful, yet excited to see her. At precisely seven o'clock a man came and unlocked the door, lit the gas lighting, and held out his hand for money. Nora paid him, then he reminded her he would be back at half eight to lock up.

Another five women and one man came in as the first arrivals took their seats. As Nora moved to bolt the door, she inclined her head to Mabel to tell her to sit on the end of the back row. Then Nora moved amongst the audience to take their money. It looked to Mabel as if they were each giving her sixpence. Some gave her small items to hold too – a brooch, a handkerchief, and one even gave her a pipe. Nora put these in the pocket of her coat.

She had mentioned that lots of diverse groups of people used this place; everything from reading lessons for illiterate adults, to dance classes and first-aid training. It smelled musty, but the wooden floor was clean and smooth. And it was cold, as there was no heating.

Finally, when everyone was settled, Nora stood on the small platform in front of everyone. She was dressed in her customary black – a loose coat, a narrow-brimmed felt hat, and thick wool stockings and stout shoes. Black made her fair skin appear sallow and aged her. Back in her little flat, she liked to put on a long, loose woolly dressing gown that was a deep sapphire blue, and with her fair hair loose she looked pretty and no older than twenty-five. But Mabel assumed that when Nora was working, she found it better to look matronly.

Nora looked at her audience in silence for a little while, going from face to face. There wasn't a sound from anyone, and the air seemed charged with something extraordinary.

Then she closed her eyes, her hands clasped in front of her. She looked like she was praying. Now the entire audience seemed to be holding their breath, Mabel found herself doing it too.

'William is here,' she said at last. Her eyes were still closed, and her voice sounded different, very flat, nothing like the bouncy way she normally spoke.

Mabel looked around at everyone and on the end of the row she was in, a young woman was straining forward, her face alight with hope.

'He is telling me he is sorry he couldn't wait until you got to the hospital. He tried to hang on. He says to call the baby Josie, after your mother, and he is watching over you.'

Even in the dim gaslight, Mabel could see the young woman was hanging on every word Nora was saying, and tears glistened on her cheeks. There was no doubt in Mabel's mind that this message meant everything to the young widow, but she wanted to know why he was apologizing for not getting to the hospital in time. Did he mean if they'd got him there, he might have lived? Or had something happened to her?

After that, the air seemed even more charged and Nora then related a message for someone called Agatha. An older woman in the front row gasped. Nora told her that her mother was with them and she was saying to give her tea set to her daughter as a wedding present.

To Mabel that was a disappointingly dull message, but she could see Agatha looking thrilled and happy.

So it went on; some messages seemed almost pointless, some cruel in their brevity, but the recipients all seemed delighted. But now Mabel was watching her friend rather than listening to these messages. It was as if she was asleep, and the voice coming out of her mouth didn't seem to belong to her. Sometimes she felt in her pocket and pulled out one of the mementos, but they didn't always achieve anything.

Finally, she opened her eyes again and said she hoped that some of them had found comfort in the messages and apologized to those who hadn't got one. 'I can't make the spirits come,' she explained. 'This is just the way it is.'

Nobody seemed disgruntled, and Mabel heard the woman called Agatha telling another woman that she'd been agonizing over whether to pass her mother's tea set on. 'It seemed disloyal not to keep it myself, but my daughter loves it so much. I can give it to her happily now.'

'Well, what did you think?' Nora asked on the way back to her flat.

'It was like magic,' Mabel said. 'I've never seen or heard anything like it.'

'I had a couple of horrible messages tonight that I didn't own up about. They were from soldiers who had died just recently, and the messages were all about their pain and terror. I didn't want to put that picture in a wife's head. They probably haven't even been told yet that their husbands are dead.'

'Well, they probably weren't in the audience anyway then,' Mabel said.

'Oh, I think they were. These messages tend to come when the person is there, close by. I think one of them was Agatha's daughter, the one who the tea set was for. The spirit asked for Alice, and I heard her called that.'

'I don't think I'd like to take the responsibility for knowing such things,' Mabel said thoughtfully.

'I don't, either. But for some reason I don't understand, I've been given this "gift", and all I can do is try to use it for the good. But speaking of this gift, a couple of times things have come to me that I know are to do with you, even when the voice calls you Betty. Both times I get the vision of a rough sea. Is this your father?'

They had just reached the gate into Nora's flat, which gave Mabel a few seconds to think of her reply as they went indoors.

'Well?' Nora said. 'I know you are hiding something, Mabel. Tell me what it is?'

Mabel realized she had to give her new friend something. 'Okay, it was my father not my uncle who was lost at sea. I didn't want to tell you before, as it's upsetting for me still. His pet name for me was Betty.'

Nora sank down on a chair, still wearing her coat and hat. She looked worried. 'There's more, though, I feel he is concerned about you.'

'Well, I did come to Bristol to get away from my mother-in-law. She was a real bloodsucker and I knew as long as I stayed near her, I could never have a life of my own.'

'But you left without telling anyone where you'd gone?' Nora's statement shocked Mabel.

'Yes, I did, it seemed the best way.'

Nora nodded. 'Fair enough. It's none of my business, in any case. Maybe your father is concerned because of what happened at your job and the beating in the alley?'

'Surely spirits don't get detailed messages of what is happening?'

'Are you laughing at me?' Nora asked.

'No, I just find it hard to imagine someone dead watching me. Until I met you, I didn't know such a thing could happen.'

'I don't think the spirits watch, or know exactly what is going on. I think they just home in on how you are feeling. But I couldn't say for sure, I can't question them.'

Mabel took off her coat and hat, then held out a hand to Nora to take hers too. 'You've been wonderful,' she said softly, finding it hard to find the right words to convey how much she owed this new friend. 'I can't imagine what would've become of me if you hadn't found me when you did.'

That night, Mabel lay awake long after Nora had gone to sleep. The idea that she got the beating as a punishment for running away, and leaving Martin, kept going round and round in her head. In a few days it would be a year since she'd left Hallsands, and she could see how much she'd changed in that year. She had learned so much; how rich people live, how they thought and spoke. She'd read books she would never have seen back in Hallsands, and they had opened windows on to places, people and other things she hadn't known about before. From Mrs Hardy and Mrs Tweed, she'd learned a great deal more than just running a house or cooking meals; she'd absorbed their stories from past times in service, their views on the upper classes.

Just living in Clifton was an education, with the beautiful houses, the history of the place, and the people who had once lived there and the ones who lived there now, such a different world to Hallsands. Her once-broad Devon accent had mellowed; no one remarked on it any more. She knew now that, even if she wanted to go back to Hallsands, she wouldn't fit in any longer, or be satisfied with such a simple life.

But she couldn't stay much longer with Nora; not only was her new friend edging nearer and nearer to the truth about her past, but Mabel had to make her own way in the world and find a life that would fulfil her and make her happy. She also didn't like the idea of being so firmly in someone's debt.

The night after she'd been to the meeting with Nora, Mabel woke to find Nora had her arm around her and was pressed up tightly to her. As Mabel had never shared a bed with anyone but her husband before, it was a little disconcerting, but as she knew people who had slept three or four to a bed as children, and heard that they would all cuddle up close, she gently removed Nora's arm and wriggled away a bit.

Nora bought a bottle of wine to see the New Year in with, and she got some steak and mushroom pies from the pie shop close by. The pies were delicious, but the red wine tasted like vinegar to Mabel. Although she pretended she liked it, not wishing to offend Nora.

At midnight, church bells rang out, and someone was banging tin trays and shouting nearby.

'Let's make a toast,' Nora said, holding up her glass. 'May 1918 bring an end to the war, and may we still be the best of friends.'

Mabel repeated what Nora had said and clinked glasses, forcing herself to drink the remains of the wine.

*

The following afternoon, the girls went for a walk along the river and came home just after one, because it was bitingly cold. They had some soup that Nora had made the previous day, then Mabel sat down to mend a small tear in Nora's skirt for her. She had tried to thank her friend for letting her stay by doing little jobs like this repair, but she felt she was just treading water staying here, she needed a wage to gain her independence.

'I must leave soon,' Mabel blurted out. 'I can't live off you any longer. I need a job.'

'You aren't better yet,' Nora said immediately, looking stricken that Mabel was even suggesting moving on.

'I'm not completely healed yet, but I soon will be. You've been so generous and kind to me. I love being here with you, but I must get work.'

'You could get a job here and stay with me forever,' Nora said, and to Mabel's astonishment her friend's eyes filled with tears.

'I can't get a decent job here as I haven't got a character. But I could write to Mrs Forester in Dorchester and tell her what happened. I think she'd speak on my behalf.'

'Why do you want to be someone's skivvy when you could help me at my meetings? You could collect the money, talk a bit to the people. Together we could move up in the world, do it in smarter places, get bigger audiences.'

There was a kind of anguish in Nora's voice and pleading in her eyes. Mabel found it a little worrying.

'I need something of my own,' she insisted, but even to her own ears that sounded weak. She didn't really know why she wanted to move on – she liked living with Nora – but a little voice in her head kept telling her she must go.

Nora moved over to where Mabel was sitting and knelt in front of her. She caught hold of Mabel's two hands, making her drop the sewing.

'I love you, Mabel,' she said and leaned forward to kiss her on the lips.

Mabel stiffened and drew back. 'What are you doing?' she asked, more puzzled than indignant.

'Surely you've realized by now?' Nora said. 'I don't like men. And I fell for you that first night, as I patched you up.'

Mabel's stomach did a little flip. Mrs Hardy had once mentioned a groom who worked at her previous employment who was sacked for having sexual relations with a footman. Mabel had been curious and asked her to explain what she meant. Mrs Hardy said that the proper word for it was 'homosexual', and women could be like it, as well as men. Mabel had wanted to ask more, but she was too embarrassed to admit to such ignorance.

But surely that wasn't what Nora was?

'I like you a great deal, but not like that. I'm sorry if you thought differently,' Mabel said gently. 'One day, I hope to find a man to replace Peter.'

Nora began to cry. She was still kneeling in front of Mabel and bent her head to her lap.

Mabel stroked her hair and tried to comfort her. 'I'll never forget your kindness to me,' she said. 'You've been an angel just when I needed help. I hope we'll always be friends too.'

'I can't be friends now that you've turned me down.' Nora's tone was petulant, and she wiped her eyes with the back of her hand. Those eyes that had pleaded earlier were hard now, and her mouth was set in a straight, determined line. 'You'd better go right now.'

'You know I don't have any money,' Mabel said in a small voice.

Nora got to her feet and looked down on Mabel. 'Then get out there and sell yourself to some dirty bastard, if you like men so much,' she snarled at her.

Mabel could hardly believe that Nora could say such a thing, or turn so dramatically against her.

'That's a mean and nasty thing to say.' Mabel got to her feet and began to look around for her belongings. 'It's not worthy of you. You are better than that.'

She found her bag and packed her things into it. She could feel Nora watching her intently, but she remained silent.

Mabel took her coat off the peg on the door, jammed her hat on her head and secured it with a hatpin. 'I'll say goodbye then, Nora. I didn't want it to end this way. I'll send you some money in a few weeks to cover the cost of keeping me.'

Nora turned her back on her, so Mabel opened the door and left.

She couldn't help but cry as she walked down the lane. She had really believed that she and Nora would be friends for life. That once she'd found a job, wherever that might be, they'd keep in touch by letter and perhaps meet up somewhere every so often.

She wasn't even horrified that her friend liked women in that way; if she'd just admitted it earlier, their friendship could've continued. But to be nasty because Mabel didn't return those feelings was every bit as bad as a man trying it on and becoming indignant when he was turned down.

Without any money, and with her ribs still hurting and the weather very cold, Mabel knew this was a crisis. It was too far to walk to Dorchester, and too cold to sleep rough. What was she going to do?

Then she thought of Mrs Hardy. She didn't want to throw herself on her, like a charity case, but the only other alternative was the workhouse. Even if Mrs Hardy wouldn't let her stay, she might lend her some money to get to Dorchester.

'Mabel, my dear! What on earth has happened to you?' Mrs Hardy exclaimed as she opened the door of the mews house to find Mabel standing there. 'You've got black eyes! Come on in, and tell me about it.'

The obvious concern from the older woman made Mabel break down and cry. She had very nearly collapsed with the pain in her ribs as she walked up the steep hill that was Park Street.

'You don't know how happy I am to see you,' Mabel said as she followed the older woman up a flight of bare wooden stairs. 'I didn't want to impose on you, but I didn't have anyone else to turn to.'

'I expected you to come to me that day when Mr Bedford told you to go,' Mrs Hardy said. 'I thought you'd give it an hour or two until he'd gone, then pop round.'

'I wish I had,' Mabel admitted. 'But I had a bit of money and I thought I'd take the train to Dorchester and see Mrs Forester. She said she would help me find work.'

'So, the black eyes?'

'A man jumped on me in an alley down near the tram terminus. He beat me up and found my money and snatched it. I thought I was going to die there in the alley. I've got broken ribs too.'

'Oh, my goodness! How terrible. But you are safe with me now.' The housekeeper led Mabel into a living room and took her bag from her hands. 'You sit down by the fire, my dear, and I'll put the kettle on.'

The relief that Mrs Hardy was prepared to help her was so great, Mabel had to fight back fresh tears. She took an upright chair; she was afraid if she sat down on a soft chair, she might not be able to get up again. She held out her icy hands to the roaring fire and looked around her in surprise to find such a cosy, comfortable flat.

The kitchen where Mrs Hardy had gone led off the living room, towards the back of Harley Place. It was tiny compared with the one at number six, but well equipped. A row of gleaming copper pans hung from hooks on the ceiling and the small central table was scrubbed white.

Mabel had never been inside this flat before, and considering how filthy Mrs Hardy had said it was, she must've worked night and day – because it was not only spotlessly clean, but cosy too.

The living-room furniture must have originally come from Mrs Gladsworthy's home, as it was all remarkably similar. There was a big, comfortable-looking dark red velvet sofa and armchairs, only a little worn on the arms, and an oak table and chairs and a matching dresser. The rugs, heavy curtains, the roaring fire, lamps and pictures all created a feeling of opulence.

'It's lovely,' Mabel called out. 'You must've worked so hard to get it this way?'

Mrs Hardy came back into the living room with cups on a tray. 'I did, non-stop. I banged things around, pretending I was banging Mr Bedford's head. It did me a power of good. I can see into number six from the kitchen, and his wife and silly daughters are flapping around, unable to sort anything. It makes me laugh. If he'd kept us on, we could've got it all lovely for them. Though his furniture is pretty shabby.'

'He deserves to be miserable,' Mabel said. 'And you deserve to be happy and rested.'

'And you must tell me where you've been since you were attacked. The whole story.'

Mabel spilled the details over tea, but when she got to the events of just a couple of hours ago, she stumbled over her words, and grew red in the face with embarrassment.

But Mrs Hardy didn't even look shocked, she just nodded. 'I have come across that myself in service a couple of times,' she said calmly. 'Both of them turned sullen when I said I didn't have the same feelings. But men who are like that, I found to be quite different. All the ones I've met were kind, fun and sweet-natured. Of course, they must keep it quiet, they can go to prison for it, but they can't help the way they are made. We had a footman at Rowledge Hall, where I worked when I was younger than you, and he became like my brother. We were always laughing, we'd go out on our afternoons off together. If he'd not been the way he was, I'd have gladly married him.'

Mabel finished off her story and then asked Mrs Hardy if she could borrow enough money for her fare to Dorchester.

'I'll gladly give you that, once we know you've got a job to go to,' she said. 'But first things first. You must write to Mrs Forester, tell her what happened with Mr Bedford. I'll put in a covering letter too. Then we'll wait to get her reply.'

'But –'

The housekeeper put her finger to her lips. 'Shh. I know you don't want to ask if you can stay here, but you can, and you must. I can see you are in pain, and walking about will take those ribs even longer to heal. There is a tiny spare room, it's full of stuff I don't know what to do with. But you only need a bed for now.'

She led Mabel across the small landing to show her. Her own bedroom was at the front of the house, the small room and the bathroom at the back. She was right, it was full of stuff, piled up with a chest of drawers, odd chairs, pictures and bedding. But there was a little truckle bed just waiting to be made up.

'You are so kind,' Mabel said. 'I didn't expect this. In fact, I thought I'd have to walk to Dorchester, sleeping in barns on the way.'

'Mabel! Mr Bedford was a nasty man, and I'm going to take you to the solicitor's tomorrow and tell him just what that man did to both of us. He might even be able to get the wages we are owed back from him.'

It was like old times to sit by the fire with Mrs Hardy and just talk. Mabel felt safe now and so incredibly grateful to the older woman. She seemed different too, more relaxed than she'd been at Harley Place, talking about things that she never would've divulged back then. Mabel supposed this was because they were no longer maid and house-keeper, where distance had to be maintained, but simply two women now with shared experiences.

'I've found myself a little job,' Mrs Hardy said with a smile. 'Just a few hours a week for a lovely gentleman, Percy Holmes. I used to see him at church, and I ran into him again at the Christmas service. He asked how I was, and I told him what had happened. He has a lovely flat overlooking the suspension bridge. Anyway, the upshot of meeting him again was him offering me some work. I've only been twice so far, a bit of cleaning, making some-thing for his dinner. I like it, the days would seem awfully long with nothing to do.'

'Is he old?' Mabel asked.

'No, only about fifty, I think. He's a professor at the university.'

'Would he make a nice husband for you?'

Mrs Hardy laughed heartily. 'Bless you, Mabel, at my time of life I couldn't adjust to living with any man. But I do like Percy, he's kind, interesting, clever – and he's not bad-looking, either. But he's been a bachelor for so long that I don't think he's looking for a wife.'

'Shame,' Mabel said.

Mrs Hardy laughed again. 'I'd sooner get you married off,' she said. 'But you've had an upsetting day today, so why don't I run you a bath? And then you can go to bed early with a hot-water bottle. Then tomorrow we'll write that letter to Mrs Forester and see the solicitor.'

'That sounds good,' Mabel agreed. She was tired, and

her ribs hurt less lying down. But the prospect of a bath was best of all. She hadn't had one since she left Harley Place.

'I'll make up your bed while you are in there,' Mrs Hardy said with a smile. 'Maybe wash your pretty hair too – you can come and dry it in front of the fire afterwards.'

6

Mrs Hardy came in the front door of the mews flat and picked up the letter lying on the floor. It was for Mabel.

'Cooee!' she called out, knowing her young guest had been on tenterhooks waiting for the reply from Dorchester. 'Looks like your reply has come.'

Mabel scampered to meet the older woman and almost snatched the letter from her hand in her eagerness. 'Sorry,' she said, suddenly realizing that was rude. 'I'm actually frightened to open it, in case she's turned me down. But I've just made a pot of tea, I'll read it to you as soon as I've poured it.'

Once they were both sitting down in the kitchen with their tea, Mabel opened the letter. '"My dear Mabel,"' she read. '"I was horrified to read how badly Mr Bedford treated both you and Mrs Hardy. I know how much you both did for my sister-in-law, and she will be turning in her grave at such nastiness. I am, of course, very relieved to know she took care of Mrs Hardy and Mrs Tweed in her will, though that doesn't really make up for the unpleasantness, but I wish them both every happiness in this New Year.

"But I am concerned for you, Mabel. I know how ridiculously hard it is to get a job without a character. Even worse to hear that you were robbed and beaten. Thank goodness you had Mrs Hardy to go to for help.

"Sadly, at this present time I have a full complement of staff, but I have asked around amongst my friends locally, and one has shown a great deal of interest.

"Miss Clarissa May is an illustrator of children's books. She lives in a cottage in rather splendid isolation about five miles from me. Like most artists (and I'm sure she won't mind me telling you this), she lives in a bit of a muddle. What she wants is not a conventional house-keeper, like Mrs Hardy, but someone who can adapt to her lifestyle. Cook some meals, do the laundry, perhaps a bit of gardening, and in general add a bit of order to her home.

"Clarissa jokes that she needs an invisible fairy god-mother! I think by that she means someone who can see what needs doing without instruction and doesn't disturb her when she's working.

"Accommodation is in a tiny cottage across her garden. She is willing to pay eight shillings a week –"'

Mabel broke off to look at Mrs Hardy. 'That's a very good wage, isn't it?'

'On the face of it perhaps. But I doubt it's "all found", as it was at number six. You may have to get your own food, and maybe wood for the fire. But it all sounds rather nice, with a separate little cottage and being left to use your initiative.'

Mabel looked back at the letter. 'She's given me Claris-sa's address. She said to write to her and say when I can come, and she'll get someone to meet me at the station. I'll get a month's trial.'

'That sounds good to me – in fact, I'd say it was perfect for you. Mrs Forester wouldn't suggest this for you unless she knew what the accommodation was like and felt you were ideal for the job.'

'Then I'll write and accept as soon as I've found out the train times.'

Mrs Hardy smiled. 'I can do that for you. I've got to go over to Percy's this afternoon. He has train timetables; I noticed when I was there last.'

'What's Dorchester like?' Mabel asked. 'All I know about it is from Thomas Hardy books.'

'I've never been there, so I'm not much help to you. But I believe Dorset is a beautiful county.'

Ten days later, Mabel arrived at Dorchester West station, late in the afternoon, in a snowstorm. The snow had started during the long journey, and she'd been afraid the train would break down and she and the other passengers would be stranded in the middle of nowhere.

But that hadn't happened, and at last, after two weeks of thinking of little else but this job, and waiting for her ribs to heal and bruises to disappear, she was here. Further along the platform, near the way out, she could see a tall man wearing a voluminous checked coat, a thick muffler and a tweed cap. He looked expectant, as if waiting for someone, and she hoped it was her.

'Mrs Brook?' he asked as she came near to him. 'I'm Andrews. Miss May asked me to collect you. Welcome to Dorchester. Now let's get going before we get stuck in the snow.'

He grabbed her bag, but as they went out of the station Mabel noticed he had a bad limp; she wondered if he'd been wounded in France.

'Sorry, this is going to be a cold and bumpy ride,' Andrews said, helping her up into a small carriage, very like the hansom cabs she'd seen in Bristol, pulled by two piebald horses. 'The horses don't mind snow, but I'm not so keen.'

Andrews arranged a blanket across her lap, then hopped up in front, and with a flick of the reins, they were off down the snow-covered road.

It was dusk as they drove away from the station, but before long darkness fell, and they appeared to be going away from the town. The only light came from small oil lights either side of the carriage, and through the falling snow all Mabel could see were ghostly-looking trees, with no further houses or lights.

There was a little window in front so passengers could see where they were going, and she slid it back so she could speak to Andrews. 'Is Miss May's house very isolated?' she asked a little nervously. It rarely snowed on the Devon coast, so she wasn't used to it, and although it had snowed while she was in Bristol it never became a scary white-out like this – and besides, there were lights, trams and houses.

'It's a bit off the beaten track, but you'll enjoy the pretty walks by the river, and you can ride a bicycle to explore further afield,' he said, yelling back and half turning in his seat. 'But you may have to resign yourself to being snowed in for the first few days. This lot looks like it's here to stay.'

'Do you live in Miss May's house?' Mabel asked. It crossed her mind he might be her lover, along with being her driver, as he was rather handsome in a bony sort of way; even his limp gave him a sort of dashing charm, and her new employer sounded unconventional.

'Oh no, I live in the town with my wife and two small sons,' he said. 'I'm not Miss May's exclusive driver. I drive lots of different people about. Though I have to say, you are the youngest person to be in my carriage this year.'

Mabel laughed. 'The year is only two weeks old.'

'Yes, but if you ask me in December, I'll probably tell you the same thing. Most of my clients are old. Miss May isn't, of course, and she happens to be my favourite as she makes me laugh.'

'I hope she likes me,' Mabel confided. 'I'm really nervous.'

'Well, I can tell you there is nothing to be nervous about. She's looking forward to getting a bit of help, and she's a lovely lady. I'm delighted for her that you are young. The last housekeeper she had was old and very grumpy. I think Miss May was a bit scared of her. I know I was!'

Mabel laughed. 'This snow is a bit frightening. But I have every faith in you getting me there in one piece.' She wanted to add she hoped it wasn't much further, as she was frozen to the marrow, but she didn't want him to think she was a moaner.

He turned to the right quite suddenly, on to a narrow tree-lined lane where the snow looked even thicker.

'Not far now,' Andrews said. 'You'll see lights up ahead soon, she always keeps it lit up like a lighthouse.'

As the lights appeared, Mabel was able to see the house; it looked very pretty, with pointed eaves and the roof thick with snow. The house was surrounded by tall conifers, and they too were laden with snow.

'You can't see now, because of the snow, but the river is just here in front of the cottage. I'll just take you to the door and then go, or I might get stuck in a drift,' Andrews said as he drove in through a gateway. 'Duke and Bertie might like the snow but even horses have their limitations. I expect I shall see you again soon. And I wish you every happiness here.'

The door was opened by a pretty, slender woman with shiny, dark brown hair, and rather prominent, large dark eyes.

'Welcome, Mabel, and come on in out of the cold,' she said with a wide smile, waving to Andrews as he turned the carriage around.

The house felt very warm and it smelled of something spicy.

'Thank you, it's good to be here, Miss May,' Mabel said.

'You must be frozen stiff. Now forget the "Miss May", I want you to call me Clara, we'll leave the "issa" out of it. So glad the train got you here, I was half expecting a telephone call to say snow had wiped out the service. I'm sure your train was probably the last for a few days.'

'I've heard most trains leaving Southampton are packed with wounded soldiers,' Mabel said. 'I wonder how the snow will affect them?'

'They'll get through somehow – it's the passenger trains they stop first. We have many German prisoners of war coming here to Dorchester. There is a big camp here. At the last count over four thousand men. But you must be cold, hungry and dying for a cup of tea,' Clara said. 'I've got supper ready in the kitchen. Let me have your coat and hat first.'

The first thing that struck Mabel was the oil lamps. After having electricity at Harley Place, she'd imagined anyone able to employ a servant would have electricity. But at least Miss May wasn't mean with the oil lamps; in the hall alone there were three alight, and the house had been a blaze of light as they approached.

The lack of electricity didn't spoil anything. Mabel thought her new employer and her house were delightful. Clara wore a red wool dress with a red-and-white striped cardigan over it. She was also wearing red slippers. Mabel had lived in black for so long now that she felt quite envious of the bright colour, but then the cottage was full of colour too. The hall was papered in a fantastic print of multicoloured butterflies; the rug over a wooden floor was a chequered design, picking up the reds and greens in the wallpaper.

The kitchen leading off the hall was large, with French windows going on to the garden at the back, and a myriad of brightly coloured plates, jugs and other ornaments adorned a huge dresser.

Even the central table, which had been laid with supper for two, had a big cobalt-blue china elephant sitting in the middle, with four candles around it. And the kitchen was well heated, thanks to a cooking range that looked even more modern than the one at Harley Place.

'Let me draw the curtains to keep out that chilly view,' Clara said. She pulled heavy red curtains, trimmed all round with yellow and blue braid, across the window.

'What a lovely, welcoming home,' Mabel said. 'So much colour!'

Clara grinned impishly. 'I can't be doing with sombre, sensible colours. I'm not sure I've actually become an adult.'

'I expect that is why you are a children's book illustrator, then,' Mabel replied. All at once she felt she could finally breathe out, forget the worries she'd had that she wouldn't be able to cope here. Just looking around, she knew she was going to love looking after this house, and its owner.

'The weather is too bad to take you down to the little cottage tonight, so if you don't mind, you can stay here. It might be for a few days,' Clara said.

'That won't be a hardship,' Mabel said with a heartfelt smile. 'It is so lovely here.'

'If you think that, then we'll get along famously.' Clara beamed. 'Now sit down, I've made soup, and there's sandwiches too. I'm a terrible cook, so don't expect too much of the soup.'

The soup was French onion, and despite what Clara had said, it was good, as were the ham sandwiches, and some fruit cake. Over supper they talked. Mabel told Clara a shortened version of what had happened since she'd been made to leave Harley Place, and talked rather more unwillingly about her husband being killed in France.

'There is going to be a whole generation of widows and spinsters,' Clara said sadly. 'So many young men dead and injured. And for what? I ask myself. Over in the POW camp the prisoners are mainly just boys too. What is wrong with the world that we send out our finest young men to be killed and maimed? What cause could be that important?'

'There is talk that it is nearly over now, and we are winning,' Mabel said.

'There will be no winners.' Clara shook her head. 'Not

when children will never know their fathers, when women have lost their husbands and sweethearts, and mothers have lost their sons. Germans, French and English, it's the same for all of us. Women will have to shape up now and make sure they get the vote to create a fairer society. Maybe one day we'll even get women in the government to influence those who see war as an answer.'

'You sound like a Suffragette,' Mabel said.

'I am – or rather, I was – the war put much of that on a back burner. Women have been doing traditional male jobs since war broke out, and they've proved themselves more than capable. I'm ashamed I haven't done my share. I do go over to the POW camp once a week and teach art, but that's hardly helping the war effort – in fact, some would say I was collaborating with the enemy.'

'Surely not!' Mabel was shocked at that.

'Only a handful of simpletons would fail to see that a country that treats its prisoners with respect and compassion is a strong country. But happily, people round here are mostly tolerant of the POWs. Many of them help on the local farms and look after public gardens, so they are keeping things going while our men are in France. I have no doubt we'll see gangs of them out tomorrow clearing the snow off the roads. I have a man helping in the garden too. In the summer he came often, but now only occasionally – mostly to chop wood for me.'

After supper, Mabel washed up while Clara dried, and then she showed Mabel round the rest of the house. The sitting room was lovely – all soft pinks and greens, with thick carpet and a piano. Clara said she loved to play and, in fact, had wanted to be a concert pianist.

'I wasn't good enough, sadly,' she laughed. 'So I painted instead.'

There were several of her large paintings on the walls; all landscapes, and exceptionally beautiful. Then she took Mabel to show her the studio where she worked. That was upstairs at the back of the house, and very cold, as it had a huge window and no fire lit. There was no easel as Mabel had expected; Clara said she did her illustration work at the big table. She showed her some pen-and-ink sketches of a pig in women's clothes.

Mabel laughed when she saw that the pig pretended to be human, but that she was always being found out, however much she disguised herself. 'I'm liking this book already,' she said.

'I wish I could do bigger pictures for it in colour, but the publishers just want these little sketches,' Clara said wistfully.

Finally, she showed Mabel to a small room at the front. 'This is where you'll be staying until the snow clears a bit. Now, do you think you're going to like it here?'

'I know I am,' Mabel said.

'Well, you'll find I can be a bit of a recluse when I'm working. I shut myself away for lengthy periods. But you mustn't think you've offended me in some way. You just get on with whatever you think needs doing.'

It was just after ten when Mabel got to bed. The pretty blue and white room and the comfortable double bed with a thick eiderdown made her feel cared for. Her last thoughts before she fell asleep were of Nora. She wished it hadn't ended so badly, and she was resolved that in future she would be less quick to judge people who weren't quite in line with what she thought was right.

Mabel was up the next morning just as the first rays of daylight appeared in the sky. She thought it must be after seven o'clock, though she had no clock or watch to check. She reminded herself she must ask Clara if she could borrow one.

After having a quick wash and getting dressed, she crept down to the kitchen. The range was still alight, but it needed riddling to bring it to life, and more coal. When she'd finished, she put the kettle on.

Pulling back the thick curtains, she gasped involuntarily. The snow was halfway up the French windows, and the garden looked so beautiful under its blanket of snow that her eyes welled up unexpectedly.

There were humps and bumps everywhere – buried shrubs, she supposed – and the trees were bent down with the weight of snow on their branches. She could see animal tracks in the snow; a fox, or maybe a badger, had come right up to the house. She longed to go out there herself and make fresh footprints. But she had work to do.

When she pulled back the curtains in the sitting room, which looked out to the front, she got an even better surprise. Willow Cottage was less than a hundred yards from the River Frome. That too looked beautiful; the bushes and trees on both sides were laden with snow, and she could see Dorchester straight ahead, across the river, rising beyond the fields.

By the time Clara came down, at almost nine, Mabel had cleared the fire in the sitting room and laid and lit a fresh one. She'd swept the carpet in there, dusted, and plumped up the cushions on the sofas and armchairs. She'd also laid the table in the kitchen for breakfast, looked in the pantry and decided she could make a beef stew later with what she'd found there.

'Well, well, well, you've been busy, and I never heard a peep,' Clara said. Wrapped in a dusky-pink dressing gown that looked several sizes too big for her, she went over to the range to check on it.

'You've seen to it. How clever you are,' she said, looking delighted. 'The last help I had here was hopeless. Not only was she a tartar, she was always letting the stove go out. It heats the water and some radiators, so that was infuriating.'

Mabel poured her a cup of tea. 'I grew up with the oldest, nastiest old stove you can imagine,' she said. 'You had to learn how to coax it into life, to nurture it. Or it would sulk, and you couldn't even boil an egg on it. Speaking of which, what do you like for breakfast?'

If Mabel could have designed her ideal job and the place to do it in, she would have chosen to be housekeeper here at Willow Cottage, with Clara as her mistress.

There was plenty to do; the whole house looked as if it hadn't been cleaned thoroughly for some months. In the little scullery was a huge basket of clothes and bed linen waiting to be ironed, and the kitchen cupboards were very mucky. But all of that made Mabel glad that she could take pride in making everywhere lovely.

While she was cleaning Clara's studio and lighting a fire there, her mistress began playing her piano downstairs and singing. Mabel thought she must be one of the most talented women in England; her voice was like an angel's.

Clara exclaimed in delight when she went up to her studio later and found the fire lit and everything clean and tidy.

'You are a treasure,' she yelled down the stairs.

Mabel found herself smiling as she prepared the beef stew and put it in the range to cook. She made a fruit cake too, which could cook at the same temperature.

About three in the afternoon, Clara came downstairs.

'I thought we could put our coats and boots on and have a little walk, over to your cottage, so you can inspect it. Then perhaps see how much farther we can go in the snow,' she said. 'I need to get out in the fresh air, and I'm sure you do.'

Mabel happily agreed. She did want to go out; she'd looked at the pristine snow in the garden and wanted so much to run about in it like a child. She didn't feel able to reveal that yet, for fear of sounding silly. But she borrowed a spare pair of wellington boots, thick socks and a woolly hat, and grinned happily at her new mistress.

'The cottage will be like an ice house. It's some time since anyone lived in it,' Clara said as they began to trudge across the garden towards the woods. 'In a day or two I'll get Carsten to light the stove in there and we'll keep it going each day until you are ready to move over there.'

'Is Carsten your gardener?' Mabel asked as they walked outside.

'Not exactly. He's the German prisoner of war, from the camp I told you about. He does gardening, odd jobs, anything really.'

'A German?' Mabel had a picture in her head like the cartoons she'd seen, of a man with a shiny, spiked helmet. 'Isn't that a bit scary for you?'

Clara laughed. 'Not at all. He's young, very gentlemanly and pleasant – and he speaks English, which is a bonus. Back in the autumn he made a first-class job of putting the garden to bed for the winter. I showed him which plants needed cutting back and which ones to leave, and he did that and more.'

Mabel could no longer resist stamping about in the snow, feeling it crunch beneath her wellingtons. And to her astonishment Clara followed her lead and did it too, laughing like an excited child.

'We've messed it all up now!' Mabel laughed as she surveyed the area they'd trampled.

'There's plenty more in the woods and down by the cottage,' Clara replied, picking up a handful of snow, rolling it into a ball and throwing it at Mabel. 'Gotcha!'

Mabel retaliated and hit Clara directly in the chest. They threw a few more snowballs each, shrieking with laughter, before Clara put her hands in the air and yelled, 'No more!'

Suddenly they became aware of a man watching them. He was tall and slender, wearing a long blue-grey coat and a light-grey woolly hat, pulled down over his ears.

'It's Carsten,' Clara exclaimed.

'I am sorry to intrude,' he said in halting English, and doffed his hat. 'I came to see if snow was trouble for you.'

Mabel felt a bit embarrassed she hadn't instantly realized his coat and hat were army issue, but then she'd never seen a German before. He was remarkably handsome too, with bright blue eyes, blond hair and high cheekbones. He looked a similar age to her.

'We like the snow, Carsten. It makes children of us,' Clara said. 'This is Mabel, my new housekeeper. We're on our way to look at the cottage. I was going to ask you to light the stove and keep it going for a few days. I think it will be damp in there.'

'I come with you,' he said.

It seemed very odd to be walking along with a German close behind them. In Bristol, Mrs Tweed had claimed German soldiers killed babies; she said she'd read it in a newspaper. Mabel had heard other people claim they were savages and that they shot the men they took prisoner. It was so easy to just believe the things people said – after all, she knew nothing about Germany or its people. But now she knew Clara was happy to have a German working for her, and was going to the camp to teach them art, she thought perhaps people made things up – maybe in retaliation for the relatives they'd lost in the war.

'You like to come here?' Carsten asked as they went into the little cottage.

'Yes, very much,' she replied and smiled at him.

He had the kind of face that would make any woman smile; it was not just his blue eyes, but something in the way he looked at her, and at Clara too, as if he was curious about what made them tick. His mouth was lovely too, with plump lips and very white, even teeth.

'So, Mabel, how do you like the cottage?' Clara asked.

'It's really lovely,' she replied.

The room they were in was a living room cum kitchen, all painted white; but like the main house there were bright splashes of colour everywhere. The sofa in front of the fireplace was draped with a scarlet rug. Four chairs round a small circular table were painted glossy green, and the cloth on the table had green-and-white checks. A curtain across the front of the sink was the same checked material too. There were colourful books on a shelf, and several of Clara's vivid paintings. Even the oil lamps were pretty ones with coloured glass bases.

Carsten had the small range in the fireplace laid and lit within minutes. 'I get more wood and coal from shed,' he said.

As he went out, Clara said that she could boil a kettle on the range. That made Mabel smile, as she'd grown up cooking whole meals on one much older than this one.

'But you can eat with me,' Clara went on. 'I'm afraid there is no bathroom here, the lavatory is just outside. But you can have a bath whenever you like, up at the house. Are you alright with that?'

'It's lovely,' Mabel said and meant it.

In summer it would be a glorious place to live, looking out on to the garden with all its trees. The bedroom was pretty, with a big fluffy pink eiderdown on the double bed and a dressing table with a triple mirror, like one Mrs Gladsworthy had in her room. As time went by, she could add things to make it even more homely.

'I'm looking forward to the day we can have electricity in the house,' Clara said as Carsten came back in with a scuttle of coal and some more wood. 'I can't really draw after four in the winter because the oil lights are too dim to see properly. In fact, we'd better get back now, it's beginning to get dark.'

After speaking to Carsten for a few minutes about banking up the stove for the night, coming back in the morning to see to it and bringing in more logs for the fires in the main house, they left.

'Is the camp he lives in grim?' Mabel asked as they walked back through the snow.

'No, not really, especially after the terrible conditions they endured in the trenches. Wooden huts, as you'd expect, but they have a stove in each one. There are enough showers and lavatories for everyone, there is a hospital and a church too, and there are sports, art, a choir, drama clubs – and they have a band. Carsten says the men get enough to eat, and the English guards are decent to them.'

Mabel thought that all sounded surprisingly good.

'There has always been the army here in Dorchester, it's the home of the Dorset regiment, and the camp is almost an extension of the barracks, though it has grown and grown as more men arrive,' Clara went on. 'So it's not like a real prison, though of course there is barbed wire all around, with floodlights and strict security. I just hope our men who've been taken prisoner in France are as well treated.'

'Fancy them being let out to work,' Mabel said. 'Aren't they afraid they'll run away?'

'Run where?' Clara laughed. 'This is an island, they can't get off it. A few have tried, especially right back at the start of the war. I don't think any of them got out of England. But I think they are very fussy about who they let out to work; except for men like Carsten, all the other men out at work are guarded. Last year, with all our men away in France, they had to let lots of prisoners help on the farms or there would've been no crops to harvest. It worked out well too. My friend Mary has a farm near here, and she was run ragged trying to milk the cows, plant and look after vegetables, get them to market, then caring for chickens, ducks and goats. Far too much for one woman to do alone. They sent her two men, and they've been marvellous; her yard used to be like a midden, but they wash it all down every morning after the cows go back in the fields. I couldn't believe how orderly it all was when I went to visit her. She's going to miss them when the war is over, they work much harder than her husband ever did.'

'Why is Carsten an exception?'

'He's the equivalent to our rank of sergeant, for a start – there are very few NCOs at the camp. Because of his English he acts as an interpreter, and he is just very well thought of. Maybe at the start of the war, a brave, committed soldier like him would have tried to escape, to get back to Germany to fight. But now, when the war is nearing the end, I think he believes it is his duty to stay here and look after his men. He helps in the hospital too. Like I said, he is a good man.'

The snow lay thick on the garden for five days before the thaw came. As it slowly shrank back, revealing grass and soil, Mabel felt rather sad. It hadn't felt like she was working at the house, more like she was on holiday, but now she'd have to move over to the cottage, and that would remind her soon enough that she was just a servant.

That afternoon, she took her belongings, plus a box of bed linen, towels, books and other items Clara thought would make her feel at home, down to the little cottage. To her surprise it felt warm and cosy. She hadn't seen Carsten since the first time they'd met, but clearly he had been calling every day, because there was kindling, coal and logs too. She lit an oil lamp, and then noticed there was a can of oil to refill it in a cupboard, and a little carved wooden bear about three inches tall on the table, which hadn't been there before.

She picked it up and smiled at it. She guessed it was a little present from Carsten.

She had put the kettle on to have a cup of tea and fill a hot-water bottle, to air the bed, and was just about to start making the bed up, when Carsten appeared at the window.

'Hello,' Mabel said as she opened the front door to speak to him. 'Thank you for looking after the stove, it's lovely and warm now.'

He looked cold; his broad shoulders were hunched, and his face was pinched and pale.

'Would you like to come in and have a cup of tea?' she asked. 'I've got cake too.'

When he smiled, it was like the sun coming out. 'You are kind, but it is not permitted for us to have food from you.'

Mabel had been brought up to treat people as you would like to be treated. It didn't matter to her that he was a prisoner.

She shrugged. 'Who is there to see?' she said. 'Maybe a fox or a badger, no one else.'

He laughed, a real guffaw, the kind of laugh that would make anyone want to join in.

'So, it is tea then?'

He nodded and came in.

'I didn't see you coming here for the last few days,' she said, urging him to take off his coat and sit down by the range.

'I come along the riverbank and through the garden, not the front way.'

'And the bear?' she said picking it up. 'Was this from you?'

'Yah,' he said sheepishly. 'I carved it for you, I think you say a happy home present.'

'I love him, thank you so much. I'll call him Barney. He'll always remind me of you.'

'I hope good memories, not of the sadness war brings.'

'Only memories of kindness,' she said. 'You speak such good English. Where did you learn it?'

'My mother had English friend, her name Doreen. She was a widow and so she taught English. She say to me once "to keep the wolf from the door". I was only seven then and I worry about this wolf.'

Mabel giggled. 'It's a common English remark. You know the meaning now?'

'Yes, and I am glad she taught me so well. My friends back at the camp who do not speak any English, they are not so lucky like me to come out.'

'Do you get treated well at the camp?'

He shrugged. 'Good enough. Our countries are at war, we did not expect much. But food is alright, I get told we are fed better than the poor people in Dorchester. The rationing, it keeps people hungry.'

The kettle was boiling. Mabel made a pot of tea and put it on the table along with cups and the half of the fruit cake Clara had said she must take. She had noticed Clara didn't appear to have a problem with rationing. Yesterday a man had come to the door with a box of groceries, and Mabel suspected he wasn't just a friendly neighbour helping Clara out, as she claimed, but was selling her black-market stuff.

'You must miss your family,' she said, cutting him a slice of cake and pushing it close to him. 'Do you get letters okay?'

'Not enough, very slow,' he said. 'In the camp, letters from home are everything. We read again and again. But you must miss your family too, Mabel. Where are they?'

'I have no family now,' she said and quickly told him the same story she told everyone else.

'You will hate me because a German killed your husband?'

'No,' she said. 'Maybe he killed some of your men. Death in war is inevitable.'

'What does inevitable mean?'

'It is bound to happen.'

He nodded in understanding and took a bite of the cake. He rolled his eyes. 'I hear Clara say one day the word "scrumptious", another word I not know. But I think right for this cake. I could live on this. You make?'

'Yes, I make, and scrumptious is a good word.'

They drank their tea in a companionable silence. Mabel had the feeling that sitting in a warm room with tea and cake was making him think of home. Just that morning, as she was trimming the wick on an oil lamp, she had a sudden, sharp memory of doing the same at the cottage in Hallsands. It was so vivid she could smell the sea, hear the fishermen down below on the beach shouting to each other as they hauled in their boats. And she saw Martin's bright smile as he came in through the door. It made a lump come up in the back of her throat.

'You should find a new husband,' he said suddenly, breaking the silence. 'You are too young and pretty to be alone.'

Those lovely blue eyes of his were fixed on her, full of compassion, and it made her feel a little trembly inside.

'Another cup of tea and then I must make my bed and get back to Clara, to make the supper,' she said, rather than address what he had just said. As she poured the second cups, her hands were shaking.

He drank his quickly and then got up. 'Thank you, Mabel, for the tea and cake. I hope you will be happy here. I think your life not so happy in past.'

'I think I will be happy here, and I'm so glad I met you.'

7

'What a nice young man Carsten is,' Clara said as she looked out of the French windows on to the garden, where he was doing some weeding.

Mabel was peeling potatoes for their lunch, and she got a faint sense that her mistress had made this remark, fishing to see if there was anything between her and Carsten.

It was the 1st of March and Mabel had been at Willow Cottage for six weeks. Every day, she found yet another reason to be glad she had come here. And now the garden was showing signs of burgeoning into life after the long winter, she felt even happier.

'Yes, he is. So polite and correct,' Mabel said.

'That's very Germanic,' Clara said thoughtfully. 'I went to Germany a few years ago; the men are all like that, a bit too stiff and chilly for my taste.'

Mabel didn't find Carsten stiff or chilly, but she wasn't going to say that.

'What's Germany like?' she asked instead.

'Very beautiful. Well, at least the parts I saw were – forests, lakes and charming villages.'

'How come you never married?' Mabel asked. She knew now that Clara was forty-five, but she seemed much younger, with her glossy hair, her trim figure and her joyous manner. 'If that isn't too personal?'

'Not at all, my dear.' Clara turned away from the window and leaned on the draining board. 'I just never met anyone that I felt I could spend the rest of my life with. Lots of lovely chaps, parties, dances, kisses in the moonlight. But never that utter certainty that this was "the One". Were you sure when you met your husband?'

'Completely sure,' Mabel said. 'If the war hadn't come along and taken him, I'm sure we would have remained as happy in old age as we were when we met.'

'But he was your first and only sweetheart?'

'Yes, I was just fourteen when we first met, and married at sixteen.'

'I suspect that's the secret,' Clara said with a smile. 'Too much choice is never a good thing.'

Mabel finished the potatoes and put them on the range to cook. Today they were having sausages and mash for lunch, with apple pie for dessert. Carsten had brought the apples out of the shed this morning; they had been stored there over the winter, but he'd noticed some of them were going mouldy and suggested they cooked the remainder that were still edible. As a result, Clara had asked him in to have lunch with them.

As Carsten had told her when they first met, feeding a prisoner was forbidden, but Clara was by nature rebellious towards authority, and as she said, 'Why shouldn't I give him a meal when I want to?' Most days it was just a sandwich left on the garden table with a cup of tea, a slice of cake, a few biscuits, or a mug of soup. But Carsten really appreciated her offerings, as it was a long day between breakfast and his supper back at the camp.

He came and worked in the garden at least three times

a week. Clara paid sixpence an hour for his services to the POW camp, but Carsten only received one penny an hour. Something that made Clara cross. It seemed unfair to Mabel too, because he worked so hard, and they were becoming good friends. She usually left the main house at two thirty and returned later, around six, to fix their supper. Carsten always left for the day at four thirty, and his route took him past her cottage. Most days he dropped in for a cup of tea before returning to the camp.

Mabel had learned he was the eldest of three boys, that his father was a keen hunter and his mother a model housewife and great cook. He often told Mabel stories about the mischief he and his brothers got into, and it was clear to her that he'd had a happy childhood and missed his family a great deal. He had been apprenticed as an engineer back in Germany but, at nineteen, as soon as war was declared, he enlisted in the army.

'All my friends wanted to go. And we thought it was our duty too. I didn't really want to – I didn't think I would make a good soldier.'

'But you are a *Feldwebel*,' she said. She'd thought that was a joke rank when he first said it, but Clara put her straight, explaining it was the military equivalent of an English sergeant. 'You must have been a good soldier if you could lead your men.'

'I didn't manage to lead them away from becoming prisoners of war,' he said with a wry smile. 'I think I only got promoted because I spoke English. The officers thought that was useful.'

'I'm sure it was more than that,' she said.

He sighed. 'War is a nasty, bloody, dirty business. The

129

good men die, and the bad ones often survive, on both sides. I admit I was glad when I was taken prisoner. I'd had enough of the mud, the noise, lice, rats, rotten food and seeing my friends die in agony. There had been times when I almost ran away. That's how good a soldier I was!'

His honesty surprised her. Because he was German and, as such, expected to be on the winning side, she had imagined he would glorify war. But to admit the complete opposite was touching. 'I think most soldiers must feel exactly like you, if they were truthful. From what I've read in the newspapers, the battlefields are a vision of hell.'

He looked thoughtful. 'Yes, that is exactly how it is. *Hölle.* I've seen men crying, calling for their mothers, sick with fear. But such courage too, on both sides. Men who risked being shot by a sniper going back into no-man's-land to rescue wounded comrades. But soldiers, yours and mine, admire that courage. Many times, the German and English snipers don't shoot. It was because they felt the anguish of seeing a comrade injured and helpless.'

Mabel saw how his eyes filled with tears as he spoke, how he stumbled for the right words, his voice trembling, and that sensitivity moved her. In truth, each time she saw him, she knew she was growing fonder and fonder of him, waiting eagerly to see that wide smile, the brilliance of his blue eyes, and to hear his hearty guffaws.

He was strong, she'd watched him cutting up logs as easily as if he was slicing up tender meat. And when he took his coat off because he'd got too hot, she marvelled at his powerful shoulders and the muscles in his arms. Yet the gentle, sensitive side of him moved her more. She'd seen him tenderly brushing dead leaves and soil away from clumps of snowdrops, breaking the ice on the bird bath so the birds could drink. He'd cut her a little posy of daphne, a sweet-smelling blossom, too.

Mabel found herself daydreaming about kissing him; sometimes she could actually taste him, and shivers of delight ran down her spine. But she had to be so careful not to show her feelings. Clara would dismiss him, if she thought there was something between them. People around here might be tolerant enough to have prisoners working on their land. They might even grow to like the men who were sent to them. But there would be public condemnation of any English girl walking out with a German.

Besides, Mabel doubted Carsten daydreamed about her; she'd asked him once if he had a sweetheart back home, but he'd just laughed and said he'd been too busy studying to see any girls.

She told herself that she was just being silly, thinking like a schoolgirl not a grown woman. But that didn't stop her heart skipping a beat when he was at the door of her cottage or, like now, when she knew he was coming in for lunch with them.

Clara did most of the talking over lunch, asking Carsten about men she had in her art class, some of whom she felt were talented artists. Carsten had been going to her class, as he liked drawing, but he'd stopped once he came to Willow Cottage to work, in case Clara was seen to be favouring him.

'Dieter's art is getting darker and darker,' she said, talking about one of the men that shared Carsten's hut. 'How do you find him? Do you notice him having problems?'

'Many of the men have problems, they are scarred by what they've seen and frightened they will never get home. They have bad dreams. Maybe it is good for Dieter to paint and draw darkness, then he can let it go.'

'When you were in the class you drew horses, flowers, beautiful landscapes. You weren't affected in this way?'

'All people are different,' Carsten said with a shrug. 'I am lucky that I come here, working in a garden. As the snowdrops and other flowers push out, I can feel the bad memories fading. And I can talk to you too, that is good.' He paused for a moment, a cloud crossing his handsome face. 'I think we are losing the war, now the Americans have come, and soon it will all end. It will be hard to go home, knowing it was all for nothing, and to see my country in trouble. I am not bitter about this, but Dieter is. He feels betrayed. They won't let him work outside the camp because of this. So his only way to show what is in his heart is through his painting.'

'You have a great understanding of people,' Clara said. 'I hope you use that when you go home. You could be a psychiatrist.'

She had to explain what that was, by calling it a 'doctor of the mind'.

He smiled and said he doubted he was clever enough, and anyway Germany would need engineers, chemists, farmers and builders. He didn't think anyone would go to a doctor of the mind.

The conversation moved on then to the influenza epidemic, which appeared to be spreading.

'I spoke to Dr Silby at the camp,' Clara said. 'He told me the epidemic is worse in America, but so far in England it is only in small pockets and people are recovering. But he thinks it will become much worse, and they have nothing to treat it.'

'I read the other day that the people who are catching it aren't those who are usually the most vulnerable – the old and the very young – but young adults in the twenty-to-thirty age group,' Mabel said. She hadn't been alarmed at this; it all seemed far too distant from them.

'We'll be alright, I'm sure,' Clara said soothingly. 'We don't have much contact with other people. We are all healthy. And besides, I haven't heard of one case round here. Only a few in Southampton.'

'Some soldiers in France have caught it,' Carsten said. 'If it is very infectious, and if they bring it home on crowded trains, it will spread.'

'Dr Silby said they were putting suspected cases into quarantine in France. But the doctors don't know enough about the disease, the incubation period and so forth, to get to grips with it.' Clara shuddered. 'Let's move on from this subject to something more comforting, like apple pie and custard. How lucky you checked the shed, Carsten, or we might have lost the remainder of the apples.'

As March went by, and the days grew longer and warmer, Mabel had never felt happier. She liked Clara a great deal and she was easy to work for, very appreciative and fun too. Sometimes on a fine afternoon Mabel would take the spare bicycle from the shed and explore the area. She loved going into Dorchester, especially to the public gardens, which were now bright with daffodils. She bought material for a new dress with her wages and used Clara's sewing machine to run it up. It was Clara's opinion that Mabel didn't need to remain in full mourning. But to avoid risking public condemnation, she picked a pale grey with a thin white stripe. She bought a straw boater too and trimmed it with white ribbon. It felt so good to be wearing something other than black, now the sun was shining.

She loved her little cottage, especially now the weather was growing warmer. With her wages she bought little things to make it more homely, and she loved waking each morning to birdsong in the garden. Yet one of her greatest pleasures was to sit by the stove in the evening and read a book she'd borrowed from Clara's vast collection. She realized that, all her life up till now, she'd rarely had any quiet moments to please herself. In the past there had been the mending of fishing nets, darning socks, washing, cleaning and cooking. Since Martin enlisted, she'd had Agnes on her back constantly. Sometimes being answerable to no one was such a good feeling.

But most fine afternoons when Carsten was there, she helped him in the garden. As she didn't know much about flowers – she'd only ever helped her father with vegetables on his allotment – she took the lead from Carsten, who seemed to know everything.

'Not really,' he laughed when she said this. 'I just know weeds. The flowers will be a surprise to me.'

Mabel wrote to Mrs Hardy every two weeks and really enjoyed getting the gossip back about how unpopular Mr Bedford and his family were with the neighbours. So far, two maids had left in a hurry, and now the cook was leaving too. She said Mrs Bedford had asked Mrs Tweed to come back, and she'd taken sweet pleasure in refusing.

Writing to the housekeeper always made Mabel think about Nora, and sometimes she was tempted to write to her. But she resisted. She could never be what Nora wanted, and they couldn't be comfortable as friends after what had happened.

She wished too that she had someone in Hallsands who could tell her how things were there. The guilt at what she'd done hadn't gone away, and she still worried about Martin. Many a night she thought back to how sweet it had been between them when they first got married, and she wondered if he had any memory of that time at all. There was also the niggling worry that one day she might be asked for proof of her identity. She couldn't show anything, and that would look very suspicious.

Yet even greater than all these worries was the fear that she was falling in love with Carsten. She wanted him physically, dreaming of what it would be like to sleep with him or to hold him close. Sometimes the dreams were so real that she woke in a state of excitement.

He liked her too, she knew that for certain, yet he never said or did anything that would allow her to take the initiative. She told herself this was because he knew he couldn't stay here when the war ended, and she couldn't go to Germany. Perhaps, too, he was worried she would be condemned locally. But Clara had told her other prisoners at the camp were having relationships with local women, although she was at pains to point out they were 'lowly sorts', so why wouldn't Carsten at least kiss her?

All she felt she could do was make herself as attractive as possible. She washed her hair far more than she used to, and she let it dry in the sun, so it grew shiny and curlier.

Clara had said her hair was too pretty to tie back severely, so she tied it back when working in the house, then in the afternoons outside, she let it loose. Sadly, her hair did nothing to lure Carsten, nor did the dabs of lavender oil behind her ears. One very warm day, she opened her bodice and showed an inch of cleavage, but that achieved nothing. She didn't think he even noticed.

Yet Carsten noticed everything else! He was the most observant and intuitive person she'd ever met. A cut on her hand, a cat walking though the garden, Clara with a new hat, he saw them all. But it was more than that; he knew how people's minds worked and why they did things. He told Clara one day that her art had become like a shield to keep people at a distance. Later, Mabel asked her what she thought of his remark, and Clara admitted it was true.

'I've had my fingers burned with two men, Mabel. They were rather more interested in my money than my looks and personality. I began to paint more after the last man, working into the night quite often. I think a psychiatrist would call it "displacement activity".' She laughed as she said this, but Mabel sensed she didn't really see anything funny about it.

It seemed Clara was rich. Her grandfather had made a fortune building rows of houses in London before he died, in 1892. He could neither read nor write, but had superb business acumen. He sent his son, Clara's father, to Harrow, and then on to Oxford. His plan was to make him the gentleman he'd never been.

'But father liked to get his hands dirty too,' Clara explained, her eyes twinkling with humour. 'He bunked out of Oxford and trained as an architect. Instead of building rows of houses for ordinary people, as Grandpa did, he chose to design houses for the rich. Sadly, he died suddenly at the age of just fifty-five, only ten years ago. That's when I bought this cottage, here in Dorchester. I could've bought a house in London's Mayfair, if I wanted. But I loved it here in Dorchester, and I'd already discovered that with great wealth come the snakes and hyenas.'

Mabel raised her eyebrows at that. She knew exactly what her employer meant; she was just surprised Clara would voice it.

Clara laughed at her surprise. 'Oh, I know all about predators. I think my father knew this too. He gave away much of his inherited fortune to good causes, long before his death. Mother was angry, but then one could say she was one of the hyenas. She'd been a bitch to my father, and a mean mother too. She didn't understand me moving here, any more than she'd understood my father. She died a lonely, embittered woman, two years after my father. There's a lesson to be learned there.'

'Gosh!' was all Mabel could say. She couldn't imagine how anyone with a great fortune could be unhappy.

'Carsten sees it all,' Clara said with a wry smile. 'I think he comes from a good family. Not top drawer exactly, but there is money and class. Being taken prisoner has probably been the making of him, though I doubt he would agree.'

'Why would it be the making of him?'

'He was quite arrogant when I first met him, though ashamed he had been taken prisoner. He's come full circle now; the arrogance has gone, with a more compassionate man exposed. And I think working here in the garden, close to nature, has added another dimension to his character.'

'What will happen to him when the war ends? Must he leave? Or will they put all the prisoners on a boat back to Germany?'

'I don't think I've met one prisoner who wants to stay,' Clara said. 'Boredom is their biggest enemy up at the camp. They miss their families dreadfully. Especially the married ones with children. But I doubt they'll be sent away as soon as the war ends, there's far too much red tape to be tied up. I think going home will be tough too. It won't be the land of plenty they remember, and although we don't hear much about it, I suspect there are as many shell-shocked and damaged German soldiers as there are English ones.'

'Do they recover from shell shock?' Mabel asked, thinking guiltily of Martin. 'I heard about men in Plymouth with it. Some people were saying they'd never recover.'

'I don't think those with it will ever be quite the same again. But it's too soon to make predictions, Mabel. Some people break a leg and walk with a limp for the rest of their life, while others heal quickly with no lasting problem. I suspect it's down to the severity of what they experienced and the care they got when they were brought home.'

It was a few weeks later when Carsten brought the news that two cases of Spanish flu had been diagnosed in the camp. The men were in a different hut to him, but he kept his distance from Clara and Mabel, shouting his news across the garden and asking if they wanted him to stop coming to Willow Cottage.

'No, not at all,' Clara shouted back. 'You don't need to stay that far away from us, either. It's spread by sneezing and hand contact, and you haven't even got a sniffle.'

Mabel made Carsten a bacon sandwich that morning; she believed that well-fed people didn't catch things, though Carsten laughed heartily when she took it out to him in the garden and told him her theory.

'The well fed just die of different things,' he said. 'But a bacon sandwich is food of the gods to me. If they were to execute me, I'd ask for one as my last meal.'

'Who is looking after the poorly men?' she asked. 'I know you have Dr Silby who goes to the camp, but you don't have nurses, do you?'

'Only two men are ill so far,' he reminded her, and smiled. 'So stop clucking like a mother hen. Their friends will take care of them.'

Mabel woke at five the next morning to find it was already warm, and the hazy sunshine was evidence it was going to be a hot day. As she had intended to wash bed linen and towels, she jumped out of bed quickly to go and light the fire under the old copper in the wash house. If she left it till later, the heat in there would be unbearable.

By eight she was back in the kitchen, getting breakfast for Clara. Out in the garden the washing line was full of billowing, brilliant white sheets and towels.

Clara came into the kitchen and, as she glanced out the window, she laughed. 'Is that the fairies who've done all the washing? Or have you been up all night?'

'It will be too hot to do it later. Besides, there's nothing nicer than hanging washing out to dry when the sun's shining. Now, would you like a boiled egg?'

'What did I do before you came?' Clara said, sitting down at the table. 'Oh, I remember, I used the laundry service for the big stuff. You informed me that was a waste of money.'

'So it is, in weather like this.' Mabel grinned. 'It's different in the winter, when it takes forever to dry.'

'Well, I suggest you do no more work today,' Clara said. 'You should put on your nice new dress and walk into town to give Mr Bunday the list of groceries for the weekend. Then have a wander around the town.'

'That sounds good,' Mabel said.

She didn't have an official day off, because she always had a few hours free in the afternoons until it was time to make the evening meal. But then, working at Willow Cottage had never seemed like real work, anyway. How could it be when she decided what needed to be done each day?

A couple of hours later, having taken the shopping list to the grocer's, had a cool lemonade in the tea shop, and bought some sandals, as the weather was so hot, she went along to South Walks, a shady lane lined with big chestnut trees. Clara had mentioned this place on several occasions; she said courting couples walked there in the evenings, but today there were only a few overheated mothers pushing perambulators and a couple of old gentlemen taking a stroll. But under the leafy canopy it felt cool and pleasant; she just wished she had a companion, it wasn't much fun wandering around on her own.

When she reached the River Frome, she was taken

aback to see Carsten sitting on the stump of a felled tree. He hadn't been due at Willow Cottage today, but she had always imagined that when he wasn't working, he had to stay in the camp.

'What a surprise, seeing you,' she called out as she drew nearer.

He almost jumped out of his skin. Whatever it was he was thinking about, he hadn't been aware of anyone else. He looked extremely hot and grubby. His hands were black.

'Mabel!' he exclaimed. 'You look especially nice today. Is that the dress you made?'

'Yes, it is, and thank you for saying I look nice. It's awfully hot, isn't it? Why aren't you in the camp?'

'I was sent out this morning to help Mr Rawlings rebuild his chicken shed. It was disgusting, dirty work – and I have to say, he is a horrible, rude man too.'

'I don't know him,' she said. 'But then I really don't know anyone much in Dorchester. But I'm sorry if someone was mean to you.'

'I was just thinking of going along to Greys Bridge and having a swim, to get rid of all the filth and maybe chicken fleas. That man, I think he didn't clean the chickens out in years.'

A pool had been made by the bridge to use for swimming. The prisoners could often be seen walking to it along the riverbank, with towels over their arms. The guards keeping an eye on them usually looked like they wished they could join them.

'Why don't you? The water looks very inviting,' she agreed. 'I used to live by the sea, and on a day like today

I would be swimming. I miss the sea. But of course, it would raise eyebrows if I went in at Greys Bridge.'

'Then we find a spot where nobody is, and go in.'

'I can't do that,' she giggled.

'I didn't mean with no clothes,' he said, looking alarmed. '*Sie tragen ein Frauenhemd?*'

'What is that in English?' she asked.

He looked flustered. He unbuttoned his shirt and pulled out a bit of vest.

'Are you wearing a chemise?' she assumed he meant.

'Yes, I am, but I can't be seen swimming in that in daylight!'

'I take you to good place,' he said. 'I found it in winter, and I thought it would be good for swimming.'

Mabel knew, if any of the matrons of the town were to see them in the river together, she'd probably be drummed out of town. But she looked into his blue eyes, thought how lovely it would be to swim with him, and all sensible thoughts left her.

'Okay, as long as it is hidden,' she agreed.

He took her about a mile further down the riverbank, parted some thick bushes to reach the edge of the river and then, taking her hand, he led her through the bushes and pointed downwards. The river swirled into what looked like a little pond, about six feet below them. Better still, there were giant tree roots going down to the water's edge that were almost as good as steps.

It was the sort of place that Mabel would've revelled in as a child, and though she knew she shouldn't even be thinking of stripping off her dress and going in, she couldn't help herself.

Back in Hallsands during hot weather, she had never worn all the undergarments young ladies were expected to; the most she wore was a cotton chemise or petticoat, with bare legs. Today she had left off her stays, but she still had drawers, a long chemise of thin cotton, a heavy linen petticoat and thick stockings.

Carsten was already pulling off his boots, shirt and trousers, till he was left in just his grey underpants.

'Come on, off with your clothes,' he said and jumped into the river.

The sheer delight on his face as he came to the surface, rubbing the dirt off his face, was enough to galvanize Mabel into turning the other way to remove her stockings. But when she turned back, he wasn't watching her, just bobbing up and down in the water like a seal.

She was down to her chemise in a trice. She heaped her clothes together, with her straw boater on top, then followed his lead by jumping in.

Nothing had ever felt so good as the cool, almost silky river water on her hot skin. She lay back in the water and floated, laughing as Carsten climbed up on the bank to jump in again. Her chemise ballooned up around her and she had to push it down vigorously, but suddenly she really didn't care if she was exposing more of herself than she ought to.

She and Martin had often swum in the sea at night, naked; sometimes they made love on the beach too. Today was the first time since leaving Hallsands that she'd recalled that. All at once, she felt a quickening of desire, and when she looked at Carsten the feeling grew stronger.

His chest, face and arms were tanned the colour of

honey, and the sunlight was making the wet hairs on his arms and chest glisten like gold. He swam over to her, put his hands on her waist and lifted her. For a second, as she looked down into his laughing face, she thought he intended to kiss her, but instead he threw her back into the water.

Mabel dived under the water, swam towards him and grabbed his legs to pull him under too.

Again and again, they found ways of pulling or pushing each other under the water, both laughing so much they swallowed a great deal of water.

A little later they heard a couple of men approaching. Quickly they swam back, close to the riverbank where they'd got in, and stayed there while the men passed. One was talking about his sheep. The other was smoking a pipe; they could smell the tobacco.

As they stayed there, close together in the water, Carsten smoothed Mabel's hair back from her face. 'You look so pretty all wet,' he whispered.

She lifted her face up to be kissed, her heart thumping, but he just drew her closer to him and held her.

Her thin chemise was no protection from his muscular body, pressed against hers. She lifted her face again, and this time his lips met hers, but not with the passion she'd expected.

'I cannot be what you want me to be,' he whispered.

She leaned her head back to look at him and saw pain in his eyes. 'Why Carsten? Because you are German? I don't care about that.'

'I will have to go home soon. I wish I could have you in my life forever, but I can't.'

8

In the days that followed swimming in the river with Carsten, Mabel felt very confused and sad.

It was clear he felt something for her; but maybe, like her, he was afraid of his feelings. A love affair between them was bound to end in sadness, whether because of him having to return to Germany, or her having to admit she was married already. There was also the fear of becoming pregnant, and hostility from other people.

But she was prepared to risk all that. Why wasn't he?

As they walked back into the town, Carsten had twice tried to tell her something. But each time he said, 'I need to explain,' he suddenly clammed up again.

They had laughed when they had to get dressed without a towel to dry themselves. Mabel rolled up her wet chemise and put it in the bag with her new sandals. She thought Carsten had pulled on his clothes over his wet pants. They talked about how lovely it was to swim, and how shocked people would be if they saw Mabel's wet hair and guessed what they'd been doing.

They parted near the camp, and Mabel went home along the footpath by the river. When she got back, her hair was quite dry, so no explanations were needed for Clara.

That was Friday. Carsten never came to Willow Cottage at the weekend, and Clara had a friend and her husband come to stay for a few days, so Mabel was kept busier than usual, cooking and generally looking after them.

The hot weather ended suddenly with a thunderstorm on Sunday, at five in the afternoon. All that evening Mabel sat by the window of her cottage, looking out at the rain battering the garden, wondering what she could do to resolve matters. She wished she had someone to confide in, but she knew that even if she did, they would only say that a romance between her and a German POW was never going to have a happy ending.

It was Tuesday before Clara's friends left. Carsten hadn't come to work that day, or the one before. Mabel busied herself tidying the garden on both afternoons, as the heavy rain had made the weeds spring up again in defiance.

She was just laying the table for supper when a man came to the door. He was elderly but tall and slender, with military bearing, wearing a tweed jacket and cap. He asked to speak to Miss May, and Mabel invited him in to wait in the sitting room while she got Clara.

'Oh no!' she heard Clara exclaim. But even though she made an excuse to go into the hall, she couldn't hear what was being said.

When the man left, Clara came into the kitchen. Her face was ashen. 'There are fourteen diagnosed cases of Spanish flu at the camp,' she said. 'Everyone has to stay in the camp now. That's why Carsten hasn't been here for the last two days.'

'You mean he's got it?' Mabel didn't even try to modify her voice, she was so alarmed.

'No, he's okay so far,' Clara said. 'But some of the new

cases are from his hut. But even worse, Mabel, there are twenty-four cases in Dorchester. That was General Morecombe who called here. He said Southampton has over three hundred new cases, and there have been many deaths there.'

'What can we do?' Mabel asked.

'Nothing, just hope for the best.'

'But who will nurse the men at the camp?'

Clara looked at Mabel disapprovingly. 'You don't need to worry about that. They are saying this is a pandemic now, extremely serious. I'm more concerned about friends in Dorchester than POWs.'

Mabel understood that was a reproof, and she got on with doing the supper. Hearing about people becoming ill and dying miles away hadn't really registered. But now it was here, just a mile away, and that was so different.

Each day seemed longer now that she couldn't expect Carsten to appear. With no news of whether he was sick or well, she was in agony. The newspapers only spread further anxiety, because although they were confidently reporting the war was almost won, thanks to the Americans coming in to help, they weren't holding back on the severity of the Spanish flu that was now spreading worldwide.

Two weeks after Carsten stopped coming, Clara went into town. When she returned, she said the streets were almost empty of people. At the grocer's she'd been told it was because they were afraid of catching the disease.

She sat down at the kitchen table, looking very worried. 'Mr Bunday, the grocer, said that he'd had some folk telephoning him with an order and demanding he deliver it and leave it inside the gate. They even said they'd leave the money under a stone for him! He said they weren't concerned at all about him, just about getting their food. Can you believe people could be like that?'

'They'd be the rich folk who care only for themselves,' Mabel pointed out.

'It seems the vicar suggested it might be advisable for his parishioners to miss church until the pandemic ends too. Though apparently he did add that he would still hold services, as usual, for those who weren't afraid.'

'I suppose it is sensible for people to stay away from crowded places,' Mabel said thoughtfully. 'But it's a bit extreme not getting your own shopping.'

'I went down South Street afterwards and I saw Humphrey Higgins, the undertaker, taking in a large order of coffins. When he saw me, he looked embarrassed and he said it was just a precaution and he hoped there would be no call for them.' Clara sighed. 'I suppose it is sensible to be prepared, but it seems rather nasty to be making money out of a disaster.'

From the moment Mabel learned of the Spanish flu in the camp, she'd thought of little else but whether Carsten had become sick. She so much wanted to go to the camp and offer to help with the nursing, so she could at least discover if he was still healthy.

'Would you mind if I helped at the camp in the afternoons?' she blurted out now.

Clara looked stunned at such a request. 'That's a mad thing to do,' she said.

'I don't think so,' Mabel said. 'They must be needing help. And if folk around here are staying in their homes for fear of getting it, who is going to see that those poor devils up in the camp get fed and are looked after properly?'

'They are soldiers,' Clara argued. 'They can look after their own.'

'I expect my husband, and his friends who died with him, thought they'd be looked after if anything happened to them,' Mabel retorted. She instantly felt bad at saying that, as she knew the doctors and nurses worked tirelessly at the front in Flanders to save lives.

'But what if you catch it?' Clara said.

'It sounds as if this flu can strike anywhere, so I could just be here with you and get it. Or you could.' She shrugged. 'But by helping up there, keeping the sick clean, feeding them, bringing them drinks, that might save them, and others they might infect. And I'll wear a mask!'

Clara made a helpless gesture with her arms. 'Alright, go and volunteer. I'll dig out some old clothes for you to wear, but when you get back home you must wash and change before coming in here.'

The following afternoon, Mabel rode her bicycle up to the camp. It was a sunny day and a group of men were lounging on the grass just inside the high fence, topped with barbed wire. Someone whistled at her, but she ignored him and rode on to the gates.

She explained to the sergeant manning the gate why she had come.

'What on earth makes a pretty woman like you want to nurse sick Germans?' he said with a sneer.

'Maybe my husband would still be alive if there had been more nurses at the Somme,' she sniped back at him.

'English or German, the death of a soldier is always a tragedy to those who love them.'

He looked as if he wanted to say something further, but thought better of it. 'Wait there,' he said. 'I'll see if someone can come and talk to you.'

He disappeared into the small hut and she assumed he was using the telephone.

'Come in,' he said as he returned to her and opened the tall metal gate. 'Go straight ahead until you see the Red Cross sign outside the doctor's office. Someone will see you there.'

Mabel kept her eyes peeled for Carsten. She saw many tall, blond muscular young men; some were sitting on the steps outside the huts, some were reading on the grass, others playing cards. Carsten wasn't among them. But then there were over four thousand men in the camp, and their huts went on into the distance.

A deep voice commanded her to come in when she knocked on the door. Inside, a burly man, almost completely bald, smiled at her.

'So, you are Dorchester's Miss Nightingale. I didn't expect you to be so young,' he said.

'I'm not even a trained nurse, let alone a Florence Nightingale. I'm just a widow who understands nurses are in short supply for soldiers, and I can spare a few hours every afternoon to help out.'

He took details of her name and where she lived. She explained she was a housekeeper.

'I know Miss May because of her art class,' he said. 'And you had one of the prisoners working in the garden at Willow Cottage,' he said.

'Yes, Carsten Frasch,' she said. 'I hope he hasn't caught the flu?'

'No, he's fine. He's been helping with the sick, as he often does. He is an excellent nurse, along with being a first-class interpreter. If only we had a few more with his talents.'

The next day, Mabel made her way back to the camp in the afternoon to do her first few hours. She wore an old, pale blue dress of Clara's. Despite being only light cotton and rather worn, it had a stylish look, fitted into the waist, with pin-tucks down the bodice. She had fixed her hair up in a bun, run up a couple of big coverall-all aprons from old sheeting, and made a couple of masks to cover her mouth and nose.

Maybe her prime motive for volunteering was just to see Carsten, yet after a couple of minutes in the sick-bay her mind was completely focused on alleviating the suffering.

Despite the warm weather, the men lay hunched on their beds, shivering. Although their symptoms were much like a bad cold, with runny nose, cough and sore throat, the fear that it was going to escalate to an infection of the lungs, and then death, made many of them terrified, and it showed in their staring eyes and hoarse voices begging for help.

Gus Tremane, the man who'd been asked to show her the ropes, was not a doctor but a very experienced orderly. 'Firstly, don't take your mask off for any reason. Then just make them more comfortable,' he said. 'Get them to drink, wash their faces and hands with cool water, and help them to eat if they are able. But first, I'll show you the men in the other room who are unlikely to pull through.'

Checking that her mask was in place, he led her through a door to another sickroom. Before Mabel even saw the six patients, she heard their rasping breath, the struggle for their lungs to fill with air. Then she saw Carsten. He was bending over one of the men, trying to get him to drink. The man's skin had a blue tinge, and as Carsten lowered him back to the pillow and took up a wet cloth to cool him, he saw Mabel.

'You shouldn't be here,' he said quietly. 'This is no place for you.'

'We need all the help we can get,' Gus said. 'And I think she'll be invaluable.'

Gus took her back into the main room, showed her where there were clean sheets and cloths to wash the men, then indicated an adjoining sluice room with bedpans and bottles.

'Just do what you can in here for now – the other room is grim,' he said. 'It's hard, with the language barrier. But kindness works, wherever you come from.'

Mabel did find it hard. Not just because she couldn't speak German, and none of the sick men had more than a smattering of English. It was just embarrassing, assisting a man to use a bottle to urinate in. Cooling fevered brows, holding a cup for them to drink, that was the easy part. But when they coughed up disgusting phlegm, it turned her stomach. It was also hot and stuffy in the sickbay, making the various bodily smells stronger. She wasn't sure she could do a second day of it.

It was sweet relief at six, when she stepped out of the sickbay to go home. Gus had praised her efforts, but he clearly knew how hard it had been for her.

As she walked to the gate, she heard footsteps behind her, and turned to see Carsten.

'Gus told me you did fine,' he said. 'But just the way you walk now, your shoulders drooping, I think you not like.'

'I suppose I thought it would be less ugly,' she said shamefacedly. 'But someone must help, just as you are doing. Aren't you afraid of catching it too?'

'I dodged English bullets, I can dodge Spanish flu.' He gave one of his joyful guffaws that made her laugh too.

'I couldn't bear it if you did get it,' she said, looking into his lovely eyes and wishing she could kiss him. 'I miss you being in the garden at Willow Cottage.'

'I miss it too. But I will come back soon. I'd like to swim in the river again with you also.'

'I don't think I'd better do that again,' she laughed. 'But it was nice. Now I must go home and make supper. Are you going back into the sickbay?'

'Yes, I stay till midnight, and sleep and eat in the hut with other men who help. Men in my old hut are afraid I bring back the infection to them.'

'You are doing a very good thing,' she said softly. She wanted to say it was brave and noble, but she knew he would dismiss that. 'Goodnight, Carsten.'

'It was good to see you,' he said. 'I have missed you.'

For just a second the words 'I love you' formed in her head. But she bit them back, then turned and walked towards the gate where she had left her bicycle. She knew she would be back tomorrow, and the next day. Every man who was sick in that room was as precious to someone as Carsten was to her. She had to try and get them well.

*

The days that followed were not as tough as the first one. It was good to see faint smiles from the sick men when she came in. She grew used to dealing with bodily functions and clearing up messes. Two men died in the room where Carsten worked, and their places were taken by another three from her ward. She washed the men, helped them eat a little, propped them up to ease the coughing, sometimes even helped them out of the hut to sit in the sun as they started to recover.

So far, only one man had fully recovered and left the sickbay, and there were five new cases. She knew now that there was no set pattern to recovery, or death. Some people became ill and died within twenty-four hours; others appeared to be getting better, and more than a week later they died. Some could even come back from the brink of death and survive. But Gus said he thought that was rare.

Mabel tried to believe all the men in her ward would recover if she could just keep their temperature down, so they didn't get pneumonia. But almost every day, when she arrived to help, she found another man had succumbed and had been moved into the ward next door.

She didn't see Carsten every day, as he worked a rota with the other orderlies. Mostly she was alone in the afternoons on her ward, and she was run ragged, going from one bed to another seeing to the men's needs.

They were all such young men too. The eldest so far was just twenty-four, the youngest seventeen; she guessed he'd lied about his age to join up, just as English boys had. She wished she could understand German too, as sometimes she felt they were really trying to tell her something important. Their eyes pleaded with her, they reached out for her hands, sometimes kissing them, and all she could do to comfort them was to stroke their brow and make soothing noises.

One sultry evening in August, she got back to Willow Cottage, swaying with exhaustion. As always, she went straight to her cottage. Every morning since she'd been going to the camp, she would use the garden hose to fill up a small tin bath just outside the cottage. On hot days the water would be warm when she returned in the early evening, so she could bathe in it.

Mabel had hit upon this idea as there were thick bushes around the spot where she put the bath, and she rather enjoyed the idea of doing something so risky. But tonight, she was so tired she could barely strip off her clothes. Although the cool water perked her up enough to dry herself, dress again and put her clothes in the bathwater, she hadn't the energy to wash them and hang them on the line to dry. As she walked over to the main house, she was staggering.

As she came through the back door, Clara was in the hallway. She took one look at her housekeeper, saw the state she was in, and gasped.

'Oh, Mabel! What have you done to yourself? Are you ill, or just worn out?'

She took Mabel's hand, led her into the kitchen and sat her down.

'I'll be fine after a sleep, Clara,' Mabel said. But even her voice was slow and indistinct.

Clara made a pot of tea and poured a cup for Mabel. 'Have you fever, a sore throat, anything which might suggest you've got the . . .' She didn't finish the sentence because she couldn't bear the thought of what that would mean.

'No, nothing,' Mabel insisted.

'Then I'm going to insist you stay upstairs tonight. I'll make you some supper and come up with it.'

Sometime later, when Clara carried a tray upstairs with soup, bread and cheese and some apple pie for Mabel, she found her housekeeper fast asleep in the spare room.

Clara felt guilty then that she hadn't heated up the chicken soup that Mabel had made that morning and made her eat it before sending her to bed.

She stood for a moment or two, looking at the girl, and felt a pang of guilt at her own selfishness. No one had ever worked for her the way Mabel did. She was a good cook, she cleaned to perfection, the laundry was all done – washed, dried and ironed – without her even noticing. She mended clothes, and even cleaned Clara's shoes for her. Yet with this big house to look after, she still insisted on helping nurse those men at the camp!

No one else around here would do it. There were some in Dorchester who'd be happy if every POW died. And these were people who went to church every Sunday and claimed to be Christians.

Clara did find Mabel a bit puzzling. She didn't ever talk about her past – at least, no further back than the time she'd spent in Bristol. If she mentioned her husband, it was only in passing; she didn't seem to be suffering from grief. But more than that, she'd never given Clara a sense of what her family background was.

Yet despite this puzzle, looking down at the girl with

her glorious red hair spread over the pillow, she felt a surge of real affection for her. Mabel had made her life ordered, comfortable and easy. She didn't demand anything, she was always pleasant and interested in anything Clara had to say. A paragon of virtue, really, along with being very pretty.

But for all that, Clara knew there was something dark in Mabel's past!

9

Clara was concerned when Mabel didn't wake up the next morning. She had gone into the room to check on her the previous night, and she was totally out for the count, which was good. But considering she was usually up at six every day, it was worrying to find her sleeping soundly at eight. At ten she was still asleep, but by then Clara could see that she seemed completely relaxed, and the pallor she'd had the previous evening had been replaced by pink cheeks.

Clara was relieved she wasn't ill, so she let her sleep on. She even went down to the cottage and, on seeing Mabel's clothes still in the tin bath, she fished them out, wrung them out, and then hung them on the line to dry.

Around four in the afternoon, Clara was in her studio painting when the spare-room door opened and Mabel came out, looking like a little girl with her hair cascading over the shoulders of one of Clara's voluminous nightdresses.

'I'm so sorry,' she said as the clock downstairs chimed the hour. 'I can't believe I've slept so long.'

Clara laughed. 'Well, I'm glad you were only suffering from exhaustion. Last night I was afraid you might be coming down with something. You've been doing too much. It's so truly kind and noble of you to help at the camp, but if it wears you out, you must stop.'

'I can't, Clara,' she said. 'Those poor men need my help.'

Clara could see complete determination in Mabel's eyes,

and knew no reproving words were going to stop her. 'Yes, I suppose they do, but just promise me you won't let yourself get into that state again. All sorts of nasty diseases can take hold when your body is at a low ebb. I want you here for many more years yet.'

Spanish flu was the only thing people wanted to discuss. It had completely eclipsed the war as a topic of conversation, but then everyone believed the war was all over bar the shouting. This wasn't true, of course, as Clara and Mabel realized when they studied reports in *The Times*. The fighting was every bit as fierce as it had been all along, but it was true that the American troops, fresh to battle, had managed to push the Germans back.

No one even seemed that shocked when news broke that Tsar Nicholas and his whole family had been executed in Moscow, in July. It was as if everyone was wearing blinkers and couldn't see anything but the Spanish flu.

Maybe Dorchester wasn't as severely affected by the pandemic as the cities they read about in the newspaper, but here in Dorset the farmers were worried about who would be left to get the harvest in. The previous year there had been plenty of prisoners to call on, but now they were confined to the camp. The farmers' sons had either been killed in France, were still fighting there, or were at home recovering from serious wounds. On most farms there was only one elderly man and his womenfolk and children, and though they would all do their best when the time came, they too had the fear of catching this terrible disease.

All the towns and villages were quiet. Publicans claimed

they'd be ruined; shopkeepers saw produce going bad through lack of customers. No one wanted to buy or sell in markets, it was too risky being in crowded places. Schools were badly attended before the holiday in August, and some teachers said they wouldn't be opening again in September. And almost every single person could speak of a family member who had succumbed to the disease. If this person hadn't died, they spoke of curious remedies they'd used to save them. Clara claimed it was like going back to the Middle Ages and that, before long, people would start believing in witches and spells.

For those, like Mabel, who saw the disease at close quarters, they took a calmer stance. So far in the camp seven men had died, but over thirty had recovered and gone back to their own huts. Granted, there were new cases almost daily; but it was hoped, with increased awareness of hygiene, that most would survive.

Then, at the end of August, Carsten became sick.

Mabel arrived at the camp on Monday afternoon, as usual, and was shocked to find him in bed in the ward where she always worked. He was shivering, although it was a very warm day. He was hunched up in the bed, the way most of her patients lay in the first stage of the disease.

She immediately got another blanket for him and tucked it round him. 'How are you feeling, Carsten?' she asked, putting her hand on his forehead and finding it red-hot.

'Not good,' he admitted in a small voice. 'It came on last night, my throat is so sore.'

'Don't try to speak, then,' she said. 'I'll get some saltwater for you to gargle, and some aspirin. You must try and drink water too, even if it's hard to swallow.'

The onslaught of the disease was often rapid, but she didn't think she'd seen any other patient's symptoms increase as rapidly as Carsten's did. She'd barely got him to gargle with the saltwater, and to swallow the aspirin with a large glass of water, before the sneezing, coughing and runny nose came on vigorously.

Gus came in then and asked her to come and help him in the acute ward. She wanted to refuse and stay to look after Carsten, but she knew that was wrong when other men were even sicker. As Carsten had always worked in the acute ward, and the other orderlies were sick too, they had no one else experienced enough to take his place.

To see men fighting for their breath, their skin taking on a blue tinge, was even more alarming than usual, knowing that the man she loved could easily be in this ward soon, breathing his last.

But somehow she had to squash down that terror, and help soothe these men. They too were loved by someone who would be distraught if they died.

It was quite the worst afternoon of her life, struggling to change sheets on beds, cooling brows, holding kidney dishes to be vomited in, and all the time avoiding spray from sneezes and violent coughs.

The afternoon grew even worse when, just before five, Dieter Kahn died. It was an ugly, violent death; his lungs were full of fluid, and he tried desperately to fight it, throwing himself around in the bed. The sound he made as he tried to breathe was hideous and his skin had turned blue. Gus had to hold him down while Mabel kept swabbing him with cool water and tried to soothe him.

He was just twenty. Still just a boy. It was a relief to all three of them when his body finally gave up the battle to live. Mabel washed his face one last time, closed his eyes and covered him with a sheet. When she finished, she found herself crying. Not just for Dieter, but for everyone who had, or would get, this terrible disease.

Aware that she was possibly splattered with spray from Dieter's nose and mouth, she didn't go near Carsten as she was leaving. He was lying on his bed, looking towards the door she'd come from, and she felt cheered a little when she saw recognition in his eyes. She blew him a kiss and said she'd see him the next day.

As she walked home, she offered up a little prayer that she would indeed see him, and that he wouldn't go into the final stages of the disease during the night.

Carsten was gravely ill for three days. The night after she'd left him, he was moved into the acute ward. Gus told Mabel the next day that he'd called out her name several times during the night when he was delirious.

'You know him well?' he asked her, his eyes alight with suspicion.

'Quite well, he comes to work in the garden of the house where I'm housekeeper.'

'Is he the reason why you volunteered?'

'No, although I wouldn't have known much about the camp but for Carsten telling me things. You know I am a war widow? I like to think if my husband had been taken prisoner, a German woman would've looked after him.'

'People don't like it that we help Germans,' Gus said. 'I've been called names and spat at. A couple of times I've had our soldiers picking on me in the pub. You be careful, Mabel. I wouldn't like that to happen to you.'

For two days after Gus's words, Mabel found it hard to concentrate on anything; she was so worried about Carsten. But while she was up at the camp she made sure she didn't spend all her time at his bedside, as she guessed there were gossipmongers amongst the English soldiers guarding the camp. It was hard to keep her distance and make out he was of no more importance to her than the other men. The sweat poured off him, yet still he shivered, but Gus said it was a hopeful sign that his lungs seemed reasonably clear. When Mabel did go to him to sponge him down, he caught hold of her hands and held them tightly. He was still delirious, and she didn't understand when he spoke in German, but she liked to think he was begging her not to leave him.

When she arrived at the camp on Friday, to her utmost surprise and delight, he was sitting up in bed in the first ward, reserved for less serious cases, and when he saw her, his smile stretched from ear to ear.

'They told me you healed me,' he said.

'That's rubbish, I only sponged you down and things.' She wasn't going to tell him what the 'and things' were, as he'd be embarrassed. 'You were lucky your lungs didn't become infected. Sponging you down wouldn't have saved you, if they had been. But how do you feel now?'

'A bit weak. But hungry.'

'It just so happens I've got some meat pie in my bag,' she said. 'I was going to give it to Gus, as I didn't expect you to be well enough for food. But I've got some cake I can give to him.'

She reached into her bag and told him he was to eat it secretly, or he'd get her into trouble. Then she popped in to see Gus.

Gus smiled. 'Glad to see him a lot better?'

'Yes, very, but how is everyone else?'

'No change, except for Carsten, from yesterday. But as you know, things happen fast around here.'

She gave him the cake and went back to see the patients in the adjoining room. She felt so happy she could sing.

As September began, there were no new patients. Another man died, but the rest gradually recovered, aided by fine weather so they could sit outside in the sunshine. Mabel was pleased to see Carsten and the other men getting their colour back and eating well again.

None of those who worked in the sickbay dared to ask whether the pandemic had run its course, but there was an air of optimism around. Then the news came that selected prisoners were going to be allowed to help with the harvest locally.

Carsten was told he could go back to Willow Cottage for one week only, to do light work prior to joining the other men on farms.

'So, I guess that's the last I'll see of you?' Gus said to Mabel.

'I'll come straight back if you get more cases,' she said. 'But there's no point in staying now, when all the men are recovering.'

'I'll miss you,' he said. 'You ought to train as a nurse. You're made for it.'

'I can't say I've really enjoyed it,' she said. 'But I am glad I came, and I hope I made a difference. I'm going to miss you too. But you know where I am if you need further help.'

The weather was lovely during the week Carsten came back to Willow Cottage. It was warm and sunny, but not too hot, and local people were hoping it would last until all the crops were harvested.

At Clara's suggestion Mabel got her chores done early in the morning so that they could both enjoy what might be the last of the summer sunshine. They had a late breakfast outside, then Clara would paint, capturing the voluptuous beauty of the garden before it went into a decline in the autumn. The asters were particularly lovely – huge clumps of violet flowers with bright yellow centres.

Mabel sat in a deck chair, either doing mending or reading a book. Sometimes she got up and busied herself with a bit of weeding and dead-heading until Carsten arrived.

No one would have believed he'd been so ill; his face had filled out again and he was suntanned, his eyes bright and his blond hair shiny. He looked strong and healthy, which was just as well; he was thinning out some of the trees down in the heavily wooded part of the garden that led to the river, before cutting them into logs for the winter.

'You might be home by winter,' Clara said to him, when he came up to ask if he should chop down an old and diseased plum tree. 'I'll have to try and get someone else to care for the garden.'

'Let's hope the war is over soon,' Carsten agreed. 'I think a returning soldier would be glad to come and work here. I've loved this garden – it, and the two of you, will be my best memories of England.'

'That's a lovely thing to say Carsten,' Clara said. 'But I suggest you prune that plum tree hard. It might recover. I see the other plum tree is laden with fruit, we ought to pick the ripe ones today and bottle them.'

All the while he was talking to Clara, Mabel couldn't stop looking at him. Her heart seemed to be swelling with love, so much so that it hurt. She couldn't bear the thought of him leaving; facing the day without that wide smile, that loud, joyous laugh, would be too sad to contemplate.

She wondered if Clara too had grown fond of him, because she suggested picnic lunches in the garden all that week and included him. In the cool of the evenings Mabel bottled the plums, made bacon and egg pie – which was delicious eaten cold – little meat pasties, and bread pudding from the left-over stale bread. There were lettuces, tomatoes and radishes in the garden, and pears, apples and gooseberries too. It was so easy to put together a feast of simple foods. Then to eat them outdoors in the sunshine was a delight.

'You are a little wonder,' Clara said to Mabel as she cleared away another picnic lunch. 'You prepare food with such thought, imagination and care. Tell me about your childhood. Did your mother do this too?'

'She died when I was eight,' Mabel said, sitting back down at the garden table. 'I was too young to remember much. But yes, I think perhaps she did. We ate a lot of fish, because my father was a fisherman, but I remember her making it into little fishcakes, or pies. I suppose that was so it wasn't as boring for us to have fish every day. She liked me to pick wild flowers too for the kitchen. She loved flowers, she would have been so happy to be in this garden.'

'I think she'd hope that you will marry again.'

Mabel was startled by that statement. Why did Clara make it? And why was she asking about childhood and her mother?

'I hope that one day I'll meet another man I want to marry,' Mabel said. 'But not yet, I need more time.'

'A friend told me recently that there won't be enough young men to go around when they come back from the war,' Clara said. 'I assume that means there won't be enough middle-aged men, either. Not that I want one.'

Mabel laughed. 'I think you'd like to be wooed.'

'Maybe, as long as he didn't get the idea that I would wait on him or agree with him about everything.'

Carsten came back up the garden at nearly five. Mabel was reading, and Clara had dozed off in the deck chair, but hearing Carsten's voice, she woke up.

'Time for you to leave?' she asked.

Carsten nodded. 'I won't be back until after the harvest is in. But in case that means I can't come back at all, thank you, Miss May, for employing me, and treating me so well. I've cut up all the logs and put them in the shed. There's enough kindling too to last the whole winter.'

'It's been a pleasure having you here, Carsten,' Clara said. 'But I hope I will see you again.'

Carsten looked at Mabel. 'Maybe I'll see you back at the

camp. I've been allocated to work from next week at the farm on the other side of the river, for a Mr Laithwaite.'

As he walked down the garden to return to the camp, Clara turned to Mabel. 'He told you that, hoping you'd go over there and see him,' she said.

'I don't think so,' Mabel retorted, but the thought cheered her.

10

Mabel yawned once again, and Clara laughed.

'Were you up half the night?'

'No,' Mabel replied. 'I think it's just sitting here in the sun making me sleepy.'

She was, in fact, bored. The days seemed so long since she'd stopped working at the camp and Carsten had gone. It didn't help that it was such pleasant weather; if it was to rain, she'd find something to do inside, even if it was only turning out some cupboards or cleaning silver.

Going for a walk or a bicycle ride on her own had no appeal. In the two weeks since Carsten had left, she'd read five books. Now this afternoon was spread out in front of her, and she had the choice of doing some weeding, or finding another book.

Clara looked round from her sketching. She'd recently been asked to submit her ideas for illustrations for a book of fairy tales, a full-page picture for each of the fourteen stories. She had been extremely excited when she first got the offer, but she was a bit panicked now, reading and rereading each of the stories to try and decide which aspect of the tale was best to highlight so the publishers would give her the job.

'I'm not getting inspired. Why don't we go and see how well Carsten is coping with a scythe?'

'Isn't Mr Laithwaite a grumpy old devil?'

'He certainly is. The worst! But we could take a few of those buns you made this morning to sweeten him up. I've been sitting so long, my legs are likely to seize up.'

They put on their straw hats, put the buns in a tin, and walked through the front garden to the path along the river. The hedges and shrubs on the riverbank had become very overgrown in recent weeks; in some places it was quite hard to get through.

'If Carsten does come back to me, I'll ask him to cut all this back,' Clara said. 'If no one does it, soon it will be impassable, and we'll have to go the long way around to town.'

Some distance along, there was a bridge over a stream leading to an old thatched cottage that had been abandoned; again, the vegetation was taking over. Just past the cottage and across a big field they could see Laithwaite's farmhouse. The mellow grey stone, with a porch covered in roses, looked very picturesque from a distance, and Mabel admired it.

'It might look pretty from here, but he's never done anything to the inside of the house It's still the same as it was in his grandfather's day, or so they tell me,' Clara said. 'Tight-fisted old chap! His poor wife suffers with arthritis. They say in the winter it's so cold in there she hobbles around with her coat and a woolly hat on. When the war began, no one could've been more vocal about the Germans. He was full of hate, sounding off in the pub about what monsters they were, citing all the propaganda in the newspapers. But as soon as he knew he could get POWs as cheap labour on his farm, he backed right down and took the help eagerly. But I heard he treats them badly too.'

'His poor wife!' Mabel said. 'It must be dreadful being married to someone like that.'

'She's a poor downtrodden soul and no mistake. They've got one son, and he enlisted at the first bugle call. Everyone remarked that it was so he could get away from the farm and his father. Even as young as seven or eight, he was expected to milk the cows and do other chores before going to school. Yet that man boasts about his son to anyone who will listen. To hear him talk, you'd think the lad was a hero.'

'Aren't they all heroes?' Mabel said. 'But I pity Carsten being sent there to work. It must be awful after his job with you.' She shielded her eyes from the sun and peered at the place. She could see someone by the barn at the side of the farmhouse. 'I think that's him up there.'

Clara looked. 'Yes. Looks like he's mending the tractor. I can't see any other prisoners, though. I know six were sent there. The rest must be up in one of the fields behind the farmhouse.'

'Oh gosh! There's the telegram boy,' Mabel exclaimed, pointing out a young lad peddling his bicycle for all he was worth up the track to the farmhouse. 'They always make shivers run down my spine. You don't ever hear of anyone sending good news by telegram.'

'As unpleasant as Laithwaite is, I do hope it isn't his son,' Clara said thoughtfully. 'Maybe we ought to go back home. He won't want visitors if it is bad news.'

Clara stopped walking, but Mabel carried on. If nothing else, she would take the buns to Carsten and just see how he was. He hadn't seen her yet, as he was bent over the tractor.

The telegram boy was at the front door now, and an elderly woman appeared in the doorway and took the envelope.

Mabel stopped dead and put the tin of buns down on the grass. She felt she was looking at an idyllic rural scene in an oil painting. The bright sunshine, with Carsten bent over the tractor, the barn set back a bit from the farmhouse. Chickens pecking around the yard, doves cooing in a large dovecote. A chestnut horse looking out from a stable door. Yet at the centre of this pretty scene was the anxious telegram boy, who was watching the old lady open the envelope.

It was his job to wait until it was read, because she might need to send a response. Mabel could sense the boy literally holding his breath.

As the old lady turned her head to look back inside the house, her call, 'Henry, a telegram!' changed everything. Suddenly she sagged against the door post. A low, terrible wail came from her.

A man, presumably Laithwaite, appeared beside her, and snatched the telegram from her hands.

Mabel's instinctive reaction was to run to them, to offer sympathy and comfort. But Clara guessed that and came up behind her and grabbed her shoulder. 'No, you can't, folk like them are very private,' she said.

Yet as they stood there, rooted to the spot, Laithwaite pushed his wife to one side, nearly knocked down the telegram boy, and tore across the farmyard, roaring like a bull in pain.

In a flash of intuition Mabel knew what he was going to do. She shook off Clara's hand, and started to run.

'Carsten!' she yelled.

He stood up next to the tractor, looked towards her and waved. Clearly, he couldn't see along to the farmhouse from the barn where he was working.

'Get away,' she screamed out.

But to her further horror, as Laithwaite ran, he snatched up a pitchfork propped against the wall. Carsten, meanwhile, continued to just stand there and wave at her.

'Heaven help us!' Clara exclaimed behind her. 'Carsten, *look out*!' she yelled.

They were now less than thirty yards from Carsten. Finally, he looked round in alarm. Whether that was because of their yells or Laithwaite's roar, they didn't know. But he appeared frozen to the spot, not moving at all, as the man came charging towards him holding the pitchfork in both hands in front of him, like he was carrying a rifle.

The man's roar became even louder now he could see Carsten. A terrible, agonized roar. Mabel and Clara were running at full tilt towards him, screaming at the man to stop and for Carsten to get away. But before they could get there, Laithwaite plunged the pitchfork into Carsten's chest. The force was such that Carsten was driven back to the barn wall and pinned there.

'Death to the Hun,' the man shrieked out. 'Death to the Hun.'

'I'll get the telegram boy to bring help,' Clara shouted, and swerved off in that direction, running like the wind. Mabel heard her screaming at him to get the police. 'Go now, top speed on your bike, and ask for a doctor too. A man's life depends on you.'

He didn't need telling twice. He was off down the track in an instant.

Meanwhile, Mabel ran towards Carsten, shouting at Laithwaite to get away from him. The man was still yelling 'death to the Hun' as Mabel reached him. Aware he had to be stopped before he did something more to Carsten, or turned on her, she snatched up a large wrench lying on the ground. With all her might she hit him with it across the back of his neck, and he fell to the ground.

She didn't look, or even care, if she'd killed the farmer. Her only concern was Carsten. But even to someone with no real medical knowledge, it was obvious he couldn't survive the attack.

He had been struck with such force that the fork had gone right through him and out through his back, literally pinning him to the wooden side of the barn. His expression was one of complete shock, eyes wide open, mouth trying to voice a single word, 'Why?' Blood was pumping out of two chest wounds. His shirt was already soaked.

'I can't pull it out, or it will make it worse,' she said, pulling off her petticoat and using it to staunch the blood. Even though her instinct told her that nothing she could do would save him, she didn't want him to know that.

'Hold on, Carsten, until help comes. Just hold on. The telegram boy has ridden to get help.'

'What did I do to him?' He struggled to get the words out.

'He got a telegram to say his son was killed in France. You were here. The enemy.'

Clara came back then. But when she saw how bad Carsten was, she moved right back, as if she was afraid.

'Just keep that old bastard away from him,' Mabel ordered her, inclining her head towards Laithwaite, who was attempting to get up from the ground. 'Hit him again if necessary.'

She wet a handkerchief in a water butt and wiped Carsten's face tenderly. She could see he was fading fast; it looked as if one of the prongs had gone right through his heart. 'I love you, Carsten,' she whispered, tears running down her cheeks. 'I love everything about you.'

He opened his eyes again and looked right into her eyes.

'*Ich liebe dich auch, Mabel . . .*' His voice was so faint it was barely there, and there was a wheezing coming from his chest. '*Du hast England glücklich gemacht für mich.*'

There was a sound from within him which she knew was his last attempt to breathe. His blue eyes took on a grey look, and then he was gone.

She stood beside him, her head on his shoulder, still holding her petticoat to his chest, and sobbed her heart out.

'Come away now,' Clara said gently. 'You've done all you could.'

But Mabel couldn't and wouldn't leave him. She stood beside him, caressing his face with one hand, while still trying pointlessly to staunch the blood coming out of his chest with the other.

It was only when the doctor arrived with his pony and trap, and two policemen came on their bicycles, that she allowed herself to be drawn away.

'Take her home,' the doctor said to Clara. 'She needs a brandy for the shock.'

As Mabel sat in the kitchen back home, a cup of tea laced with brandy on the table in front of her, she remembered something her father had said to a neighbour when her mother died: 'I feel like I'm in a thick grey mist and I'll never find my way out of it.'

That was how she felt too. The sunshine coming in through the kitchen window, the bright colours in the room, Clara coming over to embrace her and cradle her to her chest, none of it seemed real. It was as if she didn't know this room, or the woman who was trying to comfort her. The only real thing was the knowledge that Carsten was dead. That she would never again hear that big laugh, or his German accent and his strange way of pronouncing words, never again see those bright-blue eyes or the sun glinting on his blond hair.

She hurt all over; her head, arms, legs and, most of all, her heart. There would never be enough tears to wash away the terrible anguish she felt.

Through the grey mist she could hear, as if from a distance, Clara making a statement to a policeman about what had happened.

She heard the policeman ask why Mabel was so upset. 'Was he her lover?' he asked.

Mabel neither knew nor cared what Clara's reply to his question was. She wished he had been her lover, her fiancé or husband. That way she would have a right to be in this grey mist. She even wished she was in India, where she would have the right to throw herself on her husband's funeral pyre.

She drank the tea, but only because she hoped the brandy would numb her, and then, getting up, she made her way across the garden to her little cottage so that she could be alone.

Mabel woke to find Clara coming into the cottage. She had a little tray in her hands with tea, toast and a boiled egg. Birds were singing; it was morning.

'Sit up and eat this,' Clara said. 'And that isn't a suggestion, it's an order.'

Mabel had cried for hours, both yesterday evening and through the night. Finally, she must have exhausted herself and fallen asleep.

'What time is it?' she asked as she sat up. The little wooden bear Carsten had carved fell out of the bodice of her nightdress where she'd put it to keep it close to her heart.

Clara looked at the bear lying on the sheet but made no remark. 'Nine o'clock, and PC Lessing will be round at ten thirty to take your statement. What we witnessed yesterday was terrible. I know now that you were far more involved with Carsten than I had realized. But you must pull yourself together, Mabel. It doesn't do to wallow in self-pity for long.'

'I wasn't involved with Carsten. I loved him, but nothing, not even a kiss, happened between us,' she said indignantly.

'I cared for him too, Mabel,' Clara said reprovingly. 'He was a lovely young man, kind, hardworking and honest, and I am grieving for him too because no one should die in such a brutal manner. I hate this war, which has made big-hearted men like Carsten the enemy to some people. I hate that it's taken so many, many good men, including

177

your husband. But it is the role of women to hold everything together. So you are going to wash and get dressed. When you've eaten that breakfast, you'll come over to the house and make your statement. Then we carry on, as we've always done. Because you and I are both stronger than we think we are.'

Mabel just looked at Clara hopelessly.

'Do you know what his last words to you in German meant?'

Mabel shook her head.

Clara picked up the little bear and put it into Mabel's hand. 'He said he loved you too and that you made it happy here for him. He wouldn't want you to fall to pieces now, would he?'

11

As autumn leaves began to fall, and the temperature dropped, so the Spanish flu came back. Mabel was too distracted by the tragedy of Carsten's death to notice the rain and high winds. If she heard Spanish flu was in the town again, it didn't resister. She was so wrapped up in her own misery, she didn't even care about the camp enough to go there and see how things were there.

She did her work around the house diligently but silently, and in the afternoons she walked for miles, but without noticing anything. Maybe Clara sensed there was no point in trying to talk her out of it. She got on with her painting and hoped that time would be the healer.

One evening, Mabel picked up the little bear Carsten had carved for her, closed her eyes and thought of him. All at once, that strange feeling she'd experienced after Mrs Gladsworthy died came again. She could feel herself sliding into what felt like sleep, but wasn't, and Carsten's voice came to her. 'Enough grieving, Mabel,' he said. But although she could see him, it was like he was in deep shadow and indistinct. 'You have so much more to give. I do not like this sad person you have become.'

The picture of him faded. She came to, and saw she'd been holding the bear so tightly that her hand hurt.

'Are you there, Carsten? Watching over me?' she asked.

But nothing more came, all she could hear was the wind in the trees outside.

In the days that followed she told herself she'd imagined seeing him and hearing his voice. But it did make her feel just a little less miserable.

Only a couple of days after the incident, Mabel found Clara sitting on the stairs, coughing her lungs out, and that woke Mabel up to reality. Spanish flu wasn't just in the town or camp, she realized, it was here in the house. She scooped Clara up in her arms, carried her up to her bedroom and put her to bed. She got extra blankets and the eiderdown from the guest room to help her sweat it out.

'I'll get you aspirin and a hot drink,' she said, tucking the covers tightly around Clara. 'I'll telephone the doctor too.'

'Will I die?' Clara asked in a feeble, croaky voice. 'My throat is so sore and my chest hurts.'

'You won't die if I can help it,' Mabel said. 'You are too important to me. I can't lose anyone else.'

As she went back down to the kitchen to make the drink and fill a hot-water bottle, her mind turned to Carsten again and his funeral three weeks earlier. She had gone to his funeral in Fordington church with Clara. Like previous funerals from the camp, the coffin was draped with the German flag and was carried to the churchyard on a gun carriage at six thirty in the morning. Hundreds of other prisoners followed it, their faces wreathed in sorrow, as Carsten had been very well known and popular with the other men. The guards looked equally sad; they too had thought a lot of him, and the nature of his death had shocked them all.

It was a chilly morning, but the sun came out as they reached the churchyard.

Reverend Masters, the vicar who often went to the camp to hold services, spoke of the dangers of blind hatred between nations. He pointed out that Carsten Frasch was an example of a man who had been a good soldier and a patriot, yet he'd found his way into many English people's affections during his time here in England. He recalled his first meeting with Carsten, one day when he'd been called to the camp hospital to give the last rites to a soldier.

'I was very moved to find that Carsten had volunteered to help in the hospital, willing to risk being infected himself, in order to care for men he often didn't know personally. To him they were his comrades, and it was his duty to care for them.'

Mabel heard some of the mourners complaining that Laithwaite was getting away with murder, as it appeared the crime was being swept under the table. She wished then she'd hit him harder with the wrench and killed him.

It seemed the police couldn't make up their mind if the crime came under the jurisdiction of the army or a civil court. Laithwaite was considered unfit to stand trial anyway, as he was thought to be insane. He'd been taken away to an asylum, and the farmer whose land lay next to Laithwaite's was tending his animals and his crops. As for his wife, she was apparently still in the farmhouse alone.

As Carsten's body was lowered into the grave, and the Last Post was played on a bugle, the only thought in Mabel's head was that this was God's judgement on her for leaving Martin. She believed Carsten had been sent to her intentionally to show her just how terrible it is to love someone, and then to be left alone.

But now, the realization that Clara, who she'd also come to care deeply for, was sick was like having a plaster torn off a wound. She *had* been immersed in self-pity, she'd barely spoken to Clara in the past three weeks, and she'd let herself go completely. Her hair was dull and in need of a wash, and she couldn't remember when she had last cleaned her shoes, or even washed her dress.

As soon as she'd tucked the hot-water bottle into bed with Clara and given her the aspirin and a drink, she went over to her cottage and dug out the dresses, aprons and masks she'd worn at the camp. She would sleep in the house until Clara was better. And she would make damn sure she recovered.

As Mabel had discovered when she'd nursed at the camp, Spanish flu didn't have a set pattern. Some victims went straight into the final symptoms, their skin took on the dreaded blue tinge, their lungs filled with fluid and they died. Others appeared to have nothing more than a bad cold for several days, then it suddenly grew much worse. Others might seem to be at death's door, but they could wake up the next day feeling much better. Alongside these various manifestations there were other, less dramatic versions.

What Mabel did know was that it was vital to get as much water into patients as possible, to keep them warm, and propping them up with pillows appeared to help the coughing and prevent their lungs filling with fluid. It was a peculiar disease in that it took young, healthy adults rather than children and old people. Mabel hoped, as Clara was in her forties, her age would help her recovery.

*

For the next three days, Clara's temperature soared, she was delirious, and her skin felt like she was on fire. Her doctor came, and gave Mabel some medicine for her, but he shook his head gravely as if he didn't expect her to survive.

But with or without his support, Mabel was determined Clara would pull through. She stayed in Clara's room all night, dozing in a chair, so she'd be on the spot if needed. Every hour she lifted Clara's head to make her drink. Sometimes Clara clenched her teeth together and the water dripped on to her nightdress, but that didn't stop Mabel from trying. Clara went from being soaked with sweat to shivering with cold all the time. Mabel lost count of the times she sponged her down with cool water, put a clean nightdress on her and changed the bed sheets. Then, when she shivered, on went extra blankets and eiderdowns.

Each morning that Clara was still alive Mabel counted as a battle won. Yet the war raged on; Clara's coughing racked her body, the wheezing in her chest was terrible, and often she vomited stinking mucus. But to Mabel this had to be good, at least the infection wasn't in her lungs. Yet Clara didn't seem to know Mabel, she didn't try to speak, and her eyes were blank.

On the fourth day, Mabel went down to the kitchen. When she found the bread had gone mouldy, and there were no eggs or cheese, and virtually nothing left in the cupboards to make a meal, she burst into tears.

She was exhausted from lack of sleep. She hadn't been able to leave Clara even to make food, let alone go out and buy something. She had been surviving on tea, biscuits, the occasional chunk of cheese and an apple here and there.

She could still make tea, as the milk was delivered, and there were plenty of apples, also the bottled plums. But she wanted a real dinner, with meat and vegetables. She needed a bath and a long night's sleep.

Looking out of the window did nothing to lift her spirits; the wind was so strong it had stripped the last of the leaves from the trees, and it was bending the bare branches down to the ground. She could see the old tree trunk that Carsten had used as a bench to chop logs and imagined him as he'd often been in summer, bare-chested, his blond hair shining in the sun, wielding the axe like it weighed nothing.

Turning away from the window and biting back her grief, she realized she'd let the range go out – so even if she'd had something to cook, she couldn't make a decent meal for herself.

But the image of Carsten stayed in her head, along with his message to her. He'd never complained about anything. Always that wide smile, and the roaring laugh. And she knew now he was watching over her.

'So stop feeling sorry for yourself,' she said aloud. 'Light the range and make a rice pudding, you've got milk. But first go and see how Clara is.'

As she walked into the bedroom, she saw Clara's eyes were open, and for the first time in days there was clear recognition.

Mabel lifted Clara's head and held a glass of water to her lips. This time, she drank deeply.

'Good girl,' Mabel said, as if her patient was a little child. 'And can you tell me how you feel?'

There was a faint smile. 'I don't know.'

Mabel patted Clara's cheek. 'Well, while you are thinking on that one, I've got to light the range. Here's the bell in case you need me.' And she put the little silver bell on the bed.

The misery she'd felt was replaced by joy as she went downstairs. It was possible, but not likely, that Clara could relapse. Anyway, she wasn't even going to consider that possibility, and so she set to work to rake out the range with new vigour.

When she went to the wood shed outside, the sight of a basket of kindling, chopped and ready for her, brought Carsten back into her mind again. There was a great deal more stacked up in a big box, just as the shed was full of logs. But he'd put this smaller amount into a basket, to make it easier for her to carry. Just another example of his thoughtfulness.

That evening was the first happy one since Carsten's death. Clara was on the mend; she felt able to use the lavatory, with Mabel supporting her, and said she wanted a bath too, but she wasn't strong enough for that yet.

She sat in a chair while Mabel stripped her bed and put clean linen on it, then Mabel brought her up a tray with a bowl of rice pudding.

'We've got nothing left to eat,' Mabel explained. 'But as we had milk and rice, I thought of this.'

Clara raised a small spoonful to her mouth, looking doubtful. But she ate it and smiled. 'It's lovely. I didn't think I could eat anything, but this is perfect.'

It was pure joy to see Clara eat the whole bowl, even though she struggled towards the end.

'So now back to bed with you.' Mabel took her tray

away. 'I don't want you thinking you are completely recovered, because you aren't. But it looks like you are on the mend.'

Day by day, Clara grew stronger, until she felt fit enough to go downstairs and play her piano. As the happy music of Mozart wafted through Willow Cottage, shutting out the sound of the wind and rain outside, at last Mabel felt they were both recovering.

On the 11th of November, 1918, the Armistice was signed, and the war officially ended. But although there was absolute delight and relief that it was finally over, the celebrations were muted because the Spanish flu was still with them and increasing its number of victims daily.

The press announced that fighting continued in some places in Europe, and reprisals from both soldiers and civilians were reported too. On top of that, husbands, sons and brothers were not expected back immediately.

But it was the stealthy, invisible enemy of Spanish flu that distressed most people. You could be perfectly healthy at breakfast, and dead by supper time. The government were not helping the anxiety, either; no doubt they had the idea that admitting this pandemic was out of control would create mass panic. But everyone knew someone who had caught it, died of it, or even had it themselves and recovered, so they would all have preferred honesty to lies, subterfuge and smokescreens.

For those like Clara and Mabel who read *The Times*, they knew it had spread worldwide now, and that the death toll was up in the millions.

*

'I think we need to go away somewhere for a couple of days,' Clara said, the day after Armistice Day. 'Let's plan something. We could go to London, or Bath. It will be fun. We'll buy some material for a new dress each, buy new hats, and eat in smart restaurants. It would be lovely, especially if we go in December when all the shop windows have been dressed for Christmas.'

'Umm,' Mabel said. 'Sounds wonderful.'

'But there is something else we ought to do before that. We should write to Carsten's parents and tell him how much he meant to us.'

'Won't it upset them more to know their son died at the hands of a German-hating farmer?'

Clara shook her head. 'I doubt his senior officer has told them the exact details of his death. Most likely he'll have said something like "died in the line of duty". We can ask about that. But I'm sure we can find a softer way to tell them about his death. A farming accident maybe? I'll tell them about his work in the garden, and I can say how you nursed us both through the flu. We'll tell them he was a son to be proud of.'

'But they live in a little village, they won't be able to read English. I know you speak some German, but not enough.'

'Remember the English officer from the camp who acted as interpreter for the vicar at the funeral? I will ask him to translate our letter for us. He'll get us Carsten's parents' address in Germany too.'

Finding the words for that letter was the hardest thing either woman had ever done. Carsten's parents would be grieving. They might be feeling as much hatred for the English as Mr Laithwaite had for the Germans. They might have assumed that their beloved son was safe as a prisoner of war and would soon be home with them, only to then get the news that he was dead, not from the Spanish flu – which, though tragic, could have happened anywhere – but while working on a farm.

Captain Dale, the English officer who had acted as an interpreter, believed that the Germans would record Carsten's death in general terms, as having occurred while carrying out his military duties. He also agreed with Clara that any parent would be needing to know more, as they had believed their son to be safe at the prison camp.

'A farming accident sounds best,' he said. 'They are country people, so they will know harvesting machinery can be dangerous. Unless they write back insisting on the full details, it's better for them to think he went quickly, out in the fields.'

'To me that is as potentially horrible as being killed by a sniper. If I was his mother, I'd imagine him being gored by a bull or falling into a threshing machine.'

'Perhaps, but for him to be murdered in anger with a pitchfork is far worse,' the captain said. 'We don't want to put that image in his mother's head, or the hate that provoked it. So talk about what he did in your garden, and when he helped in the sickbay. If you word it with enough warmth and genuine sorrow that he's gone, she'll take comfort in that.'

But writing the letter was a lot harder than talking about it. Eventually, after many drafts, it was done.

Mabel insisted they write that she and Clara were there as he died, having taken a walk to the farm to take some buns for him.

'I'd like to know my son died with someone who cared about him there for him, offering comfort,' she insisted. 'And we can say that it was a quick death too, without going into details of how it happened.'

Clara was doubtful, but she agreed it would go in the letter.

They went on then to tell his parents about how he had tirelessly nursed the most seriously ill men in the camp and how, when he eventually caught the Spanish flu too, Mabel had nursed him in turn. They mentioned that his funeral had taken place at Fordington church with full military honours, and that the English soldiers were as sad at his death as his German comrades.

'My housekeeper, Mabel, and I came to think of him as almost family,' Clara wrote. 'Each time we go into the log shed we see his work, with enough logs to see us right through the winter. The bench he painted blue, the flower beds that were so overgrown with weeds before he came, and the plums we've bottled, picked by him, all are reminders of his hard work, kindness and cheerful disposition. We miss him still and will never forget him. You can be very proud of your son.'

After Captain Dale had translated the letter and Clara and Mabel had signed it, he intended to pass it over to the correct authorities for sending to Germany, just in case it was picked up by the censor.

Mabel looked at Carsten's home address written on the envelope. It was in a place called Crailsheim, a village near

Stuttgart. She hoped that one day she might travel to Germany and go there.

'That's that now,' Clara said as they left the camp to walk home. It was another raw, windy day. 'I know it's hard to think happy thoughts, Mabel, when your heart aches, and people are still dying like flies from that dreadful disease. The captain said they had another six deaths in the camp this week, and more still in the town. But we must try to look forward. So let's go home, toast some crumpets on the fire and plan our little break.'

12

'I didn't expect Bath to be so lovely,' Clara said as they walked up Milsom Street, looking into the windows of all the fine shops.

They had arrived by train on the previous day and booked into Meads Hotel in Great Pulteney Street, which Mabel likened to a palace as they had two adjoining rooms on the first floor, and their own bathroom. She couldn't get over the grandeur; there was a huge chandelier in the hall, vast ornate gold-framed mirrors and thick carpets everywhere. The hotel even employed a man in white breeches, a green tail coat and top hat just to open the door.

Their two rooms had sumptuous double beds and furniture that wouldn't have looked out of place in the Palace of Versailles. Mabel was terribly worried about how much it cost, but Clara said she wasn't to worry about that, as they needed a treat to celebrate the end of the war.

Mabel loved that the bridge over the River Avon had little shops on it. Clara told her the only other one like it in Europe was the Ponte Vecchio in Florence. It felt very exotic and glamorous. But then so many places in Bath were like that: smart restaurants, jewellers with stock that cost a king's ransom, beautiful shoe shops, and even ready-to-wear dresses, something Mabel had never seen before. Rich people used a dressmaker, and the poor made their own.

Clara said she thought that ready-to-wear was the trend for the future. 'Who wants to wait weeks for a new dress? And all that bother of going for fittings. I suppose for cocktail outfits, ball gowns and wedding dresses there will always be a need for good dressmakers. But for most women in a hurry, only wanting a day dress, why not sell them ready-made in shops?'

The hotel had electricity, which could be expected, but it was a real surprise to find that an ancient city like Bath had electric trams and electric street lighting. But as Clara was happy to point out, it had always been the playground of rich aristocrats who came to take the healing waters, and the town still considered itself to be a cut above anywhere else in England.

'We'll pretend to be a couple of toffs while we're here,' she laughed. 'Now let's look for hats.'

Two hours later, after having been into five different hat shops, the two women came out of Hermione's Hats with a hat box each. Clara's hat was crimson velvet, with a droopy brim pinned up on one side with a brooch. She had placed the brooch centre-forehead at first and Mabel mocked her, saying she looked like a pirate. The owner of the shop came forward and placed the brooch correctly, and suddenly Clara looked stylish and glamorous.

Mabel, who was still concerned about mourning, was persuaded to choose a very dark green hat, also in velvet, which was perfectly correct for a death that had occurred a few years ago. It was almost a beret, only more generous, strikingly modern and youthful. The dress material she had bought earlier in the day was dark green shantung; she intended to have it made into a costume with a peplum-style jacket and a mid-calf-length skirt, as she'd seen on all the well-dressed ladies here in Bath. Her new hat would go well with it.

'You've got to get out of this country bumpkin way of thinking,' Clara whispered to her. 'You are a very pretty young woman, and it's such a waste. Now let's get some lunch, and then we'll look for more dress material.'

They had gone back to their hotel to leave their shopping and came out again at six to look for somewhere to have dinner. They were on their way back towards the Pump Room, where they had seen a restaurant that looked inviting, when they passed a big sign outside a meeting hall on a street corner. The sign said: 'Get in touch with your dear departed relatives tonight. Madam Coral Atwell, Psychic.'

Mabel stopped dead to look at it, reminded instantly of Nora.

'Would you like to go?' Clara asked, looking at Mabel's intent expression. 'I know I would.'

Mabel had that strange sensation she'd felt twice before, but this time it felt like she was being gently pulled, the way a magnet would pull a piece of metal. She was reminded of that evening with Nora, and it all seemed to fit in some way.

'I . . . I . . . d-d-don't know,' she stammered.

Clara looked at her curiously. 'What's the matter?'

'It was like a goose running over my grave,' Mabel said. She looked back at the sign, and again felt the strange pulling sensation. 'Okay, then. Let's do it.'

The meeting was due to start in just five minutes and

people were pushing past them to go in; not just older women, but a mixture of young and old, male and female. Some of them looked poor, others affluent.

They paid sixpence each to go in, the same as Nora had charged. The money was taken by an elderly woman wearing a fox fur over her tweed coat.

The hall was a much smarter place than the one Nora had used. This venue felt warm, clean and well maintained. It wasn't that big; there were about fifty chairs facing a raised platform, which was carpeted.

Mabel and Clara took seats at the back, closest to the central aisle, so they could leave early if they wanted to. The audience all seemed eager, and Mabel overheard snippets of conversation about previous meetings of Coral Atwell's.

'My friend got a message from her grandmother. She told her that Bill died saying her name and he said he'd always loved her.'

'All predictable stuff,' Mabel whispered to Clara. 'I expect we'll get a lot of Spanish flu messages too, and ones from men who died in France.'

'Don't be a cynic,' Clara whispered back. 'I'm hoping my father will come with a message for me.'

Mabel was surprised to hear that. Firstly, Clara had always seemed so well grounded that she hadn't expected her to believe in spiritualists or psychics; she had pooh-poohed the whole thing about Nora, when Mabel told her about the meeting she attended with her. Secondly, Clara had only ever mentioned her father once in all the time Mabel had worked for her. But then she knew very well how people could keep serious things incredibly quiet.

The doors were closed and the lady with the fox fur went up on to the little stage.

'I am delighted to see so many people here to experience an evening with Coral Atwell. For those of you who haven't been to any of her previous meetings in Bath, I need to explain that Madam Atwell cannot control which spirits want to speak through her. Sometimes the messages are jumbled or unclear, sometimes an angry spirit can manifest. Lately, because of the many deaths – both in Flanders and here in England, due to the Spanish flu – some of the messages have proved upsetting. I hope you can understand why this is. Coral doesn't, of course, know the direction messages will take, so if at any time you feel uncomfortable, it is fine for you to leave.'

The woman looked around the audience, as if doing a quick head count.

'Now, without further ado, I give you Coral Atwell.'

Everyone clapped, and to Mabel's surprise a big woman came on to the stage. She didn't know what she had expected, perhaps someone a bit like Nora, but this woman couldn't have been more different.

She wasn't fat, just tall – perhaps nearly six foot – and big boned. She must have been in her fifties, with her grey hair pinned up in a severe bun, and she wore a plain grey dress and round gold-rimmed spectacles. She looked like a headmistress or a missionary – certainly the pretty name Coral didn't seem to belong to her.

'Good evening,' she said. 'I am pleased to see so many people here tonight and I hope that for some of you there will be messages from the other side.'

However stern and even masculine she looked, her

voice was gentle, well modulated, with a hint of an accent that Mabel couldn't place.

She sat down on the chair that had been placed on the stage for her and closed her eyes. The woman with the fox fur turned off some of the lights and then seated herself next to the stage.

There was absolute silence as everyone waited, and it seemed an awfully long time before Coral spoke.

'I have Jimmy,' she said eventually. 'He wants to tell his wife it was too quick for him to be scared. He's saying a name, but it doesn't make sense to me. Bubba?'

Coral opened her eyes and looked around the audience.

A woman in the middle of the audience stood up. To Mabel she looked genuinely shocked and delighted.

'Was the message a good one?' Coral asked.

The woman nodded, she looked too flabbergasted to speak.

'Jimmy said to kiss the children and keep them close.'

The woman Bubba sat down, and now she was crying.

The fox-fur lady held up her hands for silence and once again Coral closed her eyes. She didn't keep still this time but kept moving her head and her hands, as if she was having a private conversation with someone.

'There is someone here at the meeting tonight who also receives messages from the other side,' she said at last, her eyes open again. She started scanning the people in front of her. 'This person does not know she has the power yet, but she was drawn in here tonight because of it. The spirit does not want to come through me.'

Mabel and Clara looked at one another. Mabel wondered

if that strange pulling sensation was what this woman was talking about.

'Your given name is Betty. But more recently you have changed it. I think it is Mabel.'

Mabel felt herself go hot and then cold. She felt Clara's hand on her arm, urging her to stand up.

Coral got up and walked down the aisle in the centre of two blocks of chairs, straight towards Mabel. She stopped, looking right at her.

'Come,' she said, holding out her hand. 'There is nothing to fear.'

Mabel got up, as if she had no control over her own movements, and reached for the woman's hand. As it closed over hers, she heard a message inside her head. She closed her eyes and a peculiar power took over. A voice was asking to pass a message to Violet.

The next thing Mabel heard was the sound of clapping. She opened her eyes and she was still in the same place, but without any idea of what had happened after the name Violet came to her.

'Can I speak to you later?' Coral asked and let go of her hand so she could go back to her seat.

Throughout the rest of the meeting Mabel felt as if she was floating away somewhere. It wasn't unpleasant or frightening, but it prevented her from concentrating or even hearing what was going on around her.

It was applause again that brought her out of this strange state, and she saw that everyone was standing to clap.

'My God, that was incredible,' Clara said. 'But you were the most amazing part of it.'

People began to leave, and one young woman came up to her and put her hands gently on Mabel's cheeks. 'Thank you for that, Mabel. You have made me feel I can deal with it all now. I hope you will be here again.'

'That was Violet, you know, the girl you had the message for,' Clara whispered in her ear. 'And do close your mouth, you look like you are catching flies.'

Coral came down the aisle. 'Mabel, I sensed you had no idea you had the power for spirits to speak through you. That must be so unnerving. Please take my card. And if it is at all possible, please call on me before you leave Bath. I need to talk to you.'

Mabel agreed she would and then, still stunned, she left with Clara. They went into the first restaurant they came to and ate their meal in virtual silence.

Back at Meads Hotel, an hour later, with a glass of brandy in her hand, Mabel felt she was back to normal and was eager to discuss what had happened.

'I don't understand. Why did this happen to me, Clara? Tell me what I said, as I don't remember anything.'

'You clearly do have a calling. You seem able to speak to the dead.' Clara looked at her housekeeper as if she'd never seen her before. 'I couldn't believe my ears.'

She went on to tell Mabel that she'd asked Violet to stand up and told her that her husband had walked away from the trenches and been shot for desertion. 'He said he wasn't deserting, he just couldn't stand the noise any longer. He wanted her to know he wasn't a coward. He'd intended to go back. But they arrested him before he could.'

Mabel gasped in horror. 'I told his poor wife that? I wouldn't be that cruel!'

'Violet knew you weren't being cruel. She was notified that he was executed by a firing squad for desertion some time ago. You mustn't feel bad, Mabel, because Violet found real comfort in the message that her husband intended to go back.'

Mabel was once again catching flies, with her mouth wide open. She couldn't believe all this had been said without her knowledge or having any memory of it.

'This is too strange for me to cope with,' she said. 'I've had a couple of weird little incidents before, and I got a peculiar feeling when I looked at the board outside the meeting hall, but I had no idea it would lead to this.'

'Mabel, whether you like it or not, you've got a gift,' Clara said. 'I think you should use it. But before we go any further, what is this about you being Betty? Would you like to explain that?'

Mabel couldn't stop herself from bursting into tears. The evening had been so strange and unsettling, especially when the woman Coral brought up her real name.

'I don't dare tell you,' she sobbed. 'You might hate or despise me. You might even want to expose me for living a lie.'

'You will have to tell me now, or I'll think you killed someone and hid the body. Whatever you tell me will not go beyond this hotel room.'

It was so like Clara to make a glib remark that Mabel gave a ghost of a smile.

'I only killed myself – at least, I let people think I'd died.'

She explained then about Agnes and her shell-shocked husband, and how the houses had been washed away. 'I think Agnes wanted me to be killed that night, and I gave her what she wanted. But I've always felt bad about poor Martin. He didn't know me any more, but that's no real excuse for walking away and playing dead. I called myself Mabel Brook. And you know the rest of the fibs I told you.'

'Oh, Mabel, sweetheart,' Clara said with a huge sigh. 'What a shocking experience for you. Strangely enough, I remember reading about Hallsands being washed away. There were several places on the Devon and Dorset coast that took a hammering too back then, but not as bad of course. I don't blame you for leaving, that woman sounds like a witch. As for poor Martin, he's got his mother and grandfather taking care of him. You did deserve a better life than that.'

Mabel hung her head. She had intended to take her story to her grave, but now it was out; she was afraid and ashamed.

Clara reached out, put her hand under Mabel's chin and lifted it gently. 'Listen to me! You will not feel ashamed, remorseful or scared. Since you started working for me you have more than redeemed yourself. You nursed Carsten and me through the flu – not to mention all those other prisoners. You are a strong, brave and kind woman who deserves far more than you've been given. And I also believe that whatever it was that happened tonight, it is a God-given gift, and you must use it.'

Mabel looked doubtful. 'How?' She shrugged. 'I can't set myself up as a psychic, clairvoyant, spiritualist – whatever you want to call it – based on tonight's message.'

'It wasn't one message, it was three,' Clara said. 'The second one was from a woman's grandmother who died a year ago when she was staying with her granddaughter in Bath. She wanted to tell the woman to start the guest house she had planned. Then the third was about a child's death from drowning in Pulteney Weir. His name was John and he was sorry for disobeying his mother and playing down there.'

'Really!' Mabel was so amazed that all this could have happened without her having any knowledge of it. She was inclined to believe Clara was making it up. 'I can't believe it. It's like one of those mad dreams that makes no sense.'

'Those messages made perfect sense to the people who they were for,' Clara said. 'But perhaps if you go and see Coral tomorrow, she can explain it all to you.'

Coral lived close to Meads Hotel, in Henrietta Street, just off Great Pulteney Street. It was a street of much smaller, two-storey houses, some of which might have been coach houses in Bath's Georgian times.

Mabel went alone, much to Clara's dismay, as she'd wanted to be part of it. But Mabel felt she needed to make her own judgement about this woman, not have her feelings clouded by Clara's enthusiasm.

It was a neat little honey-coloured stone house, with snowy lace curtains preventing a glimpse inside. Coral answered the door at the first tentative tap.

'I am so glad you came, Mabel,' she said, drawing her into a small hallway. 'I was afraid you'd back off. You seemed very shocked and bewildered by what happened.'

'I was.' Mabel let the older woman take her coat and hat, then followed her into a small cluttered parlour with a blazing fire. Coral was a big woman and all the furniture was big too; there were large chintz-covered armchairs and a huge glass-fronted cabinet against one wall which held dozens of pottery figurines. 'I've had no inkling that I possessed this ability.'

'Most of us don't – it seems to find us,' she said with a smile, before telling her to sit down. 'I saw things from the age of about six. My parents got angry when I told them what I saw. They thought I was making it up for attention. But many other psychics tell me it came to them as they were recovering from an illness, or some other major upset. Have you lost someone recently?'

'Yes,' Mabel admitted. 'I also nursed Spanish flu victims, too. I'm going back to that when I return to Dorchester. I work as a housekeeper for the lady I was with at the meeting. She nearly died of the flu. That's why we came here, to celebrate her recovery and the end of the war.'

'I really think you should use your gift,' Coral said, looking right into her eyes. Hers were very dark, almost black, and seen close up her skin was very lined, almost lizard-like. She was much older than Mabel had at first thought. 'It is a gift, even though right now you might think otherwise. If you lived nearby, I would suggest you worked with me. It's a big draw for people when there are two of us. But clearly that isn't practical, although I have a psychic friend in Southampton. I'd like to put you in touch with her, she's one of the best, and has a huge following.'

'Tell me why I should do it?' Mabel said. 'It seems wrong to me to encourage grieving people to believe that they can communicate with the dead. You see, I would never have gone to your meeting if I'd known I could tap into that world. For me, the dead should stay dead.'

'This person you lost recently, you wouldn't want a message from him?'

It was uncanny, Mabel felt Coral was looking right into her soul and knew she had already heard from him.

'Yes, I suppose I would. I mean, I was so happy when I got a message from him, because he died a cruel, untimely death. But I didn't know that's what it was, I thought it was just my imagination, or wishful thinking. I've lost both my parents too, but I don't think I'd want messages from them.'

'Messages tend to come when the recipient is still grieving, or if he or she has unanswered questions. I expect your parents don't fall into that category.'

Coral seemed to have an answer for everything. Mabel wanted to get out before this odd woman started delving into her mind and soul.

'Another thing – though it seems crass to mention it – talking to the dead can be very lucrative. I was left this house by a grateful follower. I have the kind of life now that I dreamed of when I was a kitchen maid and sleeping in a garret. Surely, you'd like to have money of your own, to be able to travel, to choose the way you want to live and where?'

'That doesn't seem right to me,' Mabel said.

'If you nursed someone and they died and left you a house and money, would you feel bad about that?'

Mabel thought of Mrs Hardy inheriting her mews cottage. 'No, but I'd have worked for that.'

'To bring messages from the dead is to work too. You

must tap into something that can drain you, and sometimes you face ridicule if the messages don't come. Believe me, you earn your money. But listen to me, Mabel. We have lost the cream of our young men in this war, and still more are dying as we speak from this flu. Pretty young women like you could once take the pick of young men as husbands. But now they are in short supply. The war will change everything, you mark my words. Women will get the vote, they won't kowtow to men any longer. They will be able to own property soon, they will be in charge of their own destiny, not subservient to their husbands or fathers. Strong, resourceful woman like you, Mabel, will be able to climb as high as you like.'

'I need to get back to Miss May now, she'll be needing me,' Mabel said, feeling intimidated.

Coral got up, opened a drawer in a side table and drew out a card. 'This is my friend in Southampton. Don't rule it out until you've met her. Promise me?'

Clara lay on her bed in her hotel room, listening to Mabel's report of the meeting with Coral without interrupting even once. When she'd finished, Clara exhaled rather noisily.

'Whew!' she exclaimed. 'So will you see this woman in Southampton?'

'I really don't know,' Mabel said. 'Last night might have been a fluke. It might never happen again. Besides, is it right?'

'I can't see what's wrong with giving people a bit of comfort,' Clara said. 'If you do find no messages come, you just apologize, and pack it in.'

'What I don't understand was why it came on so suddenly. I mean why, if I am psychic, can't I just close my eyes and summon up your father, my father, or Carsten? What was it about that hall that made it happen?'

'Maybe because you were in the presence of people thinking hard about their loved ones? Let me think hard about my father, and you close your eyes, and let's see if that works.'

Mabel moved to a chair by the window, folded her hands in her lap and closed her eyes. She waited and waited. It was so quiet in the room she could hear Clara breathing; she could hear someone on the landing outside the room, and a carriage going by on the street below. But she couldn't make herself go into that sleep-like state – or 'trance', as Nora had called it.

'You see, it doesn't work,' she said eventually.

'And I thought really hard about my father. I imagined him in evening dress, going out with Mother to a party or ball. He was a very handsome man.'

'Handsome or not, his spirit didn't come flitting through this room,' Mabel giggled. 'Come on, let's go out. We were going to see the Roman Baths, if you remember.'

They had a lovely three days in Bath; they went to the theatre to see a comedy, they looked around the cathedral, shopped and walked miles exploring the town. On their last evening they decided to eat in the hotel restaurant, as it had begun to rain heavily.

Mabel got changed and then went into Clara's room to see if she was ready. She was sitting at the little desk in the window writing a letter.

'Just finishing,' Clara said. 'I thought I'd better write something to my friend Polly, in Cheltenham. We were at school together and were once inseparable, but she got married and had five children. Now we only see each other about once every five years.'

Clara signed the letter, blotted it on the blotter, put it in an envelope and addressed it. 'I'll give that to the concierge to post for me,' she said as she got up from her chair to fetch her wrap.

Mabel looked at the silver pen lying on the desk, feeling drawn towards it. It was a rather masculine pen, chunky and heavy. As she picked it up, she experienced that same strange feeling of being pulled, just as she had the night they went to the meeting with Coral.

'This is your father's pen, isn't it?' she asked. 'I can feel him.'

That warm, sleepy feeling engulfed her again.

'Mabel, wake up! You are scaring me.'

Mabel heard Clara's voice, from what seemed a long way off. But it pulled her back to the present, and she was once again standing in the hotel bedroom, the pen still in her hand. 'What happened?' she asked.

Clara was very pale. 'You spoke in my father's voice,' she said in hushed tones. 'For a moment I thought he was here in this room. But I suppose he was – he'd come through you.'

'What did he say?'

'That he was relieved I had recovered from my illness, that he is glad I'm playing the piano again, and soon I'm going to be known for my picture-book illustrations. He said I should get out and meet more people, and it isn't good to be alone so much.'

'All that came out of my mouth?' Mabel was incredulous. 'I mean it's all stuff I could say, but not in his voice.'

'I didn't tell you, but before we came away my editor telephoned me to say she was excited about the sketches I'd sent in for the fairy-tales book, and so were the rest of the Board of Directors. She said the contract was in the bag. I didn't tell you about it, because all too often these things don't come off. So how would you know? You weren't even in the house when the editor telephoned me.'

'It was your father's pen, then?'

'Yes. He gave it to me a few weeks before he died. I'd always loved the heaviness of it. So you must have channelled him through picking it up.'

'I suppose so. Then it wasn't just a fluke the other night?'

'It doesn't appear to be,' Clara smiled. 'You talking in his voice was scary, though. I've heard about people doing that, but I always thought it was faked.'

'You know I didn't fake anything. I'd just come in the room.'

'Of course, Mabel, but the one thing this does prove is that you really have got a gift. I don't know why you've only just found it, but I suspect it was brought to the surface by Carsten's death. Maybe it works either when you are close to someone who is distressed, like those people the other night, or like now, just touching a personal item of someone who has died.'

'Nora, the woman I told you about, she liked to hold

things from people,' Mabel said, still rather dazed by what had just taken place. 'I feel really shaky now.'

Clara sat her down in the chair. 'We'll go down in a minute and I'll get us both a brandy before we go out. I'm in shock too.'

13

Encouraged by Clara, Mabel wrote to Beatrice Langdon, the psychic in Southampton, soon after they returned from Bath. But because it was nearly Christmas, and there was no immediate response, Mabel put her thoughts about it to one side, and she was soon thinking it was for the best that she couldn't pursue it.

They spent the Christmas of 1918 and the New Year of 1919 at home, just the two of them. The Spanish flu was raging in the town – as it was all over England, and indeed the world – so it seemed inappropriate to celebrate. It certainly wasn't advisable to spend time in any crowded place. The churchyard was completely full, and they were transporting bodies to a mass grave far away from the town.

Mabel went up to the camp to help with nursing on several afternoons, but she was even more conscious than before of the importance of keeping her mask on, boiling her aprons after each visit, and endless handwashing.

Gus was still there, and healthy, and it was good to see him. He said he'd missed her and had worried she might have been taken ill too.

'We are up to thirty deaths now,' he said. 'Considering there are over four thousand men in this camp, that's a pretty low ratio, especially if you compare it with civilian prisons that have a death toll of one in ten. I think it's because we've maintained such good hygiene.'

That first afternoon back, two more men died, and four new cases came into the sickbay. Clearly, the pandemic wasn't going to disappear just yet.

It was early February when Clara answered the telephone and called up the stairs to Mabel that it was for her.

When Mabel was halfway down, Clara whispered, 'I think it's "that" woman.'

Beatrice Langdon sounded a very gentle soul – on the telephone, at least. She apologized profusely for not responding more quickly and said she'd been helping her daughter, who'd had her sixth child just before Christmas.

'Why don't you come down on the train to Southampton and we can talk face-to-face?' she said. 'Coral spoke so enthusiastically about you that I am a bit worried she might have pushed you too hard.'

'That would be good,' Mabel agreed. 'This is all new to me, and I know I need advice and guidance. I didn't get carried away by Coral's enthusiasm.'

'Glad to hear it. What about if you came one afternoon, stayed the night with me and went home the next day? The trains are still all over the place. And travelling in winter, with it getting dark so early – and the cold, of course – makes it all very unpleasant.'

Mabel agreed she'd come the following Tuesday afternoon, and Beatrice promised to put a little map in the post to her. 'I live just a five-minute walk from the station.'

'Well, well, well, that's exciting,' Clara said when Mabel related what had been said. 'Did she sound normal?'

'Can we judge from a telephone call?' Mabel laughed. 'She sounded motherly. But I'll soon find out if she really is.'

On the following Tuesday, Mabel went off to Southampton. As she sat on the train, staring out of the window at the winter landscape, she was reminded of a similar view as she left Totnes. How things had changed since then! She was so much more worldly-wise; she knew things now she would never have dreamed of back in Hallsands.

Even her relationship with Clara had changed completely since her illness. She was still officially her housekeeper, but she wasn't a servant any longer, more like a companion. It was a pleasant and rewarding arrangement but, in some ways, Mabel wished they'd kept the old one. She knew her place then – what was expected of her – and it was so much simpler. What would happen now, if they fell out and she wanted to leave?

She hadn't believed Nora would ever turn nasty, but she did, as soon as she couldn't get her own way. Clara wasn't that way inclined, but she'd come to rely on Mabel, and people reacted badly to change sometimes. Would she go to the police and tell them what she knew, out of spite?

Thoughts of Martin and Hallsands kept coming to her; perhaps that was because she'd told Clara about them. But a small voice inside kept whispering that the right thing to do would be to go back there and find out how Martin was.

But she was scared to do that. Martin might have died in the Spanish flu pandemic. Although that would solve her problems, she'd be at the mercy of Agnes, and probably vilified by all her old neighbours. Whatever she found in Hallsands, it wasn't going to make anything better, and it might make things a great deal worse.

As for this psychic nonsense, she wished it had never reared its ugly head. To be telling people things that she didn't even remember afterwards was crazy. What if something came out all wrong, and she upset the person badly? Where would that leave her?

It was just after four when she arrived at Beatrice Langdon's house. It was bigger than Coral's, and terraced, a double-fronted house built at the end of the last century. Mabel liked the chequered tiles leading to the front door, and the pretty tiles in the porch, which were decorated with bunches of grapes and flowers.

An elderly maid, wearing a white frilly apron over her black uniform dress, answered the door.

'You must be Mrs Brook,' she said with a warm smile. 'Come on in, Mrs Langdon is waiting in the drawing room. Let me take your hat, coat and that bag.'

The drawing room was lovely; one wall was entirely covered by books, the others with dark green wallpaper. The sofa and armchairs were a dark russet colour and the patterned carpet was also predominantly dark green with splashes of russet and brown. The pictures with their gold frames, the lamps, and even the lovely white marble fireplace, all gave the impression of wealth and comfort.

Beatrice jumped up from her chair as Mabel came in. 'I trust you had a pleasant journey?' she said.

She was elderly, as Mabel had guessed by her voice, but she had vivid green eyes and a creamy complexion. Her hair was covered by a gold and emerald-green brocade turban, giving her a regal and exotic appearance.

'Uneventful, which is good these days,' Mabel said. 'I think people are staying home more because of this flu.'

'Let's get to the point,' Beatrice said, after asking the maid to bring them tea and cake. 'Coral said you had no idea you had psychic powers, your gift just manifested itself that night at her meeting.'

'That's right. I never sought it or wanted it. I did have a couple of unexplained incidents before, but I put those down to an overactive imagination. I'm puzzled, and I don't understand where this came from.'

'We are all just vessels for spirits,' Beatrice said vaguely. 'They pick us, seemingly at random. But I believe, from what I've witnessed, they have a knowledge of those who are sympathetic, sensitive people. Hence, of course, why we are called "spiritualists" by many. I think Coral told you that, for some mediums, they have a few visitations, then it ends. Others the gift never leaves.'

'Coral said it's often people who are grieving or who've had other difficulties.'

'Maybe, sometimes, but since this war started so many are grieving. If they all began getting messages from the other side, it would be quite worrying. It's my firm belief that we are chosen, and some of us have a special role, but once it has been achieved, the spirits no longer come to us.'

'I've read about people faking it. They sometimes have a partner in the audience.'

'Yes, there are those people,' Beatrice agreed. 'But I'm not one of those, and I know from Coral you certainly aren't.'

Over a very tasty supper of a chicken and mushroom

pie, they talked a little about their backgrounds. Mabel spoke mostly of being in service in both Bristol and now in Dorchester, only touching briefly on her father being a fisherman and her husband being killed at the Somme.

Beatrice said she too went into service as a young girl and rose through the ranks to being assistant housekeeper on a big estate in Surrey.

'I found my psychic powers in the servants' hall,' she said, and chuckled as if the memory still amused her. 'I was very junior, and the senior staff tended to hold forth about where they had worked before, grand people they'd met through their work. We juniors were supposed to be really impressed. I was, at first. But then, one day, a footman by the name of Rogers began telling us about how a titled young lady who had been to the house for a weekend party had propositioned him and asked him to come to her room later that night. He was a good-looking man, but I knew he was lying, even when everyone else was hanging on his every word. I also sensed that he had made a pass at the young lady, and because he was afraid she was going to talk, he'd made up this other story.'

'When you say you knew he was lying, do you mean that was a psychic message? Or you just sensed it?'

'They are often the same thing,' Beatrice said a bit sharply. 'But that doesn't matter now. The following evening, down in the servants' hall, Rogers began embellishing his story and all at once I felt something come over me. Next thing I knew, Cook was fussing over me and said I'd suddenly begun speaking in the young lady's voice, telling Rogers that if he so much as spoke to her again, she would make sure he was dismissed without a character.

'Apparently, Rogers got up and went to slap me, but the other servants stopped him, and he rushed out. Well, I think all the other servants just thought I was good at mimicry. They didn't understand. But as it turned out, Rogers made a nuisance of himself a second time. Unluckily for him, the young lady's maid was within earshot and reported him to the mistress of the house, telling her what had been said, and what had happened the previous time.

'When this reached the servants' hall, they were naturally astounded to find her story matched mine. I became a minor celebrity for a short while. Of course, I didn't understand what I'd done, or how I'd done it. It was sometime later, when I'd seen or sensed more things, heard messages, that I began to realize I had this ... well, I don't know what to call it. Power? Gift? Anyway, it's been both a blessing and a curse.'

'Yes, I can see that,' Mabel said. 'I'm almost hoping mine will never erupt again.'

'Are you willing to join me at a meeting to see what happens?' Beatrice looked hard at her, and Mabel didn't know if she wanted her to say yes or no.

'I think I have to, don't I? If only to satisfy my own curiosity.'

'I believe so.' Beatrice smiled. 'Well, I'm holding a meeting in a week's time, and I'd like to introduce you to my audience. Come down in the afternoon and stay the night again with me. We can discuss after the meeting how you want to proceed.'

Clara could hardly wait for Mabel to get through the door to hear how she'd got on.

'Was she nice? Old? Weird? Were you scared?' She directed questions at Mabel like rifle fire.

'Yes, she was nice, oldish, not weird really. Lovely home, and I'm going there again next week for my first meeting.'

Over a cup of tea Mabel told her friend what had been said, especially the story about the footman in the big house.

'She was cagey about who she worked for,' Mabel said. 'They must have been top drawer to have footmen. I'm not keen on staying with her, though. It makes me feel like I'm caught in a web.'

Clara smirked. 'You are funny, Mabel. I'd be far more worried about you going to stay in a guest house than staying with another woman. But I suppose you mean it makes you beholden to her?'

'Yes, that's about it. I didn't like to ask about money, either.'

'That will come after you've done the first public meeting with her.'

'Yes, I suppose, but I *am* doing this for the money, Clara, not for the good of my soul. Is that bad of me?'

Clara roared with laughter. 'You have more sides than a thruppenny bit,' she said. 'You'd nurse sick men, who might give you a disease that will kill you, for nothing more than love, but you want money for getting messages from the dead!'

'You should've seen Beatrice's house,' Mabel said indignantly. 'She was in service and got the house by her "powers". Why shouldn't I get something out of it too?'

'Well, I love my art, but I expect to be paid for it, so I suppose there's no difference between us, really.'

'You are always so reasonable about everything,' Mabel sighed. 'But I have my real work to do now; fires to light, dinner to cook. I don't want you sacking me just yet!'

'As if I would,' Clara said. 'I'd be living in a pigsty within a few weeks, and be half-starved too.'

Mabel was extremely nervous when she arrived at the meeting with Beatrice. On the train journey down she'd been tempted to catch the next train back and forget all about it.

But Beatrice reminded her that the worst thing that could happen was nothing; no spirits with messages coming through, and she'd be left feeling a bit silly. And she reassured Mabel that, if this happened, everyone would understand.

The hall was packed – nearly a hundred people – and Beatrice charged them each a shilling for entrance. She first explained to her audience that Mabel was a novice, and therefore they couldn't be sure whether she would receive any messages at all. She asked if anyone wanted to give a special item to Mabel to hold.

Several small items were handed to Mabel, which she laid on the table next to where she was sitting. While Beatrice began her display, which Mabel felt was somewhat theatrical, with much waving of arms and strange guttural sounds from her throat, Mabel rested her hands gently on the items. There was a pocket watch, a penknife, a tie pin, a brooch and a small silver box. She concentrated on how they felt under her fingers, ignoring what Beatrice was saying close by her, and the audience in front of her.

She was getting a reaction from the penknife, almost like a tingle in the tips of her fingers. She took her hand away because Beatrice was in mid-flow, talking about someone at a party. From what Mabel could gather, because she hadn't heard the start of it, this person must have upset someone here tonight and it had never been resolved.

'She is apologizing,' Beatrice proclaimed, once again making very flamboyant gestures with her hands. 'She said she always knew she should have come to you, Amy, and explained. But you were so angry with her, she was afraid.'

A round of applause appeared to be the end of that little story. Mabel just wished she knew what the person had done to poor Amy. The woman in question was in the front row, beaming like a Cheshire cat, so presumably she had accepted the apology and forgiven the now dead person.

Beatrice then turned towards Mabel. 'Do you have any messages for anyone here tonight?'

In a flash of intuition Mabel realized the older woman didn't really want her to display any evidence that a spirit was talking through her. But the suspicion the woman could be a fraud was enough to make Mabel more determined.

She lifted the penknife, and immediately that faint sensation in her fingertips came back and she felt herself slipping into that same sleepy trance-like state she'd experienced before.

Mabel came out of the trance to a storm of applause.

For a moment or two she thought she'd fainted, because she felt so strange and light-headed. But a shabbily dressed woman was standing in front of her, tears streaming down her face. She looked at least thirty-five but was extremely thin and clearly worn down by hardship, so was probably younger.

'I can't believe you could know so much about us,' she said. 'Bless you, Mabel. Thank you so much. I have new hope now.'

'What is your name? I don't know what you are thanking me for,' Mabel said, panicking a little. 'I have no memory of what I said or did. Please tell me.'

'I'm Sarah Painter. You told me it was Harold's penknife. Harold is my husband. He joined up in 1916, and after only a couple of months I got a telegram to say he was missing, presumed dead. It was awful. I have three small children – at that time, the youngest was still a babe in arms. But you said he's a prisoner of war and he'll be coming home, just as soon as they've signed some treaty.'

'The Treaty of Versailles,' Mabel said. 'That will be later this year, I think. But why didn't he let you know he was a POW?'

'You asked him that, Mabel. We all heard you, and you told us he said he couldn't read or write. That was true. He couldn't. He was so ashamed of it, he never told anyone if he could help it. Even I didn't know till after we were married.'

'He could have got someone else to write to you,' Mabel said. 'Why didn't he?'

Sarah shrugged and wiped her nose on the back of her hand. 'Silly bugger was too proud, I expect. You told him off and said he was lucky I still loved him.'

Mabel was astounded. She really couldn't believe it was possible to have a conversation with a spirit in such depth. And if Harold was alive, why was a spirit even involved?

But as shaky as she was, she knew she had to put Sarah on the right track to get help.

'Well, Sarah, you don't need to go through someone like me. You get in touch with the Red Cross and they'll tell you where he is. If he's alive, you should've been getting money too. I presume you do want him back with you?'

Sarah's face broke into a wide smile. 'Oh yes, of course I do.'

'Well, that about wraps that one up.' Beatrice interrupted, her tone a little abrasive. 'Let's just hope the message from Harold was accurate.'

Mabel decided in that moment she would not stay the night with Beatrice. She had a strong suspicion the woman had set her up to fail. Why? It was a mystery to her. Maybe Coral had been overly enthusiastic about the young woman she'd just met, and it had made her jealous? Or possibly Beatrice had fooled Coral about her abilities, and now she was afraid Mabel would find her out and denounce her.

Whatever was going on, Mabel wasn't going to stay. She stood up, thanked everyone in the room, and said she was sorry she couldn't help anyone else tonight, because she had to go home.

'I'm sorry, Beatrice,' she said, turning to the older woman. 'But these people here want to see you, anyway. Thank you for supper tonight.'

With that she picked up her coat and bag and made for the door as quickly as possible.

Her luck was in; she caught the last train back to Dorchester. It was fortunate she hadn't taken her nightdress and washing things out of her bag and left them at Beatrice's.

But once she'd congratulated herself on that, and how she'd taken the wind out of the older woman's sails, her mind then turned to how communicating with the dead worked.

Why would a man's voice come to her because she'd held his penknife? It was weird enough if he was dead, but astoundingly strange if Harold was alive! This didn't work like a telephone, after all. Unless, of course, a spirit was acting as a mediator?

What if Harold was, in fact, dead and she'd got the message wrong?

That possibility made her stomach lurch and she thought she was going to be sick. He might have been taken prisoner but had recently died of Spanish flu. That could explain it. But now she'd given poor Sarah false hope he was coming back!

She really wished she'd never gone to the meeting tonight. When she'd thought of catching the train back home on her way to Southampton, she should've trusted her instincts.

14

Clara was still up when Mabel got home, and over a cup of cocoa Mabel blurted out what had happened.

'I'm not doing it again, and that's that,' Mabel said. 'It's wrong. That poor woman, I've told her that her husband is coming home, and she is so happy. What is it going to do to her if I'm wrong?'

But to her surprise, Clara thought she was overreacting. 'I don't believe you got it wrong. You came out with stuff that only Harold's wife knew about. I can't explain why a message from someone who is alive should come through, but why not? Perhaps poor Harold was worried sick about Sarah not knowing, and that's why it got to you.'

'A bit too convenient, if you ask me,' Mabel said.

'You are just doubting your ability, and that's partly to do with that Beatrice woman. If she is putting on a kind of show, and faking it, that is very tasteless and cruel. So maybe the spirits wanted to show her up by speaking through you, with something important.'

'Pigs might fly,' Mabel said dourly.

'I believe in you, Mabel. I've no explanation as to how you could speak in my father's voice, but I'm so glad you did. It made me happy to hear him. Other people deserve to have that experience too.'

'Maybe so. But I'm not doing it any more.'

'You didn't intend to do it for me,' Clara reminded her.

'Besides, what about the doing it for money, like you said you were going to do?'

Mabel laughed then; Clara always seemed to be able to make her see the funny side of things.

'There must be a way to make some money without calling up the dead,' she said. 'Maybe I need to ask the spirits to tell me how?'

'Don't close the door on this just yet. There could be some reason why you've been chosen to receive messages. Your gift might help someone, like it did me when I heard from my father.'

Mabel pondered on that for a moment or two.

'I'll sleep on it,' she said thoughtfully. 'But I know one thing. I'll never be prepared to do it in a big hall like that again. One on one, maybe.'

The rest of February slipped past and all at once March came in. As the daffodils sprang up in the garden, so the reported cases of Spanish flu subsided. Mabel wasn't needed at the camp any more, and the men were all waiting for the day when they could return home.

At the end of March, Mabel and Clara went into Southampton to do some shopping.

They went down to the quayside first, where they saw a boat docking with hundreds of British soldiers on the decks, cheering and waving. As they watched, jostled by a throng of women waiting eagerly for husbands, sons and sweethearts, the wounded and stretcher cases were brought off.

They had seen pictures of this very scene in the newspapers many times. But this was the first time they'd witnessed first-hand the real savagery of war, seeing men who had given everything for their country and would now struggle to live a normal life again and to find work. It was just one more reminder of what this war had cost.

The sight of the wounded took the shine off the day. They still went to the shops, but their hearts weren't really in it, and although they had intended to stay later and have a meal out, they went back to the station early.

As they got there, a train was about to leave. A young man leapt out of the train and took the few packages they had in their hands. He helped them both into the carriage, where an elderly couple and another man were already seated.

The man who had helped them was around thirty, slim, dark-haired with a neat little moustache. He was very well dressed in a dark suit. He lifted their packages into the luggage rack before sitting down opposite them, next to the other lone man who was similarly dressed, and rather alike, but a few years older.

'That was terribly good of you,' Clara said. 'I think the guard would've signalled to the driver to leave, if not for your timely intervention.'

'May I ask where you are going?' he said, looking so intently at Mabel that she blushed.

'Dorchester,' Clara responded. 'And you?'

'We're going to Dorchester too,' he said with a smile. 'I'm Thomas Kellaway, and this is my brother Michael. We are going to see our aunt. Perhaps you know her? Leticia Kellaway.'

'Indeed, I do,' Clara said, suddenly a lot more animated. 'She paints in watercolours, and we met at an art exhibition a couple of years before the war. We got on like a house on fire, and every now and then we meet up for tea in town. But I haven't seen her in a while. Like everyone else, I've kept away from tea shops and other crowded places because of the flu. Do give her my best wishes and suggest we meet up again soon. I do hope she is well?'

'When we spoke on the telephone a couple of days ago, she was fine – delighted that spring seemed to have arrived.'

'I'm happy to hear that. But I didn't tell you who we are,' Clara said. 'I'm Clara May, and this is my friend and companion, Mabel Brook.'

'You must be the illustrator Aunt Leticia spoke of,' Michael, the older brother, said. 'You live in that pretty cottage by the river. We usually walk along there when we are visiting. A lovely spot. But what about you, Miss Brook, do you paint or draw?'

Mabel was touched that Clara had said she was her friend and companion, and she had the sneaky feeling it was because she thought Thomas was ideal for her.

'No, I'm afraid not.'

'She's a wonderful cook, though,' Clara said quickly. 'And so kind, she volunteered to nurse at the POW camp. I was always terrified she would get the flu too. But as it turned out, I got it, and then she nursed me back to health.'

'That was kind, and very brave,' Thomas said, his dark eyes looking right into hers. 'I can't draw or paint, and I wasn't a terribly good soldier either, but now that's all over I'm hoping I can still remember enough about law to pick up my old career.'

'You've just got back from France?' Mabel ventured.

'I was wounded in the leg last October, and I was shipped home,' he said with a smile. 'Michael had a far worse wound in the stomach, so he'd been back for three months before I arrived. Aunt Leticia must have moved heaven and earth for us, as we ended up convalescing in the same place in Bridport. They set us free three weeks ago.'

'Are your parents in Dorchester too?' Clara asked.

'No, they lived in Shaftesbury. We grew up there,' Michael said. 'Father died back in 1915, and Mother sadly caught the Spanish flu last year and died too. I assume that's why our aunt worked so hard to get us into the same place, I think she felt that on top of the horrors of war, our parents departing might be too much to bear.'

'I'm sorry,' Mabel said. 'That is incredibly sad for you both. But are you intending to stay in Dorchester now?'

'Yes, I'm hoping to join a law practice there and stay with my aunt for the time being. Michael is a surveyor, but he hasn't yet decided where he wants to live and work.'

Michael smiled. 'He wants me to stay close to him, poor baby brother!'

They chatted about general things for the rest of the journey, leaving aside the war, Spanish flu and rationing. Then suddenly, in what seemed no time at all, they were coming into Dorchester.

Thomas put on his hat and jumped out of the train first, before helping Mabel and Clara down with their packages. He then returned to the carriage and retrieved both his and Michael's suitcases. It was only when he took his brother's arm that they saw he walked with some difficulty.

'May we call on you both sometime soon,' Thomas asked.

'I sincerely hope you will,' Clara said. 'But telephone first, so Mabel can bake one of her lovely cakes.'

Andrews was waiting for them with his cab, and when Mabel looked back, she saw the two men walking out of the station, Thomas holding Michael's arm.

'Don't worry,' Clara said, guessing she was worried about them. 'Their aunt lives close by. Michael will be fine to walk that far, I think.'

'They were a pleasant surprise,' Mabel said as the horses trotted away from the station.

'Very!' Clara arched one eyebrow, making Mabel laugh.

Thomas telephoned two days later, in the morning.

'May we call in on you this afternoon? We thought we'd walk along the riverbank, as Michael needs to exercise more.'

'It would be a pleasure to see you both again. Please come to tea,' Clara said, waving her hand at Mabel joyfully. 'About three?'

'Are you matchmaking?' Mabel chuckled. 'Tea, indeed. I'd better rustle up some scones and a sponge.'

'You liked Thomas, didn't you?' Clara asked.

'Yes, of course, but why would a gentleman like him be interested in me?'

'Because you are pretty, kind and stimulating company.' Clara put her hands on her hips and glared at Mabel. 'Don't you dare put up obstacles. It will be soon enough to consider those if you fall in love and want to share a life together. For now, you just get to know him, have some fun, and be happy. That's been in short supply for some time!'

As Mabel made the sponge cake and the scones, all at once she thought of Carsten when he was eating the picnics she'd made last summer. She had a clear picture of him stripped to the waist, muscles rippling, and the sun on his blond hair making him look like a Greek god. When she called him to eat, he always put on his shirt, much to her disappointment. She wondered what Thomas would look like without his, and almost immediately felt cross with herself for thinking such cheeky thoughts.

Thomas and Michael arrived almost on the dot of three, wearing light-coloured linen jackets and panama hats. This time, Michael had a walking stick. Both men were more handsome than she'd remembered, with golden-tinged skin, thick shiny hair and perfect teeth. But it was their eyes that she focused on – deep, dark forest pools, with the kind of long eyelashes any girl would wish for.

Clara had decided it wasn't warm enough to have tea in the garden, but she'd opened the French windows to let the garden in. She'd also dressed the table in a very pretty green cloth with matching napkins, and got out her best china.

Mabel's sponge cake with chocolate butter icing was on a raised cake plate, and the scones and dainty sandwiches were on a two-tier cake stand.

Thomas looked at the table and smiled. 'This is the kind of image we used to imagine in the trenches,' he said. 'Not just me either, the enlisted men too. As they drank their big mugs of strong tea I'd hear them talking about their grandmother's best tea set, scones, chocolate cake and dainty sandwiches.'

'Really?' Mabel said. 'I would never have thought that.'

'One day I heard a rather rough chap say, "I could never

understand why the wife liked to go to tea shops. If I get back, I'll take her to as many as she wants to go to. I'll sip the tea from a bone china cup, delicately wipe my lips on a napkin, and never, ever say I'd rather have a mug of strong tea and a slice of bread and dripping." Some of the other men clapped. They knew just what he meant.'

'Let's hope when the soldiers get home, they show a bit more appreciation for their wives,' Clara said as they all sat down. 'At the art class I used to run in Dorchester, the things some of the wives told me! One of their husbands complained his wife didn't write him enough letters. She was writing to him most days. But except for that letter of complaint, he'd never written one to her!'

'Yes, Aunt Leticia has told us a few stories like that. One farmer's wife told her that she'd delivered their first baby, all by herself in the morning, when her husband was out in the fields. He came home at noon for his dinner and flew into a temper because she hadn't got it ready,' Michael said.

'Has she left him now?' Clara asked. 'I'd have gone, at once.'

'I doubt it,' Thomas said. 'But you've got to remember, there is nowhere for most women to go if the marriage turns out to be a bad one. I'm hoping now the war is over, the government will show more flexibility on many things, especially giving women the vote and finding ways to help the very poorest people in our society.'

'Sandwiches?' Clara said, passing the plate round. 'Egg and cress, or cheese and tomato. You've made me feel guilty now, Thomas, that I have so much. And I don't do guilt very well.'

The men laughed at that. Mabel smiled too, but she knew that, despite Clara's privileged upbringing, the comfort she lived in, and her sometimes quite harsh remarks about the working classes, she was in fact very sympathetic towards them, and kind-hearted and generous to everyone. She just never wanted to expose that side of her personality.

It was refreshing to find that neither Thomas nor Michael were snobs, even though it was clear that they were the products of good schools, money and loving parents. They'd gone straight into the army as officers, with probably less ability to lead men than their milkman or greengrocer. The war had few plus points, but it may have made real men out of many of the Thomases and Michaels of this world.

Thomas was twenty-nine. Clara asked him directly, even though she always claimed it was rude to ask a person's age or what work they did. Michael was two years older. Mabel couldn't help but think how difficult she would've found a tea such as this back when she lived in Hallsands. All the people she knew there, aside from the vicar, were involved in fishing. Simple people, many without any real education. They didn't own pretty china tea sets, or napkins; the men sat down to meals in their working clothes, and they wouldn't give a thank you for dainty sandwiches with the crusts cut off.

She wondered how she was ever going to get around to telling Thomas she was Clara's housekeeper. Neither man had mentioned her being a widow, either – though they probably realized that, as she wore a wedding ring. She found it odd that she cared what Thomas thought; she hadn't imagined she would ever care about a man's opinion again.

It was a very jolly afternoon, the first Clara and Mabel had spent since the week before Carsten's death. The two men were great company – not too serious, but not shallow, either. They talked about so many different things, from a discussion on when England would get back on its feet and rationing might be abandoned, to the new motor cars. Thomas was dead set on buying one, as he'd learned to drive a truck while in France. Clara said she wanted to learn to drive, so she could get one too.

Mabel hadn't any intention of revealing her 'psychic power', as Clara liked to call it. But that came out quite by accident. Clara asked Michael about his war wound, and he said the reason he was still alive was because of his grandfather's pocket watch.

'I mostly kept it in the breast pocket of my uniform, more of a good luck talisman than anything else. But I had moved it into a small pocket on the waistband of my trousers, some call it a ticket pocket, because I needed space for a notepad and various other things. The sniper's bullet hit me right on the watch, splintering it. But without the watch to absorb the main impact, I would've been torn right open. I was quite badly hurt as it was. Luckily, the doctor at the field station was determined to save me. I owe my life to him really; another doctor would've moved on to a man who wasn't so severely injured and was more likely to be saved.'

'Did they really pick who to treat and who to leave?' Mabel said in horror.

The two men looked at one another and grimaced.

'Well, yes, no point in trying to save one dying man if there are two others who are treatable.'

'What happened to the watch?' Clara asked. Ever the practical one.

'I've still got the pieces. It means even more to me now. It's as if my grandfather saved me,' Michael said.

'You should let Mabel hold it. She can probably get a message from your grandfather.' As soon as the words came out of her mouth, she clapped her hand over it and looked aghast. 'Sorry, I wasn't supposed to mention that,' she said.

But of course, both men immediately wanted to know what she meant, and Mabel reluctantly told them she did sometimes get messages by holding something personal.

'That's a wonderful talent,' Michael said. 'Gosh, I hope you'll try and reach Grandfather for us. We were both very fond of him.'

'I had decided I wasn't going to do it any more.'

'You said publicly,' Clara reminded her.

The two men looked puzzled, so Mabel felt compelled to tell them about the night in Southampton and how she'd told a woman who believed her husband was dead that her husband was, in fact, coming home. 'I don't know what I'm saying when these messages come through, it's like I'm asleep. It transpired that her husband couldn't read or write, and that's why he hadn't contacted her to say he was in a POW camp. But what if I got it wrong? Built up her hopes that he's coming home, and he's dead?'

Thomas frowned. 'Then it isn't just the dead that messages come from?'

'I thought it was, and it should be. I'm really doubting

myself now,' Mabel said. 'This gift, or whatever you call it, came on suddenly, so I'm a real novice. I wish I could find out if I was right, and he really was in a POW camp. I know I was right on some of it – after all, I got her name correct, and the fact that he couldn't read or write. But what I don't understand is why he didn't let her know he was alive?'

Thomas reached out his hand and squeezed Mabel's arm. 'If you got her name right, then the message was a real one – or how else would you have got it? As for why he didn't let his wife know he was alive, one thing I learned while doing law is that people do behave very oddly sometimes. There is the possibility that he hoped, by playing dead, he could take on a new identity once he got home and slip out of his marriage and responsibilities. I know you ladies can't imagine anyone could be that callous, but it happens.'

Mabel felt her stomach turn over. When she glanced at Clara, she could see that she too felt disturbed.

'Do let's talk about something more cheerful,' Clara said brightly. 'And do eat some more, or Mabel and I will be eating curled-up sandwiches and stale scones for the next two days.'

The men left at five thirty, apologizing for outstaying their welcome. Both Clara and Mabel laughed, as they hadn't enjoyed an afternoon so much for ages.

'Do come again,' Clara said. 'Interesting, entertaining visitors have been rather thin on the ground for some time now.'

After the men had gone and Mabel was washing up the tea things, she said she was worried about Thomas thinking she was Clara's companion.

Clara laughed. 'For goodness' sake, you silly goose. You are my companion, my friend, my everything, truth to tell! You may have come as a housekeeper, but you've kind of expanded into other roles.'

'It's lovely that you feel that way,' Mabel said. 'But a lady's companion isn't really classed as a servant, is she? Aren't they usually a poor relation, or the daughter of an impoverished vicar?'

'You've been reading too many Victorian novels!' Clara snorted with laughter. 'The world has moved on a bit since that sort of silliness. But if it is worrying you, next time you see him – and I'm sure that will be soon, judging by the way he was looking at you – he's bound to ask how we met. Then you tell the truth, that a friend of mine met you in Bristol and told you I was looking for a housekeeper/ companion. He can see for himself that I don't see you as a servant! And I don't think he's the kind of man who is looking for an heiress. His family have enough money of their own. Also, he's a lawyer.'

'But what about me being married?' Mabel could hardly bring herself to ask that question.

'We worry about that when he proposes to you.' Clara grinned, and when she saw how stricken Mabel looked, she roared with laughter.

'That was a joke, really,' she admitted. 'He does like you, but perhaps not in that way. It may be the same for you too. So just enjoy getting to know him, and be happy. God knows, we could all do with a dose of that!'

15

June 1919

Mabel stood looking at the garden from the door of her little cottage, remembering how often she'd stood in this exact same place and watched Carsten working.

The memory of him had stopped hurting now. She wished their parting had been her seeing him on to a train to go home, leaving her with the consolation of how happy his family would be to have him back, instead of the hideous memory of his tragic death. But time was a great healer, as everyone always said. The pain had faded, first into a dull ache, but now she mostly recalled the happy times and smiled about him.

A reply had come from Carsten's parents. Mabel had to take it to the camp to get it translated. It was clear that, as devastated as they were by their son's death, they had taken comfort from Mabel and Clara writing to them. Apparently, in his letters to them he'd said what a pleasant town Dorchester was, and how lucky he felt being allowed to work in Clara's garden. He spoke of both her and Mabel in every letter home and said many times how sad he'd be to say goodbye to them when the time came to leave.

His parents thanked them both for looking after their son's grave and gave special thanks to Mabel for nursing him through the flu. Many people they knew had died of it too, and life was exceedingly difficult now in Germany, with shortages of almost everything. They finished up by saying there would be a chasm in their family without Carsten; he was their first-born and they loved him so much. But they had received a letter of condolence from a senior officer who said he was a fine, brave soldier who had been held in high regard by the men he led.

The letter made Mabel cry again. She went up to Carsten's grave with some flowers and sat there for an hour just remembering him. That day, she felt she'd never be happy again.

Yet Thomas and Michael had been responsible for changing that. Hardly a week went by without them inviting her and Clara to something. Yesterday it had just been an invitation to attend a flower show organized by one of their aunt's friends. But there had been a couple of concerts, dinner twice with their Aunt Leticia, afternoon tea in the Black Cat tearooms, and walks too.

Clara had said she was going to turn down the next invitation, in the hope that Michael would bow out too and Mabel would have a chance to be alone with Thomas. But Mabel liked being with Clara and both the men; it was fun, with no awkward silences, and she'd got to know Thomas better.

She knew now that he liked to rebel against rules. He couldn't stand stuffy people, he could eat absolutely anything, and he could play the violin. He said he played it badly, but Michael said that was nonsense. He liked cricket and had just joined the local team. He liked swimming too, and Mabel wondered whether he'd swim in the river with her one day. He liked adventure books – *The Scarlet*

Pimpernel, White Fang and Sherlock Holmes – and said there was nothing he liked better than lying in a hammock in the sun with an exciting book.

She knew his last lady friend had been Hester, from Shaftesbury, who had an impeccable pedigree, but he said she was as dull as ditchwater. His parents had pushed him into it, and he went along with it. Hester found a new beau, though, just before he joined up. The new man was a farmer and was exempt from call-up. Thomas laughed as he told Mabel this. 'I was glad to be getting away. I wondered how long it would take the new man to wish he would be called up too.'

There was an openness about Thomas; he didn't ponder on things, just said what he felt. Mabel realized she was growing fond of him, and she had a feeling the only reason he was holding back with her was because of her widowed status. He had hardly asked her anything about Martin – or Peter, as she always called him, when speaking to other people. She was relieved about that, because she didn't want to tell him any lies. It was bad enough living one.

Tonight, he had invited her to come alone with him to Borough Gardens, to listen to the band. That was far better than Clara engineering it. It would be lovely, as it was going to be a warm night, and people would dance to the band, too. She was going to wear her new dress that she'd made with material she'd bought in Bath; it was a dark blue, but sprigged with little white flowers, sober enough for half-mourning, but still pretty.

He said he wanted to celebrate with her, as he'd completed his two-month probationary period at Shaldon,

Peacock and Grace, the law firm, and they had agreed to take him on permanently.

Right on the stroke of seven, Thomas called at Willow Cottage.

When she answered the door, he handed her a posy of flowers. 'You look beautiful,' he said. 'You always do, but tonight especially so.'

'You look rather handsome yourself,' she said. His face was very tanned from the recent warm weather and he wore a cream linen jacket, navy trousers and a navy-and-cream spotted cravat, along with his panama hat. 'You'll be showing all the farmers up who come wearing their hairy tweed jackets and corduroy trousers.'

'My aunt suggested I looked a bit too Parisian for Dorchester. I think that was a reproach. Maybe she wants me in hairy tweed too?'

'Well, I don't,' Mabel said, before calling back to say goodbye to Clara, who was drawing in her studio.

As they left, Thomas tucked her hand into his arm, and they headed for the footpath by the river.

'It's good to be on our own for a change,' he said.

'Didn't Michael want to come tonight?'

'I didn't ask him.' Thomas grinned. 'But he has got his eye on someone. Harriet Trott. Do you know her?'

Mabel shook her head.

'Her father has his fingers in lots of pies. A couple of hotels, a building company, and property he rents out. Bit of a big-head, likes to show off. I don't like him at all, but Harriet is rather sweet. I think she might be good for Michael. He likes goody-goody girls, and I know he really wants to marry and settle down.'

'Nothing worse, though, than marrying someone with an overbearing parent,' Mabel said, without thinking.

'Did that happen to you?' he asked.

'Yes, my mother-in-law was a real shrew. But maybe Harriet's father will keep his distance. And anyway, they are a long way off marrying, aren't they?'

'Have you thought any more about doing a little spirit raising?' he asked.

'I have been tempted by Michael's broken watch,' she admitted. 'But I'm scared too. I don't like the way it makes me lose control, so I don't know what I'm saying.'

'Yes, that would be somewhat daunting,' he said. 'Apparently, I was delirious when my leg got smashed. I was told afterwards I was saying all kinds of weird things. I just hoped I hadn't revealed anything embarrassing.'

'Have you got embarrassing secrets, then?'

'Well, there is one current one.'

'Go on, can you tell me?'

'I think I'm falling in love with this beautiful and elusive redhead.'

That was the last thing Mabel had expected to hear and, worse still, he had turned her round so she was facing him. She knew she ought to lift her head up and say something. But what? She had no sharp retort, no joke or banter.

'So, we are being even more elusive by not answering,' he said. 'You are a puzzle, Mabel, so bright, funny and competent, yet you hold so much back. Why is that?'

'Right now, it's because I don't know what to say,' she said, lifting her head to look at him. 'I didn't expect you to tell me something like that.'

'Does that mean you don't like to be told such a thing?'

'No, it is very flattering. But –' She stopped, unable to explain.

'Too soon?' he asked. 'But Mabel, I've been seeing you every few days for nearly three months. I think about you when I wake up, I go to sleep thinking of you. I can never wait to see you. I know you like being with me too, I feel it.'

'I do like being with you,' she admitted. 'Very much. I've been so happy since we met.'

'You weren't happy before?'

'They were troubled times, with the war and the Spanish flu. But there's so much about me that you don't know. I'm not of your class, for a start.'

All at once, he had his hands either side of her face and he lifted it up tenderly to kiss her. Just a light touch on the lips at first, as if to stop her protest, but then his arms went right around her, and he was kissing her with such passion she couldn't help but be swept away by it.

A glorious, wonderful kiss that started a tingle at the tip of her toes, then ran up throughout her body to her head. She knew then she was lost, in more ways than one. It was as if her whole life had been spent waiting for this one moment.

Footsteps and chatter further along the riverbank made them separate, but Mabel couldn't let go of his hand, it felt too good in hers. She started to giggle like a schoolgirl, and Thomas laughed too, and the middle-aged couple who passed them looked at them curiously.

It was the best of nights; the warm, gentle breeze, the beauty of the park with its pretty flower beds, and the band playing numbers like 'Alexander's Ragtime Band',

'Anytime Is Kissing Time' and 'After You've Gone'. Everyone around them was dancing. Some couples were trying to fit ballroom dances to the music, but the vast majority were just happily jigging about, with their arms wrapped around one another.

'I don't want this night to end,' Thomas whispered in Mabel's ear. 'I want to kiss you till the dawn comes creeping over the hill, then take you home, kissing you all the way.'

But they did go home, not at dawn but soon after ten, as the light was fading fast. The riverbank wasn't a good place to walk in darkness.

'There's a full moon tonight,' Thomas said when Mabel urged him to leave her and go home. 'Besides, what sort of cad would let his girl walk home alone along a riverbank?'

'Am I your girl?' she asked.

'I do hope so, after kissing me like that,' he said, stopping to kiss her yet again.

Later, when Mabel was in her bed, with the window open so she could hear the wading birds on the river and the owls, she felt too happy to think seriously about where this might end. She had loved Martin, but his kisses had never made her feel the way Thomas's did. As for Carsten, she'd never found out what his kisses were like; perhaps some of his attraction for her was because she knew in her heart of hearts that it could never be. Maybe that's what he'd meant when he said, 'I cannot be what you want me to be.'

Clara was all agog the next morning, unusually rising soon after eight, while Mabel was riddling the range. 'Well, how did it go?' she asked eagerly, dark eyes shining. 'Have you got anything to tell me?'

'No, I haven't,' Mabel said. 'Don't be so nosy.'

But over a cup of tea, a little later, Mabel admitted she'd had a wonderful evening and she couldn't wait to see Thomas again.

Later that morning, in church, Mabel drifted off during the sermon, thinking about Thomas. But all at once, reality hit her. She couldn't expect to hide her past from him for long; he was a lawyer, and such men delved into people's pasts. If he found out himself, then he'd be angry at her for not telling him. On the other hand, if she told him, he might decide she was too much trouble for him and end it all with her anyway.

16

'Please can we do the watch thing now,' Michael begged.

He and Thomas had come to dinner at Willow Cottage and at almost the moment they arrived, Michael had produced a little velvet jewellery bag from his pocket and asked if she would try to reach their grandfather.

There were times when Michael and Thomas reminded Mabel of small boys. They competed with each other, making bets on the silliest things like which of their paper boats would sail the furthest, or who could stand on one leg the longest. When they played cards with Mabel and Clara, they played to win – not minding so much if one of the women won, but hating to lose to their brother.

It was the same when Michael asked her about the watch; both their faces were alight with excitement, and they immediately began arguing about who their grandfather liked the most. To get some peace, Mabel agreed she would try after dinner.

Mabel had managed to buy a brace of pheasant from a man she often ran into along the riverbank. He'd offered her duck first, but when she didn't look too enthusiastic about that, he suggested pheasant. There was no doubt he was a poacher, and he shouldn't have been shooting pheasant in July, but Mabel still bought them. As she said to Clara, 'Well, he'd killed them already. Someone had to eat them.'

The recipe was an old one Clara said she'd got from an

aunt and remembered it being wonderful. It wasn't too difficult, as basically it was just half a bottle of red wine, lots of vegetables and long, slow cooking.

Thomas and Michael loved it, and they raved about the plum crumble for pudding. But all the time Mabel was aware they were rushing through the meal, just so she'd try with the watch.

'Look, it doesn't always work,' she reminded them. 'For one thing, your grandfather might not want to come down to earth – for you two, or anything else. And I'm not an expert. So if you don't expect anything, then you won't be disappointed.'

Finally, after turning off all the oil lamps, leaving only a group of three candles on a side table, they sat down. Mabel was seated on an armchair, Thomas and Michael at either end of the sofa, and Clara in the middle of them.

Mabel turned the watch parts out of their bag on to a table mat. She rested her hands on the pieces, closing her eyes and concentrating hard.

For what seemed like at least five minutes, but it was probably less, she felt nothing. She was just about to give up, as she sensed both men beginning to fidget, when she felt that familiar tingle and the strange sleepy feeling.

Once again, she came to after what seemed no time at all, hearing Clara's voice saying, 'That's enough now, she needs to wake up.'

'I am awake,' she said. 'Did you get a message?'

Both Thomas and Michael looked pale, but she thought that was just her imagination.

'Mabel, you spoke like their grandfather. Michael nearly had heart failure, as his voice was so loud.'

Mabel touched her throat. 'Is that why my throat is sore? Please get me a drink, someone.'

'He said he was with us in France, he spoke of an oak tree I used to go to behind the lines to have a smoke,' Thomas said. 'He said I was more upset when that tree was cut down by a mortar than I was when I copped it in the leg.'

'He said he saw me put the watch in my waistband pocket,' Michael said. 'He saw the bullet hit me, but I was always lucky when I was a little boy.'

'Was that it?' Mabel asked.

'No, it wasn't,' Clara spoke up. 'He said how proud he was of them both. They weren't born to be soldiers, but they rose to the task of leading their men, cared for them, and showed true courage.'

Mabel saw both men had damp eyes. She hoped what their grandfather had said was like being given a medal.

'That's it, then. No more of this,' she said, scooping the pieces of the watch up and putting them back in the bag. 'It's too distressing.'

'Thank you,' Michael said. 'If I hadn't seen and heard that with my own eyes and ears, I wouldn't have believed it.'

Thomas got up and came and sat on the arm of her chair, to embrace her. 'I don't know what to say,' he said quietly.

Mabel knew he felt the way she did, shattered by something he didn't understand, and wondering if this would stand between them. She couldn't say anything to reassure him.

Clara, as always, sensed something and rose to the occasion. 'You fill our glasses again, Mabel, and I'll play something jolly,' she said, moving over to the piano.

But no amount of drink, or jolly music, was going to banish the seriousness of what they'd experienced. It wasn't a party game, and wherever the spirit had come from, he had brought not sadness exactly – after all, their grandfather had said he was proud of them, which was something good to hear – but a weightiness to the atmosphere.

Mabel lay awake that night in her cottage, thinking on the night's events. Nora had told her that once people had experienced her getting messages from the dead, they became afraid she could see into their minds. As she pointed out, this was entirely irrational. How could she possibly do that? She wasn't a fortune teller, she didn't read palms, and in fact she wasn't even that interested in other people. But some people still thought it.

Thomas and Michael were too intelligent to think that, but this power she had might set her apart. It would be a fun topic to discuss at dinner parties; she could almost hear people gossiping that she communed with the dead. But wasn't that ultimately going to embarrass Thomas? A man whose very profession as a lawyer was one of black and white. Guilty or innocent, true or false. No grey areas. The spirit world was most definitely a grey area. You couldn't prove it existed, or that it didn't.

Then, when it came to light that she was a woman who had faked her death and abandoned her sick husband, she would be branded as at best a heartless hussy, possibly even worse. How could Thomas stand by her then?

He couldn't, of course.

So, what could she do?

She could stop the psychic thing right now. Never

attempt to do it again, and tell Thomas and Michael they shouldn't talk about it either.

That was simple.

But her past was another matter. She could carry on her romance with Thomas and hope nothing ever caused the past to come back and bite her. Or stop seeing him now. However hard that would be.

She fell asleep in the end, with no decision made.

For the next couple of weeks, Mabel tried to distance herself a little from Thomas. She made excuses not to see him so often in the evenings, and on one Saturday she claimed she was working in the garden.

She *was* working in the garden; with no Carsten now, there was a great deal of weeding, tying up unruly plants and cutting back to do. But it made her heart ache, because she wanted to see Thomas far more than she had expected to.

They did discuss the psychic problem, and he understood her fears. He promised that neither he nor Michael would mention it to anyone. But he was dismayed when she started to pull back from him.

'What is it, Mabel? I thought you felt the same as me?' he said.

'I do, but it's all going a bit fast. I want to see you, but we need a bit of time apart too. You've got your new job as well. You should be concentrating on that.'

The German prisoners finally went home. Before they left, Mabel went to see some of the men she'd nursed with the flu. It was her last connection to Carsten, and she knew she had to sever it and put the memories of him aside.

All the men had learned some English, a few had become quite fluent, and they all wanted to impress her with it. Looking at their bright faces, full of excitement that soon they'd be back with their families and friends, she felt so much affection for them. Just boys really, forced to become men too soon. But she hoped they would take some good memories of England home with them.

The day the first trainload left Dorchester for Southampton, Mabel and Clara were there to wave them off. Surprisingly, there were many other local people there too, and in conversations afterwards with some of them, they heard that sons and husbands who hadn't come home already were due back any day.

'I hope it is true that this was the War to End All Wars,' Freda Pople, who owned the haberdasher's, said to Clara and Mabel, drying her eyes with a handkerchief. She'd seen four sons go off to war, and only two had returned, yet still she'd come to wave off the Germans.

Clara squeezed her hand in agreement. 'You are a good woman, Freda, to come to the station today. I hope it helps to know some mothers will get their sons back.'

'Holding bitterness inside you isn't good for anyone,' Freda said.

The following Saturday, Clara came back from the art class she held in the town and rushed in brandishing a newspaper.

'Look, look!' she exclaimed. 'It's that man Harold. He's come home!'

Mabel had just dug up some new potatoes from the garden for dinner and she was washing them off in the sink.

She quickly dried her hands and came to look at the newspaper Clara had spread on the table.

The headline was: 'Mother of three reunited with husband she thought was dead.' Mabel read:

Just a few days ago, Private Harold Painter arrived home at Southampton on the SS *Devonshire* with other prisoners of war captured in Flanders by the German army.

Until just a few months ago, his wife Sarah (24) thought he had died in France. She received a telegram saying he was missing, presumed dead. It was devastating news for Sarah, as she was left with three children, the youngest less than a year old, when she got the telegram.

She was only told he was alive back in February by a young visiting psychic at a spiritualists' meeting in Southampton. Harold, or Harry as he is always known, spoke to the psychic while she was in a trance, and explained he couldn't read or write, which was why Sarah hadn't been notified.

It is hoped that Harold, Sarah and their three children will have a long and happy life together.

'That's marvellous! So I was right, after all,' Mabel said. 'How wonderful for Sarah. But I'm so glad they didn't use my name.'

'I bet the paper will try to follow it up, though,' Clara said. 'That's just a local paper. Wait till the nationals get hold of it. It's a happy story and, God knows, there haven't been many of those for some time.'

'I can't see Beatrice giving my name,' Mabel said thoughtfully. 'If anything, she'll want to take the credit. Let's hope so, anyway. I don't want newspaper hounds coming here.'

'I'll see them off,' Clara said. 'Though, to be honest, I don't understand why you don't want the acclaim. I would!'

'It's scary,' Mabel said. 'It would be a really tragic story if poor Sarah was meeting every ship with returning POWs aboard in the hopes her Harold was amongst them. She clearly isn't the brightest woman in the world, probably right at the bottom of the heap. If I'd made her life even grimmer, I'd never have forgiven myself. Of course, there's the other reason: the newspapers would want a photograph of me, and what a can of worms that would open up!'

Thomas and Michael were as thrilled by the newspaper article as Clara was. Thomas telephoned almost the second he had read it.

'So heart-warming,' he said. 'To think you made it happen.'

'But I didn't. Harold would've turned up at some point. The same result, except he's been shamed by everyone finding out he can't read or write.'

'Oh, Mabel,' he said reproachfully. 'You should be happy about this.'

'I am happy he's alive – and that I know for sure now – but the whole thing seems a bit shabby to me.'

'It strikes me that you've got something more on your mind than just Harold and Sarah, or being able to listen to spirits. Is it that you've changed your mind about me?'

'No, not at all,' she lied. 'But please don't talk about this article to anyone. Promise me?'

He promised, but she could tell by his tone of voice that he was concerned and perhaps suspicious.

*

The next weekend, Thomas's Aunt Leticia invited Mabel and Clara to dinner. Three other couples had been invited, as well as Harriet Trott, the young lady Michael was seeing.

'So Leticia and I are to be the two dull old spinsters,' Clara remarked. 'Or are we chaperones?'

'You may both be unmarried, but neither of you is dull,' Mabel said. 'And I don't think any of us need chaperones.'

'I think you and Thomas do. I can feel the lust simmering when you are together. Why don't you just invite him into your little cottage one night and get it over with.'

'Clara!' Mabel exclaimed. 'I can't believe you'd make such a suggestion.'

'Well, my dear, if you are holding out for marriage, you have to tell him first about the impediment.'

'How can I do that?' Mabel asked. 'He'd be so shocked he'd drop me like a hot potato.'

'I don't think he would, he's far too besotted with you. I think as a lawyer he'll think of divorce, and so he'll want to contact Martin. Of course, I can't imagine how that would pan out. Apart from non-consummation, as far as I know one of the couple must have committed adultery. If he is living with someone now, or even married to them, believing you are dead, that could be plain sailing. But if he's still as he was when you left, that won't work.'

Mabel hung her head. Whenever she thought of Martin, she felt so guilty. She would be happy for him if he'd recovered and got another lady in his life, but somehow, she couldn't imagine that.

'I know,' Clara said in sympathy. 'However you look at it, there are problems. But if it was me, I'd say I had an aversion to the married state – which I really have, believe me – and ask him to live with me without the blessing of the Church.'

'I don't think he'd approve of that for one moment,' Mabel said. But she laughed, because Clara's dislike of convention was quite amusing.

'Get him into bed with you and he'll lose all his scruples,' Clara said with a wicked grin.

'You are incorrigible,' Mabel giggled. 'But to swiftly change the subject, what are we going to wear to this dinner? It will be quite formal, I expect.'

As there wasn't enough time for Mabel to make, or have made, a suitable evening dress, Clara said she could wear one of hers. 'Some of them haven't seen the light of day since I was your age,' she added.

Clara stored her evening dresses in a big cupboard on the upstairs landing.

Mabel had looked at them all before and wondered how anyone could have so many beautiful dresses, but not wear any of them.

'I wish I could wear the white one,' Mabel sighed, stroking the white voile reverently. 'But I have resigned myself to dull, dark clothes.'

'This one isn't dull,' Clara said, pulling out a purple satin dress. 'And you would look stunning in it.'

'Are you sure purple is allowed?' Mabel said doubtfully. She took it from Clara and held it up to herself. The contrast with her red hair was quite sensational. It had an exceptionally low neck and ruffles across the tops of the arms instead of sleeves.

'It was always a mourning colour – and still is, in some

countries. It's quite acceptable for you. Especially as you are a guest of a single gentleman!'

Mabel laughed at the way Clara had made the last sentence seem quite saucy.

The purple dress was heavenly and fitted as if it had been made for her. It made her waist look tiny.

'I was much lighter when I last wore it,' Clara said. 'I doubt very much if I could get into it now. The low neck looks very seductive on you.'

'So what are you going to wear?' Mabel asked.

'As one of the spinsters or chaperones, one mustn't attempt to outdo the other female guests. But I think the red velvet, just to warn everyone I can be dangerous.'

Andrews came to drive them to the dinner. He looked at them both very approvingly.

'If I might say, you both look stunning,' he said.

'You may indeed say it, Andrews – more than once, if you feel like it,' Clara said.

'Now there's a man I might have made a play for, if he hadn't already been boringly married,' she whispered to Mabel as they drove off. 'He was something of a hero, shot in the leg during one of the early battles in France, but he still hauled a wounded sergeant back to safety behind the lines. Sadly, his own leg didn't heal well. I believe it gives him a lot of pain.'

Thomas looked stunned at Mabel's appearance. 'You look devastatingly beautiful,' he said. 'I don't know how I'll be able to control myself if we are left alone.'

Mabel giggled. 'That sounds like fun,' she said.

The other two couples invited were Paul Henderson, a

vet, and his wife Marcia, recently married, both around thirty-something. Sylvia and Gerald Toon were just a little older; Gerald was a surgeon at a hospital in Southampton. Both couples were attractive, as was expected, because Leticia liked young, attractive people around her. Although Leticia was over sixty and white-haired, she was still a good-looking woman, with clear, virtually unlined skin. In her drawing room there was an oil painting of her when she was eighteen, with her dark hair cascading in ringlets over her bare creamy shoulders, and an unbelievably tiny waist. According to Thomas, she was the beauty of Dorchester but, for reasons unknown, she'd never married. Thomas's grandfather left his house here in Dorchester to his two grandsons, under the condition Leticia could stay in it for life. It seemed to be an arrangement which suited all three of them.

The house was Georgian and very gracious, with the customary long windows and lofty ceilings. Several generations had handed down the beautiful furniture, Persian carpets, exquisite chandeliers and beautiful paintings that made it a remarkable yet extremely comfortable home.

They had aperitifs out on the terrace, because it was such a warm night. The position of the house at Top O' Town gave it a wonderful view over the fields and river down below.

It was the first time Mabel had been close to Harriet, Michael's guest. She had seen her several times, but not talked to her, and she realized immediately that when people said how sweet she was, that translated as insipid. She was pretty – blonde, blue-eyed, small and curvy in an attractive pink dress – but she had a very tiny mouth, reminding Mabel of a doll.

Mabel went out of her way to talk to her, but she smiled rather vacantly and agreed with everything Mabel said. It was tempting to say something outrageous, just to see if that would jolt her out of her tiresome dullness.

But Clara had warned Mabel that, whatever she thought of the girl, she wasn't to show it. So Mabel admired her dress, and her hair, talked about the weather and how much she liked listening to the band in Borough Gardens.

She was very relieved when she was rescued by Paul and Marcia Henderson, who were impressed that she'd done some nursing and wanted to know about the prison camp.

Thankfully, Leticia had put Mabel between Thomas and Paul Henderson for dinner. Harriet was on the other side of the table, between Michael and Gerald.

But Clara, sitting at the top of the table, led the conversation. She sparkled with fun, drawing people out, and had clearly found out facts about the Hendersons and the Toons to aid her in this. She did try with Harriet too, but even she couldn't winkle an interesting topic or outrageous remark out of her. Clara noticed that Michael seemed tense, but all Harriet did was look at him and giggle and simper.

One thing struck Mabel as she tackled her beef Wellington: she was the girl from Hallsands who would sooner have jumped in the sea from the cliff top than be sitting at this fancy table. Somehow, in only two and a half years, she had managed to lose her fishing past, and make people believe she was a gently-brought-up young lady. She owed her table manners to Mrs Hardy and Clara, and she'd gathered enough poise to be able to talk to people who would once have terrified her.

'I just love you,' Thomas whispered to her as he retrieved his dropped napkin. 'Are you enjoying yourself?'

'Yes, of course I am. I'm here with you, after all. Everything is good with you.'

He leaned even closer to her. 'I keep looking at your breasts and wishing I could stroke and kiss them,' he whispered. 'Shall I shout it out and really shock everyone?'

Mabel blushed. 'You'll do no such thing, behave yourself.'

She wished she had the nerve to tell him she was always imagining him caressing her, and how she really wanted to make love. But until Clara had put the idea into her head about him coming to the cottage, she hadn't been able to think of anywhere they could go. Should she suggest it? But what if she got pregnant?

'What are you thinking about?' he whispered again.

'You, of course. What else?' she whispered back. 'But this isn't the place to be talking about it.'

'When, then?'

'I'm not sure, I need to think about it first.'

17

Thomas called round on Sunday afternoon as Mabel was mowing the grass in the front garden. It was hot, and he wore an open-necked shirt and grey flannel trousers.

'Hello,' she exclaimed. 'This is a surprise. If I'd known you were coming, I would've made myself more presentable.'

'You look perfectly presentable to me,' he said. 'I like the peasant look.'

Mabel laughed, but more from embarrassment than pleasure. Her dress was the old grey thing she'd been wearing when she ran away from Hallsands. She only ever wore it for gardening or dirty work. She also had a scarf tied round her head like a turban.

'You said you wanted to discuss something with me. Is this an appropriate time?'

'Hardly,' she said, wondering how men could be so stupid sometimes. As if she would want to discuss going to bed with him, in broad daylight, while she was dressed like a scullery maid, and probably smelling sweaty!

'I see. I'd better push off, then,' he said, looking hurt.

'I didn't mean to be sharp with you, but look at me! I'm dressed for gardening. What I wanted to talk about needs soft light, a glass or two of something special, and somewhere comfy to sit.'

'Oh, I see.' He leaned back on the gate, arms folded across his chest. 'So go and get changed. I can't make the light softer in full daylight, or even get a drink of champagne, as all the shops are closed. But I could lead you to a haystack.'

She had to laugh then. 'You win, I'll settle for a walk. You wait here while I get washed and changed.'

She filled her ewer from the garden tap and took it into the cottage bedroom. Washing in cold water was no hardship when it was so hot outside.

After washing she put on her grey-and-white striped dress, but only a camisole underneath; it was far too hot for petticoats or even stockings. She brushed her hair, fixed it up, with a few curls loose on her cheeks. A dab of powder on her nose, some eau de cologne on her neck and wrists, her straw boater on her head and she was ready.

Thomas smiled as she approached him. 'A transformation! I hope you've left the grumpy Mabel indoors.'

She noticed he had finished mowing the lawn while she'd been gone. 'I have, and it was kind of you to finish the lawn.'

'Always ready to offer assistance, that's me. I also popped in to tell Clara we were going for a walk, in case she needed you.' He took her hand and led her out on to the riverbank path.

'Michael told me this morning he's going to propose to Harriet,' he said. 'But I wasn't supposed to tell anyone.'

'My lips will remain sealed,' she said. 'But is he sure? She seemed a bit –' She stopped suddenly, not liking to say something insulting.

'Drippy?' he suggested, raising one eyebrow. 'Well, I said that to Michael, and he said, "Maybe, but she'll make a perfect wife and mother."'

'Really!' Mabel exclaimed. 'I can't imagine her getting across the road on her own.'

'He's not the man he was before he was wounded,' Thomas sighed. 'His body is very scarred, he is often in pain, and I think he feels he has to settle for what he can get.'

'Oh, Thomas, it's awful he feels that way. He's a handsome, intelligent man, with so much to offer. She'll bore him to death in no time.'

'Or maybe she'll just keep him alive, Mabel,' he said in a resigned tone. 'I know he's considered the quick way out. I caught him once, soon after we got here, with my father's pistol in his hand. He said he was just looking at it. But he'd found the bullets and loaded it.'

Mabel's eyes grew wide with shock. 'He seems so well balanced to me. He's not talkative like you, but I didn't pick up on melancholy.'

'He has perked up a bit since we started seeing you and Clara regularly. He feels safe with Clara, you see, not just because she takes him out of himself, but because nothing is expected of him, only to turn up and be jolly.'

'But isn't he putting his head into the lion's mouth by contemplating marriage? Does Harriet know about his injuries? Won't it affect him when they go to bed?'

'I can't ask him personal questions like that,' Thomas sighed again. 'Who could?'

'A woman who loved him could,' Mabel said.

'She's all frills and flounces – she reminds me of a fluffy day-old chick. I doubt she even has a clue about what happens on a wedding night. Much less what brutal things war and injuries can do to men's minds.'

'Has your leg injury affected you?' Mabel wondered if he had something affecting him too. 'Now's the time to own up, if it has.'

'I think all vital parts are in good working order.' He grinned. 'But even I, the most optimistic, never-say-die kind of chap, has to admit to a few trench nightmares. But Michael lay injured in no-man's-land for hours. He thought he was going to die – he told me he wished for it, he was in such pain. I was lucky. When I got shot my sergeant got me on to a stretcher and back behind the lines within half an hour. I was seen quickly at the dressing station and put on a train to the hospital before I knew it. It's true I have nightmares about the trenches – the rats, the body parts that came to light when it rained heavily – but not about my injured leg, because that was dealt with, and I was relieved to be sent home.'

'I see. I'm awfully glad to hear that.'

'May I remind you this walk was supposed to be about us discussing something personal? So is it really the moment for grisly talk of injuries, rats and trenches?'

One of the things she liked most about Thomas was his ability to make light of things, especially when the conversation was growing weighty.

'It was about you wanting to caress my –' She stopped short.

'Your breasts and any other part of your body too,' he said with a grin.

She blushed. 'I have to admit I feel the same, but we can't, can we? There's nowhere to be alone.'

'There is marriage, of course.'

She hadn't expected him to say that, and it threw her.

'Lusting after someone isn't an ideal reason for marriage,' she said.

'In my view it's the best one,' he laughed.

'I don't know if I ever want to get married again, but that isn't to say I've turned my back on love-making.'

Thomas stopped stock-still and just looked at her. 'That sounds dangerously like a proposition?' he said, his eyes glinting with amusement. 'But I never thought I'd ever meet a woman who would suggest it. Have you thought ahead to where this could take place? If not in woods or fields.'

'In the little cottage I live in,' she suggested, blushing furiously, because she couldn't really believe she was being this bold. 'You could easily slip across the garden without Clara or anyone else seeing you. Or even better, come through the fence at the side of the cottage.'

'Well, well, well,' he said, and swept her into his arms without even checking to see if anyone was coming.

As always, his kiss robbed her of even the will to open her eyes and see if they were being watched. She could feel him hardening, and that made her want him even more. A faint, discreet cough warned them someone was coming, and he had to let her go.

They pretended to be looking at some wild flowers, both shaking with laughter, while they let the elderly couple go by.

'Can we go there now?' Thomas asked, once the couple had passed, snorting their disapproval.

'There is something else, before we take the plunge,' she said, hanging her head, as it was embarrassing. 'I don't want to get pregnant.'

'I can take care of that,' he said, tilting her chin up. 'But not today, I'm afraid. So let's go to the haystack.'

Later that evening, when Mabel had retired to her cottage, she sat for a while by the open door, watching darkness fall over the garden, noting how all the white flowers showed up in the half-light. She thought how delicious it had been with Thomas during the afternoon. They had found a partially made haystack and climbed into it.

It was bliss, just pleasuring each other without penetration, and Thomas was good at it, finding places to touch and stroke that she'd never been aware of before.

But a haystack was a very prickly place, and it made them sneeze. Eventually, they had to get out of it, feeling as if they had ants inside their clothes.

'Tomorrow night,' he'd said, as they parted at the gate for Mabel to go in and make tea for her and Clara. 'I'll come to the cottage around nine. You tell Clara you are going to bed early.'

The prospect of doing something most people would consider quite wrong made the thought of it even more exciting. Mabel knew it would seem an extra-long day tomorrow, waiting till nine at night.

As darkness finally fell, Mabel lit the oil lamp, shut the door and drew the curtains to stop moths coming in, then took the oil lamp into the bedroom.

She sat at the dressing table, taking the pins out of her hair, and as she brushed it loose, a couple of bits of hay fell out, making her smile.

It was then she saw her mother's green glass beads. She'd hung them on the mirror when she first moved into the cottage and hadn't touched them since. But for some reason they seemed to be drawing her to them, so she picked them up and held them in her hand.

The green of the glass reminded her of the colour of the sea just before a storm, and the colour of her mother's eyes. She looked in the mirror then and saw her eyes were the same; her father had often joked that they were sea green.

As she let the smooth glass beads twine around her fingers, she experienced that familiar sensation of heat, as she had each time she'd had contact with a spirit.

The thought crossed her mind that, if there was no one here to listen to the message, how would she know what was said? But it didn't seem to matter, as she was slipping away, she didn't know where, but it wasn't frightening.

All at once she saw the view of the sea from the cliff top at Hallsands, a view she knew so well. As a child she'd stood in the same spot waiting to spot the shoals of herring. Then she saw Agnes, and she was crying; not the quiet, restrained crying people did at funerals, but wailing, as if she'd suffered a huge personal loss.

As quickly as the image had come, so it disappeared, and Mabel was left with the glass beads in her hands, wondering what it meant.

She was so shaken that she had to go to the door of the cottage and then outside, into the cool night air. There was only one person who would make Agnes cry that way, and that was Martin. Was the message to alert Mabel that he had died?

But the beads had belonged to Mabel's mother, so the message had come from her. Was she trying to tell her daughter she had to go back to Hallsands?

18

'What on earth is up with you this morning?' Clara asked. 'It's as if you are sleepwalking.'

Mabel couldn't tell her friend what was troubling her. She'd lain awake all night just thinking about it. She even picked up the glass beads again several times, in the hope that something else would come through. But there was nothing. The beads remained as cold in her hands as pieces of green ice.

By ten in the morning she knew she had to go to Hallsands and find out what had happened there. Another night of anxiety would be too much to bear. She finished up the normal daily chores and then went to see Clara in her studio upstairs.

'I've got to go back to Hallsands,' she blurted out. 'Something has happened there.'

Clara put down her paintbrush and wiped her fingers on a rag. 'Explain, please!'

Mabel told her about the glass beads. 'The only time I ever saw Agnes cry was when we went to see Martin in the hospital in Plymouth, when they first brought him home from France. The one thing that would make her as distressed as I saw, or sensed, last night, was if he were dead. I have to know for sure.'

'I can understand you wanting to know – he was your

husband, after all. But isn't there some way you can find out, without showing your face in the village?'

'I can't see how. I certainly don't want to see Agnes. She'll attack me, I'm sure of that. I suppose I could go to Kingsbridge and ask a few questions, I wasn't well known there. If I kept my hair covered up, I might not be recognized – it was nearly three years ago that I left.'

'I've got a pair of dark glasses somewhere, they'd be useful to hide behind. And wear black, people don't tend to notice women in mourning, let alone ask questions. Do you know the way there?'

'I can get a train to Exeter, and I think there's one from there to Kingsbridge. But Clara, I arranged for Thomas to come here tonight. I'll leave a note for him on the cottage door.'

'You can leave it with me,' Clara said.

'He wasn't going to come until nine, and not to the house,' Mabel was forced to admit.

Clara half smiled. 'I see. Well, that makes it easier for me. I won't have to tell him any lies. But where are you going to say you've gone?'

'To see Mrs Hardy in Bristol,' Mabel said on the spur of the moment. 'Yes, that's it, I'll say she's sick. And I felt I must go and see her.'

'Go, then,' Clara said. 'There's a train just after twelve. Will you telephone me? I'll be worried.' She stepped forward and embraced Mabel.

Clara never embraced people. Changing the habit of a lifetime, just when Mabel needed reassurance and affection, made the gesture even more poignant.

'Yes, of course I'll ring,' Mabel said into her neck. 'I don't know what to think about this, Clara. If I'm right, and Martin has died, it would solve so many problems, but I can't be glad of that. I did love him.'

'I know. And I also know that if it hadn't been for his hateful mother, you'd never have left. You deserve happiness, Mabel, I want that for you more than anything. Go now, put your mind at rest.'

It was after six in the evening when Mabel got to Kingsbridge. She walked in the opposite direction, away from where Mr and Mrs Porter, who she used to work for, lived. She headed towards a boarding house on the outskirts of the village; she felt she was less likely to run into anyone she knew there.

Fortunately, they had one small room free. Mabel flung herself down on the bed. She had never felt more alone. Even those first few days in Bristol before she got the job with Mrs Gladsworthy, frightening though they were, hadn't felt quite this desolate.

It was too hot to sleep well – even with the window open, there was no breeze – the bed was lumpy, the pillow even worse. At eight o'clock she gave up trying to sleep and got up.

The dining room was bleak, with stained, ancient wallpaper, and had a musty smell. None of the chairs around the large central table matched, and the carpet was threadbare in places. The table was laid for breakfast, and Mabel was just wondering if she should sit down and wait when Mrs Brewer, who she'd met the previous evening, appeared and asked if she wanted porridge.

In her stained apron, she looked as worn as her guest house. She had straggly, light-brown hair and a very lined but sun-tanned face.

'Just tea, toast and a boiled egg,' Mabel said.

'No eggs,' Mrs Brewer said in a tone that suggested Mabel had asked for something exceptional.

'Just toast and tea, then,' Mabel said.

She had hoped for a friendly landlady who would gossip, but Mrs Brewer obviously wasn't interested enough in anyone for such things.

'I don't like my boarders in the house during the day. Not before five, thank you,' she said when she brought the tea and toast.

Needing to stay outside would make it even more difficult for Mabel. But one look at Mrs Brewer's cold, inhospitable face was enough to know she couldn't be talked round.

As Mabel set off from the boarding house, her red hair tucked well under her straw hat and her sunglasses on, she was grateful it was so warm. She could at least buy a newspaper and find a secluded place to sit and while away some of the day reading, during which time she'd hope to come up with a plan of what to do next.

An hour later, when she'd walked all around Kingsbridge, she was feeling less afraid. She'd walked right past Mrs Porter, the lady she used to housekeep for. Although the woman had looked right at Mabel, there was not even the slightest flicker of recognition.

She also saw Mildred Connor, a girl she'd been at school with, and although she'd never been a real friend, they'd known each other for at least fifteen years. She didn't even look twice at Mabel.

Mabel looked in several shops, but as they all seemed to have the same owners or assistants as when she was last there, she didn't go in. She was beginning to despair when she noticed one of the thatched cottages down by the Salcombe estuary had tables and chairs in the front garden and a sign offering refreshments.

Mabel remembered that it had been very dilapidated, and people said the old lady who lived there was feeble-minded. As it now looked smart, the walls white-washed, the thatch repaired, the windows gleaming and the garden bright with flowers, she was certain it had a new owner.

She was still cautious, though. After all, it could be owned now by a close relative and a native of Kingsbridge.

It was rather dark in the cottage, and she hesitated in the doorway. There were two small tables and chairs inside.

'Good morning,' a cheery voice called out, and a beaming, rotund woman wearing a white apron came through from the back of the cottage. 'What can I get you? Tea, coffee, breakfast or just a toasted tea cake? Would you like to sit out in the sunshine?'

Mabel smiled. She didn't know the woman. 'Tea and a tea cake would be lovely. And I will sit outside. It's far too nice today to be indoors.'

She sat with her back to the garden fence, just in case someone she knew came along. There were a few more people about now, but judging by the aimless manner in which they were walking, were probably holidaymakers.

When the lady came out with a pot of tea and the toasted tea cake, Mabel asked her the best way to get to Hallsands.

'Ooh, whatever do you want to go there for?' she said. 'It's a dreary place, too much sadness. Better to get a boat up to Salcombe.'

Mabel was pleased the woman didn't recognize her as a local through her accent.

'What sadness is that?' she asked.

'The houses swept away by the sea, and that poor girl went with them.'

Mabel hadn't expected a mention of her at all. 'How dreadful. I didn't know about that,' she replied, trying to keep her expression very neutral.

'Well, they always thought it were the sea that took 'er, but when her old man was found dead on the beach from being pushed off the cliff a while ago, the police think his ma did for both of 'em.'

Mabel's heart began to thump. 'His mother?'

The older woman shook her head, as if she couldn't imagine how anyone could do something so terrible. 'I haven't lived here long, so I don't know these folks, but from what I've heard, everyone there knew she was nasty to the girl. Yet she doted on her boy, even when he came home from France doolally from the guns. Never did get better – he was a sad sight, by all accounts. I was living in Salcombe when the girl went missing, but everyone here reckons the ma-in-law pushed her off the cliff in that bad storm. The police couldn't prove it, as they never found her body. But when her boy went too, they looked a bit closer. His grandfather had not long died, and he left his house to his grandson. There was also some compensation from the ruined house. They said she were an evil, mean woman, and she pushed her boy over

269

the edge so she could have it all and be free of looking after him.'

Mabel poured her tea, trying hard not to show how shocked she was at this news.

'They found her son's body, then?'

'Yes, fishermen found him early one morning on the beach. He'd been seen up on the cliff top with his ma the night before. Shocking business. So she were arrested and taken off to Plymouth Jail. They say she'll hang for certain.'

Mabel suddenly felt faint. Agnes was a horrible woman, and perhaps she might have wanted her daughter-in-law dead, but she wouldn't kill Martin, of that she was sure.

'Are you alright?' the café owner asked. 'You've gone a bit white.'

'I do feel a bit odd. I'd better pay you and go,' Mabel said quickly.

'I hope it wasn't me telling you what went on in Hallsands?'

'No, not at all,' Mabel said and got to her feet. 'It was fascinating.'

It was only eleven in the morning, and Mabel knew there was nothing further for her to discover. What she knew now had shaken her to the core, and all she wanted was to go home.

Mrs Brewer wasn't pleased to see Mabel back so soon, and even less pleased to find she wasn't staying another night. But Mabel refused to placate the woman by paying for another night.

'Your house is grubby, the bed was lumpy, and to offer

a breakfast of only toast or porridge is appalling,' she snapped at her. 'So I'll be off.'

Fortunately, there was a train due, and Mabel couldn't get on it quickly enough.

As the train chugged through sunlit pastures, Mabel's feelings were truly mixed. Even though she ought to feel some pleasure that there was nothing now to prevent her marrying Thomas, she couldn't take any joy in the news. It was shocking to think Martin had either fallen by accident from the cliff top or had taken his own life. And she was certain it was the latter; however he had died, it was surely better than living with shell shock, terrified of sudden noises, unable to communicate with others.

If it hadn't been for her disappearance, and Agnes being suspected of sending her to her death, would anyone really believe she had pushed her son over the cliff? Mabel didn't think so.

She thought back to her vision of Agnes crying and, as much as she hated her, she knew she couldn't let her hang for her son's death. She was the one person who knew how much the woman loved her son; she had watched her spoon-feed him, wash and change him when he was incontinent, and she'd never once complained about it.

Mabel had no idea what you had to do to stop a miscarriage of justice, but she knew it had to be done quickly, and it was then she decided not to go back to Dorchester. She wanted to go back to Clara, to Thomas too. But she needed to keep this potentially ruinous situation away from them. It wouldn't help Clara's career in illustration, or Thomas's as a lawyer, if they were seen to be associated with this. It could very easily come out, if Mabel had to take a stand in the witness box at Agnes's trial.

She would go to Mrs Hardy in Bristol. She would know who to approach to sort this out.

19

'I can't let her be hanged for this,' Mabel sobbed out to Mrs Hardy. 'That would be a real sin.'

'I agree totally, my dear,' Joan Hardy said. 'At least, in as far as you have to admit you ran away that night of the storm. I'm not totally convinced she didn't push her son off the cliff – looking after him must've been exhausting – but whether she did or not, that's for a judge and jury to decide. If you speak up for her, and say her son was the one person she cared about, then you've done the right thing. You can't do more.'

Joan had been astounded when she answered the knock on her door and found Mabel there. One look at the fright in her eyes was enough to know this wasn't a social call, and once she'd got the girl in, given her a cup of tea and then listened to the whole story, so much had fallen into place.

In the time Mabel had worked at Harley Place, Joan had sometimes wondered why the girl never spoke about her past. She told the brief story about her husband being killed in the Battle of the Somme, and how she'd left Plymouth to start a new life, but there were never any further details about the kind of home they'd had, about other family members, or even the little anecdotes most people shared when they made new friends.

Joan Hardy's heart went out to Mabel now she knew the

truth. It must have been so difficult for her to always be on her guard, taking care that she never slipped up and revealed her past. Then there was the fear too that she might be caught out one day. Some might say she was a hard-hearted floozy for leaving her shell-shocked husband. But there was no doubt Agnes Wellows drove her to it.

'I told you about my gentleman friend, Percy Holmes?' Joan said.

Mabel nodded.

'Well, his closest friend, John Baring, is a lawyer, so I am going to slip over to Percy in a little while and ask him to make an appointment for you to see Mr Baring. I've met him on several occasions. He's a very pleasant, kind-hearted man. He'll be able to tell you what you have to do.'

'Is it going to cost a lot of money?' Mabel asked nervously.

Joan Hardy smiled affectionately. 'I think it's quite possible he won't charge you anything, or just a nominal fee. He only has to find out who is defending Agnes and get in touch with that person and tell him about you.'

Joan made Mabel some scrambled eggs and toast. While she ate, Mabel told her friend about Thomas, her strange psychic experiences and her relationship with Clara.

'Do you love Thomas?' Joan asked.

'Yes, but all this is going to do him damage, isn't it? It's bad enough me not being of the same social class, but once all this comes out he definitely won't want to marry me.'

'Not necessarily. He sounds like a good man. But before you start telling him anything, you must first speak to John Baring and find out how much involvement you will have in Agnes's trial. Maybe you will only have to give a statement about how and when you ran away from Hallsands and your opinion that Agnes would never hurt her son. But I don't know, Mabel, I know nothing more about the law than what I read in the newspapers.'

'It's the newspapers I'm scared of,' Mabel admitted.

Joan patted Mabel's cheek. 'Take it one step at a time. Now you make yourself comfortable here, and I'll pop over to Percy's.'

Percy telephoned John Baring while Joan was with him, told him the gist of the story, and it was agreed that Mabel would go to his offices in Bristol's Queen Square the following morning at nine thirty.

Mabel slept fitfully in Joan's spare room. Joan had cleared out all the junk Mabel remembered, the walls had been papered and painted, and it was now a comfortable, pretty room. There were many improvements in the whole place; the stairs and landing had been decorated in pale blue, and a thick, dark blue carpet had been laid. There were new curtains in the living room too. However, Mabel's mind was not on the changes here but racing ahead to all the problems she might encounter in the next few weeks. She knew she should at least write to Thomas, but what would she say? He'd been told she'd gone to see a sick old friend. How could she suddenly turn that into being a witness in a murder trial?

While she knew from experience that problems always seemed insurmountable during the hours of darkness, that knowledge didn't help. She even imagined herself being sent to prison for abandoning her sick husband.

She left Harley Place well before nine to walk down to Queen Square. She wore her grey-and-white striped dress and put her hair up in a bun beneath her straw boater, as she thought her wild, curly red hair might give this lawyer the wrong impression of her.

Joan Hardy had said that Percy was very sympathetic when she explained the story to him, as was John Baring when he was told the bare bones of it.

'Neither man thought you were wicked to run from that awful woman,' Joan said. 'They both said you clearly have a big heart to want to help her now. So if those two men feel that way, I've no doubt everyone else will too.'

Mabel wished she could be that confident. It was another warm sunny day, but she seemed unable to notice the pretty gardens full of flowers, attractive window displays in the shops, or even bonny babies in perambulators. All she noticed was the number of limbless or blinded soldiers taking up positions to beg. There were dozens of thin, gaunt-faced children in rags, while so many wealthy people drove past them in their grand carriages without even noticing.

She was ten minutes early for her appointment, so she sat on a bench in Queen Square in the sunshine. She knew this once-impressive square, close to the docks, had been built for wealthy ship owners, slave traders and merchants in the 1700s. Those same rich people later moved up to new houses in Clifton, like the ones in Harley Place, to escape the terrible stink of the docks. After several years of floundering, a riot during which people were killed and houses destroyed, plus a series of other unfortunate events, it seemed this square with its central gardens was doomed.

But fortunately, it had just managed to survive because of its proximity to the business area of Bristol. Today it was still an oasis of greenery, and a source of much-needed calm as Mabel waited for her appointment with the lawyer.

John Baring was tall, stooped and thin, with a nose like a beak. Even his eyes were like a bird's – small, dark and bead-like. But despite his unprepossessing appearance, he had a warm smile and a beautiful, sonorous voice.

'Do come in, Mrs Brook,' he said, ushering her into a very elegant office lined with books. There was a magnificent white marble fireplace, and the walls were covered in dark green paper with a little gold motif. 'I can take no credit for the office decor,' he said, perhaps seeing her surprise. 'I inherited it from a senior partner.'

'It's rather lovely,' she said, suddenly feeling completely overawed.

'Now I know the background of your story,' he said, as if sensing her nervousness. 'You disappeared from a village in Devon in a storm. Your husband was suffering very badly from shell shock. But I understand your fleeing was due to your overbearing mother-in-law?'

'Yes, she sent me out in the middle of the storm, to the house my husband and I owned, to collect more of our things. It was extremely dangerous. As you may know, the row of houses were all destroyed that night, and it was already nearly pitch dark when she sent me down there. You can have no idea how terrifying it was. The lane was strewn with shingle, and the waves were already smashing on to the road.' Mabel paused for a moment. 'She was impossible. Always on at me. Nothing I did was right, and poor Martin didn't even know me. He just sat in a chair by the fire at his grandfather's house, and all his mother's nastiness washed over him. I knew, once my house was gone, I would have to live there in his grandfather's house, with Agnes. I couldn't bear the thought of it. The idea even crossed my mind that she'd insisted I went down there in the hope that I'd be swept away. But I grabbed the last of my things, just as the sea rushed into the house, and it was then I decided I wouldn't go back. I'd disappear.'

'I can't say I blame you,' he said with a wry smile. 'As I understand it, you ended up in Bristol, working under the indomitable Mrs Hardy? And you called yourself Mabel Brook. Your real name being Betty Wellows. Is that correct?'

'Yes, sir,' she said.

'Your mistress, Mrs Gladsworthy, died and all the staff at Harley Place were dismissed, but the sister-in-law of your mistress recommended you for a position as housekeeper in Dorchester?'

'Yes, sir.'

'Did you ever seek to go back to Devon and find out if your husband's health had improved? Did you keep in touch with anyone there?'

'No, sir. I didn't dare. I was, and still am, happy working for Clara May. My parents were both dead, and I had no other family.'

'So you never knew Agnes Wellows was suspected of killing you?'

'No, it never occurred to me she might be. I thought everyone would think I'd been washed out to sea and drowned.'

'So what prompted you to go back to Devon?'

Mabel didn't want to say anything about psychic powers; that might make him think she was strange. 'I had a very real dream that Agnes was crying. So real, it shook me up. She never cried, except when they first brought Martin home from France, when he was wounded, and then she howled at the hospital. Dreaming about her crying, I felt sure something bad had happened, perhaps that Martin was dead. So I had to find out.'

'And you were told that Agnes was in Plymouth prison, charged with the murder of both you and her son?'

'Yes, that's right. Obviously, she didn't kill me, and however horrible she was to me, I know she wouldn't kill Martin. I was so distraught, I came to see Mrs Hardy.'

'Well, my dear, today I will ascertain details of the charges against her, and if she has a defence barrister. If so, I will then get in touch with him and tell him that you are very much alive, and that despite not liking Agnes Wellows, you are prepared to give evidence that you do not believe she would kill her son.'

'Does that mean I will have to go to court?' Mabel was hoping to hear that wouldn't be necessary.

'I can't say yet,' John admitted. 'You being alive and well more or less cuts the prosecution in half; the defence barrister may say that submitting a testimony from you is enough. But he is equally likely to insist that you attend the trial to support any other evidence he might be submitting. Is there a reason you couldn't be present?'

Mabel took a deep breath before answering. 'I've made a new life for myself in Dorchester, it could be difficult for me to have all this come to light.'

'Do I sense a young man?' he asked, a hint of a smile playing on his lips.

'Yes, there is someone, and he knows nothing of this. Furthermore, he is a lawyer, and he comes from a very well-respected family. This would shock everyone.'

'Yes, I can see that. You have been very brave and forthright in seeking to do the right thing, and it would be incredibly sad to see your life turned upside down by that very courage. But this young man, whatever the outcome, should know about this. You, of all people, must have learned how a big secret can haunt you?'

Mabel knew Mr Baring was right. 'Easier said than done,' she said glumly. 'But I will tell him. It's just a question of when and how.'

The appointment was over; Mr Baring advised her to stay in Bristol, at least until he had spoken to both the police and the defence barrister in Plymouth.

When Mabel asked him about his fees, he shook his head. 'I know Mrs Hardy is very fond of you, and I can understand why. I am impressed by your courage and your sense of honour, so there are no fees, Mrs Brook. And I'll be in touch just as soon as I know something.'

Mabel walked back to Clifton in a daze. On the one hand, she felt a burden had been lifted from her shoulders, with John Baring believing in her and helping her.

But on the other hand, there was Thomas. The thought of having to tell him about all this was too tough – impossible, even. She knew the right thing to do; she should write him a letter tonight and tell him absolutely everything. But although she was certain he'd stand by her, if she had to give evidence at the trial, he would do that because he was noble, and he believed in supporting his friends.

That wasn't the same as wanting to marry her, though. Or even continuing to see her as his ladyfriend. He would know that he had to end their relationship, or kiss his career goodbye.

John Baring might see her as brave and forthright, and Thomas probably would too, because they were men who understood human frailty. But once word got out around Dorchester that she'd faked her death to get away from a shell-shocked husband, she would be a social leper.

Who could blame people for their reaction? There was scarcely one family in Dorchester who hadn't been touched by the war. Husbands, fathers, brothers and sons died. Countless more had recently returned with grievous injuries. A great many had shell shock too, and their wives and families buckled down to help and support them. She would never be able to convince people that her reason for fleeing was her evil mother-in-law, especially now she was going to speak up for her in court.

Mabel stopped at the post office to telephone Clara, as Joan didn't have one at home. As she was worried about the expense, she only told Clara the main details, promising to write fully tonight. She also told her she was in Bristol, with Joan Hardy, and not to tell Thomas anything, but she would write to him.

Joan Hardy embraced Mabel when she got in and let her cry on her shoulder. She was another one who had sympathy for people's frailties, so she completely understood the dilemma Mabel now found herself in.

'If you'd done nothing – let that woman hang, and kept it to yourself – sooner or later the truth about you would've come out. You would be the villain then. But you made the choice to own up, completely selflessly, because you are a good, honest person. Now dry your eyes and sit down to write that letter to Thomas. If he's half the man you think he is, he won't abandon you.'

The letter took many hours to write, and Mabel cried endlessly as she wrote. She started out with just the drama of the storm and how she decided to run away from the village. But then she realized she needed Thomas to understand the full picture of her life in Hallsands, from meeting Martin, their marriage, then her father being lost at sea. It was only as she wrote the letter that she realized Agnes had taken control of her at that point, manipulating, demeaning and making unreasonable demands. But Mabel also saw that she had let it happen, because she was young, and she'd lost both her parents. Perhaps she foolishly thought Agnes would come to love her.

Moving on to her life once Martin had enlisted, she recalled the acceleration in Agnes's nastiness. Looking back at that time, Mabel wondered why she didn't think of moving to Kingsbridge, away from her mother-in-law's influence. She supposed it was the little house, all those happy memories of her parents, and the loving sweetness of her marriage to Martin.

Eventually, she came to the main issue, the discovery that Agnes was in prison, accused of killing both her son and daughter-in-law, and that Mabel felt she had to speak up for the woman and say she would never have killed her son. Finally, she told Thomas about John Baring.

The last paragraph, winding up the letter, was the hard-est to write.

I understand completely that this will all come as a terrible shock to you, Thomas. I am obviously not the person you thought I was. I wish now I had been brave enough to tell you about my past before. I will completely understand if you wish to sever all connections with me, and I fervently hope that when this trial begins, the newspaper reports do not reach your family, friends and clients.

She signed off, telling him she loved him and was so sorry.

Once she'd put the letter in an envelope and addressed it to him, she broke down again in tears.

Writing to Clara wasn't so bad. After all, she knew about the trial. But what was hard to bear was the thought that if Thomas rejected her, she'd have to find a new job too.

20

On Friday afternoon, John Baring telephoned his friend Percy to get a message to Mabel quickly, asking her to meet him at Percy's house at five o'clock that day.

'Why doesn't he ask me to go to his office? What can be so important it couldn't wait till Monday?' Mabel asked Joan. Percy had called at the house briefly to deliver the message, then left without further explanation.

'It must be something important, but I expect he's in court all day. As he lives near here, he probably wanted to save you and him time. Don't worry about it, I'll come over with you.'

Mabel couldn't help but worry. She spent the rest of the afternoon imagining all sorts of different problems, including the possibility that she might be arrested. But when Joan took her over to Percy's house just before five, she liked him and his house at first sight, and felt herself starting to relax.

Percy was every inch a true gentleman; he was tall, slender, elegantly dressed with a little goatee beard, fair hair and brilliant, twinkly blue eyes.

His house was in a Georgian terrace looking out on to the Clifton Suspension Bridge and the Avon Gorge. He liked colour in his living room, with a navy-blue sofa, bright yellow walls, and cushions that were vivid splashes of red and green. He had a piano, which Joan said he played very well, and thousands of books lined the walls.

'Joan and I will retire to the dining room when John gets here,' he said as he shook Mabel's hand and said how much he'd been looking forward to meeting her. 'I hope you didn't think it presumptuous of me to suggest Baring met you here? With you just a short walk away, and John only living around the corner in the Mall, it seemed ideal.'

'Not a bit presumptuous. And it's good to meet you, sir,' Mabel said.

'Not so much of the sir, it's plain Percy to you,' he said with a smile. 'Joan speaks of you so often, I'd begun to think of you as family. And now, at last, we meet!'

He went on to tell her he'd met two of the Bedford girls, at the Home and Colonial.

'What ghastly women,' he exclaimed. 'They are as rude and unpleasant as their father. What a shame his sister left them number six. I'd have sooner left it to charity than that man. The girls were being so obnoxious to the staff at the shop, acting like they were royalty, and everyone else dirt beneath their feet. I have it on good authority that the family isn't liked by anyone.'

Mabel would have loved to hear more, but John Baring was at the door.

Joan and Percy disappeared immediately after greeting him, and Mabel invited Mr Baring to sit down.

'Agnes Wellows's trial begins on Monday,' he said, 'hence my need to speak to you quickly. She is being defended by a barrister named Haines. I have to say, when I spoke to him on the telephone this morning, he didn't seem pleased or relieved that you were alive. Indeed, he reacted as if I was in some way attempting to sabotage his defence. I explained carefully that Agnes Wellows had ill-treated you and that you ran away from her, leaving your incapacitated husband too, because you could no longer bear what she was doing to you.

'I then told him that, despite your dislike and fear of Agnes, you had come forward voluntarily when you heard she had been charged with both her son's and your own murder, because you don't believe the woman capable of killing her son.'

Mabel was shocked to learn that the trial was so soon, but Baring told her Agnes had been arrested more than six weeks ago, and people suspected of murder were usually tried quickly.

'For your sake, I am glad it will begin on Monday, you don't want this hanging over you for weeks. But I am concerned for Agnes Wellows. Haines doesn't sound efficient or experienced in capital charges. At first, he said that a written testimony from you would be enough, but then he changed his mind and said he might want to call you as a witness. To be frank, Mabel, I fear for your mother-in-law if he's the only person between her and the gallows. I don't think he will push himself to prove her innocent.'

'That's terrible,' Mabel gasped. As much as she disliked Agnes, everyone deserved someone fighting their corner.

'A sloppy, inadequate defence is common for poor people who don't have their own lawyer,' Baring sighed. 'They are allocated someone, often only minutes before the trial commences, and the legal representatives are usually inexperienced and poorly trained. I've been at trials where the defence doesn't even remember the name of the person he's supposed to be representing.'

'So what do I have to do?'

'You must be at Plymouth court on Monday morning by nine. Someone at the court will tell you where to wait. Let them know you are a witness for Agnes Wellows. You will, of course, need to use your real name, Betty Wellows.

'Make yourself known to Haines. I'm hoping that when he meets you face-to-face, it might shame him into trying harder for Agnes. I wish I could come with you, my dear, but I have to represent someone on a serious fraud charge here in Bristol on Monday.'

Mabel did her best to give him a bright smile. 'I'll be fine on my own, sir, you've already been exceptionally kind and helpful.'

'Try not to worry about reporters,' he advised her. 'With luck on your side, it might only be printed in a local newspaper. Also, they will probably only hear your real name, so there is really no reason for anyone in Dorchester to associate Mabel Brook with this trial. As for your young man, he should be proud of you for doing the right thing.'

Baring had to go, but Percy insisted Joan and Mabel stayed and had supper with him.

'My housekeeper made me a steak and kidney pie this morning, and it's huge. If you don't share it, I'll be eating it till halfway through next week.'

It was clear to Mabel as the evening progressed that Joan and Percy were far more than just friends. There was a closeness between them, the way Percy smiled at Joan, and laid his hand on her shoulder when he was speaking. Joan barely took her eyes off him, and there was a flirtatious banter between them that made Mabel feel hopeful for them both.

Percy was a widower, but he'd lost his wife while still a young man. Joan had said he was a professor at the university, but he didn't say anything about his work. He spoke of several charities he supported, and that he was on the board of governors at a school and a mental asylum, so Mabel had the idea he enjoyed inherited wealth, along with his salary from the university.

'Both the school and the asylum were very badly run until I got involved, twenty years ago now,' he said. 'I cannot abide cruelty to the poorest in our society,' he continued with some passion. 'Joan feels the same, which pleases me, and we hope we can work together on some projects in the future.'

There was a lovely moment, later in the evening, when Percy played the piano and asked Joan to sing. One of the songs was 'By the Light of the Silvery Moon', and it was clear to Mabel that they'd been practising together for some time.

Percy insisted on walking them home later, one on each arm, even though it was no further than five hundred yards and still daylight. At the door he kissed Mabel's cheek and wished her well for Monday.

'Speak up clearly, look the judge in the eyes, and don't let anyone intimidate you,' he said. 'But I know you will be fine – you were born a fighter for justice.'

'Percy is such a good man,' Mabel said, once they were inside. 'You should marry him. You look like a happily married couple already.'

She noted how Joan blushed. 'I suppose I'm scared,' she admitted. 'He has asked me, but I said it was too soon.'

'Scared of what? Going to bed with him?'

Joan hung her head, blushing even more furiously. That told Mabel it was indeed the problem.

'I can imagine why it scares you, I wouldn't mind betting you haven't even kissed a man in years. Am I right?'

Joan nodded.

'Then practise kissing Percy,' she suggested. 'I don't mean on the cheek, at the front door, either. But when you are alone. If you get the feeling you want more, then it's only a hop, skip and a jump into bed.'

Joan giggled with embarrassment and scuttled off to the kitchen, no doubt cooling her flaming face with a cold, wet cloth.

Mabel had no idea how long the trial would last. Baring had said it could last a week, if there were a lot of witnesses, but conversely it could be over in just one or two days. To be at Plymouth court by nine on Monday morning, she needed to catch a train there on Sunday. That meant a minimum of two nights in a hotel or boarding house. Fortunately, when leaving Dorchester, she'd had the presence of mind to bring her savings with her, just in case of an emergency.

She was terrified, though. She had only been to Plymouth three or four times and hadn't much liked the hustle and bustle of the place then. That shouldn't be a problem now – after all, she'd got used to Bristol, and that was a bigger city. But not only was she nervous of seeing Agnes, she was afraid that some of her old neighbours would come to the court.

There was no doubt in her mind that they'd all be wanting to see Agnes sentenced to death; they certainly wouldn't want her back in their village. But none of them would be expecting to see Betty Wellows there in the courtroom.

Would they understand why she ran away that night of the storm?

She felt they might think her spineless. Living as her old neighbours did, at the mercy of the sea, they were a tough, blinkered breed who had their own set of rules. To them it was inexcusable to run out on a husband, even if he was a drunk or a wife beater. As for leaving a sick man, that would be considered beyond callous. They would have been more inclined to support her if she'd pushed Agnes off the cliff.

Mabel was very withdrawn on Saturday. She had hoped for a reply to the letter she'd written to Thomas; not knowing his reaction to it was agony. Added to that, her fear of going to Plymouth made it impossible to eat; she was worrying about everything, from where she would stay, to how the prosecution would question her.

Joan left her alone, getting on with some chores in her home as Mabel sat in a chair staring into space.

In the afternoon, Joan suggested they went across the suspension bridge and had a walk in Leigh Woods.

'That would be nice,' Mabel said. 'I'm sorry if I've been strange today.'

Joan shrugged. 'Strange? I think you are behaving

perfectly normally under the circumstances. But fresh air and sunshine will do you good. You don't need to talk, if you don't want to.'

Mabel remained silent for quite some time as they walked, but gradually the peace of the woods, the dappled sunshine coming through the leaves and the sound of birdsong, all began to make her feel she wanted to communicate with Joan.

Perhaps Joan sensed this, because she reminded Mabel of how, at her interview in Harley Place, she'd said something about catching mackerel.

'You never mentioned fishing again after you started work at number six,' she said. 'Of course, I know why now – any nostalgic anecdotes might have made you say too much. But tell me about growing up in Hallsands now?'

Mabel told her about standing up on the cliff, waiting to spot the shoals of herring, then running like mad down into the village to alert her father and the other fishermen. 'I was always the fastest,' she remembered. 'I loved everything about fishing: the boats, the sea, tough men like my father, the taste of a freshly caught herring or mackerel. I even liked the smell!' She laughed at that. 'I think I've grown out of that now.'

'Tell me about your mother?' Joan said gently.

'I think I look a lot like her. The same red, curly hair and green eyes. She was always happy. She'd met my father when she was sixteen, married within a year, and I was born the year after. I can remember how she used to take a chair to the door of our cottage and just watch the sea. She told me she used to sit there to feed me when I was a baby, so I suppose that's why I like the sea so much too. But then she died of blood poisoning after a miscarriage. She'd had another little girl, who died as a baby, before that. I used to hear my father crying in the night, and I tried so hard to fill Ma's place so he wouldn't cry. Of course, back then, I didn't know the love you feel for your wife and the love for a child are different.'

'I'm sure you did fill that big hole, though,' Joan said.

'I suppose I did, in part, but he was never quite the same again. I used to make apple dumplings for him, because Mother always made them. I suppose I was trying to fill her shoes.

'When I met Martin, and he went fishing with Father, I think he felt happy again then. He told me on our wedding day that Martin was the man he had always wanted for me. After I ran away, I kept remembering those words. It made me feel I'd let my father down.' She paused, wiping a tear from her eye. 'He was lost at sea in a storm. That was a terribly sad time, but Martin was wonderful. He always knew the right thing to do or say for me. Then the war came, and Martin enlisted. Perhaps it was as well Father died without knowing what was to come.'

'You've had some tough times, my dear,' Joan sighed. 'But in a way, I think your early years were luckier for you than mine were. My mother died when I was four, I don't really remember her, and my father just disappeared after leaving me with his sister. I didn't have the same hardships as you – there was enough food, clothes, warmth and comfort. At fourteen I was put into service and there I remained until I went to work for the Gladsworthys.'

'So why do you think I was luckier than you?' Mabel asked, puzzled by that remark.

'You were loved, Mabel. I never was. My aunt was a cold fish. She made sure I had everything I needed to stay alive, but there was no affection, no real interest in me. That's almost certainly why I am afraid to marry Percy now, and why throughout my life I've kept my distance from people. But you, Mabel, you just know how to give and accept love, that was your parents' legacy to you. There's a warmth in you that draws people to you.'

Mabel stood still, turning towards Joan. 'But I feel warmth in you too,' she said. 'I didn't feel it immediately when I got to number six, but it grew little by little. And I feel that warmth and closeness between you and Percy. It's not too late for you both. You aren't old!'

'What a long way you've come,' Joan laughed, linking her hand through Mabel's arm. 'I had to teach you so much – how to lay a table, make a bed correctly, and countless other things – but you learned so fast. Anyone now would assume you had a privileged background. But it isn't just that you know how things should be done. It's that you understand people, and you are at ease with all walks of life.

'But enough of that . . . tell me about Carsten, the German. You were always a bit vague in your letters about him.'

Mabel found it was good to talk about Carsten, remembering how he looked, his laughter and how he made her feel special. 'I'll never be able to forget how he died,' she finished up. 'That was just so terrible, but I'll never be sorry I met him.'

'Sometimes I think we need to experience true sorrow,

if only to appreciate the good things that happen to us,' Joan said. 'I know you'll be fine at the court on Monday. And in a couple of months' time, you'll look back on it all and be glad you faced it head-on.'

By the time they got home, it was nearly six in the evening, and Mabel was feeling pleasantly tired from the long walk, and much calmer. It had been good to open up about her past, and perhaps timely too, for the day after tomorrow she was going to be confronted with it again. Remembering the happy times now would help her cope if the prosecution tried to belittle her.

They made the tea together, and afterwards played a couple of card games. Then Mabel had a bath and washed her hair, in readiness for the journey to Plymouth the next day.

Mabel was woken by the sound of church bells. She knew that meant it was nearly seven, and she was astounded she'd slept so well. Hanging on the back of her bedroom door, she saw her dark green shantung costume with the flattering peplum jacket. After she'd gone to bed, Joan must have pressed it for her and primped up the green hat that went with it.

They had talked about what she should wear yesterday. Mabel thought she should wear black, but Joan didn't agree.

'You will not creep into that courtroom like a frightened little mouse,' she said vehemently. 'You must stand tall, and look confident, honest and sassy. You can't do that in black. Your skin glows in that green costume, it makes your hair like fire. You are a beauty, Mabel, and I'm not going to let you hide that under widow's weeds.'

21

Mabel watched the man coming towards her along the marble-floored court corridor and guessed it was Haines, purely because his walk matched what John Baring had said about him.

He shuffled, rather than walked, or at least didn't lift his feet right off the floor. To her that signified someone lazy who would always take the easiest route. His shoes were not polished, and his black lawyer's gown looked greasy; as for his wig, that looked a little too big, and messy, as if he was in the habit of throwing it on to the floor.

As he approached Mabel, she saw he was an unattractive man, sallow, with pockmarked skin and an exceptionally large forehead. If she was in trouble and he was sent to defend her, she thought she'd make a break for it before the trial began.

'Mr Haines?' she asked, standing up to greet him. 'I'm Betty Wellows.' It sounded so strange to give that name, yet when she married Martin, she'd delighted in it.

'Good morning, Mrs Wellows,' he said. At least he had a good, deep voice. She had expected him to have a shrill one. 'I trust you managed to find a decent hotel last night? I understand you had to come from Bristol.'

'Yes, I did, and the hotel is fine, thank you.' That, at least, had proved far nicer than she'd expected.

A couple on the train had recommended it to her.

Outside, it looked disappointingly neglected. But inside, it was a different story, with traditional fringed rugs, a spotlessly clean black-and-white tiled floor, and a sparkling chandelier over the reception desk. A young lad carried her bag to her room, which was almost as luxurious and well appointed as the hotel where she'd stayed in Bath with Clara.

Last night, as she undressed to go to bed, she almost laughed at herself for being so critical – after all, this was only the second hotel she'd stayed in in her whole life, and both were far superior to the way she'd lived in Devon.

'I have seen Agnes fleetingly this morning,' Haines said. 'She was, of course, extremely surprised to hear you are alive and are going to be a witness for her defence. I will tell you now, though, Mrs Wellows is suspicious of your intentions. Of course, she is afflicted with the problem of thinking the worst of everyone.'

Mabel couldn't help but smile. 'Yes, that's her, never a good word to say about anyone.'

'You are the only defence witness,' he said. 'I have been unable to find anyone else, not even her vicar or doctor, who would speak up for her.'

Mabel nodded. 'Is that why you've already thrown in the towel?'

The man took a step back from her, his expression one of shock and indignation. 'I have not! What makes you say such a thing?'

'I know Agnes well, remember.' Mabel shrugged. 'She doesn't endear herself to people. But believe me, she did love Martin. She hated me because he loved me more, but I know she wouldn't harm him.'

'Well, if you can speak up and let the jury hear that, loud and clear, then perhaps we have a chance of her being acquitted. I have to say, you are not what I expected, Mrs Wellows.'

Again Mabel smiled. 'You expected a timid version of Agnes? A slovenly fishwife? I was never that, not even when I was gutting fish and mending nets.'

The look in his shoe-button dark eyes was one of admiration, and suddenly Mabel felt brave.

The court door opened and a clerk looked out to call Haines in.

'You have to wait here until you are called,' Haines said, tucking his file of papers under his arm. 'It may be a long wait. And you must not talk to any witnesses for the prosecution.' He glanced further along the corridor, towards the entrance hall.

It was only after he'd gone into the court, and the door had closed behind him, that Mabel saw there were three people sitting about twenty-five yards away. They hadn't been there when she came in, and they were huddled together in conversation. At a second glance she saw one was Jack Talgarth, a fisherman who had often worked with her father. Sitting next to him was Mrs Mary George, Mabel's old neighbour in the cottages that were destroyed, and Mr Barnaby, an elderly man who used to come and stay with some relatives in the village for around six weeks every summer.

Mary was in her mid-thirties, with four children, a tubby but pretty woman with long dark hair, flashing dark eyes and a mouth like a sewer. But she knew better than anyone how hateful Agnes had been towards Betty, especially once Martin had gone off to France. She'd often stood up for her, screamed ripe abuse at Agnes, then made Betty cups of tea and offered her a shoulder to cry on. It was all Mabel could do not to go to her now and be enveloped in one of her fierce hugs.

But of course she couldn't. Nor could she hug Jack Talgarth, her father's younger friend, who often gave her a piggyback up to the cottages when she was a little girl and bought her a few sweets when they took the fish into Plymouth to sell. She guessed he was around forty now, his face as brown and wrinkled as a raisin, just the way her father's had been.

Mr Barnaby was the only one she didn't know well. People said he had come to Hallsands for his honeymoon, thirty years ago, and when his wife died years later, he came back there to remember her.

It was well over an hour before the first witness, Jack Talgarth, was called. As he went into the courtroom, he winked at her, and she was reminded of how he used to do that when he saw her in chapel with her father.

She wondered what evidence he was going to give. She remembered him pulling the boat up on the beach with her father, late one afternoon, before she and Martin were married. She was sitting mending a net, when Agnes suddenly appeared above them on the lane and began shouting. She wanted to know where Martin was, and when they acted vague, she accused Jack and Bert of covering up for him. It transpired later that Martin had gone into Kingsbridge to buy a birthday present for Betty, but neither Jack nor Bert wanted to admit that in front of her, as it would spoil her surprise on the day.

Jack, who was always one to make a bit of mischief, called back, 'We sent him round to the Hut, so he knows what to do when he gets married.' The Hut was a joke amongst the fisherman, a wooden shack said to be near Kingsbridge, where you could buy a loose woman and a beer. It didn't really exist.

Agnes flew off the handle, shouting that she wasn't going to let her boy work with depraved men like them, and how her dear departed husband hadn't made sure the boy got a good education for filthy thugs like them to lead him astray.

The two men laughed their heads off when Agnes left. But Mabel was scared, because Martin's mother was always saying cutting things to her, about her being a tomboy, or her hair needing a good brush. Mabel sensed then that once Martin and she were married, Agnes was going to be trouble.

After Jack had gone into the court, Mabel got out her book, E. M. Forster's *A Room With a View*, which Joan had lent her. She'd started it on the train journey but found it hard to concentrate. If she had to sit on a hard bench for several hours, she might be able to lessen the tedium with an absorbing story.

The courtroom door opened again, about forty minutes after Jack had gone in, and this time it was Mary who was called. She glanced at Mabel as she went in, and frowned, as if not believing what she'd seen. So perhaps the three witnesses hadn't been told she was alive. And Jack only winked because he winked at all women.

It seemed longer still before the door opened for the third time and Mr Barnaby was called. It was strangely quiet in the corridor now. Earlier, there had been people milling around, down at the entrance hall, but perhaps they were all involved in other trials now.

Then just as Mabel felt she must use the toilet or burst, the door opened, and Haines came out.

'The court is in recess, until two,' he said. 'I suggest you go and get some luncheon. There's a good place across the road.'

'How is the trial going?' she asked, shocked that he didn't make that news his priority.

'Fast,' he said with a smirk. 'I think we'll be done today. But unless you can perform miracles, she's going to hang.'

'But why? The judge must know I'm alive?'

'Yes, but the witnesses have all painted a picture of a woman who stamped on anyone that got in her way. Mr Talgarth also pointed out that Martin's grandfather had left his cottage to Martin, and he was due some compensation for the cottage that was washed into the sea. That's a powerful motive for killing, even if it's your son. The woman, Mrs George, she said that Agnes had lost patience with Martin too; she'd been heard shouting at him many times. Then Mr Barnaby saw her fighting with her son on the cliff top. She was pulling Martin around by his arms, and he was trying to get free. He said it was dusk, and he was getting ready for bed, but he got dressed again to go and intervene. When he got outside, they were nowhere to be seen, but Martin was found on the foot of the cliff the following morning.'

'It's far more likely he flung himself over the top later,' Mabel argued. 'I don't believe she pushed him.'

'I could believe anything of her, she's a horrifying

woman,' he said, dabbing at his face with a handkerchief. 'I'll see you back here at two. I think you'll be called straight after that.'

Mabel couldn't eat a meal; she just went to a tea shop and had tea and a rock cake, and read a little more. Then she walked for a while. But the streets were hot and crowded, it felt as if a storm was on its way, and so she turned back to sit in the cool foyer of the court.

She wondered if the witnesses had all gone home. They hadn't come out through the door they went in by. She wondered too if there were many people watching the trial. And indeed what the inside of the courtroom looked like.

It was just a few minutes after two when she was called in. The first thing that struck her was how gloomy the room was, as the windows were all high up and the walls panelled with dark wood. There was a gallery above the court, which was packed with observers. She saw too that the three witnesses were sitting on a bench at the back of the court.

But the thing that shook her the most wasn't the amount of people watching, or the gloom, but Agnes.

She was standing in the dock, staring balefully at Mabel. She looked old and very thin, her face the colour of putty, and she wore a shapeless grey dress that must have been from the prison where she was being held. Even her hair, which Mabel remembered being a sandy brown, was now almost white, scraped back into a bun, but so sparse that her scalp showed through. Only her eyes remained the same, still blazing the way Mabel remembered, as if she'd been born angry.

Everyone stood for the judge to come back in, and it was only then that Mabel noted the jury. They were all men, a mixture of well dressed and affluent, shabby and gaunt, some as young as twenty-five and two who looked closer to fifty. The only thing unifying them was that they were all studying her intently.

She was so nervous, her hands were clammy with sweat. When she was sworn in on the Bible, she could barely say the words.

Then the prosecution barrister, a burly man with a huge stomach and a red nose, approached the witness box. His first question was, 'Can I rely on you, Mrs Wellows?'

'Well, yes,' she replied, a little puzzled.

'It won't take almost three years, then, before you tell the truth?'

Mabel knew then what was coming, a character assassination. 'No, sir, I will tell the truth right now,' she said, looking straight at him.

'We got word only a couple of days ago that you were not, as thought, drowned in the sea near the village of Hallsands, but very much alive and living in Bristol under an assumed name. Mrs Agnes Wellows, your mother-in-law, had been arrested and charged with your murder. When you disappeared, did you not think to tell someone back in Hallsands that you were going? Or were you too ashamed to admit you were running off because you'd had enough of an overbearing relative and a shell-shocked husband?'

'On the night in question I was far too distressed and frightened to do anything but run. And for your information, as soon as I discovered Agnes Wellows had been charged with my murder, I spoke to a lawyer who contacted this court,' she said defiantly. 'Why I left Hallsands is nothing to do with anyone else, anyway. It isn't a criminal offence. I have come here of my own free will to tell the court I don't believe Agnes could kill her son. She is a hateful woman, but she loved him.'

A ripple of shock at her boldness went around the gallery.

'Mrs Wellows, you will answer questions when I put them to you,' he said curtly.

'Then ask me some sensible ones,' she retorted.

This time it was a ripple of laughter that went around the gallery.

She could see she was rattling the prosecution barrister, but she was angry now and determined not to be bullied as if she were a criminal.

'Tell me what occurred on the 27th of January, 1917,' he said. 'If you can manage that.'

'I was in Tern Cottage, the house belonging to my husband's grandfather. My mother-in-law lived there too. My husband was also staying there because he couldn't manage the steep path down to our cottage. The day before, there had been a terrible storm, and at high tide our cottage and the others on the lane down to the sea were in danger of being washed away. On January the 27th, the following day, it was thought the cottages would fall into the sea at the next high tide.

'Everyone who lived in these cottages had left to stay with friends and relatives. But in the late afternoon of the 27th, when the storm was in full spate, Agnes Wellows insisted I went down to our cottage to get the rest of our things. I refused to go, because it was almost dark and extremely dangerous, but she ridiculed me. And so, in the end, I went.

'It was terrifying, the steep lane was strewn with shingle, the wind so strong I had to clutch at walls to stay upright. The waves were already washing into the houses, and it wasn't even high tide yet. I managed to wade in, go upstairs and pack a bag with the few personal items left, and just seconds after I got out, a huge wave washed in, taking the last of the furniture with it. At that point I realized that Agnes Wellows had sent me there, hoping I'd be swept into the sea.'

Haines objected to that remark, saying it was just her opinion, not a fact.

His objection was upheld, and Mabel continued to tell how she suddenly decided she wouldn't go back to Tern Cottage, to Agnes and Martin. She walked on, through the storm, to Kingsbridge and then on to Totnes.

'And where were you going? Or maybe I should ask to whom were you going? Was there a boyfriend or lover you were running to?'

'Certainly not,' she retorted, angry at the suggestion. 'I had no clear plan at all. I made the decision on the spur of the moment, because I couldn't take Agnes's nastiness a moment longer. She had taken over nursing Martin when he came out of hospital. She barely let me near him, so it wasn't as if I was leaving him without anyone to care for him.'

The barrister went on to ask what she'd done since, but she sensed he'd lost interest in riling her, and his questions soon petered out.

Then it was Haines's turn to question her. He asked about the ownership of the destroyed cottage, and wanted to know who stood to inherit Tern Cottage from old Mr Wellows, and get the compensation for the home that had been hers.

'Well, Martin, of course,' she said.

He went on then to ask how she had managed financially while Martin was in France.

'I shared his pay with my mother-in-law,' she said. 'But I worked as a housekeeper too in Kingsbridge.'

'Agnes Wellows didn't work, then?'

'No, she didn't see why she should. She had her widow's pension. She didn't have to pay rent, either, to her father-in-law.'

'So she was a woman who thought she should be provided for?'

Mabel couldn't see that this line of questioning was helping Agnes at all. If anything, it was helping to support the idea that she killed Martin to make life easier for herself.

'Excuse me, Mr Haines, but how about asking me why I believe Agnes couldn't have killed her son?'

Someone in the gallery clapped, and a ripple of laughter ran around the court.

She could see Haines didn't like that. 'Please enlighten us,' he said waspishly.

'Martin was her life. Until he was wounded in France, he was strong, handsome, intelligent and kind. That was the man I fell in love with and married. Agnes had a happy marriage too, until her husband tragically died, and Martin was a reminder of that happy marriage and the qualities she'd loved in her husband.

'It is true she became an unpleasant harridan of a woman, but she had nursed her husband for two years before he died, and the savings they had, which were intended to pay for an apprenticeship for Martin, soon disappeared with no wage coming in. She hadn't a penny left when her husband died, and she lost her home too. Yet however embittered she was, I have seen her spoon-feeding Martin like a baby when he first came home from France and couldn't even hold a knife and fork. She got up in the night to soothe him when his terrible nightmares came, she took the trouble to shave him every day, and she kept him clean and well fed. She always thought he would get better in time.

'In my opinion, knowing both my husband and his mother well, I would say he'd had enough of being frightened by sudden noises and remembering all the horrors of the trenches, and he threw himself off that cliff so his mother could be free again.'

'I think the young Mrs Wellows has said all there is to say in defence of the accused,' the judge said. He smiled at Mabel in reassurance that she'd done a superb job. 'Let us now hear the summing up of the case.'

Mabel was led to the bench at the back of the court, where the other witnesses were sitting. Mary reached out for her hand and squeezed it affectionately. All at once, Mabel felt the kind of love she'd known when her mother was alive, coming home from school to be enveloped in a warm hug. Mary's touch had taken her home.

22

The barrister for the prosecution took his stand close to the jury, taking his time, looking along the two benches at each man in turn.

'You've heard some conflicting accounts about the accused,' he began. 'But I would advise you to listen to your inner voice and think which of the witnesses has given us the most realistic view of her.

'Mr Barnaby is totally unbiased, as he only knew the Wellows family by sight. He saw a scuffle between Agnes Wellows and her son, Martin, on the cliff top at dusk, and the next morning Martin Wellows lay dead at the foot of the cliff.

'Mrs George, who has been a lifetime neighbour of the Wellows family, clearly dislikes Agnes Wellows. So her evidence about seeing Agnes going into Tern Cottage alone, that same evening, is not necessarily reliable. She might have mixed that evening up with a different one. She also told us about Agnes Wellows shouting hysterically at her son on many occasions. She overheard her say, 'It would've been better if you'd been killed at the Somme than this everlasting hell now,' which could be taken two ways. Would Martin's death there have been better for his mother? Or better for him, instead of being only half a man now? Was that remark said from love, or bitterness?

'Mr Talgarth fished with both Martin Wellows and Bert

Grainger, Martin's father-in-law, before Martin enlisted and went to France. After he was brought back, wounded and suffering from shell shock, Mr Talgarth often popped in to see him on his way home. He told us how Wellows just stared into space, and how he didn't appear to know anyone. He also told us how, one evening, his mother dropped a plate on the floor, and Wellows dived out of his chair in panic and knocked over a mug of hot tea. Mrs Wellows attacked her son for it, slapping him around the head and kicking his leg. Do we see that as a momentary loss of patience? Or evidence of someone who has had enough and wants it to end?'

'Stop, I have something to say!'

Everyone looked startled at the shrill voice coming from the dock.

Mabel, who was behind the dock, but to the right of it, had to crane her neck to see. She couldn't see Agnes's face, but she could tell by the way she was holding herself that she was extremely agitated.

'You will get your chance to speak after the prosecution and defence have summed up the evidence,' the judge said. He looked and sounded angry.

'No, no, I have to speak now. I did kill my son.'

All sound in the court stopped dead. Every face turned towards Agnes.

'You had better explain yourself,' the judge said. 'Are you now pleading guilty?'

'Yes. I pushed him. I intended to go over the cliff with him. I couldn't bear to witness his suffering any longer, I knew he wanted to die.' She wrung her hands together and her voice was full of pain. 'I took him up there at dusk for a walk. I planned to do it. Martin was calm, I put my arms around him, and it was my intention to just push against him till we both went over together, but he struggled with me. I think he sensed what I was doing. It was like Mr Barnaby said, we were holding each other's arms, both pushing and pulling. He just let go of me, and he toppled back and went over the cliff. I wanted to jump over too, but I lost my nerve and ran home.'

It was too much for Mabel. She got up and ran out of the courtroom, up the corridor, and didn't stop running until she got to the entrance hall. Her heart was thumping, she felt sick and dizzy.

Rain had started to fall about an hour earlier; she'd seen it through the high court windows. But it was heavy now, coming down like stair rods. As upset as she was, and however much she wanted to reach the security of her hotel room, she didn't want her costume and hat to be ruined in the rain.

She sat down on one of the benches to make sense of what she'd heard. She had never understood Agnes, her bitterness, sarcasm, meanness and complete lack of joy. Yet strangely, Mabel understood her trying to take both her and Martin's lives together. Martin had nothing to live for, and neither did she. She'd made too many enemies, and she had absolutely no one in her life other than Martin. To her it was an act of love to put her arms around him and hold him close until death claimed them both.

Maybe there, in the dock, she thought they were going to find her not guilty. She'd have to go back to the same life, with everyone hating or despising her, yet without Martin, who had given some purpose to that life.

She knew by speaking out that she'd hang. But that was fine by her, it was death she wanted.

No one was coming out of the courtroom and Mabel wondered what they were doing, but she couldn't go back in there.

She didn't know how long she sat there; the clock on the wall said four thirty, but it felt like it should be later. Finally, she saw people coming out of a door right at the back of the building. In front of them, perhaps looking for her, was Haines.

'Come with me,' he said as he got closer, and he snatched up her arm roughly.

'Where are you taking me?' she squealed at him, frightened now.

'Out of the way of reporters,' he said. 'Quickly now.'

He ushered her into a small anteroom. He told her later it was a room where juries made their deliberations, but all she saw then was a big table surrounded by chairs. She was taken aback when he locked the door.

'Your friend Baring has charged me with protecting you from reporters,' he said. 'As I made such a poor show of her defence, I feel it's about time I got something right today.'

They sat down in the narrow, airless room.

'I thought you did what you could,' she said. 'It wasn't a poor show.'

'You were the only good part of it,' he said, looking at her in admiration. 'You spoke so bravely and honestly.'

'Will she hang?'

'Yes, the judge put on his black cap and said those awful words. I've heard them four times now, but it never gets any easier.'

Mabel realized by his remark that he wasn't quite the shallow, lazy man she had thought.

'She's probably the first woman in history who chose to be hanged. Do you suppose I could see her before they take her back to the prison?'

'Are you sure you want to?'

'Yes, Martin would've wanted me to forgive her. And I'm sure she's suffered enough since his death. Maybe my seeing her will ease her last days.'

'You are a remarkable woman, Betty – or is it Mabel?'

'Thank you, Mr Haines, I'm not sure I want to be remarkable. But I know you meant it as a compliment. It is Mabel now, for good.'

'While I slip out and find the custody officer, I'll keep you locked in here, as there are two reporters who worried me. One was from *The Times*. If they catch you, they'll keep on at you until you say something you meant to keep quiet, and they'll take photographs. It will be fine them using your old name, but we don't want them finding out the new one and printing that.'

While Haines was gone, Mabel closed her eyes and tried to calm herself. It was done now. Tomorrow she could go back to Bristol, and maybe there would be a letter from Thomas. She would think later about what she was going to do if he hadn't written. That was too awful to contemplate.

She wondered if Joan had remembered to telephone Clara and explain what was happening. Joan had said Percy wouldn't mind her using his phone. What she really needed now was Clara or Joan; they both seemed to have the knack of dispersing her fears.

The door was unlocked, and there was Haines. 'Quickly now, I've got you just ten minutes with her, though the custody officer said he couldn't imagine why anyone would want to see her.'

The cells below the court were frightening. The lights were dim, the walls were a shade of light brown, but stained with what could be blood, or worse. There was a smell of damp, unwashed bodies and lavatories. The floor beneath her feet was bare stone, and Mabel imagined rats coming out when no one was about.

Agnes was in the last of the cells. It was tiny, with a window up by the ceiling, so small it hardly counted as a window. The only furniture was the bench Agnes was sitting on, and another upright chair. The walls had initials and names gouged into them here and there.

'You shouldn't have come,' Agnes said, and for once her tone wasn't sharp, a mere mild reproach, as if she thought Mabel was in danger here.

'I wanted to see you because I needed to tell you I understood what you said. I know how much you loved Martin.'

Agnes looked up at Mabel. Her pale brown eyes were darker now with sorrow, and the anger that had always been in them was gone. 'You know I'm to be hanged?'

Mabel nodded. 'You were truly courageous to admit what really happened.'

'I don't want to live,' she said. 'Everyone I care for is on the other side. If I'd been kinder to you, maybe it could all have been different.'

Mabel took a chance of being rejected and went to her, taking her two hands in her own. 'Don't let's dwell on the past, it's over and done with. I know Martin would want the last words I say to you to be kind ones. I came here to help you, and I hoped I'd see you walk free. Can I hug you now? We never did that, not even once.'

She gently pulled on Agnes's hands. The older woman got to her feet and let Mabel pull her into her arms. For the first few seconds she was like a plank, every fibre of her body resisting, but slowly she softened, leaning into Mabel. Then she began to cry.

Mabel let her, and her own eyes filled with tears too, remembering that this woman had given birth to her husband, had loved and cared for him as a child, and if fate had been less cruel and her own husband hadn't died, maybe she could have been so different.

'I do forgive you, Agnes,' she whispered, stroking the woman's heaving shoulders. 'For everything. I understand losing your husband changed you, grief can do that to people. I had so much happiness with your son, I really loved him too. We were both victims of circumstance.'

Agnes drew away and wiped her eyes with the back of her hand.

Mabel took a handkerchief from her pocket and wiped the older woman's face gently, putting the handkerchief in her hand to keep. 'I have to go now. Stay strong, and you will be in my thoughts and prayers.'

She kissed her mother-in-law on both cheeks. Then, blinded by her own tears, she went to the cell door to be let out.

'Thank you, Betty,' she heard Agnes say softly as she left. 'I'm glad you came.'

*

'Oh dear!' Haines said when he saw her face as the custody officer led her back upstairs. 'Was it harrowing?'

'Not really. That was the nicest she's ever been to me. The night I left Hallsands, I remember thinking, "You'll never see me again." Meaning her. Yet in a strange way I'm glad I did see her again. I feel sort of healed.'

He smiled, and all at once he looked more attractive. 'Good luck for the future, I really hope your part in this trial doesn't reach Dorchester.'

'I wish I'd brought an umbrella,' she said. 'I'm going to get soaked going to the hotel.'

Haines chuckled. 'They say the sun shines on the righteous. Look!'

She looked ahead, at the front doors of the court, to see the rain had stopped and the sun was shining.

'Thank you, Mr Haines,' she said, shaking his hand.

'It looks like those reporters have given up,' he said. 'Safe journey home.'

Mabel walked down the court steps and across the pavement to cross the road and go back to her hotel. She was just waiting for a carriage to pass when she felt a light touch on her shoulder. She wheeled round, expecting it to be one of the reporters, but to her shock it was Thomas.

Her mouth dropped open.

'You were magnificent,' he said. 'But I thought you'd skipped off through some other door. I was just about to leave.'

'You were in the courtroom?' she asked, her voice just a squeak with the shock.

'Of course. I kept my face turned away once they'd called you, as I thought I might put you off.'

'But how did you know?'

He laughed. 'Shall we get across this road safely first? Then let's find somewhere to sit down and have some tea or champagne.'

She saw what he meant; they were teetering on the edge of the pavement with the traffic, carriages, carts and trams careering past them.

A few minutes later, he led her into an elegant, expensive-looking hotel and into a drawing room furnished in dark reds with comfortable armchairs, highly polished tables and thickly draped curtains.

'A bottle of champagne, please,' he said to the waiter who escorted them to seats by the window.

'So how did you know?' Mabel was frantic to find out.

'Clara came to me and told me. Her words were, "I know it's none of my business, and snub me if you like, but you need to get to Plymouth court if you do love Mabel."'

Mabel blushed. She could just imagine Clara saying that. 'And you came?'

'Of course I did. What Clara didn't know was that I'd already posted a reply to your letter, telling you I would do anything in my powers to help you, and I couldn't care less about other people's opinions. It was a good thing I'd just bought an automobile, like I said I was going to. So I hopped in it and drove here.'

Mabel could only sit back and smile. There would be time later to find out all the whys and wherefores, for now it was enough to know he loved her, and he'd come when she needed him most.

By the time they'd finished the first glass of champagne, Thomas was back to talking about the trial.

'What a nasty piece of work your mother-in-law was!' he exclaimed. 'No wonder you ran away. Any sane person would. But as a lawyer I loved the sheer drama of it when she admitted she'd done it! Oh my goodness, I was so excited at that moment, I wanted to cheer.'

Mabel got the giggles then. She wondered how she could have gone through so many different emotions in one day. From terror in the morning to anxiety while she waited for her turn in court, humiliation when the lawyer tried to belittle her, and anger when she finally said what needed to be said. There was shock when Agnes admitted what really happened and distress later when she went down to the cells, followed by resignation and a feeling of everything completed at the end. But then just when she thought it was all over, and she'd go back to the hotel and try to sleep, Thomas appeared.

Now it was joy unconfined. She could happily sit here forever, looking at his handsome, smiling face, wondering how soon she'd get to kiss him properly. She knew she ought to telephone Percy so he could tell Joan what had happened. But for now she couldn't move.

23

Mabel felt quite tiddly by the time she and Thomas went into the restaurant for dinner.

She tried to tell him earlier that she needed to go back to her hotel to change her clothes, but he kept pouring the champagne, kissing the tips of her fingers and telling her how fetching she looked in her green outfit.

He had a room in The Royal, but as much as they would have liked to creep up the stairs to it, they knew the hotel staff would be disapproving, and it would make Mabel look like a scarlet woman.

'We'll just have to get married quickly,' Thomas said. 'I can't think of anything better than holding you in my arms every night, forever.'

Mabel had told him everything that had happened since she left Dorchester, and how indebted she felt to Joan, Percy and John Baring. She would have liked them to meet Thomas, but he said it was better that she went straight back to Dorchester with him.

'You can invite them to our wedding,' he suggested.

'You've got weddings on the brain,' she laughed. But she loved the fact that he felt that way.

The dinner was delicious; rare roast beef so tender the knife went through it like butter, fluffy roast potatoes and several different vegetables.

'I think that was the best meal I've ever eaten,' Mabel said as she finished hers.

'That might be the company, or just that you haven't eaten properly for days,' he said. 'And I'm going to insist you have a pudding too.'

A little later she asked him what he had thought when he got to Willow Cottage and found she'd gone.

'I believed your note – well, at least, until later that night when some doubts crept in. You see, Clara came out while I was at your little cottage, and I had a feeling she wasn't telling me the whole story. I couldn't understand why you hadn't at least telephoned my office. Clara passed that off as you being worried about your friend, and having to leave in a hurry, but how long would it have taken?

'Then I started to consider how little I knew about you, where you grew up, your family and the like. I wouldn't say you'd been evasive, just not forthcoming.'

'I know, and I felt bad about it. But if I told you part of it, that would lead to questions, and more lies. Besides, if I'd told you the whole story, what would you have done? Suggest we commit bigamy? In truth, if it hadn't been for all this, I might have just run away again.'

'I understand,' he said, taking her hand and squeezing it. 'At least, I did once I got your letter. I sat through that court case in a state of shock. Your life back then was so hard, so different to the pretty picture I'd had in my head before.'

'Tell me what that was like.'

'It was all rural bliss really, roses round a cottage door, you in a white apron and sun bonnet, shucking peas and feeding chickens. I certainly didn't imagine you living on a fast-eroding cliff, gutting fish and having a witch like

Agnes wiping her feet on you. But I liked what that first witness said about you.'

'Jack? What did he say?'

'That after your mother died you were the little house-keeper for your father, and how you used to come out fishing on the boat with them, and you were as good as an adult deck hand. He said you had the sunniest nature, and you were the fastest runner in the village. Though I'm not sure why he brought the running up.'

Mabel laughed. 'We kids would keep lookout for the shoals of fish coming in. I was always the fastest at reaching the beach to tell the fishermen when we spotted them.'

'That talent should come in handy in Dorchester,' he teased her.

A little while later, Mabel whispered to him. 'They want us to leave.' She could see waiters hovering in the background, and all the other diners had left.

'I know, but I don't want to take you back to your hotel and leave you there. I want you in my bed.'

'I'd like that too, but we must be sensible and show some respect to the poor staff who have jobs to do,' she admonished him. 'What time do we leave in the morning?'

'Straight after breakfast, I'll be at your hotel,' he said. 'I suppose we can always find some little backwater to do some canoodling on the way back?'

'You, Thomas Kellaway, are incorrigible,' she said. 'Now we must go.'

Mabel couldn't sleep that night for what seemed like hours. It had, after all, been an incredible day. She didn't like to dwell on that picture of Martin and Agnes struggling on the cliff top, and then him going over the edge alone. Neither did she want to dwell on the hangman putting the noose around the poor woman's neck. But perhaps it would be best to think, as Agnes did, that there was nothing left on earth for either of them.

But however distressing the court case had been, that was all blown away by Thomas turning up.

Now she was free to marry him. She could abandon the guilt, the mourning clothes and – at least in Dorchester – never again be afraid of the past catching up with her, and look ahead to a glorious future with Thomas.

What of the psychic powers, though? They worried her. Were they, as Beatrice suggested, something which could come after a trauma and disappear later? Or had they always been there, and she just hadn't tapped into them before?

She certainly didn't want such powers; they smacked of fairground booths, of seances and fortune-telling. The people who sought such messages appeared to have a rather unhealthy desperation about them too, and it wasn't kind to encourage them. Yet how could she stop it happening? What if she just picked up some item one day and all at once she found herself falling into a trance? How on earth could she stop that happening?

Mabel woke to bright sunshine, and bounced out of bed in excitement. But seeing her home-made grey and white dress hanging on the wardrobe door, she instantly wished she had something prettier to wear. The green costume she'd worn for court was attractive, especially the cheeky hat, but it wouldn't be comfortable on the long journey home, and she hadn't anything else.

Scooping up her washbag and a towel, she flung a wrap over her nightdress and ran along to the bathroom before anyone else beat her to it.

Sitting in the bath, she thought how amazing it was that the previous morning she'd been so scared, she couldn't stomach breakfast. But today she intended to eat everything the waitress offered her.

Thomas arrived right on the dot of nine, just as he'd said he would. Mabel was waiting, having paid her bill a few moments before. She had no doubt Thomas would offer to pay it for her, but she intended to keep her independence.

After he'd kissed her cheek and picked up her bag, it was the first thing he asked about.

Mabel smirked. 'I've already seen to it.'

'Before we hit the road for Dorchester, I'd like to take you on a little detour,' Thomas said, once he'd helped her into his shiny white Wolseley with red leather seats. Mabel knew that's what the vehicle was, because he'd mentioned it with pride several times the previous evening. She was impressed too; it was beautiful, and it was exciting to have her first ride in an automobile. She remembered how people used to call them 'horseless carriages', but that expression seemed to have vanished now.

She clung on to the door as Thomas started her up and pulled away. But she soon realized there was more danger of someone running out in front of them than the vehicle tipping over.

'So where is this detour taking us?' she shouted above the noise of the engine.

'Hallsands,' he said. 'I think you need to see it one last time.'

'Must I?' She was alarmed at the thought.

'Yes, you must. If you don't, you'll always be wondering about it. I'd like to see where you grew up too. We don't have to speak to anyone, just look around and leave.'

It was only when they had passed through Kingsbridge, emerging on to the narrow dirt lane she remembered so well, that images of childhood began to come back to her. Walking with her mother to visit an old lady who lived in a tiny, very isolated cottage. She didn't think she was a real aunt, but they used to call her Auntie Winnie. She used to kiss Mabel, which she didn't like, as the old lady had whiskers on her chin. They walked along part of this lane to get to Huckham school too; her teacher felt sorry that her pupils had to walk so far, so she made them cocoa on winter mornings.

Most of her memories, though, were from when she first started walking out with Martin; they often came this way on a fine summer's evening, holding hands and kissing till they were flushed and dizzy. He had lifted her up and sat her on the milestone to Hallsands to ask her to marry him.

A not so nice memory was of walking along this road every day once she'd got her housekeeping job. It was horrible when wet, her feet slipping and sliding, and sometimes she found herself wading through puddles. It was eighteen miles, the round trip. Although she used to set off in the morning at a lively pace, on the way home she was often so tired she could've lain down in one of the fields and gone to sleep.

It was especially hard in the winter. She would take a lantern to light the way, and if she was lucky she'd get a lift on Mr Hubert's cart. But she remembered the biting cold, and the wind nearly blowing her over on some days.

When they got close to Hallsands, Mabel's heart began to beat faster; she didn't want to confront any more memories, she just wanted to go back to Dorchester and put this place, and all that went with it, behind her.

The village looked far smaller than she remembered. A hamlet really, not a village. There was the mission hall, the chapel, the little shop and the coastguard station, and a few new cottages that must have been built after the disaster. But it didn't seem to have a heart, not the way it had when she was growing up.

They left the car parked at the side of the road and walked for a bit. She showed Thomas the lane that used to lead down to the sea, past the cottages. There was a rudimentary bridge made of planks across the part of the lane that had been damaged, so at least the fishermen could get down to the shore. There were a few fishermen down on the beach making new lobster pots, but they weren't looking her way.

All that was left of her old house was a bit of the end wall. Everything else was gone.

Warm sun on her face should have dispelled her memories of that last night, but it didn't; she was right back there, scrabbling along over washed-up shingle in the dark, buffeted by the wind and icy rain like nails in her face and soaking through her cloak.

She could still see the way the front door was split by the force of the storm, as if it was wet cardboard, and she remembered stepping into a foot of water in the old kitchen. But the clearest memory was of coming back down the stairs and seeing a huge wave charge into the cottage and then withdraw, taking the last chair. She was lucky she managed to get out before the next wave. Even above the noise of the sea, wind and rain, she heard the creak of timbers, masonry falling, and saw the remains of the front door float off out to sea.

'Ah you alright?' Thomas's concerned question brought her back to the present.

She shook herself to make the images go away. 'You can't imagine how dreadful that last trip to my house was,' she said. 'You wouldn't want to.'

Next, she showed him Tern Cottage where Agnes lived with Ted and, latterly, Martin. As a child Mabel had always thought the people who lived in this little terrace were rich, but she could see now that the cottages were every bit as shabby and poor as one she'd been born in. They peeped through the window of Tern Cottage. The wooden Windsor armchair that Martin used to sit on was still there, but little else. She wondered who had taken the table and the easy chairs, or the china cabinet Martin's grandfather had been so proud of because it had been made by his son, Martin's father.

'Let's go now, I've seen enough,' Mabel said suddenly.

A woman was looking out of her front door at them. Although she knew the Talbots, who lived there, she had no wish to talk to them now.

'Will that cottage come to you now?' Thomas asked as they walked back to his Wolseley. 'It ought to – unless old Mr Wellows had children other than Martin's father?'

'He didn't,' Mabel said. 'He was very friendly with my father, and before Agnes and Martin came to the village, I remember him bemoaning the fact he had only the one son – no daughter to housekeep for him, as I did for my father.'

'Then it should come to you. I can't imagine it's worth more than a couple of hundred, but it could be let out for holidays. Also, I should look into that compensation for your own house too. Agnes hadn't received it, that was spoken about during the trial.'

'I don't like to think of getting any money from here,' she said.

'Now that is plain silly. Your father would be horrified if you didn't value the house he worked so hard to maintain. As would old Mr Wellows. But I can sort all that out for you, it will be good for you to have a little nest egg of your own.'

'There's just one more thing,' he said as they got back to his automobile. He reached in the back and pulled out two bunches of roses. 'I thought you might like to throw one of these in the sea for your father and Martin. Maybe put the other on your mother's grave?'

Mabel really wanted to leave immediately, fearing she might break down and cry if she stayed any longer. But she was touched by Thomas's sensitivity, and it was such a kind thought.

She assumed that Martin was buried in the churchyard in Stokenham – her mother and father were there too – yet Thomas understood that Martin's heart, like her father's, had always been in the sea.

He drove up to the cliff top near the Hallsands Hotel

and the row of homes called Mildmay Cottages. They had been built to house some of the villagers who had lost their homes that tragic night. Mabel remembered when she was in Bristol reading in a newspaper how a councillor called Mildmay had helped to publicize what had happened. He took on the parties responsible for dredging up huge quantities of shingle for the construction of Devonport docks, ignoring warnings that they were putting the village at risk. Mabel was pleased that they'd named the cottages after him.

Walking to the cliff edge, Mabel tossed the roses in, one by one. She made herself remember their wedding day, how Martin had tears in his eyes as he put the ring on her finger. Then her mind slipped forward a few years and she remembered how smart and proud Martin had looked in his uniform when he went off to war. He needn't have gone, fishing was a reserved occupation, but he felt it was his duty. He was never able to share with her the details of the hell he went through in France, but at least now he was no longer tortured by the memories.

As for her father, there were so many good memories of him, it was hard to choose her favourite. There was going out on the boat with him to pull up the lobster and crab pots. When he found he had a good haul, he would sing on the way back, and some of the other fishermen would join in. Mabel could hear that joyous sound still. After her mother died, he would often take her on his lap in front of the fire in the evenings, brush her hair and tell her stories. Often, she fell asleep in his arms and he'd carry her up and put her to bed. He never made her feel she was a burden, he didn't go to the pub and drink like his friends, but stayed in with her, and he always told her she was his darling.

At Stokenham church it took a little while to find where her parents were buried in the churchyard. Although most people went to the chapel in Hallsands on Sunday, they preferred the Church of England for weddings, christenings and funerals. Mabel and Martin were married here, as Mabel's parents had been.

She remembered coming here with her father, picking wild flowers on the way, to put on her mother's grave. As far as she recalled, there was only a small headstone and it was close to the wall. Her father had been laid to rest there too, once his body was washed up, but there had been no money to have another headstone made.

Thomas found it, scraping off weeds and moss on several old graves before he found the right one. The headstone read: 'Patience Grainger, born 1877, died 1903. Beloved wife to Bertram and mother to Betty.'

'Far too young to die,' Thomas said sadly.

'Maybe if the doctor had come sooner,' Mabel said. 'Dad had to go nearly into Kingsbridge to get him, he said he ran almost the whole way, but the doctor was out with another patient and he didn't arrive on his horse till the next morning. Ma had already died.'

Thomas wandered off while Mabel put some of the flowers on her mother's grave.

'Over here,' Thomas called a few minutes later. 'I think Martin may have been buried with his grandfather.'

This headstone read simply: 'Edward Wellows, 1844 to 1918.' But there were signs that the grave had been opened fairly recently to make room for Martin's body. There were flowers too, but they were all dead now. Mabel put the last few roses she had in a vase.

'I'd rather imagine him and my father in the sea,' she said. 'But I suppose it's good he's with his grandfather.'

'Shall we go now?' Thomas asked, once she'd tidied up the dead flowers and pulled up a few weeds. 'It's going to be a long journey.'

The journey was over ninety miles, but despite the distance it was a lovely ride through beautiful countryside. The leaves on the trees were just beginning to take on their autumn colouring, a reminder that the summer was fading fast. It was good to just be alone with Thomas, knowing they had everything ahead of them. Every now and then, Thomas would tell her something that had happened while she'd been gone.

'Clara told me she thought you ought to move into the guest room, that after a winter out in the little cottage, without Carsten to look after the stove for you, you'll be really cold. I told her if I had my way, she'd have to find a new companion soon.'

'Thomas!' Mabel said indignantly. 'That was very naughty of you to blurt it out like that. But tell me how it's going with Michael and Harriet?'

'A spring wedding, I'm told. Michael is going to get a new house built – he bought the land just a few weeks ago. Harriet is an odd girl. Michael was trying to get her to tell him what special things she'd like. All she could say was, "I'll like whatever you decide on." How feeble is that?'

'You won't have that problem with me. I'll be so bossy you'll have no choice on furnishings!'

'I will bow to your excellent taste,' he said with a smile. 'In point of fact, I never met a man who had any idea of how to furnish or decorate a house.'

It was nearly seven in the evening, and chilly now the sun had gone down, when they got to Willow Cottage.

'I won't come in,' he said, taking her into his arms. 'You look very tired, and I know you and Clara will have a lot to talk about.' He kissed her, and then leapt out of the Wolseley to come round and open her door.

'Tomorrow night?' he said.

Mabel smiled. She knew it would be safer to say, 'Not until a ring is on my finger'. But she'd never been one for 'safe'.

24

'So much excitement!' Clara exclaimed as Mabel got to the end of her story about the trial, and then the shock of discovering that Thomas had been there all along. 'I don't know which woman was the more remarkable – Agnes for admitting she pushed Martin over the edge, or you for going to see her afterwards to tell her you'd forgiven her!'

'I think you would've done the same. Besides, I can afford to be generous, I've got a good life now.'

'You didn't know you'd got Thomas then,' Clara reminded her.

'I would still have had you, Clara,' she said. 'I've been so happy here – well, except when Carsten was killed.'

'And now it looks like you're going to leave me!'

'I'm not going far. And anyway, you'll always be a big part of my life, even after Thomas and I marry.'

Clara lifted a handkerchief to her eyes and pretended to cry. 'Until a baby comes along! Then I'll be cast aside like an old wash rag.'

Mabel laughed. 'Where I come from, we keep old wash rags. Now don't be a silly goose. But you could make life a little easier for yourself by moving into the town. You could have electricity, and it would be easier to get help in the house and garden without so far for people to come.'

'I might even do that and move right next door to you, so I can pester you,' Clara said, pulling a silly face. 'But then I expect you know what's going to happen to both of us, with your psychic powers.'

'You know perfectly well that those so-called powers don't run to fortune-telling. But speaking of those powers, I'm worried about them. I don't want them any more. Do you think there's any way I could stop it happening?'

Clara shrugged. 'You could go back to see Coral in Bath. She seemed very genuine. But maybe it just won't happen again. It could have started because of Carsten, or anxiety about your past coming out. That's over now.'

'Should I try again, just to see?'

'Go on, then. Shall I get some objects from different people? And maybe put my father's pen amongst them too?'

Mabel nodded; she didn't really want to do it, but if it didn't work, she'd feel a lot easier.

Clara collected a few small items from around the sitting room – a silver thimble, a small china owl, her father's pen, an old prayer book. And she removed a small cameo brooch from the neck of her blouse, then put them all on a small tray and handed it to Mabel.

Once Clara had sat down, Mabel rested her hands on all the items, then one by one she picked them up and held them for a couple of minutes each. Nothing happened, not even a faint sense of anything unusual. Without speaking to Clara, she began again, taking her time with each one, concentrating on the object in her hand and thinking about what it looked like, how old it was, anything that might help.

But there was nothing.

She didn't know whether to be delighted or a bit sad. Clara looked disappointed.

'Don't look so glum,' Mabel said to her. 'It's what I wanted.'

'I know, but the cameo was my grandmother's, and it would've been good to get a message from her. The china owl is nothing, just a little present from a friend who stayed here once. The old prayer book was my mother's, and the thimble is mine.'

'At least it proves I can't do it to order, so it's just as well I wasn't planning to make a business from it.'

'My grandmother died so suddenly I didn't get to say goodbye,' Clara said. 'I was close to her, possibly because Mother was so chilly. She used to paint too – it was always said that I got my talent from her.'

'Maybe that's all the message you need? To inherit looks or skills from someone must, in its way, mean you keep a connection with them. I've got my mother's red hair and green eyes, so when I look in the mirror, I'm often reminded of her,' Mabel said. 'But we ought to go to bed now, it's getting late.'

'I put a hot-water bottle in your bed earlier, just to make it cosier. But really, Mabel, I think you should move back into the house.'

'Thomas told me you'd said that. It would be nice, once it gets colder, but for now I'd like to stay over there in the cottage.'

'You mean you want a few nights of passion away from me?' Clara said.

Mabel just laughed. And Clara could make what she liked of that.

Once tucked up in bed in the little cottage, sleep didn't come to Mabel as easily as she'd expected. She kept rerunning all the events of the previous day and seeing Agnes's face as she said goodbye to her, down in the cells beneath the court.

Then her mind moved on to the future with Thomas, and instead of just imagining and planning their wedding and their shared home, as she wanted to do, niggling doubts began to appear.

While there were no legal obstacles to her marrying Thomas now, she couldn't erase her upbringing and background. She imagined Thomas's Aunt Leticia saying, 'Oh, Mabel, you didn't let on your father was a fisherman. How quaint!'

While she knew perfectly well that Aunt Leticia's good breeding would prevent her from voicing any such thing, she'd be thinking it.

Then there were the many people who would rejoice in discovering her humble beginnings. They wouldn't be coy in gossiping about it.

Despite her disturbed night of anxiety, Mabel was back in Clara's house the next morning at seven thirty, like always, raking the stove, getting it going again, and lighting the fire under the boiler to do some washing.

Clara came down at nine, still in her dressing gown. She looked astonished to see the table laid for breakfast, and eggs boiling on the stove.

'Why are you doing this?' she asked.

'Because it's my job,' Mabel replied, wondering why she would ask such a silly question.

'But surely now that you are going to marry Thomas you know you can't be my housekeeper? I mean, what would people say?'

Mabel tried to make a joke of it and looked out of the window. 'I don't see hordes of people out there checking to see what I'm doing,' she said lightly. 'Stop paying me if that makes you feel I'm no longer an employee, but I'll still do all the jobs I've always done.'

Clara sat down at the table, looking very worried. 'We need to talk this through,' she insisted. 'Try and see it through everyone else's eyes, Mabel. Thomas is a lawyer, and they'll be expecting him to marry someone of his class.'

'Oh, for goodness' sake,' Mabel said impatiently. 'You've very kindly implied to people that I'm your companion, rather than saying I'm your housekeeper. But I really don't see what the difference between them is. Surely a companion is allowed to lift a poker and a coal scuttle? Even do a bit of washing and cook the dinner?'

'You are missing the point,' Clara said impatiently. 'It's not about you doing a few chores here for me, it's where you fit in the social structure. I meant to talk to you about this as soon as you got home yesterday, but I couldn't. You were so happy, everything had turned out well. So I put it off.'

'Put what off, Clara?'

'I was invited to lunch at Lily Hargreaves's house while you were away. She told me people in town were talking about you and Thomas. Of course they don't know about the murder trial, or indeed anything about your past, thank goodness, but Lily said there's talk of you being a servant.'

'So I am, what's wrong with that?' Mabel poured boiling water into the teapot and put it on the table.

'To me and Thomas, nothing, but once you are

married, you might find some of these people won't invite you and Thomas to dinners and parties.'

Mabel put her hands on her hips and glared at Clara. 'I wouldn't want to be invited if they were like that.'

Clara sighed. 'I suspected you'd take it like this. But before you get on your high horse, think, Mabel. How will Thomas increase his clients in Dorchester if people disapprove of you as a couple for flouting social rules?'

'Have we gone back into Victorian times? Are you trying to tell me one of these silly women wouldn't let her husband hire Thomas because his wife doesn't measure up to their standards?' Mabel's voice rose in anger.

'That's about the size of it. Why do you think Michael is marrying simpering little Harriet? I assure you, it isn't for her scintillating conversation, or even her homemaking skills. She's out of the top drawer, that's why. Everyone approves of her.'

'So we live in a town where people would rather see a brave man like Michael, who nearly died for his country, live in purgatory with a drippy wife he can't even hold a real conversation with, because she's the right sort?'

'That's just the way it is, Mabel.'

'Then I'm not sure I want to live in this town.'

Clara sighed, and poured tea into both of their cups. 'You are so stubborn sometimes. I want to explain how we can get around this, but I sense you don't want to listen.'

'I am listening,' Mabel said, folding her arms and looking insolently at the ceiling.

Clara sighed. 'Remember, Mabel, I am on your side. I want you and Thomas to be happy, and everyone in this town to like you as much as I do. We can get around this ridiculous prejudice by showing people we are friends, not mistress and servant. We go to town together, arm in arm like we are sisters. Help each other shop for hats, gloves, whatever. We can also invite people here for tea or dinner, and maybe get a girl to act as our maid. Dorchester people know I'm a bit eccentric, so they won't expect a lot of fuss. But we play the game their way, and they'll come around. In no time at all they'll forget they once heard you were a servant.'

That word 'servant' seared through Mabel's brain. All at once, she saw that the fears she'd had at the back of her mind – namely that she wasn't good enough for Thomas – were not just fears, but reality.

Back in Hallsands she would never have thought it possible to self-educate herself to go on to better things. Yet when she joined Mrs Gladsworthy's staff in Bristol, something woke up inside her and told her this was a golden opportunity. So she had watched and listened, learning how to speak and behave. She managed to modulate her Devon accent and learned, amongst other things, the right cutlery to use, how to lay a table, how to address people and when to stay silent and be almost invisible.

But now it dawned on her that these were skills for a better position in service; they didn't equip her for marriage to a lawyer in the way an immaculate pedigree would. She had foolishly imagined that her new name, Mabel Brook, wiped out Betty Wellows, and all that went with her.

'I'll have to think on this. Am I allowed to dish out your breakfast and be your housekeeper for the rest of the day?'

'Mabel!' Clara said reproachfully. 'I'm really sorry I had to be the one to tell you all this. It must sound to you as if I'm purposely trying to derail your intended marriage, especially as I've never said anything along these lines before. But in my defence, I'm a bit of a bohemian, and I've never conformed, so I didn't anticipate you and Thomas being a problem to anyone.'

'Thomas didn't seem to think I was a problem, and he knows everything about me,' Mabel said defiantly.

'He should have considered it. He was brought up in a conventional manner, educated at the right school, taught to make the right friends, and duty came before everything. The law firm he's joined is a prestigious one, their clients are some of the wealthiest and most influential in Dorset. When he came here that night after you'd left for Kingsbridge, he kept on and on at me until he wore me down to tell him the truth.'

'So, you told him why I had to go?'

'Yes. I didn't want to. It wasn't my story to tell. At that point I expected him to back away. But he surprised me in that he was far more concerned for you than for how it might affect him if it all became public. I saw then how much he loves you.'

'Isn't that enough?' Mabel asked. Despite trying not to cry, her eyes filled up and the tears spilled over.

'It isn't for families like his,' Clara said sadly. 'They put upholding the family name before everything. I've no doubt that even if the whole story was printed in the papers, naming you, he would still go ahead and marry you, he's brave and noble enough for that. Thankfully, that hasn't happened. But it could in the future – secrets have a way of getting out. How would you feel, a few years down the line, if he has to resign from that law firm and has no choice but to take any job he can get? He's not his father's heir, remember – the bulk of the family fortune will go to Michael. How would you feel if he had to work as a school-master, or a clerk?'

'I'd be happy with him, even if we had to live in a barn,' Mabel said defiantly. 'I never thought of him as being a good catch, or any of the other callous phrases women like Harriet or Lily would use. I love him for him-self.' She put Clara's boiled egg in front of her. 'I'll go upstairs and change the sheets on your bed while you eat your breakfast.'

'Don't run away from me, stay here and we'll plan ways of showing Dorchester society that I am firmly behind you. Leticia will support us too, she says you are a breath of fresh air. Together we can show these stuffy, small-minded people that you are a force to be reckoned with.'

Mabel didn't choose to sit down with Clara and talk. She felt bruised and disappointed, and she needed to keep herself busy.

While she'd been away, Clara hadn't cleaned or tidied anything. But as Mabel made everything straight, put bed linen in the boiler, took the rugs outside to shake, her mind was whirling.

Deep down inside her, she knew Clara was right. If she married Thomas, she would be his downfall. He would never understand that now, but in the future, when doors didn't open for him, eventually he would become bitter at losing opportunities, and he would blame her.

She had to leave.

If she stayed, Clara would come up with a plan that would never work. It was preposterous to imagine that the pair of them going shopping together in town and inviting people here to tea was going to stop the gossip and convince everyone she was a gentlewoman.

Thomas would insist that her lowly birth and past didn't matter, and she would inevitably let them both convince her to stay. But the things that had been said today couldn't be unsaid. She would always be waiting for trouble, just as she'd always been waiting to be caught out at living a lie for nearly three years.

It seemed so cowardly to run away, and this time she didn't even have a nasty mother-in-law to justify her flight. Clara loved her, she knew that; she hadn't said these things from spite, her fears came from her heart. Thomas was blinded by love, and unable to use his head. So, she had to be the one to sort out the problem.

Putting bread and cheese on the table for Clara's lunch, she then called up the stairs that she'd made soup, which was on the stove, and she was going into town to get some groceries.

Going first to her cottage, she packed her bag, making sure she had the bear from Carsten and her mother's green beads. She tucked her savings into the pocket on the inside of her skirt waistband, put on her black coat, black straw hat and good shoes, and left. She was a real widow now, and she might as well look like one. Her cottage and the little path out on to the riverbank were only visible from the guest room, and it was unlikely Clara would look out of that window.

Walking as fast as she could, she made her way to the station. She didn't look back.

25

On the walk to the station Mabel told herself she would get on whichever train was due in first. She had no intention of going to Bristol to stay with Joan; Clara knew that address and would give it to Thomas. Maybe Exeter would be a good place to go to, or Southampton. Both big enough cities to hide away and lick her wounds. That was just how she felt, like a wounded dog in need of shelter. She would find a cheap guest house and then look around for work.

The first train was going to Exeter. Once she'd settled herself in the carriage, she felt she could breathe out again.

As reality hit her, she wondered how she had ever really thought it would work being married to Thomas. Each time he'd seen her at Willow Cottage, the colour, comfort and warmth of that cottage must have made him imagine she'd always lived that way. Clara saying she was her 'companion' had fed the idea into his head and heart that she was genteel but without money of her own.

So what a shock it must have been to him as the trial unfolded and he learned how different her childhood and early adult years had been to his own! He was a kind man; he would have felt deep sympathy and want to make a better life for her.

Even now, two days on from hearing all that, she doubted he'd thought through what an obstacle her background was to their future happiness. It might be weeks before he did. But eventually, as he planned their wedding, who they were going to invite and where they were going to live, he would start to think about whether she'd be able to hold her own with his relatives and friends. He might even worry that she would want to invite people from her old village.

But she knew he would remain protective of her. If he felt anyone was looking down on her, he was likely to round on them. But that wouldn't help anyone. It would just create a vicious circle of gossip and retaliation until it spiralled out of control.

The same evening as Mabel was checking into a guest house near Exeter station, Thomas was knocking on the door of Willow Cottage.

He'd telephoned earlier to plan this evening with Mabel, only to find Clara had just discovered that Mabel had packed her bag and run away. Clara was in floods of tears and wasn't making much sense, so Thomas went around to her home.

'It's all my fault,' she sobbed out to him when he arrived. 'I should've been much more careful about what I said.'

It was a surprise to see Clara so upset, she was usually so calm and measured, never emotional. Thomas sat down with her and listened to the whole tale.

When Clara explained how Mabel had finished her work and then, without saying a word, had packed her bag and just disappeared, she cried even harder. 'I was so shocked,' she sobbed. 'I ran down the path by the river, hoping to catch her, but she was long gone.'

'That Lily Hargreaves is such an unpleasant woman,

I'm surprised you even shared the same lunch table with her, let alone listened to anything she had to say,' Thomas said. He was very angry. Not so much that Clara hadn't realized Mabel would take what she said so personally, but that people would make such cruel and unfounded remarks about Mabel when they hadn't even met her.

'Lily Hargreaves had me earmarked for her half-witted daughter, and since I made it clear I had interests elsewhere, she's probably been waiting for an opportunity to spite me. Odious woman.'

Clara looked at him with such a bleak expression, it made Thomas feel even worse. 'I can't bear the thought of her being all alone somewhere. Do you think she's gone to Bristol?' she asked.

'I doubt it,' Thomas said. 'One thing I know for absolute certain about Mabel is that she would not want to foist herself on anyone. It's more likely she's in an unfamiliar city somewhere now, feeling like she's utterly worthless.'

'I was only trying to say we should make people see us as friends and companions, rather than mistress and housekeeper,' Clara said, desperate for him to understand that she hadn't intentionally hurt Mabel. 'I see now that I was tactless in the way I said it. But you know, Thomas, that to me she *is* a friend, I have never thought of her as a servant.'

Thomas sighed deeply. 'Don't blame yourself, Clara. Blame the stupid, snobbish people who make such a big deal about this class thing. But now I know how hard her childhood was, especially losing her mother so young, I can understand how far she has come since leaving that village, and how sensitive she is about her background.

From the age of eight onwards she was virtually her father's housekeeper and assistant. Then, of course, that witch Agnes took over and made it her business to order her about, so it's hardly surprising she feels she is doomed to stay in a lowly station in life.

'But I'm not going to let her go, Clara. I love her, I'm going to find her and marry her, and if anyone dares to say she isn't good enough for me, I shall make them eat their words.'

'But how will you find her?' Clara asked. 'She could be anywhere?'

'She would go to a big town or city where there's more chance of finding a job. Southampton, maybe. Or even London. But I'm going to go up to the station now and ask the porter if he saw her today, and which train she caught.'

The porter hadn't noticed anyone much that afternoon; he went on to say his back was killing him, as if that would prevent him noticing passengers.

It was too late to start looking for Mabel that night, but Thomas thought he'd start looking in Southampton the next day.

He postponed all his appointments and drove off to Southampton first thing in the morning. He left his car by the station and then, working systematically along the streets nearest to the station, he checked every single guest house. Some of the landladies and landlords were helpful, others less so, but they all said they hadn't got a guest who fitted her description.

The second day, he made a wider sweep of the streets further from the station, but still with no joy.

He was beginning to lose heart.

But on the third day, just as he was about to set off for Bridport, a letter from Mabel fell through his letter box.

He read her letter several times, at first disappointed by its brevity, and upset that she hadn't enlarged on her reasons for going, but by the fourth reading it dawned on him that she just didn't know what to say. He rang Percy, Joan's friend in Bristol. When Percy rushed across to Joan, to bring her to the phone, he discovered she too had received a letter, as had Clara.

Both women were clear on certain things. Mabel did love Thomas, but she was very aware of the social gulf that separated them. And she had a noble nature, which meant she would sacrifice herself for Thomas's happiness.

'For heaven's sake,' Thomas exclaimed to Joan over the phone. 'I love her, she's the woman I want as my wife and the mother to my children. Without her, I'm nothing. I don't care if I lose a few clients because they don't approve. Such people are stuck in the dark ages.'

'You've got to understand that she's put aside her own feelings and needs,' Joan said. 'She's spent her whole life so far looking after others, she can't change that selflessness now. She really believes she can only hold you back.'

'But she's intelligent, how can she believe that?' Thomas said, exasperated now.

'I don't think you fully appreciate that it is people from the upper classes, with their high-handed ways and the demands they make on their servants, who create this belief in working people that they are inferior,' Joan snapped back at him.

'I'm so sorry, Mrs Hardy,' Thomas said, realizing she

felt intimidated by him. 'I didn't mean to offend you, but if Mabel does contact you, please tell her that I love her and always will.'

'I will,' she said. 'But Thomas, if it's any help, the postmark on the letter she sent me is Exeter. Maybe you should try looking for her there.'

The next day, Thomas took the train to Exeter but, like Southampton, he drew a blank at all the guest houses near the station. Feeling completely deflated by five in the afternoon, Thomas sank down on to a bench and put his head in his hands.

'Can I help?' a voice asked close to him. 'You look so dejected.'

He sat up and saw a plump middle-aged woman with cheeks like apples, standing in front of him.

'I am, I'm trying to find someone,' he replied. 'Without any luck.'

She sat down on the bench beside him and he told her an edited version of his story. She asked how old Mabel was.

'What's that got to do with it?' he asked.

'Well, a younger woman might walk further, and look for somewhere pretty to stay, even if she was unhappy. So why not try the guest houses overlooking the river.'

Thomas realized it was too late now to go on searching, it was already dusk and starting to rain. If he got a move on, he could catch the five-thirty train back to Dorchester and try again in the morning. He thanked the woman effusively and hurried back to the station.

He told himself, that night, if he couldn't find her the

next day he was going to give up. Even as he silently told himself that, he knew he would continue, resorting to putting a private detective on the case if necessary. Saying it to himself made him feel more empowered.

It was tipping down with rain in the morning and a strong wind had sprung up. Autumn had arrived with a vengeance, and the Indian summer was over.

Thomas put on an overcoat, and took an umbrella; it paid to be prepared. As he stood on the station platform waiting for the train, the bleak outlook, the driving rain and the hopelessness he felt, all reminded him of those endless days and nights in the trenches. Sometimes, it felt better to have to blow the whistle and go over the top, rather than spend further hours in the mud just waiting.

He had a vision then of all the young soldiers, braced, shoulders back, ready to go. Such earnest, trusting faces, believing that courage and serving your country was everything. Each day fewer of them came back, and he had to write yet another letter to parents who would sooner have given their own arms and legs than see their sons killed or maimed.

Pulling himself out of such dark thoughts, Thomas concentrated on the day ahead. He had a map of Exeter, and last night he'd marked the streets overlooking the river.

At the Byways Guest House Mabel returned to her room after her breakfast and packed her bag. She was leaving now, to go to the Red Griffin public house in the centre of

Exeter, where she had managed to get a live-in job, without any character.

The Red Griffin was a bit of a rough place, the kind that working men went to after work. It was an ancient inn, and very gloomy; her room was damp and dark, with only the most basic of furniture. But all the other positions she'd inquired about wouldn't take her on without a character.

She was extremely tempted to stay longer at the guest house. It overlooked the river, not too far from the station and close to lovely shops, it was clean, comfortable and reasonably priced too. If she spoke to the owners, she was sure she'd get a reduced weekly rate as the season was over now. But common sense prevailed, if she didn't get another job soon her money would all be gone. Besides, she needed to work to take her mind off Thomas.

She had spent her first few days in Exeter crying almost continually. She had never felt so alone and abandoned. The things Clara had said kept going round and round in her head, and she smarted to think she had imagined a one-time fishwife could raise herself up enough to marry a lawyer.

On the third day, she rallied herself to go out and buy a newspaper and have something to eat. There was a paragraph or two in the newspaper about the date of Agnes's execution. It was scheduled for the 2nd of November, at Plymouth prison. That was in five weeks' time, and Mabel wished for Agnes's sake they'd made it sooner. It seemed as if the main story had been told a couple of days before. All this piece did was give the bare bones of the trial, stating that the accused had confessed to murder just minutes before the jurors were being asked to vote. Thankfully, Mabel wasn't mentioned, but she wondered if her name had been given in the previous article.

Having a meal and being out in the fresh air had made her feel marginally better that day. When she'd got back to Byways, she'd felt able to write letters to Thomas, Clara and Joan, to explain her sudden disappearance. But she didn't put an address on them.

Clara's was easy enough to write; she just said that after thinking over what Clara had said, she felt it best to get out of Thomas's life before she spoiled it for him. She told Joan what had happened at the trial, and that Thomas had turned up, but said she'd realized she would only ever hold him back and so had decided to go away.

The letter to Thomas was extremely hard to write, especially as her tears kept falling on to the paper and making the ink run. In the end she kept it simple and short, saying she wasn't right for him, and she hoped he'd find happiness with someone who was better suited to be his wife.

All three letters were badly written and disjointed, but she hadn't the energy to rewrite them. She thought that all three recipients would see the letters as proof of her lack of breeding and education, and perhaps think that she'd made the right decision.

Now, as she fastened her bag, she felt like bursting into tears again. The thought of starting again in a new job, meeting new people and being asked about her past, was awful. She knew in a public house she would need to be jolly, appear interested in her customers, and make an effort to sparkle. She didn't think she could ever do that again, but she had to try. She'd come through so much before this, a broken heart could be considered the least of her worries.

Fixing the buckles on her bag, she lifted it on to her shoulder and said a silent farewell to a room that had been a sanctuary when she most needed it.

She glanced at herself in the mirror by the door. She was always astounded that her curly red hair was invariably the same, day after day – shiny, bouncy, the kind of hair that ought to belong to one of life's winners. But she looked pale, too much crying had made her eyes puffy, and redness around green eyes wasn't attractive.

'Good luck at the new job,' Mrs Wyatt, the guest-house owner, said as she left. 'I'll always have a room for you here if you need it.'

Mabel turned to smile and blow a kiss. Mrs Wyatt was a good woman, one of those who realized when people had a problem, but didn't pry, yet gave the impression you could tell her anything.

Out along the quayside, by the river, the rain was so fierce it was like being showered with darning needles. Mabel hunched her shoulders and, with one hand holding her hat on securely, she began walking towards the centre of town.

Thomas arrived in Exeter just after twelve noon. He paused before leaving the shelter of the station. The driving rain was so heavy that he felt most people would say it was madness to walk in it, unless it was absolutely necessary. To him it was; he had to find Mabel, however soggy he became. So turning up his collar, and opening up his umbrella, he stepped out into the downpour.

Two hours later, he was completely dispirited. Water had got into his shoes, down his neck and he felt like a block of ice. He had called at dozens of boarding houses, guest houses and small hotels to ask if Mabel Brook was staying there, and had asked many shopkeepers if they'd seen a pretty red-headed woman. Most of the shopkeepers seemed suspicious of him, as if he was searching for a prostitute. Thomas realized that, without a photograph of Mabel, it was a pointless exercise.

'Just four more places, then I go home,' he told himself as his umbrella blew inside out for the third time. The rain stung his face and he had to cling on to his bowler hat.

Byways Guest House was the second of the final four. The door was opened by a middle-aged woman with a pleasant face and a welcoming smile.

'Goodness me, you look wet,' she said in sympathy. 'Are you after a room?'

'No, I'm sorry I'm not,' Thomas said. 'I'm trying to find a dear friend of mine. Her name is Mrs Mabel Brook. Would she happen to be staying here?'

'Oh, my dear, you've missed her by just a couple of hours,' she said. 'But do come in, sir, at least get warm and have a cup of tea.'

Nothing had felt so good as to be ushered into a warm, cosy living room at the back of the house. The woman, who introduced herself as Mrs Wyatt, shooed a tabby cat off one of the chairs by the fire, then told him to take his coat off and sit down.

'So where did she go when she left here today?' Thomas asked as he hung his coat and hat on the back of the door.

The kettle was whistling in the scullery that led off the living room. Mrs Wyatt scuttled off to make some tea.

'She'd found herself a job,' she called back. 'A live-in one, so she won't be back, I'm sorry to say.'

Thomas's heart sank. He thought she'd meant at first that Mabel had only popped out on an errand. He felt this woman was the motherly sort and, as such, he could be frank and honest with her.

'Such a nice young lady,' she said as she came back with a pot of tea. 'I was really sorry to see her go, but I hope she'll be happy in her new job.'

'What is her new job?'

'She didn't say, only that she'd be living in. I'm hoping she'll find happiness, anyway – she seemed awfully sad to me. It's a shame you didn't get here before she left. Maybe you could've cheered her up?'

'I think, Mrs Wyatt, I was partly the cause of her sadness,' Thomas said, taking the proffered cup of tea. 'I want to marry her, but she got the idea into her head that I'll be marrying beneath me.'

'Ahh . . .' Mrs Wyatt sighed as she sat down on the other side of the fire to Thomas. 'She told me she'd done housekeeping. Was she your housekeeper?'

'Oh no! For a lady in Dorchester. In fact, it was she who inadvertently gave Mabel the idea she might wreck my career. She wouldn't – and anyway, I have no time for snobs who care about such things. I love Mabel, and I want to marry her. I don't believe people are that small-minded, not since the war,'

'Well, many are.' Mrs Wyatt sighed again. 'But Mabel would be a fool to turn down a personable young man like you. If she was still here, I'd tell her so. I was surprised when she said she'd been in service, I thought she was the school teacher kind, or perhaps a vicar's daughter.'

'Quite,' Thomas said, pleased by Mrs Wyatt's perceptiveness. 'So will you help me to find her?'

'I don't know what I can do,' she said, shaking her head. 'She avoided telling me where her new job was. Whether that was because she felt ashamed of it, or because she thought you might find your way here and didn't want you getting any closer, I don't know. But if she does come back, I'll be sure to tell her she's a silly girl passing up a lovely man like you.'

Thomas was disappointed. 'Will you telephone me if she comes here, or if you see or hear anything about her? Don't let on you've seen me, it might send her running again. I'll come immediately.'

They had another cup of tea while Thomas got warm again. Mrs Wyatt gave him a dry pair of her husband's socks to wear home. Apparently, he worked as a guard on the railways. They chatted for a while, about rationing, the holidaymakers she had as guests here in the summer, and Thomas told her about his childhood in Shaftesbury, which she knew well.

'I hoped the rain might have stopped by the time you wanted to go,' she said, as she opened the front door for him. 'But it looks like it's here to stay.'

'As is my sadness,' Thomas said. 'At least, until I find Mabel. But thank you for your kindness, Mrs Wyatt. It was much appreciated.'

26

At ten a.m., Mabel regretted taking the barmaid's position at the Red Griffin from the moment she walked through the saloon door.

'About bloody time too!' Mr Murphy called out to her from behind the bar. 'I said first thing. That means seven o'clock.'

Mabel was startled by both his appearance and his aggression. He was wearing a grubby vest and no shirt, and he had a glass of what looked like whisky in his hand.

'When you said a seven o'clock start, I assumed you meant once I'd settled in,' she said in her defence. 'I've never heard of any new live-in employee being expected to be on duty at the crack of dawn before she has even had time to put her clothes away.'

'Don't you speak to me in that hoity-toity manner,' he shouted back at her. 'Now put that bag out the back and come in here so I can show you what needs doing.'

Mr Seamus Murphy, known as Paddy to customers, was a big man, six foot tall, with shoulders like a barn door. His hair had been red, but there was little of it left, just a few strands that reached his vest. His face was red too, and his teeth were bad, but then Mabel had noticed at her interview that his regulars were all an unattractive, grubby bunch. Many of them, like him, had come to Exeter from Ireland with road-building jobs and stayed.

She assumed he was going to show her that the floor behind the bar needed scrubbing, or that most of the glasses on the shelves were smeared. The shelves themselves didn't look as if they'd ever been cleaned, and the lights above the bar had strings of dusty cobwebs hanging from them. As for the customers' side of the bar, the wooden floor was ankle deep in cigarette butts, globules of spit and other assorted rubbish, including bus tickets and peanut shells.

Mabel had noted all this when she came for her interview; it was only desperation for a job that had made her agree to work here.

As she took her bag to the area he called 'out the back', she was horrified to see that his living room was even filthier than the bar. But beyond that was the kitchen, and one quick glance into it made her retch.

It was beyond filthy – it was a hellhole with mountains of dirty crockery and saucepans, much of which still had food in or on them that was going mouldy. There was an overflowing kitchen bin, a cooker so dirty it was a miracle that gas even came out of the jets, and piles of old fish and chip wrappings – presumably from Murphy's staple diet, as there wasn't anything clean to cook in or put food on.

After seeing this, she wondered what the lavatories were like.

She wanted to run away, recognizing her acceptance of the job here as a moment of pure madness. She could go straight back to Byways, and she knew Mrs Wyatt would be pleased to see her.

'Come on, I'm waiting for you!' Murphy said from behind her.

She hadn't heard him come into the living room. She wheeled round, unable to contain her disgust.

'How do you expect anyone to work or live in such terrible filth?' she shouted at him. 'You should be ashamed of yourself. Even animals wouldn't want to go into these rooms. And have your customers no standards? How can they drink in that midden of a bar?'

'Why do you think I took you on?' he said. He even grinned, as if he found her disgust amusing.

'You really thought for six shillings a week I'd clean this sewer?' she asked incredulously. 'And serve your customers too?'

'I told you I'd let things slide since my wife died,' he said, his voice taking on a touch of a self-pitying whine. 'I can't do everything myself.'

Mabel thought for a moment. 'You make my wages a pound a week, and give me a couple of days to sort this room and the kitchen out, and then I might stay. If not, I'm off.'

'But I need a barmaid now,' he retorted.

'I think you are more than capable of looking after that bar alone for two days,' she snapped at him. 'Now have we got a deal, or not? And I'll have my wages in advance, or I don't lift a finger.'

'You're a shrew and no mistake,' he said, but she sensed he quite admired her spirit. 'Okay. You win. A pound a week, up front, but after two days you are in the bar during opening hours.'

After seeing the appalling rooms downstairs, her room at the top of the house didn't seem quite as bad as she remembered. It was gloomy and smelled of damp, but then it was an old building. She hung her dresses on the hooks on the back of the door, took off her good black clothes and changed into her old grey dress to start the cleaning. After tying her hair back, she went down to begin on the kitchen.

It took two hours just to get rid of the rubbish and scrape the plates and pots, ready for washing. Surprisingly, she found wire wool and soda crystals under the sink, and there was a constant supply of hot water from the geyser.

Mabel had never worked so hard. Yet in some strange way she quite enjoyed it. There was something mindless yet satisfying about transforming a room as disgusting as this one into a clean and tidy place. She had to boil the saucepans on the stove, with soda in them, to get rid of burned-on food. But as the pile of clean dishes and plates grew higher, the cutlery gleamed and the saucepans returned to a useable condition, she felt good, and it stopped her thinking about Thomas.

The insides of the cupboards had to be cleaned next, to put everything away. She threw out chipped and cracked cups, and ancient food packets, and scrubbed the shelves clean.

It was four in the afternoon when she finally put all the crockery, pans and still-edible food stuffs away, and then she had to tackle the floor.

That was a hands-and-knees, hot-soapy-water-and-a-scrubbing-brush job, but beneath the grime she found handsome, dark red tiles. Several buckets of water later, she stood up, stretched her aching back and smiled at the result.

The room was a far cry from Clara's pretty kitchen or

Joan Hardy's highly organized scullery. Its battered cupboards and the gloomy aspect, looking out on to a small yard filled with beer barrels, would never delight anyone. But it was clean now and could be cooked in.

Murphy came to see how she was getting on.

'That's a fine job you've done there,' he said, looking surprised – as if he imagined a genie had visited them to transform it. 'I was going to get meself some fish and chips when they open. Do you want some?'

Mabel was suddenly aware she was starving. 'Yes, please. But if I find you've dumped the paper in here later, instead of putting it in the dustbin, I'll swing for you.'

He laughed. 'Fair enough.'

In the days that followed, Mabel spring-cleaned the living room, tackled the filthy bar before opening hours, and scrubbed the lavatory and bathroom in the living quarters. They were shocking, but nowhere near as bad as the outside lavatory for the customers. For that she had to wait until closing time, at night. By the light of a candle, she put spirit of salts down the lavatory, while holding her nose. Then she stood well back as the chemical fizzed dramatically. It was quite a revelation to look at it the next morning and find the porcelain was white again. At least then she felt brave enough to go in and scrub the walls and floor. Murphy asked her to do his bedroom next, but she refused.

'Get some other drudge to do it,' she said. 'I've done enough.'

It was perfectly obvious to her that she was never going to like Murphy; he was lazy, ignorant and uncouth. She didn't like his customers, either. They were all cut from the same cloth as Murphy, ignorant and brutish, and with no conversation. Each day, before starting her morning shift behind the bar, she studied the local newspaper for more suitable work. But every situation that looked hopeful had 'character required' at the bottom of it.

In the afternoons she made a meal for the evening. Beef stew was Murphy's favourite, which he would cheerfully eat every day. But the way he ate, chewing with his mouth open, belching and shovelling food in, as if he was afraid someone would snatch it away from him, forced her to go out of the room till he was finished.

She didn't even attempt to get to know him. She didn't care to know where he came from in Ireland, or anything about his wife, or his family. She just took his pound a week and in return kept the place clean, served in the bar and did his laundry. But she never sparkled.

At night in her dreary, damp, cold room she thought of Thomas, wishing his arms were round her, hoping that by some miracle he'd come and find her and whisk her away to get married.

Even as she wished and hoped, she knew she was fooling herself, for hadn't she been the one who had left? She'd got on her high horse, claiming she was saving Thomas from disgrace, but now, here in this nasty, mucky public house, her noble ideals didn't seem noble any longer, only misguided.

She got a bad cold, and it wouldn't seem to go; at night she coughed so much her chest hurt.

Just before seven on the morning of November the 2nd, when Agnes was due to be hanged, Mabel stood at the bedroom window thinking about her, and sending up a prayer that she would remain brave to the last and meet Martin in heaven.

The view over the rooftops was blurred by fog, and it reminded her of the days after Carsten was killed, when she had felt she was in a grey fog. Somehow that memory seemed to reinforce the belief that she was still being punished for running out on Martin. She had no future, just work like this job, where she would always be clearing up the mess other people made. Today she could understand why Agnes wanted to die. From where she was standing, full of cold, with a sore throat and aching limbs, death looked attractive. No more striving, no covering up, no hurt or shame.

'Goodbye, Agnes,' she said aloud as the church clock struck seven. 'I have forgiven you, and I hope God has too.'

As ill as she felt, she got dressed and went downstairs to start work. Her first job was always to clear the bar, as Murphy inevitably let his friends stay on to drink after closing time. He never washed the glasses or emptied the ashtrays, and sometimes these men he called friends vomited on the floor, even pissed in the corner, and he expected her to deal with it.

It was harder than usual today, because she was feverish; one moment she was hot, the next shivering, and all she really wanted to do was go back to bed and stay there. Thankfully, today there weren't any unpleasant messes in the corners. She cleaned and polished all the tables, swept the floor, then mopped it. Afterwards, she went to make Murphy's breakfast.

He came down at eight thirty, as always, without a shirt,

just a dirty vest, and he stank of sweat. Without speaking, Mabel got his plate of eggs, bacon, sausages and fried bread from the oven and put it on the table in front of him, poured his tea into his pint mug, then went back into the kitchen.

'It would be nice to have some conversation!' he yelled out. 'Sometimes it's like I've taken on one of those shop window dummies to work here.'

Normally she ignored Murphy's sarcasm, or what he claimed was humour, but feeling as she did – and knowing it was going to be another long, gruelling day – she snapped.

'What do you imagine I'd want to talk to you about?' she asked, coming back into the living room, her hands on her hips. 'How much spit there was on the bar floor, or how the ashtrays were overflowing? Yes, once again, I've had to clear up after your friends, and I tell you I'm sick of it.'

'Well, fuck off, then,' he said. 'I managed before you came, I can do it again, and save myself cash.'

'You managed before I came?' she exclaimed, her voice rising in anger. 'This place was like a cesspit. The only people who drank in here were drunks, derelicts and their tarts – filthy, stupid people like you.'

As soon as the words came out of her mouth, she regretted them. Not because they weren't true, but because she knew he would retaliate. He jumped to his feet, his vast belly quivering beneath his grubby vest, his face contorted with anger.

'Who are you to criticize me or my friends?' he yelled at her. 'Fat lot of good it's done you, trying to speak like a toff. Why'd you come here, anyway? Just out of prison, or got the clap so you can't flog your fanny any more?'

Mabel rushed to the door and up the stairs before he could hit her. But her chest hurt, she struggled to climb the stairs, and as she got to the landing outside her room, all at once his hand was on her shoulder.

He spun her round and slapped her face hard, first to the right, then to the left, so she staggered back and fell to the floor. 'You bitch,' he yelled at her, standing over her. 'I'll show you how Murphy deals with whores like you!'

He kicked her in the side, snatched her up by her shoulders, then punched her in the face so that she fell again, cracking her head on the door frame behind her.

'I'm sorry,' she managed to get out. 'I was feeling ill, I didn't mean it.'

'Oh, but you did, you bitch,' he said. 'I've watched you ever since you arrived, seen how much you despise me. I bet you were biding your time to rob me. Was that it? You thought that's what I deserved?'

'No, I didn't, I wouldn't,' she yelled back.

To her further horror, he was unbuttoning his trousers, and she knew he was going to rape her. She wriggled back on her bottom, towards her room, but he had his cock in his hand and he was rubbing at it, trying to get it hard. She had only ever seen Martin's, and Murphy's was twice the size, even if it was flaccid. He leaned over and shoved his hand up the skirt of her dress, bringing back the memory of the man in the alley in Bristol.

'*No!*' she yelled at the top of her voice, simultaneously leaping up.

He was taken by surprise, and he staggered back.

361

She knew if he got hold of her, she wouldn't get away, he was far too big and strong, but big men weren't always steady on their feet, so she kicked out at him, catching him on the knee. He lifted the knee she'd kicked, to rub it. Quick as a flash, with every ounce of strength she had left, she kicked his other knee, and he went down on his back like an upturned turtle, banging his head on the bannister as he fell.

There was no time to gather up her belongings. He would kill her now if he caught her. She fled down the stairs and out through the open back door. The door led into the small yard where the empty beer barrels were stored, with a gate on to an alley. She had the gate opened in a trice and ran like the wind down the alley to where it emerged on the high street.

It was icy cold, and she had no coat. She was wearing only the old grey dress she kept for dirty jobs. Her face was burning from Murphy's slaps, and the pain in her side told her she had a broken rib or two. Her money, and everything else she owned, was up in that room.

Instinctively, she was heading towards the river, perhaps because the only kindness she'd been shown since arriving in Exeter was from Mrs Wyatt at Byways.

By the time she reached the boarding house, it hurt to breathe, and she was staggering like a drunk. As she rang the doorbell she had to lean on the wall so she didn't fall over.

'Mrs Brook?' Mrs Wyatt exclaimed when she opened the door. She looked horrified. 'What on earth has happened to you? You've been attacked?'

She took Mabel's two hands and led her down the hall into her kitchen, where she sat her down at the kitchen table.

'You are like a block of ice, that's a black eye you've got coming, and your lip is cut and swollen.' She put her hand of Mabel's forehead and gasped. 'Oh, my dear Lord, you've got a fever.'

Mabel tried to explain that she'd felt ill when she woke up that morning, and that Murphy had attacked and attempted to rape her.

'I had to run from there, or he'd have killed me,' she said, beginning to cry. 'And I'm sorry I came here, but my money and everything is back there. I didn't know anyone else to go to.'

'You did right to come to me, and I'm going to take you upstairs and put you to bed.' Mrs Wyatt stroked Mabel's forehead to comfort her. 'We'll think what we are going to do about that beast later. For now you need a hot toddy, and bed.'

'I think my ribs are broken too,' Mabel sobbed out. 'It was the most awful place, Mrs Wyatt. I shouldn't have taken the job, but I was afraid I wouldn't find another one and my money would run out.'

Later, tucked up in bed and wearing one of Mrs Wyatt's flannel nightgowns, a hot-water bottle by her feet and a strong hot toddy inside her, Mabel felt woozy and comforted. If she stayed on her back, her broken ribs didn't hurt too badly.

Mrs Wyatt checked on Mabel half an hour after she'd helped her into bed, and noted that she'd fallen asleep, but her breathing had a nasty rasping sound, as if she had a chest infection. Although she hadn't got a thermometer, she knew Mabel's temperature was extremely high and, coupled with her injuries and the shock of the attempted rape, she could end up with pneumonia. She thought she would run along to the public telephone box at the end of the road and call her doctor.

'Yes, Mrs Wyatt, you were right to call me,' Dr Grant said gravely. He had examined Mabel and then asked the landlady to come out of the room so he could talk to her. 'Apart from the injuries she received – a couple of broken ribs and severe bruising – your friend's chest is infected. I am afraid it will turn to pneumonia. I would send her to the hospital, but I think she has a better chance of survival staying here. That is, of course, if you feel able to nurse her?'

Hannah Wyatt had the greatest respect for Dr Grant, as he'd taken care of her mother in her final years and shown care and patience. He was close to seventy himself now, small, thin, his face heavily lined, but he still had a brightness in his eyes and the energy of a much younger man.

'Yes, of course. When Mrs Brook first came to me, I guessed she'd had a lot of sadness and heartache. I don't know why she went to work in the Red Griffin, such a low dive. The owner is the kind of man you wouldn't want to run into on a dark night. I'm not surprised he beat her and attempted to rape her, that's about what I'd expect from such a man. Should we call the police? All her belongings are still there.'

Dr Grant looked thoughtful. 'Leave it to me, Mrs Wyatt. I need to stress to them that Mrs Brook is in no fit state to be interviewed. I think they'll take my word for her injuries, then arrest him and collect her belongings. I'd like to say she can give evidence against him when she's better, but I'm not sure she can recover from this.'

Mrs Wyatt gasped and caught hold of the bannister to support herself. 'Oh no, Doctor, she can't die! She's too young, and I know she's got a young man who adores her. He came here searching for her.'

If the doctor wondered why a woman would run out on a man who loved her, he didn't ask. 'In that case, if you know how to contact him, do it as soon as possible. Sometimes even the sickest person can recover if they have a good reason to do so.'

He told her to keep Mrs Brook warm, make her drink as much as possible, and then he gave her some medicine in a brown bottle. 'Give her two spoonfuls now, and again at six. I'll come back this evening to see how she is.'

After the doctor had gone, Mrs Wyatt went back to see Mabel, and was alarmed to find her delirious. She didn't appear to know who Mrs Wyatt was, and she was muttering. She caught the name Agnes and something about forgiveness.

Mrs Wyatt sponged Mabel down, somehow managed to get the medicine into her mouth, and a little water, then put another blanket on the bed.

It was alarming to think such a lovely young lady could die, and a terrifying responsibility to try and prevent it. But she still had the card Mr Kellaway had left with her; she must go back to that telephone box and ring him.

*

Mrs Wyatt wasn't used to using a telephone. A lady answered the phone at the solicitor's and said Mr Kellaway was in court, but would she like to leave a message? Mrs Wyatt panicked a bit, stumbling over her words and perhaps not making a lot of sense.

'Now who is sick?' the woman asked. 'I can tell you are upset, but give me their name. That's good. I heard you. Mrs Mabel Brook. Now tell me where she is, and who you are.'

'Mr Kellaway knows me, he came to my guest house in Exeter,' Mrs Wyatt blurted out. Then, suddenly realizing that perhaps she shouldn't tell this woman too much, she apologized and put the receiver down.

The thick fog of earlier was lifting now, but it had grown colder still. Mrs Wyatt hurried back home, hoping she'd said enough so that Mr Kellaway would come as soon as he could.

Thomas got the message from his secretary, Miss Gibson, when he got back from Dorchester court at four thirty in the afternoon.

He blanched. 'Mrs Wyatt sounded scared, you say? Did she say why Mabel had come back to her?'

'She could barely string a few words together. She sounded really panicked. Who is Mabel Brook? Is she a relative?'

'She's the woman I love,' Thomas said simply. 'And I must go there now.'

'Will you still be able to keep your appointments tomorrow?' Miss Gibson asked.

'I doubt it, so you'd better cancel them – or ask if they'll see someone else.'

Miss Gibson was a forty-year-old spinster and she wished, just once in her life, a man might have said 'she's the woman I love' about her.

'I hope it isn't as serious as it sounded,' she said gently. 'Do drive carefully, Mr Kellaway, it's awful weather. Don't worry, I'll sort out your clients.'

27

Thomas loved his new automobile, but to drive over fifty miles on a dark, stormy evening was a frightening experience.

His headlights were not so bright, and the road to Exeter was narrow and winding. Fallen leaves and the driving rain made the road slippery. It was also very cold. But the need to get to Mabel as soon as possible made it bearable, and at least the appalling weather meant there was nothing else on the road, not even the occasional badger or fox.

He had read in *The Times* that Agnes Wellows was to be hanged at dawn this morning, and he wondered if that had any bearing on Mabel returning to Byways in such a poorly state. He had studied newspapers carefully since Mabel disappeared, and although there had been some articles about Agnes Wellows confessing to killing her son, her daughter-in-law was only referred to as the young Mrs Wellows, nothing that would alert anyone to her new identity as Mabel Brook.

There had been a very sympathetic article about returning soldiers suffering from serious injuries and shell shock, and how little was being done to help them, or their families who suffered with them. Agnes was mentioned in the article, saying it was understandable that she had felt her son would be better off dead. The journalist stated that many such damaged men had told him they wanted to die too.

On cold nights such as this, with heavy rain and high winds, Thomas often found himself slipping back into the nightmare of trench warfare; he fancied he could hear the guns again, and the cries of the wounded still lying in no-man's-land. He had gone to his brother many a time to comfort him when he was suffering from a nightmare. But he and Michael were the lucky ones; they had money, a comfortable home with Aunt Leticia and futures to look forward to. Many ex-soldiers were sleeping rough, unable to find work, or trying to keep a roof over their family's heads with so little money that the children went hungry.

Whatever had happened to the government's claims that all soldiers would be returning to 'homes fit for heroes'?

It was well after ten when Thomas finally got to Byways. He could see a light in a window upstairs, and one in the downstairs hall, so Mrs Wyatt was still up.

She greeted him warmly when she opened the door, and quickly ushered him in. 'I'm sorry if my message alarmed you,' she said. 'But Mabel is gravely ill, and I felt I must call you.'

'You did right,' he assured her. 'Now tell me what happened, before I go up to see her.'

'Let me take your hat and coat first,' she said. 'You must be frozen, so I'll make you some tea.'

Thomas was cold and very stiff after the long drive, although the warmth of the fire in Mrs Wyatt's living room, and the welcome cup of tea, soon revived him. But her account of what had occurred at the Red Griffin sickened him. He vowed to himself that he would make that man pay dearly for what he had done to Mabel.

'The doctor came again at seven this evening,' she said. 'He told me to give her a bigger dose of the medicine every four hours. He said he thought the fever would reach crisis point tonight, but if she survives that, she should get better.'

They went up then to see Mabel.

Thomas was horrified to see her pretty face blackened with bruising and to hear her rattling breath. She was unconscious but her lips moving, as if she was talking to herself, and her fingers were picking at the sheet. He leaned over her and heard her say the word 'punishment' very faintly.

'She's been like that since soon after I got her into bed,' Mrs Wyatt said. 'I've sponged her down many times today.'

'You must be exhausted,' Thomas said to her. 'If you'll just show me where everything is, I can take over. You must go to bed – that is, of course, if you don't mind having a strange man in your house.'

She smiled wearily. 'You aren't strange, and my husband is downstairs in the parlour. Let me introduce you, and then I'll show you where everything is.'

At one in the morning, Thomas once again sponged Mabel's face, neck and chest with cool water, becoming more alarmed by the minute at the sound of her laboured breath and the incredible heat coming off her.

'Fight it, my darling,' he whispered. 'You can come out of this. Don't even think of leaving me.'

The room was like an oven, and Mrs Wyatt had said he was to keep the fire going. Thomas stripped down to his shirtsleeves and mopped his own brow as often as he mopped Mabel's.

She had moments of delirium when she called out his name, as well as Carsten's and Martin's. Agnes's name popped out now and then, as did Clara's and Joan's. It seemed to Thomas she was reliving her whole life.

Her eye had become blacker and more swollen since he arrived, and the bruising was coming out on both cheeks. Yet despite her facial injuries, her hair was as glorious as ever, red-gold on the pillows in the soft light, little tendrils curling on to her overheated face.

He couldn't count the number of times he'd lifted her with one arm and plumped up her pillows with his other hand, then poured a little water into her mouth from the jug by the bed. He wished he knew more about nursing; he felt so clumsy, comparing his efforts with the way he'd seen real nurses handle patients. Yet he felt that if it was possible to will someone back to health, he had the will of twenty men.

Outside, the wind was howling. When he pulled back the thick curtains and looked out on to the river, he saw the water level had risen, and still the rain came down in sheets.

Back at Mabel's bedside Thomas took her hand in his and talked. He described their wedding, who would be there in the church, and afterwards the reception at his aunt's house. Then he moved on to describing the house he imagined them living in, even going as far as telling her the colour of the drawing-room wallpaper, the stair carpet and what their bedroom would be like.

But there was no response to any of this. Her forehead was growing hotter and hotter as the night progressed, and her breathing was becoming still more laboured.

'Don't even think of leaving me,' he implored her, his voice rising in alarm. 'You're my love, we've got so much to do together. I can't live without you!'

He cried then, because there was no response. He leaned forward in his chair, rested his head on the bed beside her, and sobbed his heart out.

At first, he thought the light touch on his head was his imagination. But after a second or two, it dawned on him that it was Mabel's hand and she was stroking his hair.

He had never felt such joy before.

'My darling!' he said, sitting up and taking her hand. Her eyes were still shut but there was something different about her, something he couldn't put a name to. 'Can you hear me?'

'Thomas.' His name came from her lips like a soft caress.

'I'm here, my darling.' He lifted her hand to his lips and kissed it. 'I've been here all along. You are going to get better now.'

When he put his hand on her forehead, he found it cooler and he knew the crisis had passed.

She had been spared. With tears running down his cheeks, he offered up a prayer of thanks.

Thomas stayed in the room with her for the remainder of the night, dozing in the chair. He awoke and went to the window to pull the curtains back just enough to see it was dawn. The wind had dropped, and the rain had stopped.

When he looked back at Mabel in the bed, he could see she was sleeping now, not unconscious like the previous day. Her breathing was still laboured, and the sight of her battered face made him wince, but he felt such joy that she had come through it.

A couple of hours later, Mrs Wyatt peeped round the door. 'How is she?' she whispered.

'Past the worst,' Thomas whispered back. 'She's sleeping peacefully.'

'Come down and have breakfast with us, then?' she said. 'Sleep is the best healer.'

It was after ten before Mabel woke. She opened her eyes, looked at Thomas, and then smiled.

'I thought it was a dream that you were here,' she said.

'No dream,' he said, smoothing back her hair. 'And you'd better promise me you'll never frighten me again like that.'

She smiled. 'I promise. But how did you find me?'

'That's a long story, and I'll save it for when we are old and have nothing else to chat about,' he said. 'But let's just say I must have walked every street in Exeter over the past weeks. I found out you'd stayed here before, though, just hours after you'd left. Unfortunately, you hadn't told Mrs Wyatt where you were going.'

'So how did you know I was ill?'

'The lovely Mrs Wyatt telephoned my office, while I was in court. As soon as I got the message, I drove here. What a night! It was such wild weather that I was afraid trees would've fallen across the road. As it was, the road was slippery with leaves. Then I got here to find you were in an awfully bad way. But let's not dwell on that,' he said, conscious of how close he'd come to losing her. 'How do you feel now?'

'Warm and cosy,' she said. 'I'm afraid to move because of the pain in my ribs, but I think that's all that's stopping me from wanting to jump out of bed and hug you.'

'You won't be getting out of bed for a while,' he said sternly. 'I'm here to police that. Cup of tea? Or could you eat something?'

All that day, Thomas stayed with Mabel. She told him all the details of what had happened to her since leaving Dorchester.

'I realized as soon as I got to Exeter that I didn't want to live without you. I wanted to telephone you and apologize,' she admitted. 'I am so impulsive sometimes. I run away and jump into situations without thinking them through. I'm so sorry that I hurt you. But I hurt myself more!'

Thomas smiled at that. 'Mabel, let me tell you something, once and for all. People really don't care about this "station in life" thing any longer. The war, and better education for everyone, has changed our society from how it was in Victorian times. Anyone meeting you for the first time wouldn't label you as anything but an attractive, intelligent, vivacious lady. So please, for both our sakes, do drop this idea that you're not good enough. I want to marry you, and that's that. I take you as you are, just as you take me as I am. Warts and all!'

'Where are your warts?' she teased him. 'Will I find them when I pull your clothes off?'

'Enough of such smutty talk,' he said in a mock serious tone. 'Until you are completely well, there will be no talk of removing clothes.'

*

Later in the day, he went out to telephone his office to say he wasn't coming back yet. Then he spoke to Clara and told her he'd found Mabel.

That evening, Mrs Wyatt offered him a bed in one of her guest rooms, which he gratefully accepted.

On the second day, Mabel was well enough to get up, have a bath and eat a meal. Thomas really needed to get back to the office. But however much better Mabel looked and sounded, the doctor advised against taking her back to Dorchester with him.

'It's very cold in your automobile, and the road is bumpy. Her ribs need time to heal, and she shouldn't be exposed to fluctuating temperatures.'

A police sergeant came that day, bringing with him the possessions Mabel had left at the Red Griffin. He spoke only briefly to Mabel, asking how she was, but to Thomas he had more to say.

He made it quite clear that charging Murphy with assault and attempted rape would only result in embarrassment and humiliation for Mabel. He said that a judge would rule that, by going to work in a rough public house with a lone bachelor landlord, Mabel had laid herself wide open to abuse.

'I do not personally condone men hitting or forcing themselves on to women,' he said to Thomas. 'Murphy is an unpleasant character who deserves a good kicking. But sadly, the courts do not offer that little service.'

While Thomas was angry that Murphy had got away with it, Mabel agreed with the policeman.

'I brought it on myself, I should've guessed what might happen,' she said. 'Now let us forget all about it. I've got my things back, and I've got you too. My broken ribs are a reminder never to be so foolish again. And yes, you should go back to work. As much as I like you being here with me, it is a bit pointless now that I'm on the mend.'

A little later, Thomas said he had to go out. Mabel thought it was strange that he didn't say where he was going. An hour passed before he returned. He had two boxes of chocolates, one for Mrs Wyatt and one for Mabel. But as he handed them over, Mabel noticed the knuckles on his right hand were badly skinned, and she asked him how he'd done it.

He seemed sheepish and said he'd banged it against a rough wall.

'No, you didn't, you punched someone!' she exclaimed. 'Who?'

Even as she asked the question, she knew the answer: Murphy. 'But that was crazy! What if his chums had jumped on you?' she asked.

'That's why I went when the pub was closed,' he smirked. 'When he answered the door, I told him I was the licensing officer and needed to ask him a few questions. He asked me in – he was a bit inebriated, I admit – anyway, once I was in, I thumped him good and hard. Once I'd started, I couldn't stop. I told him it was from you. Once I'd knocked him down, I kicked him in the ribs too. I left then, leaving him lying on the floor of his living room, groaning and carrying on like a baby. But as I went through the bar, I turned a couple of the barrels on and left them running.'

'Thomas!' she reproached him. 'I didn't know you had that kind of violence in you!'

'We all have, when someone hurts the one you love. Revenge gets the better of common sense sometimes. But

I had an ace card up my sleeve – I've always boxed. Today I knew why I'd kept it up.'

He left about an hour later, promising to come back at the weekend, which was in two days' time.

Mrs Wyatt came into the room a little while later, to give Mabel her medicine and some hot milk.

'Thomas is such a lovely young man, and he adores you,' she said. 'God only knows what you were thinking about when you ran away from him!'

'I was just asking myself that,' Mabel said, wincing with pain as she pulled herself up in the bed. 'We ought to talk about money for my keep. As the police brought my things back, I've got some money now.'

'Thomas took care of all that.' Mrs Wyatt took the pillows from behind Mabel's back and plumped them up. 'The doctor's bill and everything. So all you've got to do is concentrate on getting better.'

'He is marvellous. I look such a fright, I wonder he didn't turn tail and run.'

While having a bath, she saw herself in the mirror and was shocked at how awful her facial bruises were – not just the black eye but both cheeks and a very swollen lip. But she wasn't coughing so much now, and her breathing was getting easier all the time.

Once Mrs Wyatt had gone downstairs again, Mabel closed her eyes and imagined Thomas fighting Murphy in his living room. Just another thing she hadn't known about her man, that he could fight. And act as a nurse. Somehow, those two new facets of his character made her love him twice as much as before.

*

377

It was another ten days before the doctor said Mabel was well enough to go home. She still coughed a little, especially at night, but her ribs didn't hurt unless she moved awkwardly. The bruises on her cheeks had gone, and her black eye had faded to a mauve colour.

She got up and dressed at eight. She was so excited to see Thomas again, as he'd been back in Dorchester all week. She'd put on the navy-blue wool dress that Clara had brought her when she came to visit three days ago. It was one of hers that she seldom wore, but Mabel had often admired it. Clara had been worried that she had nothing warm to wear to go home in.

It was just after ten thirty when Thomas drove up. Mabel still couldn't jump out of a chair, but she got up cautiously on hearing the automobile engine.

'Will you look at that!' Mrs Wyatt exclaimed. 'He's brought you a fur coat to wear.'

He had indeed. A brown musquash coat was draped over his arm as he came in.

'It's one of my aunt's but she said to bring it, to keep you snug on the way back,' he said, helping Mabel into it. 'I wasn't sure if you even had a coat with you.'

Mabel shed a few tears as she said goodbye to Mrs Wyatt, and the older woman did too.

'I'll never forget your kindness,' Mabel said as she hugged her. 'I can't bear to think what might have happened if you hadn't taken me in.'

'It was my pleasure having you here, and I'm going to miss you,' Mrs Wyatt said, drying her eyes on her apron. 'But you let me know when the wedding's going to be, don't forget!'

'We promise you'll get an invitation,' Thomas said, and hugged her too. 'You aren't going to drop out of our life now, you'll be part of it forever.'

Mabel was lost for words as they drove out of Exeter. It was a cold but sunny morning and instead of all the buildings looking grey and dull, as they had when she'd arrived, all at once they seemed to sparkle.

Once out beyond the city and into the countryside, Thomas reached out for her hand. 'When we get back to Dorchester, we'll go straight to Aunt Leticia's,' he said. 'She's gone to spend a couple of days with a friend and given the maid time off so we can be completely alone. I've told Clara too, so she doesn't worry.'

'Is this so you can have your evil way with me?' she asked.

'My priority was to make sure you rest and keep warm. We need to talk properly too, with no one interrupting us. But should you feel amorous towards me, then I would be honoured to oblige.'

Mabel giggled. Thomas had a lovely way of saying things.

They did make love later that day, but not before Thomas had given her a little lecture on suffrage and better rights for women, something he really believed in.

'Parliament passed the Representation of the People act last year, and they agreed women over thirty, with a property qualification, could vote, as well as men over twenty-one, whether or not they owned property. I know that's not perfect, Mabel. I and every sensible chap with half a brain would agree women ought to have the vote at twenty-one. But it's a step in the right direction.

'There's still the old guard, with outdated views about wives and daughters remaining in the home – or if they are from poorer families, in service. But that is all breaking down now. During the war so many servants went to work in factories that some of the best families had to get by without domestic help. Those women who went to do factory work won't go back to working as servants now. They've got a taste of freedom and they don't intend to give it up.'

He smiled at Mabel's rather bored expression. 'Yes, well, I'll get off my high horse now, but I want you to remember that the new society in England needs bright young woman like you, Mabel, and men capable of thinking like me. There have been too many doddering old fools running the country for too long, supported by their bigoted wives. But it is about to change. Even more importantly for me, my brother and aunt both adore you, and you have enchanted every other person I've introduced you to. That includes many of the old guard in Dorchester, and the senior partners in my firm.'

'Fair enough, you've made your point,' she said, pretending to yawn. 'Remind me never to go to court when you're defending someone! I might be there all week.'

He lifted her up off her chair then, pretending he was going to drag her off to bed like a caveman.

'I'll walk willingly,' she said, making for the staircase. 'I believe in equal opportunities.'

28

February 1920

The church organ wheezed into life to play Charles Wesley's hymn 'Love Divine' as Thomas and Mabel walked back down the nave together as husband and wife.

The pews on either side of the nave were packed with Thomas's relatives from far and near, clients, friends and well-wishers. Mabel had Joan, Percy, Clara and Mr and Mrs Wyatt in place of family, but she too had many friends, made more recently than Thomas's perhaps, but their delight at seeing their friend getting married today was every bit as genuine. Some were from local businesses, others she'd met while working at the POW camp, or at church.

Mabel wore a pale pink wool costume with a white fur collar and matching fur hat, while Thomas wore tails, striped trousers and carried a top hat.

Michael was the best man, dressed like his brother, and Clara was in pale blue as matron of honour.

'How does it feel to be Mrs Kellaway?' Thomas whispered.

'Very good, sir,' she whispered back and smiled lovingly at him. She hoped no one had noticed the slight swelling of her belly. Thomas claimed there was no such swelling, but even if there were, he'd be thrilled to announce they had a baby on the way.

It must have happened that day he brought her home from Exeter, and just the very thought of that afternoon of love in his bedroom at Aunt Leticia's made her blush at remembered passion.

Propriety had made it virtually impossible for any further love-making. But as Thomas had said, it was a good reason to marry quickly. He had bought a house for them to live in at Top O' Town, a lovely double-fronted Georgian house, close to Leticia's and with the same wonderful view from the back.

Painters, carpenters and plumbers had worked nonstop since it became theirs, putting in a bathroom and radiators, along with redecorating every room. The boiler in the cellar looked like a fearsome beast to Mabel, but Thomas insisted it was the absolute best that money could buy and should keep them cosy for a lifetime.

Clara had put Willow Cottage up for sale; she intended to move into town, to be closer to them and other friends.

Now they were going back to Aunt Leticia's for the wedding breakfast, and later they would catch a train to London for two nights at The Ritz, then go on by boat train to Paris where they would embark on the Orient Express all the way to Constantinople.

Thomas had bought her a beautiful grey fox coat, along with insisting she got innumerable dresses made for the honeymoon. He opened an account for her at a very smart and expensive shop in Southampton to buy her trousseau, including shoes, night clothes, underwear and stockings, and told Clara she was to go with her and spend madly. Having been brought up to be frugal, Mabel would probably have bought only the most basic of clothing. But Clara would have none of that. As she pointed out, they were stopping over in Venice and again in Paris on the way back. Mabel couldn't let Thomas down by looking like his housekeeper.

In the past few weeks, sometimes Mabel thought she was in a fabulous, beautiful dream, and she'd wake up back in Harley Place, still a maid, cleaning out fireplaces and polishing silver. It didn't seem possible that she was going to marry a lawyer, have a splendid house to move into, and would soon be travelling to places like Turkey, Italy and France.

But for now, Mabel was thinking only about how happy she was to finally be married to Thomas, and anticipating a joyful wedding breakfast with all the people she cared most about.

'So we finally got you there,' Clara said to Mabel later, in Leticia's drawing room. 'But I'm going to miss you so much.'

'By the time we get back from our honeymoon I hope you'll have sold Willow Cottage and found somewhere near us,' Mabel said. 'Then you can hire a maid and I'll train her.'

'Who would've thought that we'd end up like this today?' Clara said. 'I knew as soon as Lavinia Forester told me about you that it was going to work out with you being my housekeeper. But I didn't know then you would become such a dear, dear friend.'

'That's enough of that or you'll make me cry,' Mabel laughed. Since Thomas had brought her back from Exeter, Mabel had moved into Willow Cottage and they had become closer than ever. Clara was the only person who knew she was pregnant, and she'd sworn she would tell no one.

'I'd better go and check Joan and Percy are getting to know people,' Mabel said. 'I noticed earlier that Joan was about to start handing round canapés. Old habits die hard.'

'Speaking of old habits,' Clara said, catching hold of Mabel's arm, 'have there been any more psychic incidents?' She whispered the last bit.

Mabel hesitated. 'I'm not absolutely sure, it could've just been a dream. But when I was sick, I could hear Carsten urging me to fight to live. He said Thomas was the man I deserved, and I would be happy with him –' she broke off, looking a bit embarrassed. 'I imagined it, didn't I?'

'I don't think so, Mabel,' Clara said. 'I believe Carsten would've come back to try and save you. But there's been nothing else? Not even when Agnes was hanged?'

Mabel shook her head. 'Absolutely nothing. I feel it was all related to Carsten's death. And now it's all gone. Another thing to forget.'

'That's good, because it'll be one less thing for you to worry about. But now you'd better circulate, or I'll be accused of hogging you,' Clara laughed.

Mabel found Thomas talking to Joan and Percy in the drawing room. 'I was just telling them where we are going on our honeymoon,' Thomas said. 'Percy is jealous.'

Percy laughed. 'Not just of the honeymoon, but of you two getting married. I keep asking Joan and she says she's too old and set in her ways.'

'Oh, Joan, that's silly,' Mabel said, turning to her friend who was looking extremely attractive in lavender, with a very stylish hat to match. 'Agree at once, or I won't send you any postcards from Constantinople. Doesn't the name conjure up all kinds of magical visions?'

Joan was blushing furiously. 'It's all the fuss that scares me. Weddings are for the young.'

'Rubbish,' Thomas said firmly. 'They are nothing of the kind, and you don't have to do a big public ceremony, just two witnesses and that's it. We could be those witnesses when we get back in the spring.'

'Now there's an offer we can't turn down, Joan,' Percy said. 'How about it?'

Mabel could see by the way Joan looked at Percy that she did love him. 'Go on, say yes, and you can live in his beautiful house and stare at the stunning view of the Avon Gorge every day. Think how much it will annoy Frank Bedford too, when you sell the mews house!'

'Well, those are two of the best arguments I've heard yet for her marrying me,' Percy chuckled. 'Come on, then, light of my life, will you marry me?'

Joan's face was a picture of embarrassment, delight and coyness, all rolled into one. 'Very well then, Percy,' she said. 'But no fuss or a big party.'

Thomas turned to look at Mabel. 'Do you see what magical powers we've got? I think we could make anything in the world happen, if we just put our minds to it.'

Mabel only smiled. She already believed that Thomas could do anything he put his mind to. She just hoped their child would have the same gift.

Acknowledgements

Firstly, I wish to thank Shelagh Golding for telling me about the tragic destruction of Hallsands. Shelagh and I were close friends some thirty-five years ago, when our children were small. I confided to her my dreams of becoming a published novelist, and we talked books and more books back then.

It was wonderful that she and her husband Malcolm came back into my life last year, just in time to join the celebrations of my twenty-fifth year in publishing. I just hope they both enjoy this book and take pride in having struck the first spark.

Secondly, thank you, Rebecca Hilsdon, my editor at Penguin, for all your input and wisdom. You've been marvellous, even when I'm grumpy. A true star.

Then there was Carolyn, a lovely lady at the Courthouse Museum in Dorchester, who gave Carsten and me so much help in finding the most interesting and relevant places to look at in her home town. It was much appreciated.

Finally, Louise Moore, Emma Draude, Tim Bates, Liz Smith, Claire Bush and Shân Morley Jones for your expertise, and for keeping me going with your enthusiasm and belief in me. I'd be nowhere without you all.

Discover the gripping new
novel from Lesley Pearse

LIAR

Read on for an extract . . .

Coming summer 2020

I

1970, Shepherd's Bush

The stink from the bags of rubbish piled against a wall in Scotts Road made Amelia involuntarily gag and cover her nose. The dustbin men had gone on strike, and the council appeared disinclined to make any alternative arrangement. People had resorted to piling their rubbish on side roads like this one; anywhere just as long as it wasn't outside their own home.

Amelia lived just around the corner in Godolphin Road. It was a street of Victorian three-storey houses with basements. They were built as family homes with rooms for servants, but now practically all were in multiple occupation. The luckier tenants had a self-contained flat, but mostly the houses were divided up into bedsitters, with as many as ten rooms sharing one bathroom.

Amelia thought herself lucky. Her room on the first floor of number 22 was large and light, and there were two bathrooms in the house along with a separate lavatory. But then her landlord, who was a decent sort, lived in the basement flat and kept an eye on his tenants and his property.

Pleasant he might be, yet his house was still shabby. Cracked lino in the hall, a threadbare stair carpet and, despite all the tenants getting on quite well, no one was in favour of a cleaning rota. Mostly it was just Amelia who cleaned the common parts. She daydreamed of having a real flat, with a proper kitchen instead of a cupboard, and her own bathroom where she could arrange fluffy towels and pretty bottles of bubble bath. But on twelve pounds a week from her job at the *West London Weekly*, she couldn't afford anything better.

The record 'In The Summertime' by Mungo Jerry had been in the top twenty for most of the summer – it wafted out of shops, houses and from car radios all the time. But while that song created a lovely image of sunshine and flowers, stinking piles of rubbish were growing all over London. Now in late August, this one in Scotts Road had become a small mountain. Mike, who lived in the bedsit next to Amelia, claimed he'd seen rats running around on it the previous night. He thought the army should be called in to take it away.

Amelia usually averted her eyes from it and hurried past as fast as she could, but she saw something white out the corner of her eye and turned her head to look.

There on the rubbish was a pair of the gorgeous white boots she'd been aching to own. She'd seen an advertisement on the Tube for them, a black girl with an Afro hairstyle sitting naked on a rock wearing only the boots. A girl in the office called them Durex boots because the legs were tight and stretchy and quite difficult to get on.

Amelia couldn't believe that anyone had just dumped them there, the soles were hardly worn. Peering around first to check no one was watching, she went closer, braving the smell to look. She couldn't see a size, but they looked like a five, her size. Checking around her once more, she climbed up over a couple of bags and grabbed one of the boots.

It didn't move, so she pulled it sharply. The rubbish bags moved, and to her horror she saw the boot was attached to a human leg.

She screamed and almost toppled over backwards as she let go of it. On reaching the pavement she saw the rubbish pile had shifted even further with her weight and now a tanned, shapely thigh was exposed.

Seeing a man who lived two doors away from her coming towards her, she ran to him stammering out what she'd seen and pointing back to it. He caught hold of her shoulders to calm her.

'Okay love, horrible but you'll be all right,' he said soothingly, glancing over at the exposed leg. 'I'll go to the phone box and ring the police. You'd better stay here. They'll need to speak to you.'

Within a minute he was back, and put his arm round her as she was shaking from the shock. 'They're coming. Now let's just cross over so the smell isn't so bad. I'm Max, by the way. You aren't going to pass out on me, are you?'

'I don't think so,' she said, and gratefully let him lead her away.

She'd seen Max dozens of times, but mostly only from her window. He was perhaps thirty, slim and tall with dark hair. Always smartly dressed in a navy blue suit with well-polished shoes. Close up he was much nicer looking than she'd expected, with green eyes, a tanned face and white, even teeth.

'Do you think she's been murdered?'

'I can't think of any other reason for her being on a pile of rubbish,' he said. 'Let's hope the whole girl is there, not just a body part.'

Amelia shuddered. 'I saw the boots and thought someone had dumped them,' she admitted. 'I never expected they would be attached to legs.'

They stood together in silence. Amelia was normally something of a chatterbox, but shock had made her mute.

The police arrived soon after. They cordoned off the area, preventing anyone coming into the side street, and removed some of the rubbish around the body to take photographs.

From Max and Amelia's position inside the cordon, they were close enough to see it was a young girl, with long blonde hair. She was wearing red hot pants, the kind with straps and a bib, and a blood-stained white tee shirt or blouse beneath the straps. Somehow the outfit made it even more distressing as it was the kind Amelia yearned to wear, but she felt she was too plump.

A policeman came across to speak to them. He looked close to retirement age and his face was deeply lined. 'You'll be the young lady who found the body?' he asked. 'And is this the gentleman who telephoned us?'

Amelia nodded. 'I'm Amelia White, I live at 22 Godolphin Road. I just saw a leg and I ran to Max here as he came around the corner.' She couldn't bring herself to admit she wanted the boots. In the light of the girl being dead it sounded so ghoulish.

After taking down their names and addresses, the officer said they would be called on for a written statement.

'How was she killed?' Max asked.

'The pathologist is examining her now. Do either of you know her?'

'We haven't seen her face,' Amelia said. 'Do you want us to come closer and look?'

'No, that won't be necessary, we'll establish her identity and contact her next of kin. You can go now.'

'Well that's it, dismissed,' Max said in an obvious attempt to lighten the mood. 'You are as white as a sheet, Amelia. Shall I come in with you and get you tea or something? I don't want to leave you alone after such a shock.'

'That would be so kind,' she agreed, glad he'd offered because she felt she'd fall apart if she was left on her own. 'But only if you've got nothing more pressing to do.'

'Even if I had, I'd postpone it,' he said with a weak smile. 'Besides, I'm as shaken as you and I need a cup of tea, too.'

As he followed her up the stairs to her room, Max spoke up. 'How funny is this! I've been seeing you most days for ages, but we've never spoken before. Well, it's not funny, sad in fact that something bad had to happen to make us speak.'

Amelia had spotted him moving in about two years ago. She thought he was too 'straight' for her taste with his neatly cut hair and smart suit. Even when he wore jeans and a tee shirt he still managed to look as if he'd stepped out of a Burton's window.

'That's London for you,' she said as she unlocked her door, glad that she'd tidied up before going to work. 'The hippy scene made it more friendly for a while, but that's drifting away now.'

'You were a flower child when I first saw you,' he said. His smile was an engaging wide one that made his eyes crinkle up. 'You were wearing one of those loose cheese-cloth dresses and a beaded band round your forehead. I think you had bare feet, too.'

'Did I really?' she giggled. 'The thought of bare feet amongst the rubbish and dog's doings turns my stomach now.'

Max stood for a moment looking round once they were into her room. Amelia had painted it all white, including the table, chairs and an old wartime sideboard. She had a big jug of red gladioli on the table, a patchwork quilt covered an old armchair, and dozens of brightly coloured paintings hung on the walls. Even her bed in the corner was covered in a red blanket and cushions in primary colours. With the late afternoon sun coming through the large sash windows it looked beautiful.

'Are the pictures painted by you?' Max asked. 'It's obvious you are extremely artistic.'

Amelia smiled. 'Extremely nothing! I couldn't draw to save my life, but I appreciate art. I picked up most of those from the artists who hang their work on the railings outside Kensington Gardens. I do sew though; the patchwork quilt is my work, and I paint furniture.'

'It's a lovely room,' he said. 'Mine's pretty squalid.'

'Do sit down,' Amelia waved her hand to a small sofa covered in a vivid turquoise Moroccan mirrored throw, then pulled back a curtain in an alcove that held a sink and tiny Baby Belling cooker on a fridge. She filled and switched on an electric kettle, then took two mugs down from a shelf. 'This place was hideous when I moved in, but it was cheap, and it had potential. I've grown quite fond of it now.'

'So what happened to the Hippy Chick?' he asked.

Amelia glanced at herself in her long mirror. She liked to think of her present style as 'Girl About Town'. A black and white op-art minidress, her brown hair cut in a sleek bob. Back when Max first saw her in 1968, she modelled herself on the Pre-Raphaelites, with a curly perm dyed a deep red with henna. Flowing dresses, jingling bracelets and no bra.

'She grew up,' Amelia sighed. 'It was a fun time, but not, as it turned out, the nirvana we'd imagined. Jimi Hendrix dying of a drug overdose, then Janis Joplin, not to mention the Vietnam War still going on and so many American soldiers dying – all good reason to take life a bit more seriously. Then the Conservatives got in early this year, and that just put the lid on it. But what about you? Did the sixties change you?'

'It did internally,' he said, taking the tea she offered him. 'I liked the way it opened people up, me included! The music, the freedom to express yourself, but I'm an account-ant, for that you have to look quite "straight". So maybe I just reverted to type.'

Amelia nodded and sat down on a chair opposite him. She thought Max was rather scrumptious, with his lovely green eyes and wide, smiley mouth, plus he was articulate. He wasn't the type she normally went for, but then she'd had her fill of weak men who relied on a spliff to face the day and wanted a woman to keep them. It was true some of the hippy men she'd known were great in bed, but then they'd perfected their technique by staying in bed all day and taking mind-altering drugs.

'So, what do you do, Amelia?' he asked, breaking her reverie about hippy men.

'I work for the local paper,' she said. 'So, say a junior reporter, but the truth of the matter is I sell advertising space, make the tea and act as the office gofer.'

'So, do you write? I mean for yourself, fiction perhaps?'

No one had ever asked her that before, maybe people thought her too shallow, too much of a raver to do so.

'Yes,' she admitted sheepishly. 'I am writing a book, but I've never told anyone that until now.'

She hoped he wouldn't ask what it was about because a book about a girl growing up in the sixties sounded so trite. Free love, drugs and the inducements to abandon all morality changed her heroine, and doubtless readers would think it was an autobiography. In fact, it was based on observations she'd made about people she'd been close to. She hadn't lost her own moral compass, nor did she need drugs, but she certainly understood those who this had happened to.

'I'm not going to ask what it's about,' he said, surprising her. 'My grandmother wrote short stories and she hated us asking about them. She'd say, "Wait until it's in a magazine. You spoil it for me by asking. It makes me question too hard what I am writing about."'

'Gosh, that is so true,' Amelia said. 'When I try to write a synopsis, it sounds pathetic.'

'So, have you got secret aspirations to write a killer column in one of the broadsheets?'

Amelia spluttered with laughter, almost spilling her tea. 'No! I'm learning the craft of writing, with a view to hopefully get my book published, but not striving to be a real journalist – they are all so cynical, and jaundiced. I bet when I go in tomorrow and tell them about the girl in the rubbish, they'll all want to be my best friend for the day.'

'Speaking of which, wouldn't you like to know who the girl is, who killed her, why he dumped her there? Her background and everything else about her? I know I would.'

Amelia liked that he had that kind of curiosity. She found men generally didn't care about people's backstory the way she did. 'Yes, I would. Ideally, I'd like to be asked to write a feature on her as a person. What she did, her place in her family. But I think my paper will only be interested in sensationalizing her death, the lurid stuff. We might be a local paper, but even they take their lead from papers like the *News of the World*.'

Max smiled. 'Maybe this is serendipity? If you were to find out about her, get the real low-down, you could use that to make your book really great.'

They had more tea, then Amelia made them both cheese on toast and they talked as if they'd always been friends. She learned that until six months ago Max had a steady girlfriend called Gloria. 'I was fond of her, but not in love, whatever that is,' he said. 'She kept hinting we should get married and I thought if I'm going to marry someone, it's got to be because I can't bear to be without her. I suppose that's what real love is all about. I felt bad that I backed out. Gloria was very hurt,' he went on. 'She actually said she hoped I'd be miserable without her. Well, that didn't happen, but I think she jinxed me, because some of the dates I've had since looked promising at the beginning, but they soon wore thin. I guess that makes me very shallow?' he said.

Amelia liked him more for saying that. 'Not shallow, just honest. I don't think I've ever experienced real love either,' she admitted. 'I have found the bullies, the vain ones, the pathetic ones, the mean ones. Not to mention the ones not too keen on personal hygiene. Once or twice I've felt hurt when I was dumped, but in a day or two I felt relieved I'd escaped. So now I can't really be bothered to date anyone. I'd rather sit here at night and write.'

Max smiled at that. 'Last winter I often saw your light on late at night. I got the idea you had a wild romance going on. I never imagined you writing a book.'

'All my wild romances are fictional ones,' she admitted and laughed. 'I'm so glad you came along when you did today, you've managed to cheer me up.'

At midnight Amelia was still awake. Max had finally left about ten o'clock. She was quite staggered by how much she liked him; he wasn't what she called a 'Normal Norman' at all, and she felt a bit ashamed that until today that's how she'd seen him, without knowing a thing about him.

He was so easy to be with; he didn't talk about his work, or the people he worked with – he said that was deadly dull. Instead she found he played cricket, he belonged to an amateur dramatic society, so far only playing small parts, he liked singing, and rock climbing.

'I like the idea of a singing rock climber. *The hills are alive with the sound of music*,' she warbled for him.

He had laughed at that, but then he laughed readily. He said that being the youngest of four boys he had to learn to laugh at their cruel jokes or be labelled a cry baby. He had grown up on a moorland farm in Devon, but his parents had sold it the previous year to retire in Sidmouth. They had hoped one of their boys would want to take on the farm, but two of his brothers had joined the RAF, the third had just finished his training as a vet and moved to Edinburgh. Max had never wanted to be a farmer, even though he said his childhood spent on the farm was idyllic. He had started rock climbing at seven, back then on rocky patches of Dartmoor. Now he liked to go to Scotland or North Wales to climb.

They kept coming back to the murdered girl though. He was as interested in who she was and why she'd been killed as Amelia was. He pointed out that narrow Scotts Road, which was merely a way of giving access to all the roads that ran from Goldhawk Road to Uxbridge Road, had probably been chosen to dump her as garden walls either side obscured any view. The upper storeys of the houses couldn't see much either because of the tall plane trees that grew along the road.

'Still, a strange place to dump a body,' Max remarked. 'She wasn't there this morning; I would've seen those boots. So, she must have been put there during the day. Possibly not long before you passed by. The killer must've driven her there, so why didn't he go further out of London? Unless the rubbish dump was the attraction? Maybe he saw her as rubbish?'

Now, as Amelia lay in bed, turning things round and round in her head, she realized not only was she burning to know about the dead girl, but she also wanted to see Max again.

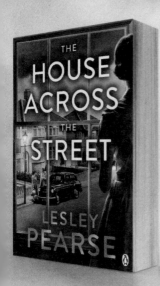

The House Across the Street
Katy is horrified when her father is charged with the murder of the people killed in a house fire over the road. Determined to prove his innocence, Katy sets out to uncover the truth about the mysterious house across the street . . .

The Woman in the Wood
Fifteen-year-old twins, Maisy and Duncan, lose their mother to an asylum one night in 1960. They are sent to their grandmother's country house, Nightingales. But one day Duncan doesn't come home from the woods . . .

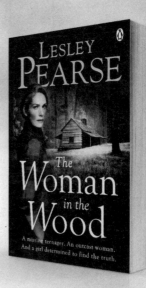

Dead to Me
Ruby and Verity become firm friends, despite coming from different worlds. However, fortunes are not set in stone and soon the girls find their situations reversed.

Without a Trace
On Coronation Day, 1953, Molly discovers that her friend is dead and her six-year-old daughter Petal has vanished. Molly is prepared to give up everything in finding Petal. But is she also risking her life?

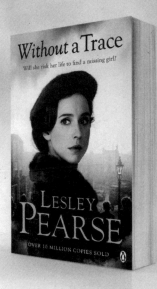

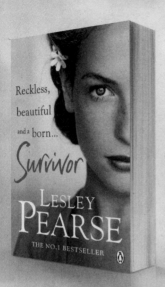

Survivor
Eighteen-year-old Mari is defiant, selfish and has given up everything in favour of glamorous parties in the West End. But, without warning, the Blitz blows her new life apart. Can Mari learn from her mistakes before it's too late?

Forgive Me
Eva's mother never told her the truth about her childhood. Now it is too late and she must retrace her mother's footsteps to look for answers. Will she ever discover the story of her birth?

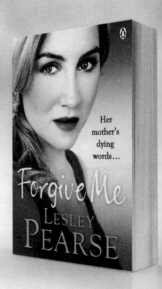

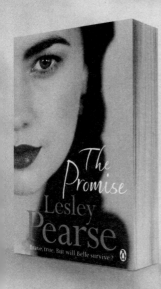

The Promise

When Belle's husband heads for the trenches of northern France, she volunteers as a Red Cross ambulance driver. There, she is brought face to face with a man from her past who she'd never quite forgotten.

Belle

London, 1910, and the beautiful and innocent Belle Reilly is cruelly snatched from her home and sold to a brothel in New Orleans where she begins her life as a courtesan. Can Belle ever find her way home?

Stolen
A beautiful young woman is discovered half-drowned on a Sussex beach. Where has she come from? Why can't she remember who she is — or what happened?

Gypsy
Liverpool, 1893, and after tragedy strikes the Bolton family, Beth and her brother Sam embark on a dangerous journey to find their fortune in America.

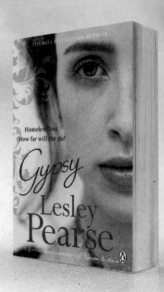

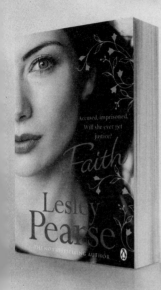

Faith
Scotland, 1995, and Laura Brannigan is in prison for a murder she claims she didn't commit.

Hope
Somerset, 1836, and baby Hope is cast out from a world of privilege as proof of her mother's adultery.

A *Lesser Evil*
Bristol, the 1960s, and young Fifi
Brown defies her parents to marry
a man they think is beneath her.

Secrets
Adele Talbot escapes a children's
home to find her grandmother —
but soon her unhappy mother is
on her trail . . .

Remember Me
Mary Broad is transported
to Australia as a convict and
encounters both cruelty and
passion. Can she make a life for
herself so far from home?

Till We Meet Again
Susan and Beth were childhood
friends. Now Susan is accused of
murder, and Beth finds she must
defend her.

Father Unknown
Daisy Buchan is left a scrapbook with details about her real mother. But should she go and find her?

Trust Me
Dulcie Taylor and her sister are sent to an orphanage and then to Australia. Is their love strong enough to keep them together?

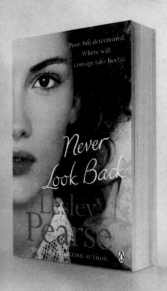

Never Look Back
An act of charity sends flower girl Matilda on a trip to the New World and a new life . . .

Charlie
Charlie helplessly watches her mother being senselessly attacked. What secrets have her parents kept from her?

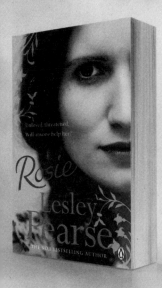

Rosie
Rosie is a girl without a mother, with a past full of trouble. But could the man who ruined her family also save Rosie?

Camellia
Orphaned Camellia discovers that the past she has always been so sure of has been built on lies. Can she bear to uncover the truth about herself?

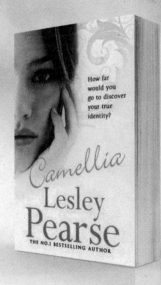

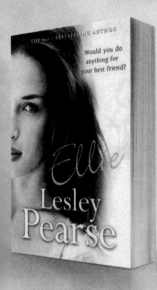

Ellie
Eastender Ellie and spoilt Bonny set off to make a living on the stage. Can their friendship survive sacrifice and ambition?

Charity
Charity Stratton's bleak life is changed for ever when her parents die in a fire. Alone and pregnant, she runs away to London . . .

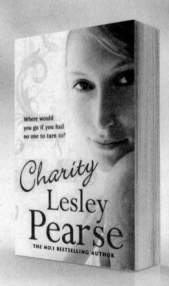